FROM
STORM
AND
SHADOW

ALSO BY RACHEL MORGAN

CREEPY HOLLOW

The Faerie Guardian

The Faerie Prince

The Faerie War

A Faerie's Secret

A Faerie's Revenge

A Faerie's Curse

Glass Faerie

Shadow Faerie

Rebel Faerie

CREEPY HOLLOW COMPANION TITLES

Of Kisses & Quests

Scarlett

Raven

RIDLEY KAYNE CHRONICLES

Elemental Thief

Elemental Power

Elemental Heir

CITY OF WISHES

The Complete Cinderella Story

FROM
STORM
AND
SHADOW

STORMFAE · BOOK 1

RACHEL MORGAN

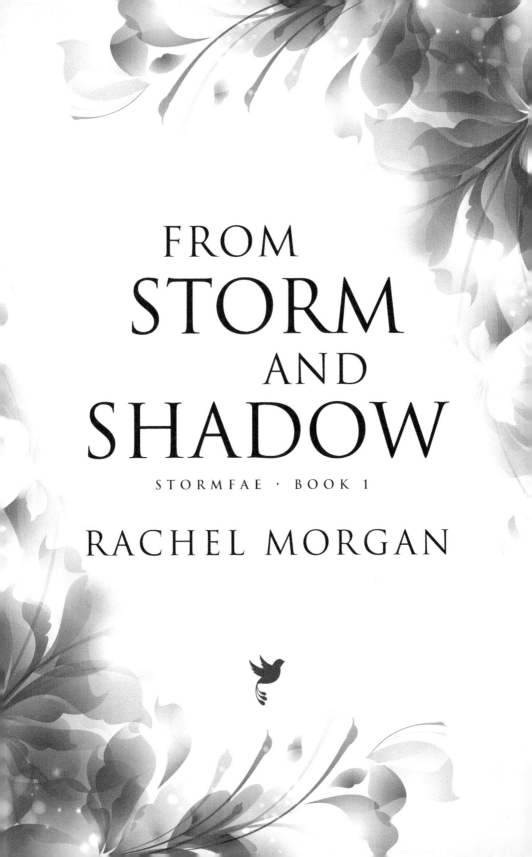

ISBN 978-1-928510-48-2 (ebook)
ISBN 978-1-928510-49-9 (paperback)
ISBN 978-1-998988-00-6 (hardback)

www.rachel-morgan.com

For Riley,
my bright sparkler child.

ONE

"THERE'S NOTHING THERE," THE GIRL SAYS TO THE GUY AS THEY squint across the street at the nondescript door tucked into the shadows between two empty storefronts. Beside them, I step silently from a hole in the air, leaving the faerie paths behind. My body casts no shadow across the moonlit sidewalk. With glamour magic concealing me, I'm as invisible as the building these two humans are trying so hard to see. Well, the guy is trying hard, staring with such force he's in danger of hurting himself. The girl continues to regard the door with arms folded over her chest.

"There *is* something there," he insists. "Gav swore to me he's been inside. He said it's completely mind-blowing. *Literally* out of this world."

The nighttime sounds of the city reach our ears: the squeal of breaks, an occasional siren wail, a dog barking somewhere nearby. Exhaust fumes fill the air, and a neon sign on the building behind us flickers and buzzes. It's tough to imagine there's anything 'out of this world' here in this unremarkable street.

"Right. Sure," the girl says as I step off the sidewalk and onto the street. "A 'magical' club owned by a 'magical' dude with actual 'magical' powers?" I can almost hear the air quotes hanging from her words. "We both know Gav is full of—"

"Babe, come on. He said you have to believe when you look at the door. You have to like … have *faith* that it's there."

"That's the stupidest thing I've ever heard."

I almost snort-laugh as I cross the street. I highly doubt those two will be making it inside Riven's club tonight. The glamour is a powerful one, hiding this place from both humans and those with magical blood. The average passerby would never know it's here. Humans have to be invited by Riven or come along in the company of someone who already knows of this place and has seen it. And those from the fae realm need to know precisely where the club is and come close enough to pass through the glamour.

I reach the sidewalk on the far side of the street and approach the door. Dull brown, plain, uninteresting. Possibly even a little creepy. But the moment my high-top sneakers touch the single doorstep, the glamour ripples and melts away. The polished marble steps appear first, then the impressive pair of arched doors, glass with gold doorknobs and gold filigree patterns curling around the edges. The entire entrance expands, the sparkling quartz walls seeming to push aside the surrounding buildings. And while the exterior now appears large, I know it's nothing compared to the size of the building hidden within. I lift my eyes to the large gold letters above the door: The Gilded Canary.

I climb the steps and reach for one of the gold doorknobs. The ring containing my employee access charm—a slim silver band with tiny flourishes etched into it—goes warm for a second. Then the door opens, releasing cool, perfumed air and the faint thump-thump of music. I step inside, leaving behind the pair of arguing humans, the guy still trying to convince the girl that the simple door they're staring at is a secret entrance to another world. That isn't entirely true. The Gilded Canary exists very much within the human realm, but it is dripping with magic. And to humans, that's probably the same thing.

The two bouncers standing inside the glittering, gold-lit foyer nod to me as I pass, my sneakers squeaking slightly on the polished floor. "Evening, Silver," one of them says.

"Shouldn't you be using the employee entrance?" the other one asks, a small frown in place.

"There's a queue there, Niko," I tell him over my shoulder. "And I'm late."

"Riven won't be happy to hear you're waltzing in through the main entrance," Niko calls after me.

"Riven won't know unless you tell him," I call back.

"Riven knows everything!"

I smile and shake my head as I reach the curtain of water droplets separating the foyer from the rest of the club. I know Niko won't say anything. The curtain sweeps itself aside and I step into the glittering, magical in-between world of Riven Xeryth's creation. A seemingly endless maze of dance floors, bar areas, VIP balconies, private rooms, a casino, a small theater, an enchanted fighting ring, and even a concert hall.

The Rainbow Room is first, where aerial acrobats spin effortlessly through the air above the patrons, twirling ribbons behind them. Sprites flit between the performers, leaving trails of shimmering bubbles in the air. Waitrons adorned in silver jewelry and glittery makeup carry exotic, colorful drinks through the crowd, which is made up of faeries, humans, and halfling fae of all types—people with slender horns, bat wings, clawed feet, shimmering scaly skin. Inside The Gilded Canary, all invisibility glamours are stripped away. The impossible becomes possible. It's a wonderland for humans. And it's all entirely illegal.

I assumed, when I first discovered this place, that the Guild knew nothing of it. Surely the Council would go into spasms of fury if they learned of such a place. But then I met Riven, creator of The Gilded Canary, and all he did was laugh when I asked how he managed to keep this all hidden from the Guild. "My dear ... Silver, is it?" He glanced at my silver-white hair, which I hadn't covered when I had my interview with him. "The Guild already knows."

Startled, I said, "But … they haven't tried to shut you down?"

"Oh, I'm sure they wish they could. But we have a mutually beneficial arrangement. As I'm sure you can imagine, my club is a breeding ground of illegal activity. Plenty of my employees are in a position to overhear … *interesting* things. As long as I continue to supply the Guild with information—in a way that can't be traced back to me—they leave us be. So." He regarded me with piercing dark eyes. "If you're thinking of running off to a Guild to share your thrilling discovery of The Gilded Canary in the hopes of gaining some sort of reward, I'm afraid that will end badly for only one person. You."

Standing there in his office, I'd almost choked on that idea. For one thing, it would break my rule of never returning to the fae world. While I use the faerie paths to travel quickly from one point to another within the human realm, I haven't crossed the veil back into my own world in a long time. And for another, it would be suicide to walk into a Guild. "I can assure you," I said to Riven, "I don't plan to go anywhere near a Guild—or any guardian—for as long as I live."

"Good. Now, *Silver*—" he said my name in a way that suggested he thought I'd made it up "—why don't you show me what you can do?"

As it turned out, he was pleased with my demonstration. I've been working here two or three nights a week ever since.

I slip between the dancing, spinning bodies in the Rainbow Room as quickly as I can and make for the mirrored passageway that connects this dance area to the next one: the Gold Floor. Inside the passage, I glance sideways to double-check the glamour enchantment for my hair. Shoulder length, dead straight, ink black. A satisfied smile touches my lips as I continue walking. More powerful than the type of glamour I could cast with my own magic, this particular spell works on fae as well as humans. My own hair—white blond streaked with literal silver—is far too noticeable, even in a place like this where almost every second person is a dazzling splash of color. Brunette and tangerine, blond and aquamarine, black and violet. Faeries are hard to miss with their two-toned hair and vibrant eyes, and I prefer to draw as little attention as possible.

The Gold Floor has a more sophisticated feel than the Rainbow Room, with metallic finishes and sparkling diamond-like embellishments, not least of which is the enormous chandelier of cut-glass crystals. Icicle-shaped drops hang from the lower part of the arrangement, the largest icicle at the center seeming to glitter with more than just refracted light. The music in here is slow, seductive, a liquid beat pulsing through my body.

I head straight for the sleek, metallic bar curving along one side of the room, aware—as I told Niko—that I'm running late, but also conscious of the fact that I need to collect something from Mel before her shift ends. I reach the bar and lean casually on it, pretending I have all the time in the world. "Hey, Mel," I call out to the woman with black hair and scaled skin.

"Silver! Hey, babe." She leans across the bar, clasping my left hand as she loops her other arm around me. Something small and hard presses against my palm as we half-hug across the bar. "For Goldilocks," she whispers in my ear before pulling back. My hand closes around the small object. It feels like a ring. What secrets or magic it may contain, I have no idea. My only job is to pass it on to Goldilocks, who will make sure whatever crime this ring-shaped item is related to doesn't happen. "You're on tonight?" Mel asks with an easy grin, as if the exchange never happened.

"Yeah, in a few minutes." I slide the small object deep into one of my pockets.

"Better hurry," she says with an arched brow. "Klyde will be getting his panties in a twist."

I laugh as I turn away. "His panties can twist themselves all the way up his—" My words die at the back of my throat as my gaze lands on the guy just a few feet away from me. He's reaching for a glass from a passing tray, and his sleeve has pulled up an inch or two to reveal something on the inside of his wrist: dark, swirling patterns.

My heart slams against my ribs, and I'm instantly lightheaded from the flood of adrenaline. The man lifts the glass to his lips, his gaze sliding toward me, but I'm already turning away. I face the bar and lift my right foot onto the nearest stool, pretending to casually redo my laces while I try to remember how to breathe.

"Everything okay?" Mel asks.

"Yeah," I manage to say, my eyes darting across my forearms as I mentally catalog the numerous charms hidden there. A thick leather cuff with an oval-shaped moonstone pressed into it encircles my left wrist. On my right is a multilayer wrap bracelet of leather braids, knots, stones of various colors, a few freshwater pearls, and a small silver bird with the number three engraved on its side. Each stone and pearl contains some form of magic. The majority are for emergency use only. *This isn't an emergency*, I remind myself as I attempt to stay calm. *Not yet.*

I straighten, still facing the bar, and pat both jacket pockets. Cell phone in one, amber in the other. I withdraw the amber. From a distance, it could be mistaken for a phone—slim, glossy, rectangular, serves the same purpose—but anyone close enough would see that its translucent surface remains blank instead of lighting up to reveal numbers, apps, and photos.

I slip my stylus out of the same pocket and write across the amber's surface. I'm not supposed to contact Riven directly, so I write a message to his assistant Lily instead. *Urgent! Just spotted a guardian on the Gold Floor. Brunette and red.* Magic flows out of my fingers and through the stylus, making the words glow as they appear on the amber. They remain visible for a few moments, then vanish. My intention, plus the magic bleeding through the stylus, are enough to send the message to the right person.

I continue walking, amber clutched in my hand, and Lily's reply comes moments later. I scan her neat, almost childlike script. *Relax. He's Riven's new contact at the Guild. They have a meeting tonight.*

My pulse slows. My hands stop sweating. I grip the stylus with a little less force as I swipe her message away and write another one. *When you see him, tell him to hide his markings better. Unless he's hoping to get himself killed.* Then I slide the amber and stylus back into my pocket and increase my pace. I'm *definitely* late now.

I leave the Gold Floor behind and head through the arched passageway that leads to the private rooms. One of the doors opens as I pass it, and I catch a glimpse of thousands of tiny purple birds fluttering toward the ceiling, which is enchanted to look like a galaxy of stars. Delighted laughter reaches my ears, and then it's gone, swallowed up by the frenetic drum beat emanating from the room next to it. I hurry past all of them, aiming for the employees-only door at the end of the passage. With a nod to the centaur who stands guard beside it, I open the door—the employee access ring warms briefly on my finger—and slip through.

The backstage area, accessible from numerous points throughout the club, is a tangle of dressing rooms, bathrooms, offices, and training areas for fighters and other performance artists to practice in. I navigate the passageways with ease and speed, ducking quickly into the room I share with five other fighters. Couch, dressing table, mirror, lockers. We don't need much else.

My phone buzzes as I reach my locker. A message from Teddy. *Got takeout! Come over when you're done.* Teddy thinks my evening shifts take place inside a university library. He'd probably faint if he knew the truth.

Thanks! I type quickly before shoving the phone back into my pocket. Then I remind myself to hurry up. Jacket off, necklace on, mask secured, locker shut. And then I'm off, the other performers in the back-stage corridors passing in a colorful blur. I hurry into Competitor Lounge A, the muffled roar of cheers and applause reaching my ears. Two other fighters—scheduled to go on after me, if I remember the line-up correctly—are already there.

"Silver!" The furious hiss comes from the other side of the room beside an open doorway filled with white mist so thick it's impossible to see through it. Klyde stands there, hands on his hips and his ever-present amber tablet floating in the air beside him. His hair, a shock of crimson and blond, is even more unruly than usual. He glares at me, and since he's a faerie and his eyes match his hair, I'm glaring back at a fiery gaze so intense it's almost burning. "You're late," he snaps, marching over and tugging me toward the mist swirling in the doorway.

"I'm perfectly on time."

"The last two fights ended earlier than expected. This is why you're supposed to be here at least—"

"Has my fight started yet?"

"No, but Hemlock's about to announce you—"

"Then I'm not late." I take a step toward the mist, but he grips my upper arm and pulls me back against his chest. "Be careful, Silver," he breathes into my ear. "You're not so good that Riven won't get rid of you if I tell him you're not taking his rules seriously. I've been here far longer than you have."

I resist the urge to shove an elbow into Klyde's gut and instead shrug him off. I wish I could tell him that I *am* that good, that I could be crowned Champion every night if I actually tried. But he would laugh in my face since he's never seen a shred of evidence to back this up. So all I say is, "Get off me. Flaming Peacock and I have a fight to get to."

"Sadly," Klyde says, a sneer in his voice, "the lovely Peacock didn't show up tonight. But we do have someone new. Someone *desperate* for a fight. So instead of starting this mysterious someone at the bottom, I mixed things up a bit. Decided to give you a little fun."

I twist to look over my shoulder. "And does Riven know you're changing things up behind his back? Throwing unvetted fighters into the—"

"Riven trusts me to put together the type of show that will keep patrons salivating for more."

"Well, I assume she's good then. I'd hate to get bored out there and disappoint the audience."

His sneer lifts a little higher. "Oh, trust me. *He* is very good."

If Klyde is hoping to scare me, he's going to be disappointed. I don't

8

care who I'm paired up with. In the end, I always choose to lose. Showing the patrons of The Gilded Canary what I'm truly capable of has never been an option.

With a sigh and a shake of my head, I turn from Klyde and face the doorway. Wrapping my hand around the chunky stone hanging from my necklace, I squeeze hard and whisper a few words. The enchantment the costume department created for me bursts into life with a prickle that runs all the way down my spine. Then I step right up to the eddying mist that separates me from the enchanted arena, breathe out a slow, steadying breath, and picture myself as the person my opponent will see when I appear on the other side: The Black Bateleur.

My clothing is simple enough—a black tank and stretchy black pants—but my mask, perfectly contoured to the upper half of my face, is covered in silky black feathers that gleam with a blueish purple sheen wherever the light catches them. The black feathers that sprout in wing formation from the enchantment running down my back shimmer with the same glossy purple blue.

This bird-of-prey persona has been my identity for the past couple of months. Before that, I was the Ruby Scorpion. Before that, the Diamond Knife. And before that … well, my identities begin to blur together after a while. I've played many parts in Riven's fighting ring. The moment I begin to gain some measure of popularity, I put that persona to rest and come up with a new one. Riven isn't a huge fan of this strategy, but I made it clear that it was the only way I could continue to work here safely. And despite Klyde's threat that he could easily get rid of me, I've always had the feeling Riven wants to keep me around.

On the other side of the mist, Hemlock's magically magnified voice shouts my name, bringing me back to the present. With a final breath, I step through the swirling whiteness and into the fighting ring.

The setting is different every night, and until this moment, I have no idea what to expect. Salty air fills my nostrils. Sea spray wets my skin. My gaze darts about and I take in a strip of beach battered on either side by a choppy sea. Though it isn't raining, bruise-dark clouds fill the sky and lightning flickers overhead. I can't see the spectators seated around the outside of the magical arena, but the distant roar of their voices reaches through the dome of magic, mingling with the crash of waves against the shore on either side.

Then my eyes settle on my opponent on the far side of the sandy strip. Tall, broad shoulders, muscular build. A simple black mask covers the whole of his face. No scales, feathers, glitter, or fangs. No animal or fae design. He's made no effort with his clothing either. Riven will not be impressed when he learns of this.

I tilt my head, watching, waiting to see what move he'll make first. He remains frozen for a heartbeat. Then another. And then he begins stalking toward me. I'll bet he's smirking beneath that dull mask of his. Probably thinks this will be the easiest win of his life. I almost smile. The bodybuilder types are always the slowest.

He heads straight for me, hands steady at his sides. No sparks, no elaborate magical displays, no impressive acrobatic stunts. Just a simple, no-nonsense stride. I cock my hips to one side, feigning boredom as I gather magic above my palms. I'm half-convinced that his plan is to simply walk straight into me, but then he comes to a halt a few feet away. He doesn't move.

"Well," I say, lips curving up in what I hope the audience interprets as a sultry smile. "What are you waiting for? Come and get me."

He steps forward. "Are you—"

I sweep both hands through the air, my magic scooping up sand and hurling it in two arcs toward him. His shield magic is up in an instant, faster than I would have thought possible. The sand blasts against it and rains down onto the beach. Then the rippling layer of magic is gone, and he's lunging forward, hands up, magic crackling—

I leap aside and dodge around him. Cartwheel, back flip, perfect landing. My head snaps up, gaze landing on him and lips curving into another smile as I straighten. All completely unnecessary, but unlike Mr.

Boring over there, I'm here to earn my keep by giving the people a good show.

A lightning bolt streaks overhead, blinding me for a second, and when it's gone I see my opponent's fingers curled toward the water on my right. A wave rises up with alarming speed, and I barely have time to duck down and tug a layer of magic over myself like a blanket before the wave crashes right over me.

I straighten again, and suddenly he's a lot closer. I lash out with magic, transforming the sparks into tiny, sharpened twigs before they reach him. He knocks them aside with one arm and a powerful gust of wind. His other arm is already up, sending blue-green flames my way. They're swallowed up within seconds by another arc of sand.

And then the fight really begins. No weapons are allowed in here, but there are almost zero restrictions on magic. And that, of course, is more fun than any weapon. A rain of razor-sharp stones, a vortex of snow, a spray of glowing-hot lava. I'm limited only by my imagination, the speed of my thoughts, and the amount of magic I have—and I'm nowhere near running out of that just yet.

We're close enough now to strike out with fists and feet as well, darting forward to punch, and then dodging back to throw more magic. Spiny leaves, twisted vines, silvery needles. No matter what I throw at him, he's ready to hurl his own magic right back at me. He comes scarily close to hitting me with a flaming boulder, but I jump, and a burst of magic plus the enchantment woven into my wings carries me higher than a normal leap. The boulder soars beneath me and explodes into tiny pebbles. I land hard, forcing a pulse of magic from my palms so that the sand flies up around me. *It's all about the show*, I think, just as I hear the muffled *Ooooh!* from the crowd.

And then we're back at it, me and Mr. Not-So-Boring-After-All, dancing, dodging, lunging, kicking. He's certainly making me work harder than anyone else I've faced in this enchanted fighting ring. On an ordinary night, I have to remind myself to slow down. To give my opponents a chance. But not with this guy. He's good. Too good. As if he knows the space I plan to occupy before I even get there.

With a flare of irritation, I wonder if he's been here before. If he's watched me and taken notes. But that shouldn't make him this good, should it? Even the people I've fought multiple times—the people who should know my moves better than anyone else—aren't this fast. This guy wields offensive magic as if he's been professionally trained. Almost as if he's …

I take a split second to glance at his wrists, but his sleeves are too long for me to tell whether his skin bears the markings of a guardian. A *guardian*, in Riven's fighting ring. What an absurd idea.

Light streaks toward me, and my moment of distraction leaves me with no time to deflect it with magic. My right arm is up instinctively, and the bolt of raw, unformed magic rebounds off my wrap bracelet. A surprised gasp comes from the crowd. *Yeah, it's more than just a few strips of leather*, I think with a satisfied curve to my lips.

But then I feel something … *different*. The swish of hair against my shoulders is gone. One hand flies up, but I realize before it even reaches my head what must have happened: My opponent's magic struck the pearl that contained the glamour for my hair. My sleek black bob is suddenly a messy tangle of silver and white atop my head.

Well. Crap. That hasn't happened before.

My opponent pauses, apparently as surprised as the audience. Then he lunges forward, grabs my wrists, and tugs me closer. We're suddenly face to face, close enough that I can see the precise color of his eyes: flecks of yellow gold in amber irises. The color is so startlingly familiar that for a moment I'm too stunned to fight back. And that's the moment I find my legs swept out from beneath me.

I land hard on my back. He's on top of me, clamping my wrists together with one hand and pinning my arms down against my chest while his other hand reaches swiftly for my mask. What the hell? There may be close to zero rules inside this fighting ring, but removing someone's—

He rips the mask clear off my face. Then he goes utterly still. His words, a hoarse whisper when they finally come, chill my blood: "I thought you were dead."

His grip loosens. My hand shoots up and I tear the mask from his face. My breath seizes. His dark hair is longer, the angles of his face sharper, but I recognize him in a heartbeat.

Ash.

Another heartbeat passes.

Then I roll us so that I'm the one on top. I shove away from him, rise swiftly, and run.

TWO

My surroundings flash past me in a blur as I hurtle through the backstage passages of The Gilded Canary. I tug sharply at my necklace and feel it snap. The wing enchantment vanishes. I drop the broken necklace and skid around a corner. I'm vaguely aware of the shouts behind me, but I can't tell if they're from the people I've almost slammed into or from Ash.

Ash.

Ash!

My heart is in my throat as I duck behind a costume rack laden with dresses, each one shot through with threads of glowing color. I raise my right arm, turn my wrist, and run one finger across the pearls threaded onto the wrap bracelet until I find the largest one. Then I squeeze it hard between my thumb and forefinger. I saved up for *months* to be able to afford the powerful—and illegal—spell hidden inside this stone. But tonight is precisely the kind of desperate situation I was preparing for when I purchased it, so I don't hesitate before whispering the two words that go along with the spell.

In an instant, I'm invisible. Still, I'm not about to take my time getting out of here. As is the case with most private buildings belonging to faeries, the paths can't be accessed from within these walls. I need to get outside. Since I have to pass my dressing room anyway, I slam to a halt against the doorframe, lunge for my locker, and grab my jacket. I have a feeling I may need the numerous small weapons concealed within it. The jacket vanishes from sight the moment I touch it, and I tug it on as I race back into the twisting passageways.

I just about throw myself through the door back into the main part of the club. I race across the Gold Floor and then the Rainbow Room, ignoring the startled cries of patrons as my invisible form shoves past them. Finally, I'm hurtling beneath the water droplet curtain and across the foyer toward the main doors. I ram into the right-hand one to shove it open, and one of the bouncers cries out behind me as I jump down the steps.

I run. My sneakers slam the sidewalk, I swing myself around the corner, and then finally I come to a gasping halt. I raise my hand—already holding my stylus—to the wall. The words I write are a shaky mess, but they're enough for the doorway spell to work. Darkness spreads across the wall, revealing an entrance to the black nothingness of the faerie paths. I lurch forward, throwing a final glance over my shoulder. No one there. I try to feel relieved as the edges of the doorway melt together, sealing me inside the safety of the paths. But there is no relief. Only panic.

I picture my apartment. Warm yellow light permeates the darkness ahead of me. I hurry toward it, my next steps carrying me out of the paths and into my lamplit bedroom. I catch myself against the edge of the bed, my chest heaving as my heart continues to pound.

Ash. *Ash.* How did he find me? After more than two years, I thought I was safe. With my stylus still clutched in my hand, I touch the simple aquamarine stud in my left earlobe—one half of the charm that's supposed to protect me from all tracking and summoning magic—and rush to the wardrobe. I reach into one of the shelves for the glass jar partially concealed behind a messy pile of half-folded T-shirts and sweaters. The jar should be filled with blue liquid. Whenever the level is within an inch of the bottom, I redo the spell and top up the jar's contents. *Always.* Except—

Right now, there is not a single drop left.

CRAP!

Fear paralyzes me, and for a moment, all I can do is stare at the empty jar. How did I let this happen? How long has it been empty? How could I have become so … complacent? I'm supposed to check it every day. It's supposed to be in my line of sight the moment I swing the door open every morning to find something to wear. The only reason I ever put anything away in this darn wardrobe is so that I'm forced to open it on a daily basis. And the jar had to hide *in* the wardrobe because I couldn't very well leave it out in the open where one of my overly inquisitive friends might see it.

Okay.

I'm okay.

Breathe. Think. Plan.

I turn blindly away from the wardrobe, leaving the jar inside. I squeeze my eyes shut, but all I see is Ash's face. His amber eyes, his angular jaw, his honey-streaked dark hair. My brain is already cataloging all the ways in which he's changed. Taller. Broader. Stronger. And yet … he's the same Ash. My heart squeezes painfully.

I force my eyes open, press my fingers to my temples, and pace to the window. The city lights are smudges of color on the other side of the dirty glass. This tiny apartment is nothing amazing, but it's been home for over a year. The thought that I may no longer be safe here makes me sick.

Logically, Ash shouldn't be able to follow me through the paths. Not without touching me. But if he tracked me to The Gilded Canary, he can track me here too. Perhaps he *has* already located this apartment. Perhaps the protective enchantments I cast when I moved in are the only thing keeping him out. I've always wondered whether they actually work. After all, what does a teenager with zero experience in that particular area of magic know? Most people would pay a professional for that sort of thing, if they can afford it. But perhaps I should have had more faith in my skills. Perhaps I did a good enough job to keep unwanted faerie visitors out.

Focus, Silver! Make a plan!

What should I do first? Grab my go-bag and run, or make more cloaking charm? If Ash can track me, then it doesn't matter where I go. I won't be safe until I can magically conceal myself. I drop my hands to my sides, my grip tightening on my stylus. *Cloaking charm*, I decide. I'll trust that the protection I placed on this apartment will keep him out while I grab all the necessary elements and prepare a new batch. Then, when I leave here and go somewhere new, he won't be able to—

"Please don't run."

I whip around, my heart jumping into my throat once more. And there he is, on the other side of my bed, so out of place in this room, in this *world*. I guess I was right to doubt those protective enchantments after all.

"Silver—"

Magic rises instantly to my palms. I hurl a handful of sparks at him. He dodges easily, but that's all the time I need. I'm across the room before my stained-glass lamp—the unintended target of my magic—hits the floor and shatters. I race through the tiny living room, dodging left past the armchair as I sense the crackle of magic behind me. Sparks shoot past and strike the couch, blasting a hole through one of the cushions and slamming the cheap piece of furniture against the wall. Ducking down behind the armchair, I raise one hand and hastily cast a shield of protective magic between Ash and me. He's in my bedroom doorway now, his mouth opening to speak. "Please just—"

But I'm up again, dashing to the nearest wall, lifting my stylus to scribble a doorway spell. Some baser part of my brain screams at me to free every weapon from inside this jacket, drop my shield, and hurl them at him. I'm faster than he is. He'd be down within seconds. But it's *Ash*, and I—

"Hey, wait! Just wait! I'm not here to hurt you."

"You just *fought* me and then told me I'm supposed to be dead." I pause halfway through the doorway spell and look back at him through the shimmering, near-transparent layer of my shield. "If all you wanted to do was *talk*, Ash, you could have knocked on my front door instead of surprising me inside a fighting ring."

"I didn't know where you lived! I found you there last night and tried to follow you, but you vanished as soon as the fight was over. And then you wouldn't let me get a word in tonight before attacking me, and I just—we don't have time—and I didn't even know for sure that it was you! Silver, I—" He cuts himself off, raking a hand through his hair. Something in his expression seems almost … desperate. "I thought you were dead. All this time, I thought you were dead. That's what we were all told."

I hesitate as his words dig their fingers into my brain. But even if what he says is true, it doesn't change what he did that night.

"Holy fae," he whispers. "I can't believe it's really you standing in front of—"

"Wonderful," I interrupt. "So people lied to you. And now that you've discovered the truth, you're here to finish the job? Well good luck with that." I return my attention to the doorway spell. The glowing half-written words have disappeared. I start again.

"What? No."

A doorway melts open across the wall. I take a step—

"*No!* Silver, just wait, please!"

Instead of disappearing into the dark opening, I hesitate. It's stupid, I know. I should be running as fast as I did the day the Guild tried to kill me. I should be turning my back on Ash and never allowing him space inside my head again. But it's him, it's *him*, and there's something inside me that simply … can't.

"No?" I repeat. "*No?*" I whip back around to face him. "You, Asher Blackburn, my best friend in the whole world, tried to *kill me*! And now you show up out of the blue as my latest opponent at The Gilded Canary, and I'm supposed to believe you're not here to try again?"

He goes silent, a look of horror crossing his face. "I—what?" he stutters. "*Kill you? Are you insane? We were told that your parents had murdered two Guild councilors because those councilors discovered your parents were Unseelie spies. We were told that you were in on it too, that you'd helped them steal information. I was trying to *catch* you, not kill you. I figured there must have been a good explanation for—*"

"Oh, you were just trying to *catch* me? That's all?" My right hand curls tightly around my stylus. "Because you believed I was an Unseelie spy and should be locked up by the Guild? Wow. I feel so much better now."

"Silver—"

"I told you the truth that night, but you chose to believe *them* over me."

"No! I didn't know *what* to believe. I was … confused. Bergenfell … she was so damn *convincing*. She said the three of you had been lying to us since the moment you stepped into Stormsdrift all those years ago. And I kept thinking that it couldn't be true, there was just no way, because I *knew* you. But also … what if it was true? What if you'd been lying to me all along? Because it wasn't just Bergenfell saying those things. I overheard multiple councilors that night. The people we'd always looked up to and respected and trusted. The people I had been trained to obey. The people *you* were trained to obey."

I release a short breath of utter disbelief. "How long did I live in Stormsdrift, Ash? Ten years? You honestly thought I'd been lying to you every single day for a *decade*?"

"No! I thought … I thought …"

"You thought what? Do tell me, Ash, exactly what was going through your mind when I was running for my life and you were the one throwing magic at me."

"Can we please just—"

"Please *nothing*," I spit at him. "Tell me what you really thought."

"Fine. At worst, I thought your parents must have lied to you about what happened that night, and you believed what they were telling you—"

"Screw you."

"—and at best, I figured there must be some huge misunderstanding between them and the Council, and that if we could all just—"

"There was no misunderstanding! No truth potion questioning. No chance for justice. My parents were good people, *excellent* guardians, and they ended up discovering something the Council wanted to keep hidden. So that was the end of it. The Council decided to get rid of them as quickly as possible. And when they came after us—when they *killed* my mom and dad—you were on their side, not mine."

His expression is wretched now. "I made a mistake. I have been heartbreakingly aware of that *every single day*. If I hadn't gone after you, you might have escaped. Instead, a bunch of councilors caught you and you ended up dead. Or so they had us believe. But your death was an *accident*, Silver. We weren't ordered to *kill* you. If someone had given me that order, I would have refused in a heartbeat."

My jaw clenches as my brows pinch together. "Do you think I'm stupid? Do you think the details of those final moments aren't seared into my brain forever? I *know* what you were all ordered to do, Ash. I heard exactly what Councilor Bergenfell said." I suck in a deep breath before finishing. "*Kill her.*"

Ash steps closer to my shield, no trace of doubt in his expression. "I remember too, and Bergenfell may have given that order to the Council, but she certainly didn't give it to the rest of us. We were told to—"

"How does that change anything? My parents are still dead, and you and I are still standing here on opposite sides of the law. You think I lied to you about—"

"I saw it," he interrupts. "The door. I know you were telling the truth."

"You—what?" I blink, my brain taking a moment to catch up with this unexpected subject change. But then my thoughts start firing again, and I know immediately what door he's talking about. The faerie door my parents discovered in the Shadow Crypt. The faerie door responsible for everything that went wrong that night.

Unlike the faerie paths, which can be used to travel almost anywhere in either realm, a faerie door has a fixed location on either side. Mom didn't tell me if she knew where that door led to, but she did tell me what came through it: a fae creature unlike anything she'd ever seen before. A monster. The real killer of the two councilors whose deaths she and my dad were blamed for.

I shake my head, banishing the memory. "You saw the faerie door?"

"Yes. Two nights ago. The councilors know what I saw, and now they're after me too. I overheard them—"

A loud banging on the door interrupts Ash. We both look toward it. "Silver?" A deep male voice.

"Who is that?" Ash asks.

"No one," I answer immediately.

"Silver, honey?" Another male voice, not as deep as the first. "You okay in there? We heard a crash."

"Multiple crashes," the deep voice adds. "Just want to make sure you're okay."

"No one?" Ash repeats, his brows climbing as he looks at me.

"My neighbors. Just ignore them. They'll go away."

"We're coming in," the deeper voice says. "Squeak now if you're fine and don't need our help."

I groan. Ash's eyebrows inch higher. "Exactly how many No Ones have a key to your apartment?"

"Look, they have nothing to do with you or the door or whatever reason you're here, so don't you *dare* hurt them."

"Why would I *hurt*—"

"Shut up," I whisper-hiss as the lock on my front door clicks. I swipe at the air, and my shield vanishes. Instinct—or just my silly, desperate heart—tells me it wasn't necessary in the first place. "Just shut up and get back in my room." I point toward my door, then give him a shove for good measure. "Or at least glamour yourself, for goodness' sake. I don't need them asking questions about you."

"We seriously don't have time for—"

"Now!" I shove harder. With a deep grumble, Ash stalks the final distance into my room. I spin around and bound toward the front door just as it swings open. "Hey! Hi!" I catch the door and keep it from opening all the way. I love Teddy and Duke—far more than I should ever have allowed myself to love a pair of humans—but if I let them in now, they'll be here all night chatting. "So sorry. I walked into a table." I roll my eyes and force out a laugh while hiding my stylus in my back pocket. "Just being clumsy."

I'm greeted by two highly suspicious gazes, one peering out of a pale, skinny face, the other from a dark, chiseled one. Teddy is ensconced in his favorite fluffy robe, while the sweat glistening on Duke's hulking form suggests he's just returned from his evening gym session. "Clumsy?" he repeats in his rumbly baritone.

Teddy flips his hair—currently dyed a horrendous shade of green—out of his eyes. "You're never clumsy. You're like … lethally graceful."

"Lethally graceful?" This time, my laugh is a little closer to genuine. I tuck a few loose strands of silver behind my ear. "How very poetic, Teddy. Those late-night creative writing classes are clearly paying off."

"You're dodging the subject," Teddy says. "There was some kind of … *scuffle* in here, and then you came racing over to the door looking highly flustered. If you weren't being attacked, then I assume you're hiding a lover."

My jaw drops at that. "A *lover?*"

"Which is totally cool," Duke adds, his hands rising in surrender. "All you needed to do was shout that you were fine. We were just worried when we heard the crashes, that's all."

"I don't *see* anyone …" Teddy cranes his head as he peers over my shoulder. "Holy poo, what happened to your couch? Is it—"

"Look, you know I love you guys, but you're being super nosy, and now is not a good time. I assure you, I'm fine. Thank you for checking on me. I really—"

"Is that *blood* on your arm?" Teddy's pale face turns a shade paler.

Crap. I curse inwardly as I look down and find a cut on my upper left arm. "Oh, that's just from ... the lamp," I finish lamely.

"The Tiffany lamp?" Teddy demands. "The one we gave you? I *knew* I heard glass shattering—"

"Silver, what's going on?" Duke asks, his eyes narrowed in concern. "Are you in some kind of trouble? You know you can tell us if you need help."

I almost laugh at the idea: Teddy and Duke, helping me out with my Ash problem. Ash could knock willowy Teddy over with one finger, and as for Duke ... well, he might spend hours at the gym working on his toned physique, but Ash could bring him down in seconds if he had to. So could I, for that matter. "Seriously, guys. I'm fine."

"You sure?" Duke looks doubtful. Lowering his voice, he adds, "Blink twice if you need us to call the—"

"Okay, we don't have time for this," Ash says from behind me.

Duke's gaze shoots over my shoulder, his expression hardening immediately. "Who the hell are—"

"Seriously?" I face Ash with my hands placed firmly on my hips. "I told you to stay in my room."

"Oh, I *knew* you had a guy in there!" Teddy crows.

I sense Duke's large form right behind me. "Is he from the cult?" he asks in a low tone.

"The cult?" Ash demands. Then he shakes his head. "There's no time for this. I'm not kidding, Silver. You're in—"

"Ooh, I didn't think of that," Teddy says. "You're right, love. We should probably call the—"

"You're in danger!" Ash says, his gaze still fixed on me. "They know you're alive. They know where to find you. We have to go."

My hands slip slowly from my hips. My next breath catches in my throat. *They know where to find you.* Is this the moment I've been hiding from for more than two years? The moment my life shatters to pieces around me all over again? *They know where to find you.*

"They?" Teddy asks from behind me. "Who's they? People from the cult?"

Ash is still staring at me, his body tense. "We have to go," he repeats, quieter this time.

I turn to face Teddy and Duke, inhaling deeply. Will I ever see them again after I close this door? My eyes scan their faces, memorizing as much detail as I can. Teddy's pursed lips. Duke's concerned gaze. Emotion constricts my throat. I knew, I *knew* I should never get close to them. I knew it would break my heart one day. Whether five, ten or twenty years from now, I knew they'd eventually notice that somehow, oddly, their friend Silver doesn't seem to age. I knew I'd have to move on at some point and that getting attached to people would only hurt me in the long run.

But they came over with their freshly baked cookies and their offer to set up my Wi-Fi—back when I didn't even know what Wi-Fi was— and I was so lonely and broken I couldn't turn them away. I soaked up Teddy's non-stop chatter and Duke's contagious, rumbly laughter like a withered flower in a drought. Their door was always open to me, and I took full advantage, stepping into their hearts and allowing them into mine, knowing it would cost me one day. But I had hoped 'one day' was still far away.

I step forward and wrap my arms around both of them. It's on the tip of my tongue to blurt out everything in a rushed whisper: *I'm a faerie, I'm from another world, but the law enforcers of that realm killed my parents, and I was forced to run for my life.* But I can't say these things. Not because I care about the Guild's laws, but because it's safer for Teddy and Duke if they don't know the truth. "I love you guys," I say instead.

"Um, what's happening?" Teddy asks.

"I'll be fine, I swear." I step back, smiling at them. "You don't have to call the police." Jerking my thumb over my shoulder at Ash, I add,

"He's just a friend from my past. We have some catching up to do, that's all. See you guys later, okay?" I close the door before they can reply, saying goodbye in my head since I can't say it out loud. It would freak them out too much.

Behind me, Ash takes a few steps closer. "Come on. We need to get out of here."

I tilt my head forward and touch my brow to the back of the door, allowing my eyes to slide shut for a moment. Pain gathers into a hard core at the center of my being. The pain of everything I lost two years ago and everything I'm about to lose now. But I should have known, the second I tugged that mask off Ash's face and saw it was him, that my current life was over. If he knows where I am, then of course the Council knows too.

I whirl around on him, and my sudden burst of raw magic is enough to throw him across the room and onto the half-burned couch. "I'm not going anywhere with you. I don't ever want to see you again. *If* what you're telling me is true, then I appreciate the heads-up. But I sure as hell don't trust you enough to go anywhere through the paths with you. I trusted you before and look where that got me."

"I'm trying to *help* you!"

"Help me? Is that what you were doing a few minutes ago when you threw magic at me? You know, the magic that burned a hole through my furniture?"

He rises slowly, his expression changing. Gone is the desperation, the wretchedness, the disbelief at finally seeing me again after so long. Even from across the room, I can see the steely determination in the set of his jaw. "Yes. That was a stunner spell."

"You tried to *stun* me?"

"Yes, and I would do it again. I failed you before and I'm not about to repeat that mistake. If I have to stun you in order to get your stubborn ass out of here, I'll do it."

"Oh for goodness' sake, don't be so dramatic."

"I THOUGHT YOU WERE DEAD!" he roars. "And you could

very well end up dead for real if you don't leave here right now, so I think I have every right to be dramatic!"

"Fine!" I yell back at him. "I am leaving, just not with *you!*" I shove past him and head for my bedroom. "I need to grab my things." My lamp is broken, lying on the floor surrounded by shattered glass, but I can see enough by the dim light that filters through the dirty window-pane. I hunker down beside the bed and swipe my hand over the section of floor I enchanted to safely house my go-bag and weapons. Several floorboards disappear, revealing a backpack, a collection of blades of varying size and shape, a bow, arrows in a leather quiver, and a few other weapons I've collected in the time since I fled the Guild. "Feel free to show yourself out," I add. "I don't need you hanging around while I—"

"Isela."

I go rigid at the sound of my name. No one's called me that in years. Not even my parents, when they were still alive. It's the name they gave me at birth, but Mom nicknamed me Silver early on and it stuck.

"I heard your name," Ash says. "Your real name. When I got close to the door. Someone on the other side was … calling to you."

Slowly, I look over my shoulder. He's standing in the bedroom door-way. "What?"

"I was expecting it to be dark, like inside the paths. That's what you see behind other faerie doors, until you actually walk through them. But this was gray and misty, and then … a shadow moved past the other side of the door. Something was definitely there."

"Wait." I stand and face him. "The door was *open?*"

"No, it was closed, but there were holes in it, so I could see a little bit of what was on the other—"

"Holes?" I repeat, my tone even sharper now.

"Yes. Here and there amid the carvings on the door. They were—" He shakes his head. "Look, can we please go somewhere else before we talk about this? We're not safe here."

"I told you I'm not going anywhere with you."

"Silver, you are involved in this whether you like it or not. You can't keep hiding in a world you don't even belong—"

"I'm not going back there."

"Please just hear me—"

"I *can't*."

"I need your help!" he all but shouts at me. "There is something strange—*very* strange—going on in Stormsdrift. Things are getting bad, and I'm pretty sure it's all happening because of that faerie door. But I can't go to the Council, because they're the ones trying to cover this all up, and I figured *you* might know something that could help because your parents—"

"Things are getting bad? What does that mean?"

Thump.

We both freeze. Then Ash turns to face the living room. "Wonderful," he mutters. With a sigh, he raises both arms. Warm light burns through the darkness, and by the time his arms are level with his shoulders, he's gripping a crossbow that glitters like a thousand golden stars. "Looks like we're out of time."

THREE

THERE'S AN ODD MOMENT WHERE THE PAST SEEMS TO OVERLAP with the present. The sight of a guardian weapon brings memories bubbling to the surface. Days in the training center, nights stalking through the forest. The sheer joy of executing a perfect series of flips, and the warm prickle of golden weapons beneath my touch. Weapons that sprang into existence with little more than a thought. Weapons that belonged to *me*. I can almost feel them, as if it were only yesterday that I held one in my grasp.

But in a blink, the moment is gone. I am not a guardian. I never will be. I lost access to my weapons the moment I destroyed the pendant that marked me as a trainee.

I blink again. My gaze focuses beyond Ash. There is a fae creature—a feathery, taloned fae creature—in my living room. In the human world. Flipping wonderful.

I reach for the leather cuff on my left wrist and rub my thumb in a quick X across the moonstone. The stone vanishes, leaving behind a tiny version of my favorite weapon: a knife made of two blades, each shaped like a crescent moon, interlocking so that the blades curve away from each other with a grip in the middle. I lift the tiny weapon between my thumb and forefinger, and it begins to expand the moment I touch it. By the time I've risen silently to my feet, I'm gripping the deadly crescent-moon knife tightly in my right hand. It's a primitive, inelegant imitation of a guardian's weapons, which are invisible and always within reach, but it was the best I could come up with when attempting to mimic the super-secret, centuries-old spells the Guild created.

My gaze settles beyond Ash on the unwelcome visitor. Larger than the couch it's currently perched on, it looks like a giant black eagle with a dragon's barbed tail and a pair of bull's horns. *Bloodtongue*, my memory whispers to me. An unofficial name, but it's the one I remember. Rare and deadly, the Guild uses them for tracking purposes. One taste of magical blood, and they can hunt that person down across both realms.

Ash takes a careful step forward, crossbow still raised. The bloodtongue cocks its head, sharp and birdlike, its black eyes missing nothing. I edge forward, my breaths steady and my grip firm on the crescent-moon knife. My left hand is free. In the absence of an invisible arsenal of guardian weapons, the next best thing is magic. Provided I'm quick enough with it.

"You should stay back," Ash warns.

"And you should stop telling me what to do," I respond, moving a step closer. The moment I reach the doorway, I see what I missed from the bedroom: a second bloodtongue. *What an honor*, I think dryly. Who knew our tiny Guild could afford such an expense? And then another thought occurs to me: the Guild shouldn't have any of my blood. It's been years since I went anywhere near …

"You," I murmur as the realization sinks in. These creatures haven't once looked at me. Their glittering obsidian gazes are pinned on Ash. "They're tracking you, not me. Did you leave a handy little sample of your blood behind after you discovered the faerie door?"

"There was a fight, so yeah, I guess I did." The bloodtongues continue to watch him. They're trained to track down and immobilize, not kill, so I suppose they'll wait until he makes a move.

"Seems you were right about us not being safe here," I add. "Turns out *you're* the one who brought the danger, though."

"Oh, come on," he says tightly. "Bergenfell discovered you work at The Gilded Canary. Wouldn't have taken her long to find this—" His words are cut off as both bloodtongues dart forward, razor-sharp beaks snapping and wings beating the air.

Okay, so my no-killing theory may have been incorrect.

Ash fires at the larger one, which swerves clear with a screech. I grip my knife tighter and slash in a wide arc as the smaller one nears me. Feathers fall, a scaly tail sweeps around, and I twist neatly out of the way. Duck, roll, spin around, swipe again. I know from the piercing cry that my blade has caught its clawed leg. I'm up again, on the other side of the smaller bloodtongue now, and Ash is no longer in sight.

I dodge and swipe, toss magic and reshape it as it flies. Stones, ice, fire. My mind withdraws. External thoughts still. The world narrows until it's only me and the bloodtongue and the weapon at the end of my arm. The creature moves surprisingly fast, diving away from most of my magic. Then fire ignites along one wing, and the smell of singed feathers fills the air. It jerks its head back, preparing to strike, and I lunge forward and swipe my curved blade across its neck. Too many feathers. Not close enough to meet flesh.

Ash's voice reaches my ears.

The world expands outward in an instant. I dodge away from the snapping beak, my gaze darting around in search of Ash—and I see the tail swinging toward me an instant too late. I dive out of the way, but it catches my shoulder, knocking me against the wall as I curse myself. I should be better than this. I *am* better than this. But Ash is here—*Ash is here!*—and it's the kind of distraction I haven't dealt with in a very long time.

I drop to the floor as the tail sweeps toward me again. I feel the air move as the tail passes mere inches overhead. And that's when, with a piercing shriek, the larger bloodtongue explodes into a flurry of feathers.

The feathers drift to the floor and vanish, leaving behind an oddly metallic scent—and Ash with a sword glittering in his hand.

Again, that sense of overlapping time. We are trainees. This is just another assignment. Another session inside the simulation ring. He's defeated his opponent before I've defeated mine. In a moment, he'll look over at me and his lips will turn up in that cocky grin I can't help but love, and he'll say something like, "Beat you again." And I'll laugh because even though the two of us are competitive, there's never been any serious rivalry between us. We're competitive because it's *fun*.

But Ash isn't smiling. And I'm not laughing.

The barbed tail. Again. I roll out of the way, my arm slashing upward, and my curved blade slices through scaly flesh. The bloodtongue flaps and whirls around, one wing still burning. Its wounded tail strikes a window. Glass shatters. The tail lashes out again, dragging a splintering gash along the wall. It occurs to me with a sudden, terrifying lurch that this creature might break right through into Teddy and Duke's apartment.

An arrow shoots past me, trailing sparkles through the air. It glances off the wall as the bloodtongue dodges. "We need to get it out of here!" I call to Ash, deciding that I'm not waiting to find out if he can kill this thing before it winds up inside my neighbors' home. "Now!"

"Doorway!" he shouts back, sending another arrow across the room. Ducking to miss another swipe of its tail, I drop to the floor. I switch the knife to my left hand, grab my stylus from my back pocket, and scribble a doorway spell. Darkness spreads across the floor: an opening to the paths.

"Now!" I shout again.

He throws himself at the bloodtongue and wrestles it toward the doorway in the floor. But the angle is off, and the bloodtongue is forcing him to the side, hissing and spitting, and they're inching closer to me instead of the doorway. I splay my fingers behind me, and with a burst of magic, I shoot toward the struggling creature. The three of us topple into the darkness.

"Don't think," Ash gasps, and though part of me wants to snap once more that he doesn't need to tell me what to do, I recognize that only one of us can direct the paths. So I let him do the thinking as utter darkness envelops us and I cling tightly to the writhing feathered creature.

Light appears. Leaves and branches and moonlight. We hit the ground. I tumble away from the bloodtongue, the scent of damp earth filling my nose. Part of me wonders if the creature may be dead by now —some fae can't survive a trip through the faerie paths—but the thought has barely taken shape when that savage tail slams down beside me. Then I'm on my back, sharp talons pressing into my chest. Its beak is open. A long, forked tongue flicks out. My hand is up between us—its head strikes down—

Shield, I think in the split second before that hard beak meets my face. The creature snaps at the layer of magic that's materialized between us, then rears back. Before it can strike again, I release the shield. My knife is up, slashing across, and this time I meet flesh. With a blood-chilling squawk, it lurches away from me. It jerks forward again and then—it bursts into a swirling mass of feathers. They float toward the ground, coming to a gentle rest before vanishing. That metallic smell is in the air again, but fainter out here, mixed with forest scents: leaves, earth, the subtle perfume of flowers.

I push myself hastily to my feet. Ash stands a few feet away, a sword raised, blood-covered blade pointed down and the hilt gripped between both hands. I'm guessing he stabbed it straight after it lurched away from me. For several moments, we simply stare at the space where the bloodtongue existed only moments ago, chests heaving as we gulp in air.

And that's when I feel it: *magic*. In the air, the trees, the ground beneath my feet. My gaze slides over giant trumpet-like flowers, their pink fluorescence lighting up the leaves around them. Purple umbrella-shaped trees hang overhead, trailing long, leafy tendrils and looking for all the world like giant, glowing jellyfish. Two winged sprites flit past, holding hands. A line of glow-bugs wiggles its way over tangled, interwoven tree roots. And all around, the quiet trill of tiny nighttime creatures fills the air.

I don't recognize this place. We could be anywhere in the fae world. But that doesn't matter. It's *my world*. My true home. I missed it so, so, so much, and I didn't even know it until this moment. My next breath is almost a sob.

"You never stopped training," Ash says quietly. The moment—which feels as though it may have stretched out across an eternity—is broken. I tear my gaze from the glow-bugs and look at him. He releases his sword, which vanishes with a trace of gold sparkles. Another twinge of nostalgia pierces my chest, but I force my mind away from the weapons I still secretly long for to the weapons I own now. Weapons of solid, cold metal. Cold metal, I realize as I blink down at the crescent-moon knife in my hand, that's now covered in black blood.

I just fought and killed a magical creature.

I'm standing in the fae realm for the first time in years.

They know where to find you.

I blink again, my eyes still on the blade. "Um, no," I say, and my voice sounds oddly distant, as though it belongs to someone else. There are too many trains of thought racing through my head, and I'm struggling to catch even one of them. "I didn't stop training." An image of light streaming through red glass joins the jumbled thoughts flashing through my mind. I squeeze my eyes shut and give my head a little shake. "Um … they're going to send more bloodtongues. If Bergenfell still has your blood, then—"

"No, we only had those two, and it took Bergenfell months to acquire them. They're even rarer than they used to be. It'll take weeks of paperwork before she's able to get her hands on another one."

"Tracking owls?"

Ash shakes his head. "Not enough time. The imprint of our magic will be gone from your apartment by the time Bergenfell can get any owls there. They won't pick up anything."

"Okay." I nod. Take another breath. Allow my eyes to dart across the scenery as my mind races back through everything that's—

Teddy and Duke.

I lurch away from Ash, holding my knife against the leather cuff on my wrist as I aim for the nearest tree. The complicated spells that took forever to weave together snatch hold of the knife, pulling it from my grip, shrinking it immediately, and returning it to the indentation in the cuff. By the time my hands are reaching inside my jacket for another stylus—because I'm not about to crawl around on the ground in search of the one I dropped—the moonstone has reappeared, hiding the tiny weapon. I write across the tree trunk with my spare stylus, rough bark grazing my hand. A doorway spreads open in front of me.

"Hey, wait, where are you—"

"I'll be back!" I call as I race into the darkness without a backward glance, thinking only of my friends. They would have heard the fight, the crashes, the screeching of the bloodtongues. If they go into my apartment and some other fae creature shows up—

I run out of the paths and into their living room, my eyes combing the space. There's no one here, and their front door is standing wide open. A second later, their voices reach my ears. I race through the open door, swing left, and dash into my own apartment. They're standing in the center of the living room, Teddy with his palms against his cheeks, and Duke with a phone pressed to his ear. For a second, I take in the demolished room I left behind: every item of furniture swept against the walls; TV shattered; window smashed; rug wrinkled and smoking in one corner.

"You're okay!" Teddy says. A moment later, I almost topple over as he collides into me and embraces me tightly.

"Oh, wait, she's here," Duke says into the phone, coming closer. "She—"

I reach around Teddy, yank the phone from Duke's hand, and say, "I'm fine, everything's fine, thank you!" before ending the call. "That was the cops, right?" I add after a beat of silence.

"Of course that was the cops," Teddy answers for Duke. "We had to call them. You were being *attacked* in here!"

"I was not being—I'm fine, okay? I promise I'm fine. But you need to stay out of this apartment." I drag them both into the hallway before tugging my door shut. Then I herd them back into their place, my gaze darting over both shoulders as we go. I close their door. "I don't know if someone else might come looking for me, so you have to promise to stay out of there."

"Silver, what the hell is going on?" Duke demands. "We didn't ask too many questions before, because you—"

"I can't tell you. It's … even if we had time, you wouldn't believe me. I—just—there's something going on and I need to figure it out. I'll be back … soon."

"Soon?" Teddy repeats. "When is soon? Where are you going? And what do we tell the landlord? I mean, that damage in there? He's going to *freak* when he finds out about it."

"I'll … figure something out. I'll take care of it. Just don't call the cops again. Please? I promise I can take care of myself." I wrap my arms around both of them and squeeze tightly. "I have to go. Please stay safe." And then, because there might be someone else in the hallway by now and I don't want to open a faerie paths doorway out there, I head for Teddy and Duke's bedroom.

"Wait!" Teddy calls after me, genuine panic in his voice now. I shut their door and write on the back of it, tears pricking behind my eyelids. "Waitwaitwait, Silver, please! You can't just—" His words slice off mid-sentence as I vanish into the faerie paths.

Four

I step silently from the paths and find Ash pacing. I watch him for a few moments, taking him in fully for the first time tonight. Broader shoulders, the angles of his face more defined. Gone is any trace of the boyishness he still possessed at age sixteen. Looking at him now, I can't imagine that only two and a bit years have passed. He seems older than that.

He turns and sees me. "You came back." His voice is deeper too. Is that possible?

"Of course I came back. I said I would, didn't I? Despite what you think, I've never lied to you before."

His brows jerk upward in disbelief.

"Fine. I've never lied about anything important," I correct.

"It seems we disagree on the definition of—"

"So an enchanted door you know nothing about has holes in it," I interrupt, folding my arms across my chest, "and you decided to *put your eye against one of those holes and peer through*? How stupid are you? What if—"

"I didn't *shove* my eyeball right up against the door."

"What if some creature from the other side stabbed you in the—"

36

"I observed from a short *distance*."

"—or shot some deadly venom into your eye."

"There's little that's deadly to a faerie, so I think I—"

"There's *plenty* that's deadly to a faerie," I argue.

"The holes aren't *tiny*, okay? I could see enough from a distance to know that a shadow passed across the other side!"

I bite down hard on my lip and suck in a steadying breath before this becomes the most pointless argument of all time. Squeezing my eyes shut, I press my fingertips against my temples and rub. "There shouldn't be any holes in the door," I say, almost to myself. "It shouldn't be possible. My dad locked it. That's the only reason my parents went back there that night. To lock the stupid door." I drop my hands to my sides and look at Ash. "And I don't mean a simple locking spell or an everyday key with no magic on it. I mean the kind of key that holds great power. The kind of key that *keeps* something locked and prevents things from getting through. I'm pretty sure that includes random holes."

"I don't know what else to tell you, Silver. The door is locked, and there are holes in it. And I know it's locked because I heard Bergenfell say as much. Although … she did say something about it not being locked *properly*."

"What does that mean?"

"I don't know."

"I mean … it's either locked or unlocked, right?"

"Silver, I don't know! Look, can we—" He holds both hands up. "Can we start again? Please? You're … *you're alive!* I just want to have a conversation with you that doesn't involve me having to defend myself after every sentence."

"I think my anger is pretty damn justified after what you and the rest of the Guild did to—"

"I know. *I know.* I'm sorry. Please just …" He trails off as he moves closer. Part of me wants to take a gigantic step back and put as much distance between us as possible. But another tiny part—the part of me I've never been able to banish entirely—wants to collapse into his arms and cry and cry and cry until there's nothing left inside me. He holds my gaze, his eyes reflecting the light of the magical forest around us, and I can't look away. "Can we please just talk?"

I manage to break eye contact. "Fine. We can talk. But I'm not going back to Stormsdrift. I hadn't planned to return to the fae realm at all until you brought us here." I look around at all the blossoms and leaves that glow different colors. I've never seen anything like it in the human world. "It's … weird," I add quietly. It's amazing. Heartbreaking. The kind of ache you feel for a place you no longer belong in. Returning home to Stormsdrift would be even worse.

"Hang on," Ash says. "You haven't been back into this world at all? Not since you were … since that night?"

"I was here at first," I correct before I can stop myself. I clamp my mouth shut and try to force my mind away from the past. Red light streaming through stained glass windows; red blood on the—

Stop. Pretty flowers, pretty trees, pretty glow-bugs.

I force myself to see my surroundings instead of the nightmare inside my head, and when I trust myself to speak again, I say, "It's been a little over a year since I was last in this world." One year and three months, to be precise, but Ash doesn't need to know how closely I keep score of the amount of freedom I've accumulated.

"You haven't been back here in over a *year*? So you don't know anything about what's been happening in Stormsdrift?"

I stand a little straighter, lifting my chin slightly. "Did you expect me to hide out nearby and keep tabs on all the people who tried to kill me? No, Ash, I don't know what's been happening in Stormsdrift. I got as far away as I could, started a new life, and didn't look back. Why?" I add as icy fear shoots through me. "Have the councilors done the same thing to other people? Is your family—"

"They're fine. At least, they were when I left. And no, the Council hasn't falsely accused anyone else of murder and then hunted them down. But there's … something else. Something that changed a little while after you were gone. A few weeks later, perhaps. I don't remember exactly. A kind of … darkness. Not something visible," he adds. "It's more … something you can feel. A strange magic in the air. And this thick fog that settles over everything, taking days to disperse each time it comes. I know we get a lot of storms—obviously, it's called Stormsdrift —but when they clear up, things are generally bright and sunny. Not this eerie, shifting mist we live with so often now. It didn't happen too often at first, but now it's almost constant."

"I guess that is weird," I admit.

"And then there are the creatures. Odd fae beasts we never encountered during our training. Creatures we can't find any record of. And they seem to be more … deadly." He says this last bit grudgingly, probably thinking of the argument we just had. *Yes, Ash*, I want to remind him. *There is plenty that's deadly to a faerie.* "We've lost some guardians," he continues quietly. "More than we should have. And a few civilians. The Guild even implemented a curfew several months ago. No one's allowed out between sunset and sunrise. Well, guardians are, of course, but no one else."

I breathe out a quiet curse. "I'm … I'm sorry." In my head, Stormsdrift has remained exactly the same all these years. How naive of me to think it wouldn't change.

Ash clears his throat. "Yeah. Not fun. And to add to all the strangeness, sometimes the faerie paths just … don't work."

"What?" Of all the things he's said so far, this is the most alarming. "How is that possible?"

"I don't know. Obviously magic exists that can block doorways to the paths. That's what they do inside the Guilds and at the Seelie Court and … I don't know. Plenty of other places, I'm sure. But this seems different. It comes and goes without warning. You can be in the middle of writing a doorway spell, watch the doorway begin to open up in front of you, and then it kind of flickers in and out of view before disappearing."

"That's … unsettling."

"We wondered if it was a widespread thing—like back in the day when Lord Draven was trying to take over—but it seems localized to Stormsdrift and the surrounding area. Which, in the beginning, we thought was odd. Nothing much used to go wrong there. Almost all of our assignments were outside of Stormsdrift, remember? We always thought it was strange that—"

"That there was even a Guild in Stormsdrift to begin with," I say.

"Yes. But lately, there's been plenty to keep us busy there. Something's definitely changed."

"And you think it's the faerie door."

"Yes. We've been trying to figure out the source of all this strangeness for months, and no one's had any success. Well, the Council *said* they had no leads, but now I know they were lying." Ash lets out a disgusted huff of breath as he shakes his head. "Two nights ago, I was following this creepy whispering sound and I ended up in the Shadow Crypt. I've searched for the door before, of course. But I could never see that archway and the extra room you told me about. They just didn't exist. But this time, everything looked different. As if a glamour or some other magic had been lifted. I found the door. And I saw something climb through one of the holes."

There's something about the way he says those last few words that sends a shiver across my skin. "Something?" I ask, not entirely sure I want to know the details.

He looks past me, frowning. "I suppose 'climb' isn't really the correct term. It was like a black mist. Like shadow come to life. It poured itself through the hole and took form once it was on the crypt side of the door. And it reached almost to the ceiling, once it was upright. It stood on two hind legs. Two arms, each ending in long claws. A snout that protruded forward with bared teeth. And its skin seemed kind of … leathery."

Ash is right. Based on his description, this doesn't sound like any fae creature I remember reading about or facing in the wild. "That's … creepy."

Ash's eyes move back to mine. "It didn't get very far. There were two councilors there—Bergenfell and Poppywood—and they stood on either side of the door and killed it the moment it took form. It was after that, while they were staring down at this dead monster, that I heard your name from the other side of the door."

This time, the shiver crawls all the way up my neck and into my hair.

"Poppywood commented that he didn't know any Isela," Ash continues quietly, looking past me again with unfocused eyes, as if watching the scene play out across his mind. "And Bergenfell said, 'Isela is Silver Wren's real name.' I clearly remember her saying 'is' and thinking it must have been a slip of the tongue, but then Poppywood asked about a guardian named Markham and …" Ash shakes his head. "I don't know, something about a dead end. And then Bergenfell said …" Ash swallows. "She said, 'No, it's definitely Silver Wren. I've sent Markham to finish her off tonight.'" Ash shakes his head, returning his gaze to me. "I … I was so … I don't even know. I don't have the words to describe what I felt. I … don't remember exactly what happened, but suddenly I was on my knees, and I must have said something, or made some kind of sound, because that's when they discovered me."

I draw in a slow breath, watching him carefully. I'm almost certain he's telling the truth, but what if I'm wrong? What if he's in on the Council's plans, whatever they may be? My parents died to make sure that door was locked and no councilor ended up with the key. I can't let them down now just because my silly heart wants to trust Asher Blackburn again.

"So they … they tried to kill you?" I ask Ash.

"Yes. I don't remember how I fought them off. My brain was … in shock? I must have acted purely on instinct. All I could think was that I had to know if it was true. I had to know if you were still alive."

He's staring so intently at me that I have to look away. I desperately want to believe everything he's saying, but those final moments of my parents' lives are stamped too firmly on the inside of my mind for me to forget. *Don't ever come back here. Don't ever let them get the key.* Even if Ash is telling the truth, I can't let him drag me back to Stormsdrift.

"I left immediately," Ash continues. "Didn't even go home. Well, I stopped at the Guild and stole a few of those indigobell seeds, the ones that are traceable for a few hours. I found Markham leaving his office, and I dropped one down the back of his jacket. Used that to track him after he left the Guild. I followed him all the way to the fighting ring inside The Gilded Canary before he noticed me. I tried to pretend Bergenfell had sent me. That she'd told me to help him. But I guess my expression must have given me away when he said ..."

I raise a brow. "When he said?"

Ash clears his throat. "When he said, 'I don't need help torturing the key's location out of her and then killing her.'"

My pulse quickens, a steady rhythm thrumming in my ears. In a low tone, I mutter, "I'd like to see him try."

"He won't be getting the chance any time soon. I stunned him, tied him up, and dumped him outside a particularly unfriendly elven community in Fallowhaven. They like to act first and ask questions later. They'll lock him up and take their time contacting a Guild."

"Too bad. Here I was looking forward to another fight."

"And then I found you," Ash says softly, ignoring my comment. "The following night, just outside that fighting ring. And it was like ... like seeing a ghost." His gaze, soft in the light of the pink trumpet blossoms, travels my face. My skin grows hot, and the world grows quiet. The forest fades away. It is just the two of us.

And the chasm of secrets that now exist between us.

This reminder slips through my mental haze and jolts me awake. I blink and look away. The world is loud again. Chirrups and warbles and water tripping over pebbles. "What, um, what did the Council tell you?" I ask. "About how I died, I mean. Magical accident? Did I fight back and Bergenfell and the others were forced to end my life?"

Ash is quiet a moment, still watching me. A flutter of wings stirs low in my belly. I imagine beating them down with one of Teddy's fancy embossed rolling pins. "Shadowfire," Ash says eventually. "In the Guild greenhouse. They said you must have started it when you ran through there trying to get away from them."

"Of course," I murmur. "I *did* start the fire in the greenhouse. I had the leftover potion my mother gave me after she set fire to our house. But I escaped through the paths straight after the fire began."

"I see. Well, Bergenfell changed that last bit. She said she and some of the others tried to get you out, but you were trapped because you'd lost your stylus somewhere along the way, so you couldn't open a doorway to escape. And because it was shadowfire, there was nothing they could do to extinguish it. So you … you died in the fire. That's what we were all told. I didn't want to believe it, but afterwards … well, there was a body."

My frown deepens. "Wow. I wonder who that was. Who had to die just so Bergenfell and the rest of our wicked Council could keep their lies buried?"

"Perhaps it wasn't even real. Bones and teeth can probably be conjured."

My gaze jerks up, landing on his. *Bones and teeth.* Another shiver crawls up my spine as I imagine that moment, walking among burned ruins and seeing the charred remains of a body.

"And no one ever mentioned anything about a faerie door or strange creatures," Ash continues. "All we ever heard was that your parents had killed those two councilors. If someone ever took a closer look to confirm Bergenfell's story, or if someone questioned her under the influence of truth potion, someone else on the Council must have been ready to cover it up. It sounded to me as though they're all in on this."

"In on *what* exactly?"

He shakes his head. "I'm not sure. They know there are creatures on the other side. Monstrous fae we've never had to fight before. And it sounded like the councilors are supposed to be guarding this door—like they've been guarding it for a very long time—but now the only thing Bergenfell wants is to get through to the other side."

"Okaaaay," I say slowly, staring at the ground and wondering what Bergenfell could possibly hope to gain by opening a door to a land of horrifying fae.

"Look, all I know is that Stormsdrift has become a dangerous place. There's a door, and there are monsters getting through it, and the councilors are supposed to be *preventing* this from happening, but instead they want to open the darn thing. How many monsters are going to wander through into our home if that happens? How many more people will die? It's just … it's crazy. It goes against everything guardians are trained to do."

"Well, I'm glad you're finally seeing Bergenfell and the rest of her corrupt little posse for who they really are." I fold my arms and add quietly, bitterly, "Since framing my parents for murder and then killing them clearly wasn't enough for you to stop trusting them."

His gaze is hard now as he stares me down. "You think that I—if you only *knew* all the—" He slices the end of his words off with a hard press of his lips and a frustrated exhale. He swings away from me, swatting several trailing leafy tendrils out of the way. His hands are on his hips as he inhales deeply. He faces me again. "I don't have time to get into all of that right now. What the councilors are doing is wrong, and that means we need to stop them."

I'm shaking my head before he's even finished speaking. "There's no 'we' here, Ash. I don't know why you came to me for help instead of—"

"I came to you because I'd just discovered that my deceased best friend was possibly *not* deceased, and my brain couldn't focus on a single thought aside from confirming that this was true. I didn't care about the door, or the monster that crept through it, or the councilors who want to kill me, or the key they're hoping to find. Just you." He pauses, and I'm not sure if he expects me to respond, but I can't. The emotion lodged in my throat makes it hard enough to swallow, let alone speak. "But now that I know it to be true," he continues, quieter, "there's just enough space in my head to start worrying about Stormsdrift again."

"Well, the—" I pause, clearing the croak from my voice. "The key isn't going to help. And besides, it's gone," I lie. "My parents didn't want anyone else to be able to find—"

"Of course the key isn't going to help. The door is already locked, and somehow monsters are finding their way through it regardless. What I want to know instead is …" He takes a breath. "How do I get rid of the door entirely?"

I blink. "You want to destroy it?"

"Yes. That seems to be the obvious solution. Then nothing can pass through from either side. I know your parents burned everything in their home that night to hide whatever they discovered, but did they tell you anything? You said they spent years hunting down whatever knowledge they could find about the door. Was there anything that led them to believe it could be destroyed?"

"I … I don't know." *Do* I know? Did they tell me if it was possible to destroy this strange, enchanted door that leads to a land filled with monsters? I can't remember …

"Okay, well did they try?" Ash presses. "What did they tell you?"

I will take this secret to my end.

I blink and tear my gaze away from his. "I—I don't know, Ash. That night was … it's kind of a blur. We were in a huge rush, and they were talking over each other, throwing things in a bag. They didn't have time to sit down and have a chat about all the discoveries they'd made." They did, however, have time to tell me they'd hidden what they discovered *outside* of our home, but I haven't figured out yet if I should share that with Ash. "Whatever I told you that night," I continue, "when you came over just before we left, is what they told me."

"I think you said they went to the door that night because they wanted to get rid of it."

I frown at him, genuinely puzzled. "I did?"

"Yes. Isn't that why they were there instead of at the Lib Day Ball with the rest of us?"

"They were there because …" My gaze slides away from Ash's as I try to remember the garbled details that flew from my mother's tongue as she and Dad dragged me from the ball that night. "I can't remember, Ash. I don't know *why* they went there that night, but I remember them saying there were two other guardians, and a creature they'd never seen before, and the guardians ended up dead, and even though Bergenfell saw what happened, she told everyone my parents were the ones who'd killed the guardians. That's what I told you, right?"

"Yes, but … you don't remember them saying the reason they went there in the first place was to try something that would destroy the door?"

My arms are crossed again, pressing tightly against my chest. "I've done my best to block out a large chunk of my life, Ash, starting with that night. Forgive me if I don't remember precisely what everyone said to everyone else."

I will take this secret to my end.

Okay, so there's one thing I do remember with absolute clarity, but it's not going to help Ash.

"A large chunk?" he asks, brows lowering further. "What else—"

"Don't you think that if it *was* possible," I continue, "then whoever told our Guild Council to guard this stupid door would have simply destroyed it instead?"

"Maybe that person didn't know how."

"Okay, well you know who might know? A thousand other guardians in a dozen other Guilds all over the world. Why don't you go to them for help?"

He gives me a pointed look. "Why didn't *you* go to another Guild after you ran? Why didn't you try to get someone to listen to you about what really happened?"

"One trainee going up against a whole Council of respected guardians? People able to forge documents and create 'truth' out of lies? Bergenfell would have killed me before any other Guild managed to get close to unearthing the truth. It was safer for me to stay hidden and get on with my life."

Ash raises both brows as if to say, *Exactly.*

I roll my eyes. "Don't tell me it's the same for you. You've graduated, at least. You're a guardian, not some child that no one will believe. And you don't have a bunch of people accusing your parents of having murdered other guardians. Another Guild will take you seriously. They'll listen to what you have to say and open an investigation."

"Okay. Perhaps that's true. *Hopefully* that's true, otherwise the entire Guild system is completely messed up. But it will still help if you can tell me whatever you remember, or if there might be someone your parents confided in. Someone I can go and speak to. Then at least I have more information to take to another Guild."

Tell me whatever you remember. Somehow, I can't help hearing those words in Bergenfell's voice. I walk past Ash, aiming for the roots of one of the purple umbrella-jellyfish-type trees. "Okay look. I just … I need to grab my things from my apartment. And—" I suddenly remember the ring in my pocket. The ring Mel gave me that I'm supposed to pass on to Goldilocks. "And something else," I finish vaguely, pulling my stylus free once more. "Give me half an hour. Then meet me outside Stormsdrift. At the signpost. If you've been telling the truth about what's happening there, then I'll consider helping you."

"Wait—just—" Ash releases a short breath as he steps toward me. "How do I know you won't disappear again?"

I crouch beside the giant, twisting roots and write a doorway spell on one of them. I want to tell Ash that perhaps I will disappear. That I owe him nothing. That he'll just have to wait and see. "I guess you don't," I end up saying. Mainly because I don't know yet either.

"Fine," he answers as dark space spreads across the roots at my feet. I straighten, sliding the stylus back inside my jacket and stepping toward the opening. I almost don't hear him grumble beneath his breath, "Won't be hard to track you down again."

I stop. I turn back, one foot inside the darkness of the paths. "Excuse me?" It occurs to me now that I forgot to ask him the first question that flashed across my mind when he showed up in my bedroom: "How exactly did you find me after I ran from The Gilded Canary?

Because I *know* you couldn't have followed me through the paths. You were nowhere near me when I opened that doorway."

Ash lets out a resigned sigh. "An indigobell seed. In your hair. I put it there just before I pulled your mask off in the fighting ring."

Anger burns hot and sudden in my veins. My hand shoots up to my hair, and my fingers feel through the tangles for several moments before curling around a small, prickly object. I pull it out—smaller than my pinky nail, a blue so dark it's almost black—and throw it on the ground at his feet. "Any other tracking items I should know about?" I ask, my tone icy.

He shakes his head. Without another word, I turn and stride into the darkness.

FIVE

Silence greets me as I step into my bedroom. At least, it seems like silence in comparison to the forest that was alive with sound. My anger fades rapidly as the reality of my situation sinks in. The Guild found me. Ash found me. He led bloodtongues to this very apartment. And even though we killed them, Bergenfell would surely have been tracking them. The Council might know about this apartment by now. They could be on their way here at this very moment. *Bergenfell* could be on her way here.

Fear digs its chilly fingers into me and tightens its grip. I can't move, think, breathe. Suddenly, I'm that sixteen-year-old girl again, stumbling through an unknown part of the fae world, my face streaked with tears, terror forcing me onward as my brain keeps reliving the killing strike Bergenfell delivered to end my mother's life. And then I'm seventeen, running once again, constantly looking over my shoulder—

Stop.

I am neither of those girls. I am eighteen now, stronger, and if I figured out how to survive before, I can do it again. I swing around to face the hole in the floorboards, forcing myself to *see* it, to stay in the present, to shove the fear to the back of my mind. I need to grab my things. I need to remain alert. I need to get out of this apartment and figure out what my next move is.

I crouch beside the hole in the floor and remove the backpack that already contains some clothes and other essentials. Then I line a duffel bag and hastily pack all my weapons into it, my ears pricked for any unexpected sound, my eyes darting up every few seconds, searching for movement in the shadows. I zip it up, press my hands against the sides, and draw on my magic so I can shrink the bag. I haven't done this in years, so even though it's a charm I used to be good at, it takes longer than I'd like to get the words right. But eventually I'm left with a duffel bag small enough to sit on the palm of my hand. Teddy would call it the cutest thing *ever*. My heart squeezes, but I push the ache aside as I shove the tiny duffel into the top of the backpack. I zip it closed and pull it onto my shoulders.

Then I stand in my bedroom doorway and take a brief look around the place I've called home for a little over a year. The damage is extensive, and though I told Teddy and Duke I'd take care of it, I'd rather not risk the time it would take to figure out the correct spells. On top of that, the fighting has drained me of some of my magic. I don't want to tire myself further when I have no idea how much more magic I'll need tonight. I push aside the guilt that niggles at me as my eyes scan the shattered window and the gouges in the walls. This is what a damage deposit is for, right?

The last two things I reach for are the empty jar that's supposed to contain the cloaking charm and a book from the shelf in my bedroom. Then I open a doorway and step out of this chapter of my life. Darkness presses against my open eyes, and I fight back the urge to cry. Memories flit across my mind—movie nights on the couch, Teddy teaching me how to bake, Duke's endless patience as I figured out how to use a phone and a laptop, the cramped chaos of make-your-own-pizza nights when we invited all our other friends over—but I gently push them aside, reminding myself that I need to choose a destination if I don't want the faerie paths to drop me somewhere completely random.

The darkness pulls apart, and I walk into a cemetery bathed in the soft peachy violet of twilight. This is one of my meeting places with the woman I know only as Goldilocks. I'll never be a guardian, but that doesn't mean I can't do my part to secretly foil the plans of the criminals who meet up at The Gilded Canary and whisper about their dealings. Riven has his agreement with the Guild, but he doesn't tell them about half the things that go on in his club—and I'm not about to go to a Guild either. After what they did to my parents, I trust a secret vigilante group more than I trust guardians.

Goldilocks has a network of at least a dozen people who work at The Gilded Canary and gather information, but I'm one of only a few people who actually meets with her to pass on that information. Or, occasionally, an actual item. I'm not sure exactly what I did to earn myself this position of trust, but I'm grateful for a way to make a difference.

With my jar and book still under one arm, I walk to one of the headstones and reach for the urn sitting atop it. Made of stone, it's merely for decorative purposes and was never meant to be opened. But Goldilocks enchanted it so we could hide things inside. I remove the lid, drop the ring into it, and close it again. Then I pull out my amber and write a message.

> *Tonight's item is in the urn. I'm sorry I can't meet you myself. Someone from my past turned up. I'll be on the run for a while. When I'm settled somewhere new, I'll let you know. I want to keep helping.*

Then I turn my back on the cemetery and head into the paths. My next destination is a flat roof in the same area as the bakery I ended up working at. Not too far from home, it's nighttime here as well. Quiet. No one else around. A space for me to think.

I stare in the direction of the bakery. Ant will be worried when I don't show up tomorrow morning. He'll call, and I won't answer. Then he'll try Teddy. I wonder what Teddy will tell him. More guilt piles itself on top of the healthy portion already sitting in my stomach, so I turn my focus to the book tucked beneath my arm.

I open it to reveal a hollow space where all the elements required for the cloaking charm are hidden. I sit on the roof, place the empty glass jar in front of me, and methodically drop the various bits and pieces into it as I recite the incantation. Less than a minute later, I watch the jar slowly fill with blue liquid as I screw the lid back on. It isn't the best anti-tracking charm out there, but it's all I've been able to afford. It takes me another minute or so to think up a good enough spell to protect the jar from breaking, but once that's done, I shove it into the backpack beside the tiny duffel bag.

Then I place my hands on my hips and stare out across the city, my heart torn. I don't have to go back. I could leave Ash there waiting. Disappear again. Let him solve his problems on his own. Except …

Things are getting bad.

Unease tugs at my mind. Stormsdrift was my home. A place dearer to my heart than any other. There are people there that I used to care about—*still* care about, if I peek beneath the hard shell I've fashioned for myself over the past few years. If what Ash said is true, then I should help them. I *want* to help them. Even though I promised Mom I would never return.

With my thumb and forefinger, I pinch the bridge of my nose. I squeeze my eyes shut, trying to quiet the war in my mind. The two sides battling it out: Trust Ash. *Don't* trust Ash.

He came to warn me. He attacked a fellow guardian in order to get to me first. The Council knows that he discovered the door, and now he's being hunted by them as much as I am. Surely that should put him on my side? Unless all of that was a lie? Nothing more than a very good act?

Possibly …

But, the other side of my brain shoots back immediately, those bloodtongues were definitely after him, which means the *Council* is definitely after him. Which would put him back on my side again. Unless that was all part of an elaborate plan to get me to trust him. Maybe Ash is just waiting for me to give up all my parents' secrets, waiting for me to tell him where the key is so the councilors can unlock the door, and *then* he'll kill me.

I press my fist against my brow. No. Ash was never a good liar. Not with me, at least. I'd be able to tell if everything he's said tonight is false. Then again … we've both changed. I'm a better killer; perhaps he's a better liar.

Stop deliberating! I all but shout at myself, dragging my hands down my face and taking a deep breath. I need to go to Stormsdrift and see for myself. *Feel* for myself. Then I'll know for sure that at least part of Ash's story is true.

And it's an excuse to spend a few more minutes with him, that small, traitorous corner of my heart whispers to me.

Shut it, I mentally snap right back.

Then I open a doorway and face the darkness. I take a breath, step forward, and think of the place I've tried for years to erase from my memories: Stormsdrift.

Six

then

THE AIR WAS FILLED WITH THE SCENT OF HONEYCINTHS AS SIX-year-old Silver stepped out of the faerie paths, her small hand inside her mother's, and looked around the forest that was her new home. Golden rays filtered through the trees, casting dappled light on the leaves and tiny asterpearl blossoms that covered the forest floor.

"Ah, there it is," Dad said, pointing to the clearing up ahead. "We were a little bit off."

"Not too far," Mom said. "We can walk the rest of the way." She inhaled deeply, and Silver looked up to see her mother's eyes closed, her face lifted toward the forest canopy. The light turned her alabaster skin a pale gold and glimmered where it caught the silver strands among her white hair. "Isn't it perfect here?" Mom murmured.

Dad caught Silver's eye and raised both brows in that exaggerated fashion that left her fighting a giggle. His eyes were round, and he nodded toward Mom as if to say, *What's up with her?* Silver couldn't help it. Laughter bubbled up and escaped her lips.

"What?" Mom asked, looking first at Silver, then at Dad.

"I didn't say anything," Dad answered.

Mom rolled her eyes, but she was smiling. "You think I'm being silly again."

"Not silly." Dad slipped an arm around Mom's shoulders. "I love that you're already so happy here. Makes it worth the back-breaking effort of moving a thousand boxes before midday."

"Oh, you mean those thousand boxes you moved with *magic*?"

"I moved two of them!" Silver reminded her parents, tugging on Mom's hand and turning her next step into a jump.

"I know, and you were amazing, Silver girl," Mom said. "You're doing so well with your magic."

"I unpacked one of my boxes with magic too," Silver added proudly. It had taken her all afternoon to lift her stuffed toys one by one from their box and send them traveling jerkily across the room to the bed, but she'd felt an enormous sense of accomplishment by the end of it.

"Well done, that's fantastic!" Mom bent and kissed the back of Silver's hand before straightening. Then she sighed and lowered her head to Dad's shoulder as they continued walking. "I know you still think I'm imagining it, but there's something here that just feels … right. As though I've finally found whatever it is I've been searching for."

"What have you been searching for, Mommy?" Silver asked, leaping over a small ring of toadstools.

"I don't know, bug. I just always felt like … something was calling to me. I've felt it for years. My whole life maybe."

Silver frowned. "Is something calling me too?"

"No, Silver girl, don't worry," Mom said with a laugh. "It's just me. But I think Stormsdrift is where we're meant to be. Don't you get that feeling?" she said to Dad.

"I don't know, Nel. We could have had illustrious careers at Bloodwood. They've had by far the most—"

"—high-profile cases in the past five years, I know, I know," Mom said. "You keep reminding me. We spent all that time climbing the career ladder and—"

"And now we're throwing it all away to come to a tiny Guild way out here in the middle of nowhere."

Silver thought of their new house, nestled between trees instead of hidden within one by a glamour, as their previous home had been. Here, where every house was out in the open, there was even space for a garden, overgrown with tiny white flowers called baby-something and wild yellow roses that Mom had told her reflected moonlight at night. Silver loved being able to *see* her new home and the homes around hers. Stairways and little bridges and vines creeping up walls. 'The middle of nowhere,' she decided, was beautiful.

Mom's voice turned teasing as she leaned into Dad and said, "*You* could have stayed at the Bloodwood Guild. It's only a short trip through the faerie paths, you know."

He shook his head and kissed her cheek. "Never. You know I'd follow you anywhere. Even if it is to the middle of nowhere."

"Look, at the end of the day," Mom said, "we'll still be fighting dangerous creatures and putting a stop to evil magical plots and protecting totally oblivious humans. Does it really matter where we do it?"

"Well, no. But I'll admit I enjoyed doing it at a Guild where there's at least *some* prestige—"

"Don't pretend there's no prestige here. It's the oldest Guild in existence. That'll look good on your CV."

"The oldest Guild *ever*?" Silver asked.

"Well, second oldest. The first Guild ever built no longer exists."

"Why?" Silver asked.

"Um …" Mom's expression turned thoughtful. "I think there was a fire. The first Guild didn't have a lot of protection on it, and it was one of those enchanted fires that couldn't be put out. Shadowfire, I think. But you know you don't have to worry because Guilds are much better protected these days."

"Especially since Lord Draven and the Distraction," Silver said. She hadn't been born yet when that happened, but her parents had explained it to her after someone at school tried to scare her with stories of Guilds blowing up and guardians dying.

"The Des*truc*tion," Dad corrected, a hint of amusement in his tone. "And yes, Guilds are even better protected now. You don't have anything to worry about, bug."

They were almost at the clearing now, and Silver could hear laughter and shouting, and had caught several glimpses of people running back and forth. "So … it's the Blackburns we're meeting?" Dad asked. "Lennox and …"

"And Iris," Mom said. "The couple we chatted to when we came for the second interview."

"Oh yes, the guy with the beard. And she was overboard friendly."

"Hey, she was *nice*," Mom protested, nudging Dad in the side. "I liked her. These are the people we'll be working with for however long we end up living here. Would you prefer it if they *weren't* friendly?"

"I'm kidding," Dad said around a laugh.

They stopped as they reached the edge of the clearing, and the first thing Silver noticed was the enormous picnic blanket laid out on one side. Her gaze traveled across the open space and landed on the opposite end, where the trees didn't quite come together. She could see all the way to a beach that lay at the end of a path, and beyond that, white-crested waves crashing onto the shore. She took a breath of the warm salty air before her attention was caught—and held—by the children racing across the clearing and the ball floating in the air between them.

They were all boys, some with streaks of orange painted on their arms and cheeks, others painted blue. They knocked the airborne ball back and forth between them, sometimes with magic, sometimes with hands or feet. The ball remained blue for the first few moments Silver watched it, flying between blue-painted figures. And then the tallest boy —a dab of orange beneath each eye—jumped higher than the rest and sent a spark of magic streaking toward the ball. The magic caught it, and the ball instantly turned orange. Then it spun around and went sailing toward another orange-painted boy.

"Hey! Hello!" Silver blinked at the sight of the woman coming toward them. "Nelina, Rowan, so nice to see you both again." The woman stopped in front of them and wrapped Silver's mom in a hug.

"Thanks, you too." Mom returned the hug. "And you can call me Nel."

"Right, yes, sorry. I remember you saying that. And this is Silver?"

"Yes. Silver, this is Iris," Mom said.

Iris crouched down and grinned at Silver. Everything about her seemed warm: chestnut hair, tanned skin, smiling eyes. Her secondary color was light brown rather than some vibrant shade of the rainbow, and even this made her seem gentler, friendlier. "It's lovely to meet you, Silver." She didn't attempt to ruffle Silver's hair in that annoying way of some adults, and she didn't force a hug on Silver either. Silver rewarded her with a smile, deciding that she agreed with Mom. This lady was nice.

"Have you ever had a toasted mallow sparkle cake pop?" Iris asked. Silver shook her head. "Oh my. They're possibly the most delicious thing in the whole world. Toasted marshmallow on the outside, and underneath that is a chocolate layer, and then the cake in the middle has these sparkles that just *explode* all over your tongue like magic. *So* good. They're over there on the picnic blanket if you want one."

Silver gripped Mom's hand tighter, hoping to communicate that yes, she definitely wanted a sparkly marshmallow pop thingy, but no, she didn't want to walk to the picnic blanket on her own. Fortunately, Mom was good at interpreting hand squeezes. She crossed the grass with Silver, and Iris went with them while Dad headed toward a bearded man who was standing near the edge of the clearing with his hands up in the air. Silver guessed he was busy with some kind of enchantment based on the tiny sparks of magic dancing above his head, and the way his hands kept moving about.

"This is such a beautiful spot," Mom said, taking a seat on the picnic blanket while Iris pulled a cloth off one of several baskets to reveal a plate of toasted marshmallow thingies on sticks.

"Isn't it?" Iris said, handing one of the sticks to Silver. "It's our absolute favorite spot in the whole of Stormsdrift. We come here all the time in summer. The boys spend hours in between the river—" she pointed through the trees "—the beach, and this clearing." She offered Mom a cake stick, which Mom politely declined, before covering the basket again. "I know you must be tired after moving in today, but I'm so glad you could join us. It's such a lovely evening for a picnic, and the boys have been looking forward to meeting Silver."

"They're … all yours?" Mom asked hesitantly, and Silver followed her gaze to the group of boys. They had just finished tackling each other to the ground in one large, rowdy heap, and it was impossible to tell how many of them there were.

"Oh! No, thank goodness," Iris said. "Four belong to me. Flynn is the oldest. Just had his eleventh birthday." She pointed to the first boy to detach himself from the pile of bodies and flailing limbs. Blue paint marked his face and hands. "Connor and Tobin are nine." Iris pointed out two boys with identical features. "And Ash is our youngest." She nodded at the boy who'd just rolled away from the group. He jumped up and sprinted away with a whoop, the ball—now blue again—in his hands. "Same age as Silver," Iris added.

"Oh, yes, I remember you saying that." Mom ran her hand up and down Silver's back. "Remember I told you about Ash? You'll be in the same class as him."

Silver nodded as she took another bite of the marshmallow wonder. This time, she bit through the chocolate layer and reached the cake in the middle. Something tingly and chocolatey and utterly delicious exploded across her tongue and danced around the inside of her mouth like teeny sparks of edible magic. Silver smacked a hand over her mouth to keep from spraying cake and sparkles everywhere as she started laughing.

"It's good, right?" Iris said, her eyes crinkling at the corners as she grinned. Silver nodded, swallowing and licking her lips. "Anyway," Iris said, turning back to Mom. "Those two—" she pointed at the pair of boys now scrambling up the side of a tree "—belong to my brother. And those two—" an orange-painted pair, screeching at the top of their voices as they tore off in the opposite direction "—are my sister's. They'll join us a bit later. My brother and sister and partners, I mean."

"That's … a lot of boys," Silver's mom said.

"I know," Iris answered with a laugh. "And I know it's unusual for *four* of them to belong to one family. And before any of the Stormsdrift gossip reaches you, no, we did not forget how to do contraceptive spells. We just decided to go against faerie tradition and have a big family."

"I like that," Mom said. "A big family. Must be nice."

"You come from a small family?" Iris asked.

Mom nodded. "I'm an only child. Rowan had a sister, but she was … well, she was killed during Draven's time. Our parents all died in the same attack. And my grandparents … I never knew them. My parents weren't in contact with them anymore. And Rowan's grandparents died before he was born. So … it's just us."

"Oh, I'm so sorry." Iris looked devastated, but this story wasn't new to Silver, so she turned her attention back to the boys' game. She hadn't ever known any of the people Mom was talking about, so while she knew Mom got sad about them sometimes, it was difficult to feel any of her own sorrow over their absence.

"You've been at quite a few Guilds over the years, haven't you?" Iris asked.

"Yes. Starsfjord was the first one, but we also spent a while at the London Guild and the Bloodwood Guild. Oh, and we were at the Creepy Hollow Guild for a couple of years after the Destruction. After Lord Draven's defeat, I mean. We helped with getting everything set up at the new Guild there."

"Oh yes. Can you believe it's been *nine years* since then? Almost a decade. Crazy how the time flies."

"I know. We didn't even have Silver then." Mom pulled Silver against her side and kissed her cheek. "It feels like a lifetime ago, hey, baby bug." Silver looked up at Mom before offering her some of the half-eaten chocolatey mallowy mess, but Mom smiled and shook her head. "You finish it, bug." Then she turned her gaze toward the sky, still golden from the light of the setting sun, and said, "So. Stormsdrift, huh?"

"Yes," Iris answered with a nod. "And don't let the 'drift' part fool you. There's nothing slow about the way they come and go. We'll have sunshine one minute, and the next thing you know, thunderheads are rolling in and you're seconds away from being soaked. I have no doubt we'll be caught in the midst of one before the evening is over. That's why Lennox is getting the canopy enchantment up now. Takes a bit of time to do one large enough for the whole clearing, but at least this way the boys can keep playing even when the storm hits."

"Though I'm sure a storm wouldn't stop them," Mom said.

Iris laughed. "You're right. It certainly wouldn't."

Silver followed the ball's progress as it flew in zigzag patterns across the clearing, switching between blue and orange every few moments. Licking the remaining chocolate from her fingers, she watched as the oldest Blackburn boy leaped from a tree, *just* touching the ball with the tips of his fingers before he hit the ground. It switched from orange back to blue, and the four Blackburn boys roared and pumped fists in the air.

"Have you been to the junior school yet?" Iris asked.

"Yes," Mom said. "We're very happy with it. I think Silver will enjoy —" She ducked down as the ball, still blue, struck the edge of the picnic blanket, bounced over the collection of baskets, and came to rest just behind Silver.

"Connor!" Iris shouted. "Please be careful!"

"Sorry, Mom!" one of the twins shouted back. He ran toward them, but Silver was already up. She grabbed the ball and raised it above her head. Then she released a jolt of magic—after practicing all afternoon, she was getting quicker at pulling it from within her and setting it free —and sent the ball flying back. Her aim was off, though, and the ball sailed right over Connor and hit the boy behind him on the head. He stumbled backward, tripped over someone else's foot, and landed on his backside.

61

Silver slapped a hand over her mouth. *Oops.* Wasn't that the boy Mom had said she would be in the same class as when she started school? Ash?

"Oh, goodness, I'm so sorry," Mom rushed to say. "Silver, that was—"

"Don't worry about it," Iris said with a laugh. "Happens all the time. These boys aren't exactly gentle."

With the ball in one hand, Ash ran up to Silver, his other hand rubbing the side of his head. "That hurt," he said.

"I'm—sorry," Silver answered haltingly. "It was an accident."

The boy lowered his hand. When he smiled, it reached all the way to his warm amber eyes. "It was a good throw. Know how to play Keep The Ball?"

Silver shook her head, though she'd guessed the gist of the game by now.

"I can show you. Wanna be on our team? My cousins are older, so I think we need one more person if we're gonna beat them."

"Yes!" she answered immediately.

"Okay, come on." Ash took off across the clearing, and Silver raced after him, a grin already in place.

SEVEN

now

MY GAZE LANDS ON THE STORMSDRIFT SIGNPOST AS I WALK OUT of the faerie paths, my thumbs hooked beneath the straps of my backpack. The weathered wooden post, wrapped in a twisting vine that glows jewel-beetle green in the dim moonlight, rises from a pile of stones. The vine winds all the way up and trails over the sign, small heart-shaped leaves partially obscuring the carved letters that form the word Stormsdrift.

Ash is facing away from me, arms folded over his chest, staring past the signpost. An orb of magical white light—his, I assume—floats nearby. At the sound of my footsteps, he tenses, head jerking to look over his shoulder, magic gathering in his palms. But the magic dissipates when he sees it's only me. He moves to stand at my side, saying nothing.

I let the backpack slip from my shoulders and slowly lower it to the ground as I peer into the shifting mist. Moonlight barely pierces through from above the treetops. I see no glow-bugs on the branches, no tiny winged creatures zipping through the air. I can just make out the oversized pega-wing flowers at the base of some of the trees, but their glimmering azure light is suppressed by the mist. And the trees themselves are little more than shadowy shapes that, thanks to the drifting mist, seem to almost … move.

Don't ever come back here, Mom said that night. *Don't ever let them get the key.* Though I know she meant the door itself when she said 'here,' it still feels like a form of betrayal to be standing at the edge of Stormsdrift, so close to the thing that brought about her death. *I won't go back there*, I silently promise her once again.

"Believe me now?" Ash asks quietly.

I fold my arms and shrug, not ready to admit that he may have been telling the truth about something. "It's just mist. Fog. A normal weather phenomenon."

He lets out a weary sigh. "Come on, Silver. It *feels* different, doesn't it? It's too quiet. Too … close."

I know what he means. I can't *see* anything sinister, but I get the sense that something is slowly, inexorably pressing in on me. A shiver creeps its way up the back of my neck. "Yeah," I say eventually. "I guess there's something that feels a bit … off." My heart does a clumsy little flop. Could it be that everything Ash has said tonight is true? Should I dare to trust him?

"I would offer to take you to my family," he says. "They'd tell you the same thing about all the strange happenings here. The fog and the creatures and how our home is no longer safe. But they don't know what I saw, and I don't want to get them involved."

"In case they end up like my parents," I finish quietly. "Silenced forever." He doesn't argue with me. I shake my head. "It's despicable," I hiss, my jaw tight, "what the Council is doing. The lengths they're going to in order to get to whatever's on the other side of that door and to keep everyone else quiet about it. They're the *leaders* of our Guild. They're supposed to be setting an example for every guardian who works there. They're supposed to be upholding the oaths they took to protect people, and instead they're *murderers.*"

I suck in a deep breath and clamp my lips shut. I didn't mean to spit that all out, but there it is. Suddenly, I'm desperate to find the information my parents hid before they died. I'm desperate to find a way to destroy this door, not only because it's an entrance to a land of monsters, but because it's made monsters of the people we're supposed to trust.

I turn to Ash. "Okay. I'll help you. I'll share what my parents discovered. But I can't go near that faerie door. Because ... I just *can't*. So you had better be telling the truth about which side you're on and what your motivations are, because if it's possible to destroy the door, *you're* going to be the one to do it."

He's quiet another moment, his eyes searching my face. Then he nods. "I understand."

He doesn't understand, but that's okay. As long as we're in agreement. "I don't currently have the information in my possession," I continue, "so we'll have to go and find it. I think I'm the only one who can read it, so I'll take a look and let you know if it says anything about destroying the door. Then we can part ways. I'll get back to my life, and, if it's possible, you can get on with saving Stormsdrift. With or without the help of another Guild. That part's up to you."

"Go and find it," Ash repeats slowly. "*Read* it. Are you saying there's a record somewhere of the things they discovered? Something that's actually *written down*? Not just the things they told you? Because that would be amazing."

"Yes. My parents burned our home to make sure no one could discover anything from the notes or drawings or whatever was left in their home office—" I pretend not to notice the quiver in my voice as I speak of the home that went up in flames "—but my mom told me that she'd recorded most of it in a journal." *A journal*, I almost repeat with a scoff. Having spent some time living like a human, it seems ridiculous that this valuable information wasn't stored digitally on a hard drive plus a backup hard drive, with a *backup* backup version in the cloud— encrypted or password protected or something. Most humans assume that magic, if it existed, would make everything better, easier, and in many ways it does. But in some ways, stepping back into my world feels like stepping back into the Stone Age.

"A journal, okay," Ash says.

"Yes. Apparently it was hidden beneath the pool in my parents' bathing room, but after those guardians were killed that night—after my parents realized no one would believe their story and they'd have to run —my dad took the journal and hid it somewhere else while my mom came to get me from … from, uh, the Lib Day Ball." I look away, stumbling over my words as I remember the precise moment my mother found me—found *us*—that night. Ash is probably picturing that moment too, and now I wish with everything in me that I hadn't mentioned it. "Anyway," I forge on, determinedly *not* looking at him, "the journal should hopefully be hidden in the same place still, waiting for us to find it."

"Wait. What do you mean *hopefully*? You don't actually *know* if it's still there? You haven't checked?"

"No." I have a feeling this is about to become a Thing, so I move to step past him. But he's in front of me again just as swiftly, blocking my path.

"Let me get this straight. Your dad told you exactly where you could find a journal detailing almost everything he and your mom discovered about this mysterious faerie door—something that was important enough for them to spend *years* trying to learn more about—and you never went looking for it?"

"No!" I answer, louder than I intended. "I left everything from my old life behind. My father locked the door, my mother got rid of the key, and that was that. End of story. Whatever was on the other side would stay there forever. So why would I want to go digging into all of that again?" Why would I want to unearth all that heartache, is what I really want to say.

"I don't know, maybe because …" His gaze softens, his tone growing gentler, as if he's aware he's treading on sensitive ground now. "Maybe because it would be a memento of your parents, if nothing else?" Though I can tell he isn't trying to hurt me, he says this like it's the most obvious thing in the world. Like I'm a terrible daughter for *not* wanting to find a journal my mother wrote in years ago.

"Look, I—" I press the palm of my hand to my brow, my eyes darting unseeingly over the ground between us. "Some stuff happened straight after I fled the Guild, and I wasn't in a position to go looking for it. And after that was over, I just … I needed to move on."

"Stuff happened?" I hear the growing concern in Ash's voice. "What stuff?"

None of your damn business, I almost tell him. My heart is a hummingbird flutter in my chest now as the paralyzing fear I lived with for so long creeps closer, threatening to shut my brain down.

Water.

The river.

The Blackburns' kitchen on a Sunday afternoon.

Cascading waves and warm cupcakes and Duke lifting me off the ground when he hugs me.

The mental images work. I exhale slowly. "Look, do you want to find this journal or not?"

"I—yes. Of course."

"Then let's go." I reach for my backpack and hike it up onto my shoulders.

"Okay then," Ash says after a pause. His eyes slide away from my face and land on the backpack. "I hope you packed something warm this time."

I blink, startled and unsure how to respond. "Is that … supposed to be a joke?"

He sighs. "It is, yes. I was also going to make a lighthearted comment about how I know you were always good at shrinking charms, but did you really manage to fit all your worldly possessions into one bag? But I think I'll keep that one to myself."

My hands tighten on the backpack straps. "Why don't you get straight to the point, Ash, and ask me if the key is hiding somewhere in this backpack? You clearly don't believe me when I say it's gone." *Probably*, I add silently, *because you can tell I'm lying.*

A flicker of confusion crosses his face, only to be replaced a moment later by something hard. "I'm not interested in the key, Silver. It isn't going to help me."

"But it would certainly help Bergenfell."

"And you still think I'm secretly working for her? You think I've tracked you down so I can pretend to be your ally until you trust me enough to tell me where this key is, and then I can take it to Bergenfell?"

I shrug. "It's an option, isn't it?"

"First of all, if you really believe that, then I don't think you ever knew me at all. Secondly, please *don't* tell me where it is; I don't want the wrong people prying its location from me. And thirdly …" He throws his hands up. "If you really believe I'm not on your side, then why agree to help me?"

I take a deep breath, wondering if perhaps I overreacted. Perhaps he really was trying to lighten the mood with his 'joke' and his 'worldly possessions' comment. I hold his gaze and say, "I guess I'm hoping you're telling the truth. Just know that if you're *not*, I will make you pay for your lies."

He watches me a moment, then turns away with a small shake of his head and walks toward the Stormsdrift signpost. "Never thought I'd hear words like that from someone I once considered my closest friend."

"And I never thought I'd have to try and figure out whether the person I once considered *my* closest friend is plotting to murder me after he gets his hands on a key I've already told him is gone," I shoot back. "But here we are."

He stops in front of the pile of stones at the base of the signpost. "I'm not even going to dignify that with a response."

"Great."

"Great." He slides his amber out of his pocket, glances at it, pauses, then puts it away.

"You know the Guild can track that," I point out.

"This isn't the amber I usually use." He bends and writes with a stylus on one of the stones. "I'm not that stupid." A doorway opens, and I'm about to take a step forward when the dark opening flickers oddly—a phenomenon I've never seen in my life—before blinking out of existence. "Wonderful," Ash mutters. "How supremely convenient."

My heart thuds too quickly in my chest. "That—was that—what you meant about—"

"The faerie paths not working sometimes? Yes. This is what I meant. So we'll need to walk a bit, then check again once we're a little further away from Stormsdrift."

I'm still staring at the blank spot on the stones where the doorway is supposed to be when Ash walks past me. "Wait," I say faintly. "Wrong way. We're heading into Stormsdrift, not away from it."

He stops. "Your father hid the journal somewhere in Stormsdrift?"

"Yes."

"He could have hidden it anywhere in the world, but he chose to hide it where the very same people he was trying to keep it from live and work every single day?"

I give him my most withering glare. "Stormsdrift is a huge area. And my dad needed a place that would mean something to him and me and to no one else, so I'd know exactly where to find it if something happened to him. I guess this was the first place that came to mind. He didn't exactly have time to think of something else."

"Terrific. So we'll be traveling through the fae world's latest and greatest monster wonderland. Should be fun."

"Look, if you're afraid of a few—"

"*Afraid?* This has nothing to do with either of us being *afraid*. You don't know what kind of—"

"I can handle myself, Ash."

"Fully trained guardians with decades of experience have been killed by the creatures that now roam Stormsdrift. You may have kept up your training since leaving here, but technically you didn't even make it past fourth year."

I pin him with the full force of my glare as I step closer to him. "I. Can. Handle. It."

"Or," he says, "we can sit here and wait until the faerie paths start working again, and then we can go straight to wherever this super-secret spot is."

"And if the paths never work again as long as that door is still there? No. I'm not waiting." I march past him into the mist.

"So where exactly are we going then?" he calls after me.

"The Canopy Way."

"You'll have to be a little more specific," he says as he catches up to me. "The Canopy Way covers almost the entire forest."

"I don't *have* to do anything. I'm not going to explain the exact location so you can stun me and run off to find the journal on your own." At that, he only shakes his head. "Not that it would do you any good," I add. "My dad put some kind of enchantment on it to protect it from other people."

"Good. Hopefully that means it's still there."

My gaze slides across the passing landscape, landing on whatever features I can make out through the mist. My senses are on high alert for any sudden movement or unexpected sound. I don't know if I should expect a guardian ambush, or if Ash might suddenly attack me, or if a monster I've never seen before may leap from the shadows.

"So," Ash says. "What, uh, what have you been up to the past few years?"

I shake my head, my gaze catching on a small flare of light near the ground. But it's only an eruptor mushroom spewing tiny streams of lava from its cap. "We're not doing this."

"Not doing what?"

"Not catching up on each other's lives like we're old friends."

"We *are* old friends." There's an edge to his voice that might be anger. Good. I'd rather he be angry than daydreaming about reconnecting or something stupid like that. When I say nothing, he adds, "So … what? We're going to pass this whole journey in silence?"

I almost roll my eyes. "It isn't going to be a 'whole journey.' If the faerie paths start working soon, it'll take us barely a few steps to get there. Then a few minutes, max, to retrieve the journal. Even if the paths remain nonfunctional and we have to climb all the way there, it still won't take us that long. We should be done before the night is over."

"So—that's it?"

I stare ahead, my eyes following the trail of a sprite as it flits between the trees and disappears into the mist. "What were you hoping for? A lengthy reunion?"

He releases a sharp exhale. "Are you going to be angry with me for the rest of our lives?"

"Don't I have the right to be?"

"Of course you have the right to be angry, but not *forever*. I've apologized. Multiple times. And even though I didn't know what to believe that night and I chose to follow Bergenfell's order to capture you, I did *not* try to kill you. So what else do I need to—"

"Just stop," I say as I come to a halt and face him. "Stop thinking you can fix everything that went wrong just by showing up and apologizing. We're not going to be friends. We're not going to hang out. We've survived just fine without each other for the past two-plus years, and we'll go on happily living the rest of our lives without each other too."

It's impossible to miss the hurt that flashes across his face, and I hate that I'm the one who put it there. I hate the guilt that rises in a wave and washes over me, leaving me cold. *I'm* the one who's supposed to be upset, not him. I'm the one who lost both parents and ran for my life and ended up—

Stop.

I shut my eyes before the blood-stained memories hit me. When I open them again, Ash's expression has hardened. "So this is how it's going to be."

I should be more relieved at his acceptance. I *am* relieved, I tell myself. That pain in my chest that's stealing my breath? That isn't my heart breaking all over again. I'm *fine*. Ash and I are on the same page now. This way it'll be easier to say goodbye in a few hours—or at the most, a day or two—and move on with our separate lives. "This is how it's going to be."

It's almost visible then, the shutters slamming closed over his features. He faces forward. "Let's get this done then."

We walk in silence. Ash tests the faerie paths. We walk a little further. He tests them again. This time, when a doorway opens, it doesn't flicker and vanish. "Good," he says quietly. "At least we don't have to spend any more time than necessary in each other's company." He looks back at me, his gaze settling somewhere to the side of my face instead of on it. "If you're done being hostile …" He holds his hand out toward me.

I stare at it, trying not to think of all those nights long ago when I dreamed of sliding my fingers between his. All the nights up until That Night. I try not to think of all the nights since then, my cheek pressed against a pillow wet with tears, alternately hating him and longing for him before falling into fitful dreams of the moment that flash of magic left his hand and streaked toward me.

"For goodness' sake, Silver," he mutters, dropping his hand to his side. "We can't go through the paths together without touching. Would you like to link pinky fingers or something, just to ensure there's as *little* physical contact between us as possible?"

I roll my eyes, step forward, and catch his hand in mine. There's no tingle of skin, no jolt in my chest, no skipping of my heart.

Liar.

I stride forward, pulling him into the paths behind me. "Clear your mind," I remind him. "I'm the one directing the paths."

His sigh is impossible to miss, but his muttered response—something that definitely includes the word 'bossy'—is harder to catch. I decide to ignore him. Despite the complete darkness surrounding us, I close my eyes to help me focus. Stepping out of the paths in the wrong place is potentially hazardous when aiming for a spot so high above the ground.

The darkness gives way to muted light. Wide branches and trailing vines and shafts of moonlight. I step forward, my hand still in Ash's. His skin on my skin, his fingers gripping mine, his thumb sliding across the back of my—

I release his hand and look around. The ground is so far down I have no hope of seeing it through the mysterious fog that swirls below. A fog that doesn't seem to reach the Canopy Way. Up here, on the path that snakes through the very tops of the trees, where glow-bugs dot the leaves and beetles like tiny jewels scuttle across the branches, it's easier to believe that nothing in Stormsdrift has changed.

"We're close," I say to Ash as my eyes land on a familiar heart-shaped knot formed between two branches. I gesture to the right with my head. "That way."

We start walking. Though no official markings indicate the Canopy Way, the path is obvious from the well-worn branches and the parts where the arms of two neighboring trees have been magically intertwined. This tree-top route isn't the only one of its kind, though it's the only one I've ever traveled. Faeries have always enjoyed wandering the canopy world—when they're not traveling almost instantly from point A to point B via the faerie paths. Long ago, in what feels like another lifetime, I came up here at least once a month with my father.

Just before we reach a walkway of braided branches, I step off the Canopy Way and climb carefully around a large trunk. Reaching the other side, I slide down the smooth, concave surface of another branch and land in the wide, flat space where four enormous branches meet. In this moment, the nostalgia that hits me is so overwhelming it almost steals my breath away. I put a hand out against one of the branches and stare past it into the night.

We're almost at the northern edge of the Stormsdrift Forest, and this particular spot provides a spectacular view of the Ellaneen River winding past before plunging down the Thunder Falls and continuing its journey toward the sea. I thought the scene might be obscured by fog, but the dense moisture has thinned out here at the edge of the forest, little more than a light mist mingling with the spray of the falls.

"Okay," I say to Ash, turning my back on the view. "The journal should be hiding somewhere around here."

"So this place meant something to you and your dad?" Ash asks, looking around.

"Yes," I answer shortly. Then, deciding I might be taking this hostile thing a step too far, I breathe deeply and add, "He used to bring me here to do my homework on those afternoons when my mom was working and he was off. He always said it would … clear my senses and help me think better." Instead of forcing the pain away like I usually do, I allow it to take shape in my chest. Allow the tears to prick behind my eyes, and the ache to tighten my throat. It's kind of impossible *not* to face the pain, here in this place where the memory of Dad is so near it's almost as if he's present. I take another breath and the pain eases a little, spreading through me instead of overwhelming me.

Ash peers out between two of the enormous branches. "He didn't think your brain might be paralyzed with fear due to the very real possibility of slipping and falling into that raging river down there?"

I almost smile. "Nah, he always put a shield up while we were sitting here." I crouch down, the backpack straps pulling taut around my shoulders as I stretch forward and nudge aside a few fern fronds. "We didn't come here that often. Most afternoons I was—" I cut myself short before I can wander too far down memory lane. I'm the one who said we wouldn't be doing this. And Ash already knows what I was about to say: Most afternoons, both my parents were working, and if I didn't have extra training or an assignment, I was hanging out at his place. "Anyway, yeah. We didn't come here that often, but I knew exactly what place he was referring to when he told me he hid the journal at our study spot."

"Um, Silver?"

I look up, something in Ash's tone catching my attention. "Yeah?"

"That seems like an obvious spot." He points at something behind me. I straighten, turn, and see the hole that's formed where a gnarled knot once existed.

"Huh. Interesting. I'm pretty sure that wasn't a hole before."

"Then I'm going to take a not-so-wild guess and say the journal's hiding in there."

"Probably a safe bet." I step closer, trying not to think of what else might be hiding in that hole. "Well. I guess I'm now the girl who sticks her hand into mysterious, dark holes in magical forests."

Ash's laugh is so quiet it's more an exhalation of breath than anything else. "You were always that girl, Silver."

And I suppose he's right. So I do what I would have done when we were children and banish all concern from my mind before reaching into the dark space. There's a moment of uncertainty as my fingers search blindly and feel nothing but rough bark, but then they nudge something smooth. My heart lurches into my throat. I rise on tiptoe, stretch a little further, and wrap my fingers around the object that most definitely feels book shaped.

My heart is pounding so hard that I feel a little lightheaded as I withdraw the journal. I hold it carefully, almost reverently. Brown leather cover, leather strap, metal clasp. Plain and yet … perfect. Whatever magic Dad placed on it has worked well. There isn't even a speck of dust, let alone damp pages or mold. "Well, that was … easy," I murmur. I'm vaguely aware that now would be a good time to say, *I told you this wouldn't take long*, but I'm too focused on the treasured item in my hand.

Then something snakes around my ankle and tightens. My heart jolts, and I swing my arm up and away from my body to keep the journal out of reach of whatever's attacking me. "What the—" My eyes land on a vine encircling my ankle. "Do you think that's part of the—"

Heat burns through my hand. My gaze darts up in time to see a flash of magic burst from the journal and strike the center of Ash's chest. The force of it throws him backward toward one of the openings between the branches. His eyes go wide for a single instant before sliding shut. His body slackens. He starts to fall. And as I throw my other hand out, his name a gasp on my tongue, he tumbles off and disappears into the night.

EIGHT

then

SILVER GRIPPED THE VINE TIGHTLY WITH BOTH HANDS, RAN TO the edge of the rock, and leaped off it with a shriek. Exhilaration flooded her thirteen-year-old body as she swept through the air. The vine reached its furthest point, and in that frozen moment before it began swinging back, she let go and dropped toward the river with a whoop. She plunged into the water, bubbles and tiny turquoise glow-fish rushing up around her. With strong strokes, she pulled herself toward the surface, emerging with a grin still on her lips.

She turned her gaze toward the rock where Ash was guiding the vine back with magic and the other three Blackburn brothers were arguing about how far Silver had made it across the river. They were near-duplicates of each other—well, Connor and Tobin *were* duplicates—with honey-colored streaks highlighting their dark hair, and year-round, sun-kissed skin that Silver couldn't help envying. No matter how many hours she spent in the sun every summer, she remained as pale as ever. Or red, if she didn't apply enough sunblock potion.

"No way," Connor was saying. "She definitely wasn't in line with the third marker."

"Exactly, she landed *further* than that," Tobin said.

"No way!"

"Yes way!" Silver called out as she treaded water.

They ignored her, looking instead to Flynn. Eighteen, recently graduated, and by far the most responsible Blackburn boy, his brothers generally looked to him for the final word. "Oh yeah, she was definitely beyond the third marker," he said. "No doubt about it."

"Yes!" Silver shouted, shaking a victorious fist in the air. She pointed at Ash and yelled, "Beat that!"

"In my sleep!" he yelled back. Then he raced to the edge of the rock and leaped off with a jubilant cry. Silver squealed and swam out of the way as Ash sailed through the air. He hit the water with a tremendous splash, emerging moments later and wiping a hand over his wet face. "Pretty sure I beat you," he said with a grin.

She stuck her tongue out at him. "You wish. But Connor's about to beat *both* of us, so don't get too excited."

"Out of the way, skinny brats!" Connor shouted before flinging himself off the rock. With the aid of a bit of magic, Silver and Ash swam swiftly back toward the riverbank. It wasn't quite sunset yet, and they could get at least a few more jumps in before they headed to the beach for the bonfire. "Beat you both!" Connor shouted from behind them as they climbed the bank.

"You used magic," Ash shouted back. "Cheater."

"No he didn't," Flynn called from somewhere above them.

Together, Silver and Ash climbed around trees and over rocks, listening to the whoops and cries as Tobin and Flynn jumped into the river, until Silver scrambled ahead and pulled herself up the final distance onto the large rock they'd been jumping from for years. She skipped to the end and stood on the very edge, her arms spread out at her sides. "You know those stories humans tell about us?" she said to Ash. "Magical creatures with wings? I sometimes feel like those should be true. We *should* be able to fly."

"Do you also want to be really tiny?" Ash asked. "Because they say that about us too."

"I think they get us mixed up with sprites."

"They get *everything* mixed up."

Silver laughed. "They do." She grabbed the vine Flynn's magic had sent swinging back to her, and then she jumped again.

Eventually, after plenty of arguments, acrobatic leaps into the water, and much laughter, Flynn, Connor and Tobin went ahead to start the bonfire. Ash and Silver stayed for another few jumps, but the sun's descent couldn't be halted, and they would miss the colors if they didn't leave soon. The sun disappeared on the other side of Stormsdrift, not over the ocean, but sunsets at this time of year were so spectacular that —provided there was no storm—the color spread across the entire sky, lighting up the high clouds with brilliant orange and pink.

They floated on their backs, watching the trees slide by as the gentle current carried them toward the beach. This was the epitome of a lazy summer afternoon, and though Silver was excited for the next chapter of her life—Guild training—to begin, she was in no hurry for perfect afternoons like this to be over.

The trees thinned out and disappeared, and before the river could take them all the way out to sea, they stood and waded onto the beach. The bonfire was already going, flames dancing and smoke rising. "Race you there?" Ash said.

"Hah, so you can watch me win again?"

"No, so *you* can watch *me* kick your ass. You know I'm faster than you now."

"Oh, *what-ever*. There's no way you're faster than me."

"I've been practicing. In secret."

"Oh yeah?" Silver danced a few paces ahead, spinning back to face him as her lips turned up in a wicked grin. "Well then. Come and get me." She dashed across the beach, struggling to gain traction on the loose sand, but somehow managing to stay just inches ahead of Ash. She slid to a halt beside the bonfire and crashed into Connor, her legs aching, her chest burning. "Beat your ass again!" she gasped as she and Connor toppled over.

"Thanks, lunatic," Connor grumbled, crawling across the sand and retrieving his stylus from where it had landed. "Do you want the fire to die? I was just getting it perfect."

Silver stood and brushed the sand off her arms and legs as best she could. "Sorry. But your fire will be fine."

"Actually, it requires careful attention," Tobin said, "and a slow but steady stream of magic to keep the—"

"It's just a fire, Tobin," Ash said breathlessly, hands on his knees as he bent to recover from the sprint.

"It isn't *just* a fire," Connor argued. "You think something this spectacular happens in no time at all if there's no magic involved?"

"Hey, are your parents still coming?" Silver asked no one in particular. "Because if not, I'm calling dibs on the extra s'mores."

"They'll be on their way soon," Flynn told her. "Dad said don't you dare touch his s'mores."

Silver laughed as she dug through the bag she'd left there earlier and pulled out a towel. "And you said Holly's coming too, right?" she asked, referring to the girl Flynn had started dating a few months earlier.

"Oooooh." Connor made some disgusting kissing noises, then jumped aside as Flynn threw a handful of sand at him.

"Shut it," Flynn told him. "If you embarrass her when she gets here, I will hurt you. That goes for all of you."

"We would never," Silver assured him. "Holly's cool." She made a half-hearted effort at drying her hair, then pulled her shorts and T-shirt back on over her bathing suit. A cool breeze drifted across her arms, and she dug a little further inside the bag. "Ugh, I forgot a sweater."

"Surprise, surprise," Ash said, then dodged out of the way as Silver flicked her towel at him.

"The fire will warm you up soon," Flynn said.

"Or I guess we could heat the air in the meantime," Tobin said, "if you're desperate."

"Nah, it's fine." Silver pushed her towel back into the bag and closed it. "I'll survive."

"Here." Ash finished pulling a dry T-shirt over his head and threw a bunched-up hoodie at her.

"Thanks," she said, catching it easily. As she pulled it over her head, she leaned closer to him and whispered, "You got the syrup spell ready?"

"Yeah," he murmured. "Want to do it now?"

"Yes. I'll distract them." She pushed the hoodie sleeves up as she stepped around Connor. He and Tobin were once again focusing intently on the bonfire. Flynn was crouched down on the other side, unpacking all the food they'd brought. Without another thought, Silver swiped the stylus from Connor's hand and danced out of reach.

"Hey, give that back!"

"Can you just let somebody else do it for once?" Silver said, pointing the stylus at the fire. "You're such a control freak."

"That's because it's *my* fire."

"It's not *your*—"

"Guys, please," Flynn interrupted. "Do we have to do this every time?"

"Yes, we have to do this every time," Silver said, "because Connor insists on being such a—"

"Because *Silver* doesn't respect the time-honored tradition of—"

"Would you both just *stop*?" Tobin said. "I'm trying to concentrate here."

"And … *now*," Ash cried out. Silver scrambled backward, her eyes on Ash as he lowered his hands in an abrupt downward-sweeping motion. A moment of confusion passed, and then the near-invisible layer of sticky syrup he'd been quietly constructing above everyone's heads cascaded over his three brothers and the fire.

Shocked silence filled the space between them as Silver stared in frozen glee. The brothers blinked. The sticky bonfire wood hissed and sizzled. Then: "Oh, you are *so* gonna pay for that, you little turds!" Connor launched himself sideways, droplets of syrup flying everywhere, and Silver squealed as she took off up the beach with Ash, their bare feet kicking up sand behind them.

They aimed for the trees, then raced between them until they reached the clearing. Silver threw a glance over her shoulder but didn't see anyone behind Ash. "Are they still … coming after us?" she asked breathlessly as she slowed.

Ash turned to face the beach, also slowing until he came to a stop. "No, I think maybe they went down to the water to wash off the syrup."

"Can you see them?"

"Uh … no. Good point. They're probably hiding in the trees, waiting to get us back."

"Probably. So worth it though." She laughed. "Did you see their faces?"

"Silver?"

Silver spun around at the sound of the new voice. "Zilph," she said, startled to see one of her classmates emerging from the trees on the other side of the clearing. His two friends, Senna and Rolph, stepped out beside him. Well, they were no longer her classmates, she reminded herself. They were all done with junior school now.

"Wow," Zilph said, his features twisting in disgust. "It is you."

All trace of laughter was gone. Silver's insides clenched. "Of course it's me. Who else has silver hair around here?"

Zilph muttered something she couldn't quite make out.

Silver folded her arms and lifted her chin as Ash moved to stand at her side. "Is there something you'd like to say to me?" She knew what Zilph was mad about, but she also knew it had nothing to do with her. Two weeks earlier, her father had arrested Zilph's older brother when he'd been found at the scene of a murder. The victim was a councilor from another Guild, and—from what Silver had overheard—Zilph's brother swore he'd been in the wrong place at the wrong time. A truth potion had determined he most likely *wasn't* the murderer, but it had also turned out he knew more than he initially admitted. He'd seen something—Silver didn't know what exactly—and had been trying to keep it from the Guild.

It would have been awkward for Silver if she and Zilph were still attending school together, but summer vacation had begun by then, and while Silver and Ash were starting at the Guild in the fall, Zilph had chosen to attend an art college outside of Stormsdrift. Silver had hoped she wouldn't run into him again, but now here he was, glaring at her as if *she'd* been the one to commit a crime.

"Yeah," he answered, his chin jutting forward. "Are you proud of having a father who's such a useless guardian?"

Anger flared in Silver's chest, but she managed to keep her magic from flashing across the space between them. "Excuse me?"

"My brother would never be involved in an 'assassination,' as the stupid Guild is calling it. Your lazy-ass father couldn't be bothered to find the right person."

Blood pounded in Silver's ears, but Ash answered before she could. "Why don't you come over here and say that?"

"Sure." Zilph took a step forward. His friends followed. "I'll come right up and spit it in her obnoxious pale—"

"I don't think you want to do that." Another voice. Connor. He moved into the space on Silver's left. From the corner of her eye, she saw Tobin and Flynn appear beside him.

Zilph shook his head and let out a derisive snort as his eyes landed on Silver again. "Got your bodyguards with you, as always. You wouldn't be so brave if you were on your—"

"Shut the hell up, Zilph," Connor snapped. "You wouldn't know bravery if it bit your scrawny ass."

"And you would?" Zilph's friend Senna challenged. "You Blackburns are just as bad as the Wrens. Think you're so damn superior, when you're really just—"

"Don't you dare finish that sentence," Silver hissed. The Blackburns were like family to her, and she wouldn't stand to hear anyone speak ill of them.

"Superior?" Flynn repeated, an icy edge to his tone. "Is that the word for people who risk their lives every day to keep others safe?"

"Yeah, that's exactly what it is," Senna retorted. "You pretend to be so noble and everything, when all you really want to do is rub it in everyone's faces. 'Look at us, we're so much better than you!'"

"Yes, I'm sure that's what a guardian thinks," Tobin said quietly, "when he lies dying in the cold beside the fae monster he tried to slay in the hopes of protecting a town of innocent humans."

A tense pause followed Tobin's words, and Silver thought Zilph and his stupid friends might be about to back down. But then he curled and uncurled his fists, lifted his chin once more, and said, "Look, this doesn't have anything to do with you stuck-up Blackburns. This is between Silver and me, so why don't you run along and leave us to finish the conversation we—"

"Leave you and Silver?" Ash repeated. "Like we'd just walk away and let you three—"

"Try it," Silver snapped. With hands clenched at her sides and magic burning at her fingertips, she marched across the clearing. "I dare you to try it. All three of you. I'll show you exactly what I'm made of."

She was almost in front of Zilph when Ash reached her side, hands raised and magic swirling and sparking in his palms. But Flynn caught them both by the arm and began dragging them back. "This is not the kind of fighting that impresses the Guild," he said quietly. "Don't get yourselves suspended before you've even started."

Silver continued glaring at Zilph, but she knew Flynn was right. *Breathe*, she told herself. *Just breathe, dammit.*

Zilph let out another humorless snort. With a superior tilt of his head, he said, "Yeah. That's what I thought."

Silver almost ripped free of Flynn's clutches so she could throw herself at Zilph. Fortunately, the idiot was now turning and heading back into the trees with Senna and Rolph. As Flynn let go of her arm, she inhaled deeply and rolled her shoulders. "I could have taken him," she said. "And his stupid friends."

"I know, but that whiny little brat isn't worth it."

"Would have been entertaining, though," Connor said as they headed back to the beach, "watching Silver beat up those three wimps."

He threw an arm around her shoulders and gave her a sideways hug, and it suddenly occurred to her that he was no longer covered in syrup. Neither were Flynn and Tobin, for that matter. Her rage cooled slightly as it made way for a vague sense of annoyance. How did the three of them clean themselves up so quickly? It really was frustrating that they knew so many more spells and enchantments than she and Ash did.

"Yeah, well, get ready to be entertained next time," she grumbled, kicking at the sand as they walked, "because if he says anything like that again about either of my parents—or you guys—I'm going to make sure he regrets it."

"Silver," Flynn started.

"No, seriously. If someone doesn't put him in his place, he's going to just keep bullying people. You should have heard what he said to Odette when she found out one of her uncles is only half faerie. He made out like it's the most disgusting thing ever, which we all know it isn't, but she was in tears after what he said."

"I understand how you feel, Quicksilver, but—"

"Hey, Silver?" It was Ash who'd interrupted.

Silver looked around, then realized he was somewhere behind her. "Yeah?" she said, turning to face him.

He grinned. "Look up."

She did—just as thick brown liquid dropped through the air and enveloped her in warm, goopy stickiness. She gasped and froze, torn halfway between shock and laughter. She blinked, meeting Ash's mischievous gaze through the syrup that trickled from her eyelashes.

"You!" Then she launched herself at him. He let out a yelp and tried to dodge away, but—as she'd proven multiple times this afternoon—she was faster than he was. She tackled him to the sand, laughter bubbling from her syrup-covered lips, and tightened her arms around him in a giant hug. He tried to fight her off, but he was laughing so hard he could barely move. She rubbed her sticky head all over his chest and neck, and soon enough there was sand stuck to their faces and in their hair and covering their clothes and crunching inside their mouths.

85

They lay there for a long time, recovering from their laughter and spitting out sand and watching the pink-orange-gold clouds shift across the sky. And eventually, after all the color had faded, they half stumbled, half chased each other into the waves and cleaned off by way of a water fight.

NINE

now

Ash is gone.

I act on instinct. My hand sweeps down, magic slicing through the vine tugging weakly at my ankle. I shove the journal inside my jacket, tug the zip up, and dive straight off the edge of the branch and into the night.

He's a dark shape below me, and we're fallingfallingfalling, water rushing up to meet us, and he's doing nothing to slow his fall, which means he's either been stunned unconscious, or he's—

Not dead.

He can't be dead.

I throw magic out ahead of us, but the words of the spell are ripped from my tongue and stolen by the night. Useless. My fingers scramble across the stacked leather braids on my right wrist. I know the pattern of stones and pearls without having to look. I know the charm I'm aiming for. One, two, across, and then up one more. I squeeze it between my fingers, my heart slamming in my throat, the river *right there*—

Magic streaks away from me. A glittering web ripples into existence and catches us. We slow but don't stop, the web stretching and stretching and—

Snap. We hit the water. Streams of bubbles and sparkling glow-fish and currents too strong for me to fight against. I don't know which way is up or down. I pull desperately at the water, aware of my backpack adding weight and resistance. As my lungs begin to scream, my head finally breaks the surface and I gulp in a deep breath of fresh air.

The swift current carries me along as I twist my head around, grateful for the turquoise glow-fish illuminating the water as I search for Ash. But I can barely make out anything from above the water. I take a deep breath and drop beneath the surface. No longer disoriented from the fall and the rush of bubbles, I release magic behind me and slide easily through the water, my eyes peeled for Ash.

Deja vu hits me then, somehow reaching through my panic. For one breathless moment, it's summer again, and Ash and I have just leaped off our favorite rock and plunged beneath the water's surface. We're racing one another to the beach, seeing who can swim the fastest—

There! I blink away the memory as my eyes make out a dark shape up ahead. A distinctly Ash-shaped shape. I release another pulse of magic and shoot toward him. Fear squashes all rational thought as I get close enough to see his lifeless limbs and closed eyelids. I hook my hands beneath his arms as magic gives me an extra boost upward.

Our heads break the surface. I suck in air and silently beg him to do the same. I'm trying to hang onto him, trying to keep my head above the water, trying to draw on enough magic to fight the current and propel us to shore, when I suddenly realize several things at once: The water is far choppier here, the current is dragging us along even faster than before, and that fist-shaped rock protruding from the water is alarmingly familiar.

"Crap," I gasp. Because I know from experience—one terrifying and highly unpleasant experience—that that rock is the last thing one can grab hold of before vanishing down the Thunder Falls. And we've just been swept right past it. I struggle to pull Ash against me, one arm squeezing around his chest as I release the smallest jolt of magic. "Wake up, dammit!" I risk a slightly stronger pulse of magic. "Wake—"

A scream swallows my words as we're swept clear over the edge of the falls and plunge toward the thunderous, frothing spray below. Ash slips from my one-armed grasp. I can barely see or breathe or hear, and even though I'm a magical being, I'm utterly useless in this moment.

There's plenty *that's deadly to a faerie.*

My own words flash through my head an instant before my body strikes the river and I'm submerged in its bubbling, churning depths. Up is down, I'm spinning around, and there's a dark, jagged shape speeding toward me. My heart slams in my chest as I miss the rocks by mere inches, a current dragging me over them. My arms pull, my legs kick, my hands release magic behind me, and finally, finally, finally—

Air.

I suck in a great gasp of it, my arms and legs still working to keep me above the turbulent surface. I look around, fighting the cold, bone-deep fear that Ash is still trapped somewhere beneath the seething water. Gone forever. I dive down, my eyes searching the blue-green depths. But despite the illumination the fish provide, I can't see much down here where the water is so choppy.

I come up for air, swiping the water out of my eyes and trying to remember the spell we learned years ago to create bubble-like structures over our heads so we could—

"Silver!"

My hands beat the water, spinning me around in the direction of the gasp. I see him, *alive*, slicing through the river toward me, and I'm doused instantly in body-weakening relief. He loops an arm around me before I can protest—not that I want to; I suddenly feel as though I barely have the strength left to keep myself afloat—and propels us to shore.

We crawl up the bank, where I allow myself a moment to collapse onto the sand and pebbles. I breathe. In … out. In … out. Then I push myself up onto my knees and look over at Ash. "Hey," he says, dragging in another breath. "You're okay."

"You idiot!" I shove his shoulder roughly. "Why the hell would you touch the journal?"

He blinks at me as his heaving breaths begin to slow. "You literally shoved it against my chest!"

"I was—holding it slightly away from my body."

"A little more than *slightly*."

I press my lips together and look anywhere except at his face because it's impossible to hide from the fact that this was very definitely my fault. "I'm … sorry," I manage to mutter. Then I take a breath and quietly repeat, "I'm sorry. And I'm sorry about that too." I point at his chest where his T-shirt now displays a roughly circular singed hole.

He frowns as he looks at it. "That was you?"

"Um, yeah. Raw magic. Just a little bit," I add quickly, well aware that throwing pure, unformed magic at someone generally isn't a friendly move. "I was trying to wake you before we reached the falls. Trying to shock the stunner magic out of you."

"Right. I guess it worked. I woke up just before we hit the bottom of the waterfall. Bit of a shock to see *that* when I opened my eyes." He searches the pockets of his pants, then groans and says, "My amber's gone."

I check my jacket pockets and let out a curse. "So is mine. And my stylus."

"You don't carry a spare?"

"Of course I carry a spare. Multiple spares." I tug down the front zip of my jacket. The journal's still there, as well as the various small weapons discreetly secured by straps and zips, and two more spare styluses tucked into a tiny pocket. It was only the items that were shoved into the open outer pocket that are now taking a trip down the Ellaneen River.

Still kneeling, I place the journal carefully on the ground and shrug free of the backpack straps. I dump the soaking wet bag on the ground in front of me. "Crap it," I mutter as I open the top, already knowing what I'll see inside. "Everything is drenched."

Ash hunches down on the other side of the bag. "You didn't have a waterproof charm on it?"

"No, Ash, clearly I did not. I wasn't expecting some moron to go flailing down a river in need of immediate assistance." A moron who was only in the river in the first place because of me.

"There was no *flailing*," he replies, his voice containing just a hint of defensiveness.

I exhale sharply before quietly muttering, "Yeah. I guess there wasn't." It was the complete *lack* of flailing that made it so damn scary, but I'm not about to admit out loud just how terrified I was.

"Silver, come on," he says, tone gentler now. "This river is practically our second home. You knew we'd be fine. Right?"

I didn't, though. He could have drowned, and it would have been my fault. I would have hated myself for the rest of time—for bringing about the death of someone who may or may not have tried to kill me once upon a time. A guy I still don't know if I can trust. I hold onto this thought as I continue digging through my wet belongings, stubbornly avoiding his gaze. "We survived the falls before," he adds. "Of course we'd survive them again."

My hands go still. My eyes rise to meet his. Across my vision plays the memory of us accidentally hurtling over the edge of the Thunder Falls many years ago. I was sure we were plunging to our deaths, but, in the end, we were fine. We never told anyone, though. We knew our parents would be furious that our reckless antics had brought us so close to death.

I realize I'm still staring at Ash. He returns the gaze from beneath long lashes glistening with droplets of water, eyes almost shimmering in the moonlight. My breath quickens as my heart stumbles over itself. I clear my throat and tug the zip of the backpack closed. "We're not doing this," I remind him as I pick up the journal and stand.

He remains crouched down for a moment longer, then rises. "Right, I forgot. We're pretending we have no shared history. And since you're the one who put us in this sopping wet situation, Miss Let Me Smack

You In The Chest With An Enchanted Book, you only have yourself to thank for the state of your belongings."

Well. Annoying as that is, it's the truth, so I can't exactly argue with him.

"Now that we've almost drowned for this journal," Ash continues, "care to take a look inside and let me know if it says anything useful about getting rid of the door?"

A hot-cold flash of anticipation goes through me at the mention of the journal. I look down at it. Brush my thumb over the leather and then up over the metal clasp. I press, and it releases with a quiet click. My heart rate jumps another notch. I take a step backward, putting some distance between Ash and me. I think Dad said something about me being the only one who could read it—aside from him and Mom— but if I'm wrong about that, I'd rather not have Ash peering over as I open it for the first time. I know the most important secret *isn't* in here, so neither he nor Bergenfell can use it, but there's no harm in being extra careful.

I hold my breath and slowly open the cover, waiting for the pain I know will pierce my chest at the sight of Mom's handwriting. But it doesn't come.

The page is blank.

Next page, I think, turning the wet paper carefully. *She left the first page blank.* But the following two pages containing nothing either. I release the breath, telling myself not to panic as I wait, because this is surely part of the protective magic Dad placed on the journal. If I just give it some time, the words will reveal themselves to me. Except … nothing happens. I turn to the next soggy page, and then the next. I turn to the back and separate another few pages, but nothing changes. "It's … empty. Blank." I lower it so Ash can see. "Is it blank for you too?"

He steps closer and nods. "You said you're the only one who can read it, so perhaps you have to … I don't know, identify yourself some-how. So the journal knows it's you."

"Surely the journal already knows it's me," I argue, ignoring how stupid it sounds for a journal to 'know' anything at all. "If it didn't, I wouldn't be able to touch it without being shoved away by magic like you were." I turn the journal over, examining the back and spine, and then all three sides of the page edges, looking for some sign or marking. But there's nothing. "Maybe the charm malfunctioned? Or … do you think … can a charm expire?" Guilt grips my chest and squeezes. Did I wait too long to come and find the journal? Is it my fault we'll never know what secrets lay between these pages?

"I don't know. Maybe?"

"Perhaps I'm supposed to do something or say something to reveal the words." I turn the journal over thoughtfully. "I don't remember my dad telling me that, but like I said before, everything was a rush that night, and my head was still spinning from—"

Oops, scratch that.

"From, um, everything. So it's more than possible that I missed something he said." Ash doesn't answer, and I'm worried his brain might be stuck on the awkward moment I almost brought up. For the *second* time tonight, because that's how much of an idiot I am. Eventually I look up and find him watching me with an expectant expression. "What?"

"I'm just giving you a moment. You know, to run things through in your head, maybe remember something you didn't remember before."

"I can't *make* a memory simply pop into my head, especially if the memory might not even be there to start with."

He holds both hands up. "Okay, fine, sorry."

I frown at the journal again as I turn to another random blank page. "Maybe it's not showing me anything because the pages are wet. Maybe I need to dry it."

"Worth a try."

I crouch down and stand the journal upright, fanning the pages open as best I can, then take an energy-mustering breath before gently heating the air with both hands. My fingers shake slightly, and I hope

Ash doesn't notice. It's stupid, but I don't want him knowing how tired I am.

"If this doesn't work," he says, raking a hand through his wet hair, "then do you think there might be someone your parents confided in about all this? Someone we can go and talk to?"

"I don't know." I stare at the journal, my mind working. "Do you think … maybe your parents know anything about this?"

"No. I wondered the same thing. I mean, they were really close to your parents. But I told them everything you told me about the door and the key and … well, everything that happened that night, and they had no idea what I was talking about. They searched the crypt at some point—unofficially—and didn't find anything. They were aware that the councilors had asked everyone to keep an eye out for this key years ago, but they had no idea your parents had actually found it."

"Well then … I wonder if …"

"If?" Ash prompts as the gears in my brain continue turning.

I look up at him. "There's someone we used to visit occasionally. An old friend of my parents. He was my dad's mentor when my dad was a trainee, and they remained close after my parents graduated. He retired a while ago, so I was thinking that perhaps, if my parents wanted to confide in someone no longer affiliated with any Guild, they might have spoken to him."

Ash is quiet for a moment, then asks, "Ostin Fairwend?"

Surprise jolts through me. "You remember him?"

"Yeah, well, you mentioned him a bunch of times. And your parents spoke about him too. I think I actually met him once when he was visiting you guys."

"Oh." I frown as wisps of a memory take shape in my mind. Ostin sitting in our living room. Mom laughing. Dad pouring drinks. Ash and me successfully sneaking past them into the kitchen to steal some of the mini raspberry cakes Mom had baked that morning. "Yeah, I think you did," I say quietly.

"Have you visited him since … you know. Your parents died?"

I shake my head, feeling intensely weary all of a sudden, as if that memory sucked the last of my strength from me. "I meant what I said earlier. I left this life behind and started a new one."

"So he thinks you died too."

"Yes. I did actually consider going to him for help, but then …" I trail off, my brain scrambling to come up with a believable reason for why I wouldn't have run straight to one of my parents' oldest friends after everything that happened that night. I shouldn't have admitted I thought of Ostin at all. Now I have to try to explain—

"You thought Bergenfell might know he was still close to your parents and that she would go straight to him if she was still looking for you?"

"Um, yeah." I grab the lifeline Ash has unintentionally thrown me, telling myself it isn't really a lie. That thought probably did occur to me at the time. "Hopefully she won't think of him again now. I mean, if I haven't gone to him for help in over two years, why would I go to him now?"

"Yeah. Still, we should be careful."

I almost roll my eyes at that. "Really? I was thinking we dress up in ruffled skirts and sparkly makeup and dance burlesque-style outside his front door."

"Well," Ash says, "that does sound more like the old you."

I pin him with a glare.

"But clearly you've changed."

"Like I had a choice," I mutter. I lower my shaking hands and feel a few of the journal's pages. "Almost dry. I know we're in a rush to find answers, but I don't want to damage the paper by heating it too much."

Ash nods as I stand. "Agreed. Rather let it air dry. In the meantime, we could go to Ostin. If you remember where he lives?"

"Um … I don't know."

"You don't know if you remember?"

"I don't know if we should go to him. I mean … maybe *you* should go to him. That would be simpler. He lives in, um … what's it called? Firecove? It's on that volcano island, the one with the name that sounds like dragon."

Ash's frown deepens. "You don't want him to know you're actually alive?"

"I just—I don't know, okay? I wasn't prepared for any of this. I—" I close my eyes and press my fists against them, trying to still my turbulent thoughts. I don't even know what I'm trying to say. Everything feels like it's getting away from me. Like I'm losing control. And that is *not* a state I want to be in.

I open my eyes, and my gaze lands on the journal still standing on the ground. Its pages remain blank. If I'm hoping for this to be over as soon as possible—if I want to leave Ash and Stormsdrift and everything else behind and start a new life once again—then I'm probably going to have more luck talking to Ostin than waiting for a journal that may never reveal anything.

But the faerie paths have probably decided to be non-functional again, and that'll mean walking all the way back to the edge of Stormsdrift to find a place where the paths *are* accessible. And just the thought of that is enough to make me wilt. After all the fighting tonight, almost falling to our deaths, battling against the river currents, using far more magic than I'm used to on an ordinary night, and the emotional upheaval of having my life once again tugged out from beneath me—not to mention almost losing Ash—I don't think I can handle much more physical activity. All I want to do is curl up in a ball at the base of the nearest tree and ignore the real world. Preferably after I use whatever remaining energy I possess to dry myself off. But—

"What was that?" Ash murmurs, turning to look behind him.

I hold my breath, listening. A faint hiss and the sound of something slithering over dead leaves reaches my ears. My skin prickles as goosebumps raise the hairs on my arms. I turn slowly, my gaze jumping from shadow to shadow. "See anything?" I ask.

"No," he answers quietly.

"We should get moving." It's the last thing I want to do, but sitting down to rest against a tree doesn't seem like the best idea. "I guess our next step is to go and find …" My words die on my tongue. My fingers go cold and my palms start to sweat. Because further up the bank, barely a stone's throw away, a wolf-like creature prowls from the shadows.

TEN

THE WOLF SPREADS ITS SHIMMERING SCALED WINGS, LIFTS ITS head toward the sky, and howls. Every hair on my body stands on end. Another two emerge from the darkness, then three more. The single reassuring thought at the front of my mind is that I recognize these beasts. Wulfentynes, I think they're called. And if I recognize them, that means they didn't come through the faerie door.

They pad toward us, their long, snake-like tails slithering along the ground. My hands are up, shield magic rippling away from me as I turn slowly, instinctively, so that my back is to Ash's. We have the river on one side, and the wulfentynes in a roughly semicircular formation on the other. I suppose we could escape via the river, though the idea makes me droop with exhaustion.

"Just wait," Ash says quietly as one of the creatures sniffs my shield. "No sudden movements."

"I know," I murmur, though it's been so long that I've almost forgotten what we were taught: Don't attack first. Don't make the first move. Our world is full of dangerous creatures, but many of them don't want any trouble. They're curious more than anything else. But my heart continues to thump wildly. I put it down to the fact that I've spent too much time in the human world where creatures that could eat a person don't generally wander out of the shadows in the middle of town. And if they do, no one knows about it because guardians take care of the problem.

I watch the wulfentynes pace slowly on the other side of our shield magic, some pawing at the ground, some sniffing the air. One cocks its head, watching me with unblinking yellow eyes. I stare back, sending a little more magic into my shield. A headache begins to pound behind my eyes.

Are you so weak, little—

Stop. I physically flinch at the mental rebuke that whispers without warning in my head.

"You okay?" Ash asks.

I focus on my magic, on the tingle at my fingertips and the smell of wet sand and the muted roar of the falls a little further upriver. "I'm fine."

"Just a little longer. Looks like they're growing bored. I think they'll leave soon. Then we can check the paths."

Ash is right. The wulfentynes don't stick around much longer. After another howl that sends a shiver skittering up the back of my neck, they wander away along the bank, then disappear into the trees further downstream. The moment they're out of sight, I release my shield magic while Ash hunches down and writes on the ground. He curses beneath his breath when nothing happens. "Not working."

I bite back a groan. Of course the paths aren't working. This is turning into a 'whole journey' just as he predicted. Not that I'm about to point that out. I don't want to hear 'I told you so.'

I exhale and raise my fingers to pinch the bridge of my nose. The headache is growing worse. "Okay, let's … um …"

"Silver," Ash says. "Don't hate me for suggesting this, but—"

"Oh dear."

"But I think we need to find somewhere safe to rest for the night. I promise," he adds quickly, holding his hands up in a show of surrender,

"I'm not trying to annoy you by dragging this out any longer than necessary. Trust me. Monsters are roaming Stormsdrift and people I care about are in danger. The sooner I can get rid of that door, the better. But I know you're tired after that whole ordeal—" he gestures vaguely at the river "—and wandering through Stormsdrift with anything less than lightning-fast reflexes is basically a death wish these days."

I notice he doesn't admit that *he* might be tired, but I decide not to point this out. I release a long, slow breath. "You're right."

His eyebrows jerk upward. "I am?"

I roll my eyes. "I'm stubborn, but I'm not stupid. The question, though, is *where* should we rest? Back in the day, we could have taken our chances sleeping beneath the stars, but that's clearly out of the question now."

"I'm not sure *where*, exactly. I was expecting you to argue with me for a lot longer, which was supposed to give me time to come up with something." He shakes his head and looks around. "We can't go anywhere public where people will recognize us. Bergenfell will hear about it within minutes. We can't go to any of my family members because it isn't safe to involve them until I can get to another Guild and explain everything. We obviously can't go to my place because Bergenfell will definitely have someone watching it. And to complicate matters, we're far away from pretty much *everything*, and the darn faerie paths aren't—"

"You have your own place?" For some reason, this concept is as weird as everything else that's now going on in Stormsdrift.

Ash gives me a bemused look. "You have *your* own place. Is it inconceivable that I'd have my own too?"

"Um … no. Sorry. I suppose I just pictured you at your parents' house because that's the only place I've ever known you to live. And it's only been a few months since you graduated, so … I don't know. Never mind. Forget I said anything about it."

He opens his mouth, then appears to think better of whatever he was about to say. "Okay, well …" He presses his fingers to his temples and rubs. "I'm just trying to picture exactly where we—Oh." He lowers his hands and looks over his shoulder. "The Gauntlet. It's back there, just over that hill."

"That's still outdoors, nitwit," I remind him, picturing the enormous obstacle course belonging to our Guild. With its ropes, planks, poles, nets, ditches, and walls of varying heights and angles, it was one of the more challenging parts of our training. The Gauntlet is a fitting name for it.

"The changing house is indoors," Ash says. "And only accessible by guardians and trainees. We'll be safe there."

"Safe? Inside a place that belongs to the Guild? I'd rather take my chances out here with nameless monsters."

"No one's going to know we're there. The changing house isn't monitored inside—obviously—and it's the middle of the night. We can dry off without having to use our own magic, and we can sleep without worrying we'll end up eaten by something before sunrise."

"Were you always this dramatic?"

"I think the word you're looking for is 'realistic.'"

I cross my arms. "Do the mentors still keep snacks there?"

"Yes."

"Okay. I'm in."

A minute later, with the journal safely inside my backpack, we begin climbing the hill. "This faerie paths problem is a pain in the freaking ass," I grumble.

"Yeah."

"What happens if they're not working and you're outside of Stormsdrift? How do you even know? Do you just … get stuck inside the paths?"

"No. You end up falling out of the paths somewhere outside of Stormsdrift. The closest spot the paths *are* working, I suppose."

"And then you walk," I say. "Must take a while to get home sometimes."

"Yes. It's strange after spending a lifetime traveling from one place to another in a matter of seconds. The idea of 'travel time' takes a bit of getting used to. We never had to take it into account before."

"I guess the Canopy Way is used a lot more now than it used to be."

"Yes." Ash pats his pocket, then lets out a breath of frustration.

"What?"

"Just ... I keep forgetting my amber is gone. I was going to check for messages."

Another few moments pass before I say, "Your family must be really worried about you right now. You simply disappeared two nights ago." I know I'm going against my own rules here, bringing up the other people in his life, but it feels too insensitive not to say it. And I'm finding it harder and harder to fight the side of me that's desperate to know more about the people I once adored with my whole heart.

"Yes," he answers. "They are worried." He doesn't add anything else, and I know it's my fault. My stupid, desperate need to keep our lives as separate as possible so we can part ways without it breaking my heart again. But when I say nothing, Ash seems to decide to continue. "I used the throwaway amber—the one I've now lost—to tell my dad not to worry about me. I sent that message two nights ago a few hours after I left Stormsdrift. I haven't answered any of his questions since then. I want him to be able to answer honestly that he doesn't know anything if someone from the Guild questions him."

"So ... do you know if Bergenfell's told him anything about what happened the other night? When you overheard her and Poppywood and then they tried to kill you?"

"Well, the last message I received from him asked if it's true that I attacked and stunned another guardian."

My jaw tightens. "Wonderful."

"Yeah. So I guess that's the story that's currently going around."

My exhale is sharp. "After we're done with this—when we've figured out what my parents knew—you can go to another Guild. You can get this mess cleared up." Ash looks at me, an expression I can't decipher on his face. "What?" I ask.

"Just … seems like you forgot for a moment that you think everything I'm telling you is a lie."

I look away with a shake of my head, my gaze sliding across the shadows. I don't tell him he's right. That I *did* forget for a moment. Because it's so easy, here in this forest that used to be my home, to slip back into thinking that he's the Ash I knew before everything turned upside down.

We continue our steady climb through the trees in silence. Step after step after step, the thin mist swirling around our feet, and clusters of silver oyster mushrooms pulsing faintly with light as we pass them. We stop to free a sprite entangled in a giant spider's web, but even that we do in silence. We're almost near the top of the hill, so close to the promise of safety and sleep, when Ash breaks the quiet. "Earlier, with your friends … what was all that about a cult?"

"Oh." I suppose it wouldn't kill me to explain that bit. "I, uh, told them when I first met them that I'd escaped an extreme religious cult. I needed a good reason to explain why a teenage girl barely had a clue how to use a computer or the internet or a phone or … basically any technology in that world."

"You weren't worried they would try to notify the authorities? The police or something?"

"They wanted to. But I told them I was too scared. I was finally free and didn't want to draw attention to myself. I said the leader was smart and had contacts in law enforcement and would find me. I just wanted to forget it all and move on."

"And they believed you?"

"Yes. They seemed to."

Ash nods. I'm grateful he doesn't make some snarky comment about building friendship on top of a lie. It's something I've always felt guilty about, but what else was I supposed to do? Tell Teddy and Duke the truth about the magical world I'd run away from? They would have thought I was nuts.

We reach the top of the hill. The ground dips down a little on the other side, then levels out, revealing the Gauntlet laid out among the trees. Complex structures of crisscrossing wooden poles, a giant net, a series of wooden rings suspended high above a mud pit, ladders strung horizontally between trees, and ropes swaying eerily in the darkness. We make our way between a balance beam and a wall of wooden planks. I remember slipping off that balance beam at the beginning of first year and breaking my wrist. A few months later, I could somersault off it with ease.

"There," Ash says, nodding toward the building that's barely visible between the trees on the other side of the Gauntlet, as if I've forgotten where the changing house is. Its uneven edges become clearer as we walk closer. A simple stone structure with dark windows and no door, it appears unassuming from the outside. I know better, however. It may not be *hidden* by a glamour, but there is undoubtedly glamour magic placed upon it.

We stop in front of the building, and Ash pushes one sleeve back. He holds his marked wrist against the stone wall and waits. A moment passes in which I wonder if it always took this long—but then the magic begins. A dazzling gold line runs up, across, and down, forming the outline of a door. Textured wood appears where a moment ago there was only dull stone, and elegant metal leaves spread across the top of the door and down one side. Finally, a metal handle pushes through the wood, curves into an embellished floral design, and solidifies. Ash reaches for the handle and opens the door.

Warm light spills out, bathing the area in gold. Ash moves back to let me walk in ahead of him, and I'm too distracted by the odd sensation of my current life once again overlapping with my old one to be annoyed by this. I step inside and look around. Though little has changed, I see it all with new eyes. Considering the sole purpose of this building is to provide a space for trainees to shower and change their clothing, it's unnecessarily extravagant. The main room is long, the floor covered in a plush carpet—complete with self-cleaning spells to rid itself of the mud we used to traipse in here. Comfortable chairs, enormous couches, and gold-embellished cushions fill the space. A fire designed to heat the room to the perfect temperature, no matter the season or time of day, crackles happily on one side.

I can't help the derisive huff of breath that escapes my lips. Nothing but the best for the young guardians in training who will grow up to be heroes and save the world. *Of course* they need a place like this to gather with their mentors, enjoy revitalizing drinks and snacks, and relax in a pool of bubbles to wash away the mud and grime of the Gauntlet. But despite my cynicism, I can't ignore the guilt that sits in the pit of my stomach, reminding me that once upon a time I was one of those entitled trainees. I loved it here. I loved everything about the Guild.

I push the uncomfortable thought aside as my eyes travel over the Gauntlet leaderboard on the wall above the fireplace, enchanted to display the top ten all-time record holders for fastest completion of the course. I notice the names Lennox Blackburn and Flynn Blackburn are still there. Along with a new name that wasn't there before: Asher Blackburn. Of course.

I force my gaze away from the leaderboard and look to the right where the wall is lined with doors leading to individual bathing rooms. A staircase winds up to the second level and more bathing rooms. The pull toward hot water and scented bubbles is almost magnetic, but I need food first. I look to the far side of the room and the kitchen door. Without a word to Ash, I head for it. The gold numbers that shimmer on the wall beside it tell me it's earlier than I thought. Just past eight in the evening. Wasn't it already after nine when I got to The Gilded Canary? And that feels like a lifetime ago. But it makes sense, now that I think about it. This part of the fae realm isn't in the same zone of time as the part of the human world I've been living in. This is good, I think as I reach the door and push it open. More hours to sleep. More hours before trainees and mentors show up here.

In the kitchen, I find a bowl of fruit on the table. I help myself to an apple and a handful of strawberries, then check the cupboards and find a collection of glass bottles containing that disgusting green tonic the mentors used to give us after a particularly tough round of the Gauntlet. I grimace and almost close the cupboard door—seriously, I think the stuff Teddy smears on his face every self-care Sunday tastes better than what's in those bottles—but then give in with a sigh and take one. I know it'll make me feel better. I tuck the bottle beneath my arm and open another cupboard, and that's where I find the real prize: chocolate.

I leave the kitchen with my makeshift meal and find Ash standing in front of the fireplace, staring at one of the couches. "Um, I'm just gonna use one of the bathing rooms," I tell him.

He looks up. "Right. Yes. I should probably do that too." Then, with a small twist to his lips, he adds, "I see you still have no problem stealing the mentors' snacks."

I stick my tongue out at him—*wow, hello, ten-year-old Silver*—then disappear quickly into the nearest bathing room. The floor is tiled with slate, but that's where any similarity to bathrooms in the human world ends. A pool deep enough for me to comfortably submerge myself in sits in the center of the room at floor level. Small pebbles and moss surround it, and water cascades over a rock formation on one side. This is completely normal for the world I grew up in, but having spent a few years living like a human, it's a little strange now to see no bath or shower. I also have to work hard to remind myself that the pool is self-cleaning, just like the carpet out there. *Don't think about the other people who have bathed in here*, I tell myself.

I take a bite of the apple, lower my backpack to the floor, and balance the rest of my food collection on top of it. A basket containing tiny bottles of bubble enchantments sits on top of the rocks, and I examine the labels as I continue crunching on the apple. My gaze catches on the bottle with the shimmery purple-pink label. *That's the one*, I decide with a small smile as I reach for it. I need something light-hearted in my life right now. I pour a few drops into the water at the base of the miniature waterfall. Bubbles begin to form almost immediately. They take the shape of winged unicorns and gallop across the water's surface before rising into the air, flapping a few times, and then popping.

After removing my damp, dirty clothing, I slip into the water. I don't want to admit to myself that I missed this, submerging myself in a pool of steaming hot water, but I did. It's not as though I used to use this changing house often—I only bathed here a handful of times, when I got particularly dirty going through the Gauntlet—but we had a bathing room like this at home, and I definitely took it for granted.

I hold my hand out, palm up, and one of the unicorn bubbles jumps onto it. I lift it closer to my face, admiring the translucent rainbow-shimmer surface. What if this was still my life? What if there was no mysterious faerie door, and Mom and Dad had never died, and we still lived here in Stormsdrift, and I was sitting in my own pool of bubbles?

The unicorn pops and vanishes.

Yeah, I think as I shut my eyes, bend my knees, and slide below the water. *There goes that daydream.* In the dark silence below the surface, images flicker lightning-fast across my mind—Mom's hand gripping mine, the panicked rush of our last few moments at home, fire consuming everything, a guardian sword slashing down—

I straighten, my feet connecting with the bottom of the pool and my head breaking the surface. I take the unbearable ache that's constricting my chest and twist it into something else: determination. I will not let what happened to me happen to anyone else in Stormsdrift. That damn door needs to go, and so do the councilors.

After eating the remainder of my scrounged-up dinner while floating in the water, and then drying some clean clothes and my jacket with the same spell I use to dry my hair, I get dressed. I shove my dirty, damp clothes into the backpack—future-Silver will not thank me for this, but I don't care right now—and look around to find that the towel I dropped on the floor has disappeared. A new towel, already folded, has appeared on the rocks beside the basket of bubble enchantments. Right. I forgot that happened here.

When I leave the bathing room, jacket and sneakers in my hands and my backpack on one shoulder, Ash is pulling a couch to the far side of the room near the staircase. The other one is still on this side, near the kitchen door, with his sweater draped over one of the arms. My gaze bounces back to him. Yep, he is now in a T-shirt, which gives me an excellent view of his bare arms and the muscles cording beneath his skin as he finishes moving the couch. When did his forearms become so … defined? And why the heck am I even noticing?

I avert my gaze and see a gray blanket folded on the couch beside Ash's sweater. There's one on the couch he's just moved as well. Of course the changing house has a supply of blankets. Why wouldn't it? That seems totally necessary. "Uh, is that one mine?" I ask awkwardly, pointing to the couch he's just finished moving. The sweater suggests he's claimed the one I'm standing beside.

"Yeah, if you don't mind. The other one's longer, and I'm taller, so …" He trails off.

"Yeah, of course."

"I considered moving them into two separate bathing rooms," he adds, "so we don't have to breathe the same air tonight, but there isn't enough space beside the pools."

I refrain from rolling my eyes at the 'breathe the same air' comment, which I'm pretty sure is supposed to be a joke. "This is fine. Thanks." He strides back toward his couch, and I head for mine. This is not weird. This is not weird at all.

I drop my backpack, shoes and jacket on the floor and slowly lower myself to the edge of the couch, looking back across the room at Ash. He doesn't have a bag, which I suppose makes sense considering he left Stormsdrift in a hurry and hasn't been home since. Has he been wearing the same clothes for three days? Probably, but knowing him, he would have used a quick laundry spell or two while he was in the bathing room. I should ask him if he can remind me how to do those. I haven't cleaned my clothes with magic in … um … okay, I've never cleaned my clothes with magic. Mom used to take care of that.

Ash sits on his couch and moves all the extra decorative pillows onto the floor. I know I should stop staring at him, but I can't. I absently twist the Gilded Canary ring around and around my finger as my gaze travels down his bare arms once again, landing on the dark, entwined markings on the inside of his wrists. An ache shudders through me, stealing my breath. I'm surprised by the intensity of it, the sudden, desperate longing curling in my stomach. I'm supposed to hate the Guild and everyone who works there. I *do* hate them. And yet … that was supposed to be *my* life. *I* was supposed to have markings just like the ones imprinted on Ash's skin. I was supposed to graduate alongside him.

I force myself to look away, remembering that it was all for the best that I never had the chance to graduate. Better that I found out what those two-faced guardians are really like *before* becoming one of them instead of afterwards. I reach for the blanket and unfold it, but I don't lie down yet. I won't until Ash does. Just in case … in case what? He tries to hurt me? Kill me? The thought is so ridiculous I almost laugh. Here, in this place where the memories of the life I used to have are so close to the surface, I can't think of Ash as anything but the boy I grew up with. I knew him better than I knew anyone else, and he would never in a million years do anything to hurt me, and I miss him I miss him *I miss him so much*, and now he's *right here* and all I want is to be able to trust him again.

"Silver?"

I blink and look across the room at him. "Hmm?"

"Are you okay? You were just … staring. At the floor."

I blink again. The Ash I miss isn't the one in this room with me. This Ash is quieter, older, stronger, deadlier. I mustn't forget that. It's too soon for me to know if I can trust him. "Yeah, sorry. I'm just … tired."

He doesn't lie down yet. He just sits there. Watching me. He opens his mouth, shuts it, exhales, opens it again. He doesn't quite look at me when he asks, "Are we … ever going to talk about what happened? Between us. That night, before everything went—"

I turn swiftly away before he can finish, immediately defensive, immediately … *something*. Angry-hurt-embarrassed-heartbroken something. They're all twisted together, and I'm so darn tired, and how dare he bring this up now? "That night before you turned on me along with everyone else I had planned to dedicate my entire life to working alongside?" I lie down, facing away from him, and pull the blanket over me. "No, Ash, I don't think we need to talk about that."

For an uncomfortably long moment, I hear nothing. Ash doesn't move. He doesn't speak. Then I hear the quiet creak of the couch, and I imagine him lying down. The light suddenly vanishes, and we're plunged into semi-darkness. Only the gold numbers on the wall provide any illumination now.

I relax the tiniest bit. Time passes. I try to figure out whether he's asleep. His breathing is steady, a little slower now than when we first lay down, so … maybe? This is so freaking awkward. I should have just shrunk my couch a little, pushed it into one of the bathing rooms, and shut the door so I could have a peaceful night of sleep. I'm sure I have enough magic left for that. Now that I think about, I could probably still—

No, don't be so silly, I tell myself. *Go to sleep. Just go to sleep. Go to—*

"Silver?" Ash says, startling me from my stupid thoughts. "Have you honestly spent the past four—I mean two—years thinking I tried to kill you?"

I press my lips together and shut my eyes. My brain has gone back and forth a thousand times over the years, torn between the certainty that I must have been mistaken—that Ash *wasn't* trying to kill me—and acceptance of the cold, heart-breaking truth that he chose the Guild over me. I let out a breath. "Mostly," I say quietly, "I've tried not to think of you at all."

He doesn't answer, and I hate myself for lying to him. I turn onto my other side, hoping sleep will steal me away from this world.

And eventually, it does.

ELEVEN

then

A THRILL RACED THROUGH SILVER'S BODY AS SHE STOOD OUTSIDE the grand entrance to the Stormsdrift Guild for the first time. Gleaming white stone, columns, arched windows. An elaborately carved wooden door so large she could have sat on Dad's shoulders and not reached the top of it. This building had stood here for centuries, the forest slowly growing around it. Mom and Dad had told her that most of the newer Guilds were hidden by complex glamours, and only guardians knew exactly where to find the entrances. Which was kind of a cool idea, Silver thought, but also a little bit sad. How could you truly appreciate just how impressive a Guild was if you couldn't see it?

She climbed the steps, her eyes drinking in every detail of the impressive door as Mom and Dad held their wrists up so a guard could scan their markings. Dad signed Silver in as a new trainee who hadn't yet received her access pendant—Silver had to press her lips together to contain her squeal of excitement at the reminder that she was now an *actual trainee*—and then they were crossing the threshold into the Guild's magnificent entrance hall.

Though Mom and Dad had worked here for years, Silver had never been inside. There had never been a need for this. If both her parents happened to be working late, she would hang out at the Blackburns' house where either Iris or Lennox were generally at home. If they were both working late as well, then Flynn was on duty, trusted to look after his younger brothers and Silver.

She stood just inside the entrance, a grin on her lips as her eyes traveled the large, circular space. Arched doorways led off the sides of the room, a majestic staircase wound up to another level, and on the far side of the entrance hall, a wide doorway opened out to a courtyard. Her gaze continued upward until it settled on the stained glass domed ceiling where protective enchantments mingled like wisps of multicolored cloud.

Her entire body hummed with the thrill of being here. It was finally happening. She was *inside the Guild!* She was a *real trainee!* No more dancing around the forest clearing with wooden swords while the older Blackburn brothers laughed at her and Ash. No more landing on her backside when she tried to mimic their spins and somersaults. She was going to learn to fight for *real*.

"Silver!"

She pulled her gaze from the dome of magic and looked across the entrance hall. Ash waved to her as he walked in from the courtyard, the grin on his face even wider than hers. Excitement flared inside her again, and this time, her squeal couldn't be entirely contained. She bounced up and down on her toes, waving madly back at him. She was about to take off with little more than a "Bye, Mom! Bye, Dad!" when Dad pulled her into a quick hug against his side.

"Good luck, baby bug," he whispered into her ear.

"Have fun!" Mom added as she raced away.

She dodged neatly around the guardians and trainees crossing the entrance hall and almost collided with Ash. Gripping his arm, she bounced up and down and said, "I can't believe we're really here!"

He laughed. "You are *so* not playing it cool right now."

"Shut up. I don't care. Odette!" She waved at the girl who was hurrying toward them.

Dark curls bounced on Odette's shoulders and a nervous smile pulled her lips tight. She had attended the small junior school in Stormsdrift with Silver and Ash, and she was the only one of their class-mates who'd applied to join the Guild. Everyone else had chosen to attend different institutions elsewhere in the fae realm. "I'm so glad I found you guys," she said. Her large fuchsia-colored eyes, bright against her dark skin, darted around. "The only other person I know is—oh, there he is." Her features relaxed a bit as her gaze landed on someone behind Silver. "This is my cousin, Remy," she told Silver and Ash as a boy with midnight blue highlighting his dark hair joined their group.

"Oh yeah, you said he'd be joining us here," Ash said. "Welcome."

"Thank you," Remy said. He let out an anxious chuckle. "I was told to go to a courtyard and I somehow lost myself in a room full of portraits instead?" His words were accented, but Silver couldn't remember which part of the world Odette said he came from. "I swear the one of the Seelie King was watching me for real," Remy added.

"Oh, I know that one," Ash said with a nod. "It's definitely creepy."

"Do you think someone enchanted it so the king can watch what's happening here?" Odette whispered, as if King Idrind of the Seelie Court might be standing right there in the Guild's entrance hall.

"I'm sure he has better things to do with his time," Silver said. "Although …" Her expression turned thoughtful. "The royal family are a little bit nuts, so maybe he did send an enchanted portrait of himself to every Guild."

Odette's eyes widened. "You can't say things like that! Especially inside a Guild. We have to follow the Seelie Court laws."

"Relax," Silver said with a roll of her eyes. "I'm not about to commit treason or something. I'm just saying there's definitely some crazy blood in that family. I mean, that's where Lord Draven came from, and look at what he tried to do."

"And remember what happened when we were kids?" Ash said. "With his mother and the veil?"

"Definitely crazy," Silver said, nodding along. "Can you imagine what life would be like if she'd succeeded? If she'd torn through the veil properly and revealed our whole world to humans?"

"I actually have a friend whose mom is on the guard rotation there," Remy said. "Next to the gap in the veil, I mean. Since no one knows how to fix it. She says it's the most boring job ever."

"Look, I'm not saying I *disagree* with you," Odette said, her voice still low. "I'm just saying that it's safer to keep our opinions about certain people's mental stability to our—"

"First years! Gather in the courtyard please!"

All thoughts of the Seelie royal family were forgotten then as Silver, Ash, Remy and Odette hurried out to the courtyard with the rest of the new trainees. A fountain took up the courtyard's center. A stone figure stood in the water, holding aloft a bow with an arrow pointed at the sky. Water shot straight up from the arrowhead and rained down into the fountain. Around the outer edge of the courtyard stood statues of various fae creatures in between huge stone urns containing rose bushes. Nine chairs had been placed along one side of the courtyard, and Silver took a seat next to Ash.

The hushed whispers and quiet giggles came to an end as the steady click of high heels across the stone paving made everyone sit up a little straighter. A woman strode toward them, a line of guardians walking behind her. She was perfectly put together, not a hair on her head out of place. Her two colors were so close—both different shades of red—that she could have passed for human if not for her red eyes. But Silver knew who she was: the councilor in charge of the Stormsdrift Guild.

"Good morning," she said, her lips pulling up in a warm smile as she came to a stop in front of the nine first-year trainees. She laced her fingers together in front of her black pencil skirt. "My name is Ursula Bergenfell. I am one of the councilors at this Guild. You won't see much of me during your day-to-day training—the Council is in charge of the overall running of this particular Guild—but I wanted to extend a warm welcome to all of you anyway. You have chosen an honorable path, and while this Guild may be one of the smallest, it is also the oldest, which means you have just become part of a great legacy."

Silver's eyes scanned the guardians standing behind Councilor Bergenfell as she went on about 'great risk' and 'enormous reward' and 'huge responsibility.' She explained the role of Seers, the faeries who were trained to See visions of magical attacks and crimes that hadn't yet come to pass. These were the visions that most guardian assignments were based on. Then she covered the type of training they would undergo during their five years as trainees—a mix of theory, physical training, and practical assignments out in the field. Those assignments would progress over the years from group to paired to individual with mentor supervision, until finally, they would be expected to handle assignments on their own.

With two parents who worked at the Guild, and having hung out with the older Blackburn boys since she was little, Silver already knew all of this. So she listened with only half her brain, while the other half performed cartwheels of glee. *I can't believe I'm really here!* she kept thinking.

"And now," Councilor Bergenfell said, grabbing Silver's full attention again, "it's time for you to meet your mentors." She looked over her right shoulder and then her left, smiling at the guardians lined up behind her. "They will give you your pendants, which identify you as trainees of this Guild. The pendants have numerous protective enchantments woven into them, and—more importantly—they contain the magic that gives you access to your guardian weapons. This magic will be transferred to you when you first put the pendant on and will remain functional unless the pendant is broken in some way. When you graduate one day, this magic will become part of the markings that are permanently etched onto your wrists."

Silver's excitement level was so high at this point that she was ready to jump from her seat and pump her fists in the air. She settled for jiggling her left leg up and down in a movement she hoped was too small for anyone to notice.

"But before that …" Councilor Bergenfell paused. Her lips stretched into another smile. "A demonstration from some of our older trainees." She swept her arm out wide as she and the other guardians behind her stood aside. "Enjoy."

Six trainees marched around the side of the fountain and formed a perfectly straight line. Ash's brother Connor was one of them, and Silver tried to catch his eye. But he stared determinedly above the heads of the new trainees, a superior tilt to his chin. Then, with a single cry, the six trainees extended their right hands and each gripped a sword from the air. Silver clasped her hands tightly together as her breath caught and her lips pulled into an awestruck grin. The trainees stepped forward and swung their swords in perfect unison. The neat slice of blades through the air sent a thrill racing through Silver's body.

Then the blades vanished, and in a single movement, each trainee held a bow, pointed toward the sky, arrows already nocked. They released an arrow one after the other—one, two, three, four, five, six— then swept their arms down, releasing the bows.

And then there were throwing stars, and curved blades, and tiny knives, and acrobatic leaps and flips across the courtyard, and it was all so dramatic and impressive that Silver barely spared a thought for where these thrown weapons were actually landing. Presumably there were targets hidden among the flowers and statues, but she was too caught up in the performance to look for them.

The demonstration ended with the six trainees doing backflips off the edge of the fountain, each landing in a perfect crouch. The courtyard erupted into applause, from both the new trainees and the assembled guardians.

Silver clapped as hard as anyone else. She was ready to leap from her seat and begin her own training that very second. Without a doubt, this was going to be the best five years of her life.

TWELVE

now

I WAKE TO THE SOUND OF SCRATCHING. IT'S INSISTENT, THIS *scrape, scrape, scrape* that pulls me from my dreams. Insistently annoying, when all I want to do is burrow further into sleep.

Scrape, scritch-scritch, scraaaaape.

I force my heavy eyelids open, and for one disorienting moment I have absolutely no idea where I am. Then everything crashes into my brain at once. I sit up quickly, my hand reaching instinctively into the air, my fingers expecting to connect with something—before I remember a split second later that of course I have no magical weapons to reach for. Stupid dreams, confusing my brain, melding the past with the present. My thumb swipes an X across the moonstone on my wrist, and the crescent-moon knife is in my grip within seconds.

Scrape. Scrape, scrape.

A warm glow illuminates the room, and I twist around to see that Ash is sitting up with a guardian dagger in his hand. "What's that noise?" he whispers.

"No idea. I just woke up."

Scrape, scraaaape.

Within seconds, we're both on our feet. "Sounds like it's coming from the front door," Ash says.

"You said we'd be safe here," I hiss at him as I snatch my jacket up from the floor and pull it on. Sneakers next. Then backpack. Then the knife is in my hand again.

"It's probably nothing. Probably just some regular fae creature wandering around out there."

"Yeah, well, I'm not taking any chances." A quick glance at the numbers on the wall tells me it's an hour before sunrise. We were due to wake up soon anyway. May as well get the heck out of here now.

"Yeah, probably a good time to leave," Ash says, tugging his boots on.

Scraaaaaape. The sound is like a sharp fingernail being dragged slowly along a wall.

And then I hear it. A whisper. *"Iselaaaaa."*

My mouth goes dry. A shiver creeps into my hair and sweat breaks out across my palms. "What the *hell*?" I whisper. I look over my shoulder at Ash. "Is that what you heard in the crypt? From the other side of the faerie door?"

Ash's eyes are narrow as he stares at the door. "Possibly."

"What the hell, Ash? What the *actual freaking hell*?"

His gaze slides to mine. "How does it know you? How does it know you're *here*?"

"You're asking *me* that? I should be asking *you*! You're the one who heard my name being spoken from the other side of a magical door and then saw some creature climbing through it!" I pin my eyes on the door again. "It shouldn't be able to get inside. It can't even see the door from the outside."

"Correct. There's protection on this building. Not nearly as much as the Guild itself, but there's at least *some*—"

A long black claw slides beneath the bottom edge of the door. My heart misses a beat. I clench my curved double blade tightly and resist the urge to scramble backward. That's not what I was trained to do. I was trained to face threats, not run from them. "Well," I say, the shudder in my voice betraying my shock, "it looks like this thing has magic that trumps whatever protection this place supposedly has."

The claw disappears. I hear my shallow breath. My heart pounding. Ash inching closer.

And then a black mist like heavy shadow begins seeping under the door. "That's it," Ash says, suddenly at my side. "Same as the thing I saw in the crypt. Go that way—" He points to the left side of the door as he lunges right, but I'm already moving, remembering what he told me about Bergenfell and Poppywood. They stood on either side of the faerie door, ready to kill whatever had come through.

The mist begins to take shape, rising rapidly from the floor, and I raise my crescent knife with both hands. A longer blade, like the sword in Ash's hands, would probably be better, but at least I know the curved edge is as deadly as—

A sound like the sizzle-crack of lightning splits the air. The reverberating boom of thunder rockets through my body. I'm flying clear across the room before I know it. Ash and I land in a heap on the couch he slept on, which skids across the floor and crashes against the wall. Within moments, we're back on our feet, weapons brandished.

And there it stands. Bare and leathery, a creature tall enough to brush the ceiling with its head. A head that seems a little bit wolf, a little bit dragon, but somehow neither. Bared teeth. A snout that sniffs at the air. Bright white sparks of magic jumping around its clawed fingers. No, not magic, I realize as I stare at those curved, black claws. More like … jagged little forks of lightning, snapping and crackling.

"Iselaaaaa," it says in a low tone that sounds like the rustle of dry leaves across a forest floor. My skin prickles.

Suddenly, it slashes at the air with both hands. I throw up a hasty shield of magic. "We can take it down," I tell Ash. The creature drops to all fours and hunches over. It shudders, then becomes dark, heavy mist again, pooling just above the floor. "It'll be easy. I'll hold the shield while you draw power—stunner magic—and when I drop the shield—"

The black mist passes right through my shield, leaving the rippling layer of magic intact. We both curse out loud at the same time. "It can go through *shields?*" I demand.

"Clearly!" Ash snaps. Then his hand is around my wrist. "We need to run."

I don't hesitate. If Asher Blackburn, who's never backed down from a challenge in his life, would rather run than fight this thing, that tells me all I need to know. I hurl myself around the side of the couch along with Ash. There's another way out, a door on the other side of the kitchen. Trainees don't use it, but mentors come and go—

Something yanks me backward. I let out a yelp. Surprise and fear collide in a hot, dizzying haze. I see things in split-second blinks: Ash's eyes as his head snaps back around, his hand reaching for mine, talons slicing down my right arm. Then a weight is suddenly gone from my back, and I'm falling against Ash as he drags me out of the creature's clutches and into the kitchen. A second later, two things happen: my brain registers the pain of the gouges running down my arm, and I realize why I suddenly feel lighter: my backpack is gone. "The journal," I gasp, pulling Ash to a halt.

"Leave it."

"But how—"

"It's not worth your life!" he shouts as his magic hurls the table out of the way. He launches for the door on the other side of the room, almost yanking my arm from its socket. His hand is up, wrist pressed against the door, and then the door is gone.

We race into the predawn darkness. Icy droplets slam into us immediately. Of course. Because this is Stormsdrift, so why wouldn't it be raining? My magic reserves have been replenished after a good few hours of sleep, so it's easy to push at the air and raise a layer of magic around my head. I'm drenched already, so there's no use trying to prevent that, but I'd like to at least keep the rivulets of water out of my eyes so I can see properly.

A glance over my shoulder reveals the creature leaping out of the changing house after us. Crap. I skid across the muddy ground as flashes of lightning illuminate our surroundings—and the balance beam that's suddenly right in front of us. We vault over it without slowing. And then there's the mud pit and the rows of wooden rings hanging above it, and another backward glance shows the creature *right there*, claws raking the air, teeth snapping—

I launch forward and grab hold of one of the rings. *Pain, pain, pain in my arm!* My fingers slip on the wet surface of the ring, but I manage not to lose my grip. Momentum carries me far enough to reach out with one arm and grab another ring, while below me, a snarling screech suggests the creature has just landed in the mud pit. I swing from ring to ring, teeth gritted against the pain. Beside me, Ash is traversing the mud pit in the same way. Beating me, darn it, because of course he's the very best at almost *everything* in the Gauntlet.

A bubble of hysterical laughter threatens to burst from me. Who would have guessed when I stepped into that fighting ring last night that in less than twenty-four hours, I'd be back in Stormsdrift, halfway across the Gauntlet, trying to beat my ex-best friend while some creepy creature that knows my name chases after us?

We land on solid ground on the other side, my feet hitting the earth moments after Ash's. We race forward. "Check the paths!" I shout to him above the pattering rain and rumbling thunder. "I'll hold that thing off!"

"You can't—"

"Just do it!" My mind is already turning to the charms on my wrist, thinking of the one that could buy us an extra few moments. "There." I point to the wall of wooden planks up ahead. "Write on that." The words have barely left my tongue when an angry roar reaches my ears. Then that same sizzle-crack sound, followed instantly by a bolt of lightning streaking past me and burning a hole right through the wooden wall.

I gasp in fright, lurching sideways instinctively. Ahead of me, Ash veers sideways and brings himself to a sudden halt against the wall beside the smoldering hole. I don't stop yet. My fingers slide across the pearls. I find the correct stone. *Twist, press.* Then I spin around, drop down, and slam my palm against the ground.

For a single moment, the world seems to move in slow motion. I see the creature soaring through the air toward me, rain dripping from bared canines, mud flying from its body. Then my magic bursts away from me, amplified at least a dozen times, and the shockwave hurls the monster back toward the pit.

I suck in a gasp of breath.

Then something tightens around my arm—my left arm, no pain—and drags me backward. "Paths are working!" Ash's voice. Then darkness envelops us.

For a moment, I hear nothing but our labored breathing, and then we stagger out of the paths into a different part of the forest. The rain is little more than a drizzle here. Within moments, it stops completely. Cool mist swirls around us. Quiet forest sounds—the occasional chirp and the drip, drip of raindrops from leaves—soothe the pounding rush of my pulse.

"What *was* that?" Ash asks, still breathing heavily. "You shouldn't have been able to draw that much power so quickly."

I lift my wrist—the pain in my upper arm seems, oddly enough, to have dulled a little—and point vaguely to the layered bracelet and its numerous pearls and stones. "Amplifier spell. Hidden in a stone. Never used it before, so I wasn't entirely sure how it would work. But it seems like it amplified my own magic, as I'd hoped."

He nods and takes another deep breath. Then, eyes trained on me, he moves closer. "Silver. Why does a monstrous creature with magic that appears to be stronger than a guardian's shield *know your name*? Why does it appear to be *hunting* you?"

I lower my arm and give him an incredulous look. "I told you already. I don't know! Maybe it … maybe …" I trail off, still breathing heavily as something occurs to me for the first time. Something that should have been obvious the moment Ash said he heard my name from the other side of the door. "Maybe they went through," I say quietly. "My parents. Maybe they went through to the other side of the door."

"Why would they do that if they were there to destroy it?"

"I don't know. Maybe they *weren't* there to destroy it. Or maybe … maybe they went through *before* that night? I don't know, Ash, they didn't tell me enough. But how else would some creature on the other side know my name?"

"I suppose that could be what happened," he says slowly. "Or perhaps it's some kind of tracking creature, and after it got through to this side, Bergenfell sent it after you."

"Maybe. Either way, I'd prefer it if you stop demanding answers from me like I'm supposed to have them all."

His gaze narrows. "Don't pretend you're not keeping things from me."

"Of course I'm keeping things from you. We've already been over the part where I don't know if I can trust you."

Suddenly he's right in front of me. His hands are framing my face, and though I could pull free if I wanted to, I can barely breathe let alone move because he's *so close* and I can't fight the part of me that's wanted him this near for so long. "Tell me I've been lying to you," he says fiercely, eyes burning into mine. "Look at me, Silver, and tell me you can't trust me."

I finally manage to gulp in a breath. I blink and shove him away. I know what my answer is, but I'm afraid that I'm wrong. I'm terrified that I have a blind spot where he's concerned, that my judgement is off, that I'm only seeing what my silly heart *wants* to see. I'm seeing …

My surroundings. My gaze slides past Ash. The mist around us has slowly cleared, and by the blue-green light of the everstar leaves, I suddenly realize exactly where we are. The clearing in the forest. Golden pinpricks of light—glow-bugs—appear as the mist recedes. The river is on my left, and right of it, through the trees, I can see to the beach. The ocean. It's still dark out there—not quite time for the sun to rise—but luminescence lights the waves and crashes onto the sand like a thousand sapphires spilling from the water.

I suck in a shuddering breath as pain hits me square in the chest. This place. *This place.* It symbolizes everything I lost the night my parents died, and I just … I can't … I swallow, trying, trying, *trying* to pull my gaze away from the ocean. Away from the beach. Away from the memories bombarding me. But I can't.

"Silver?"

I hear Ash's voice, the concern in his tone, but still I can't look away. I miss this—Stormsdrift and my parents and the river and the beach and Ash and his family and my friends and the life I had here—*so much that I can barely breathe.*

But I do. I force a breath in. A breath out. And then I turn my back on the beach and finally manage to speak. "I can't do this." I shake my head. "This was a bad idea. The journal is gone, and it's not like we could read what's inside it anyway, and to be honest, Ash, I don't think it's possible to get rid of the faerie door." I fumble with the zip of my jacket. I'm sure I must have a spare stylus inside it somewhere. I always carry far too many of them around with me. "If it was possible, someone else would have done it by now. This is … this is up to you now. You need to go to another Guild and ask them for help. That's what you should have done in the first place." My fingers finally wrap around a stylus, and I move to the nearest tree. "You shouldn't have come looking for—"

"Stop."

"I'm not *stopping*, Ash. I need to get away from all of this. From—from *you* and—"

"Stop!" he repeats, louder now, and it's the anger in his voice that makes my hand pause against the tree. "You don't get to just walk away from all this like you're the only one who's suffered."

I swivel slowly to face him, my face growing hot. "I don't think I'm the only one who's suffered, but—"

"Oh really? That's exactly how you're behaving."

"I'm not—"

"Have you asked me what *I've* been through over the past four—*two* —years? No. All you have to say about the time that's passed since we last saw each other is 'We're not doing this.'" He throws my own words back at me with such bitterness that all I can do is stare at him. "I get that you were angry with me, that you thought I'd betrayed you or something, so concern for me was probably not the first thing on your mind when you saw me last night. But now you know that wasn't true. I *know* you know I never intentionally hurt you. But it still hasn't crossed your mind to ask how *I'm* doing?"

I give him a withering glare, my jaw tightening. "Have you also spent the past two years terrified of your past catching up to you and *killing* you? Have you also lost the people you love more than anything in the world?"

"I lost you!"

My next breath catches in my throat.

I lost you.

I lost you.

I never really considered it from his perspective. I spent so much time agonizing over his betrayal that I never stopped to appreciate the fact that perhaps that awful night two years ago left him as heartbroken as it left me. To him, I died. *I died.*

"And not only that," he continues, looking away, "but then …" He hesitates, his chest heaving with heavy breaths. He presses his lips together, as if he's trying to hold his next words back. But they tumble from his mouth anyway. "Remy is dead."

My stomach drops to my toes. "What?" I whisper.

"Like, actually dead. Not let's-lie-to-everyone-and-say-he-died-in-an-enchanted-fire dead. No, this was a sometimes-assignments-have-tragic-endings kind of dead. A yes-it-sucks-but-you-should-have-expected-this-to-happen-to-at-least-one-of-your-friends kind of dead."

I can't speak. I can't move.

"It was one of the first strange creatures to show up after the mist started hanging around," Ash continues, still not looking at me. "Remy got the assignment." He shrugs. "Could have been any of us. But it was him. And he died." He shakes his head. "We were all just starting to figure out how to live without *you*, and then he was gone too. Such a damn, freaking waste."

My hand reaches for the tree beside me. I use it to prop myself up, to keep myself from sinking to the ground. "Ash, I … I …"

"And then we had to get through the rest of our training like we didn't have this shadow hanging over us. We all had to pretend like graduation was a *celebration*. As if it was just *fine* that you and Remy weren't with us anymore." He shakes his head. "I couldn't wait to get out of here. So that's what I did. I left. And after years alone, I finally return here, ready to face this place again and try to move on, and it turns out things are even worse."

"Years—years alone?" I croak. I clear my throat and swallow. "What are you talking about? You just graduated a few months ago."

"And then I discover you're still alive," Ash continues, amber eyes on me again, "and it's like *something* in this messed-up world might actually be right. But then it turns out I'm the last person you want to see. You can't wait to get away from me. You can barely stand to *look* at me. And then you want to walk away from all of this because it's too much for you? No. That's not the way this works. You don't get to leave without—"

"I'm sorry, Ash, I'm *sorry*. About Remy, about … everything. I can't even imagine … after everything else … but I can't stay here and—"

"Don't keep telling me you're sorry when it's clear all you want to do is get the hell out of here as fast as possible. Do you even care—"

"Of course I *care*! I'm just trying to *survive*, okay? You don't know what I've … what I've …" I press the heels of my hands against my eyes. I'm straying too close to the things I can't tell him. The things he'll never understand. The things he'll never forgive.

"No, I don't know exactly what you've been through," he says, his voice a little quieter now. "Because you won't *talk* to me. But I know how much you loved your parents, and I know what it felt like to lose a friend—to lose *two* friends—so I can imagine how hard it was for you. How it might still feel like all you're doing is *surviving*—"

I'm shaking my head before I can stop myself. "It's not that."

"It's not … what?"

I bite the inside of my cheek. *Don't. Say. ANYTHING*, I silently scream at myself. Ash is the last person who will ever understand.

"Silver …"

I squeeze my eyes shut, red images flashing across my closed eyeballs, my heart pounding, my hands sweating. My breathing is elevated, shallow, but I can't seem to slow it down, and she's there in the shadows, stalking toward me on glossy high heels, almost close enough now to—

"Silver?" Ash's hand on my shoulder is gentle, but I can't help flinching away. My eyelids snap open in time to see the hurt in his gaze. "We used to talk about everything," he says after a moment.

"I … I can't believe Remy is gone," I say, turning away from Ash, pressing my fingers to my temples, changing the subject from one kind of pain to another. "How can he be *gone*?" The idea that there's now a Remy-shaped hole in the world stabs me in the chest and sucks my breath away. I embrace the pain, allowing tears to burn in my eyes.

"I know," Ash says quietly.

"Is … is Odette okay?" I pace away from Ash as my body starts to overheat. All this emotion is doing weird things to me. I'm sweaty, sticky, uncomfortable.

"Um, yeah. Silver, what's—"

"And your brothers? What are they … um … what are they doing?" A jittery feeling has begun to steal through my limbs. I can't keep still. I'm dizzy and breathless, and my arm won't stop throbbing. "Are they … are they well?" I know I said we wouldn't be doing this, catching up on each other's lives, but the world is starting to spin, and maybe I'm not even awake. I think I'm dreaming this. The pain in my arm, and the pain in my heart. So much pain.

I blink, and suddenly I'm … horizontal? I feel the ground beneath me. Ash is standing over me, and then his face is right in front of mine, cool hands on my cheeks, his beautiful eyes searching my face, and … crap, where did those other two people come from? I blink a little more forcefully, trying to clear the haze from my head. It helps a tiny bit, and the words 'Asher Blackburn' and 'under arrest' manage to reach my brain.

Oh. I see. Guardians. Wonderful.

It seems Ash feels the same way I do, because I'm pretty sure I hear him curse loudly and then yell, "*Are you freaking kidding me?*"

I want to laugh. In fact, I think I am laughing. But then I'm also falling …

And then …

I'm nothing.

THIRTEEN

then

THE SMELL OF BURNED SUGAR FILLED SILVER'S NOSE AS SHE hurried out of the faerie paths and into the clearing. On the far side, near the path that led to the beach, Ash, Remy and Odette were gathered around a fire. "How do you burn them *every time*?" Odette was asking as she laughed.

"How do you *not* burn them?" Remy countered.

"You're not supposed to hold them *in a flame*. You're supposed to hold them near the hot coals, and that way they toast slowly. Otherwise you're just burning the outside."

Remy tossed his stick into the fire and sat back with a defeated sigh. "There should be a spell for this. The perfectly toasted marshmallow."

"There is," Ash said, "but it never tastes as good as one that's toasted for real."

"I'll bet it tastes better than a burned one."

"Hey, you guys are here already," Silver said as she bounded over. The contents of the bowl in her arms sloshed around, and she slowed down, relieved she'd decided to put a lid on top of the bowl before leaving her kitchen.

"Yeah, because we said we'd meet here like an hour ago," Ash said.

"I was finishing the waffle batter!" Silver exclaimed in defense.

"Oh my gosh, you were serious about that?" Odette said, laughing again.

"Of course. Why would I joke about waffles?"

"Um, because all we have out here is a simple fire?"

"Odette." Silver sat on the ground between Ash and Remy. "This is Iris's No-Fail Waffle Enchantment. That means it doesn't fail. Ever."

"Okay then." Odette removed her perfectly toasted marshmallow from the end of a stick and added, "I'm watching."

Silver glanced at Ash, a knowing smile on her lips. His expression mirrored hers. He knew as well as she did that this recipe enchantment never failed. It was his mom's, after all. He'd witnessed it many times. Silver removed the lid from the bowl, then began muttering the words Iris had taught her months ago while coaxing magic from her core. It seeped from her palms in wisps and sparkles, and she wove it together with neat flicks of her fingers, exactly the way Iris did it. Then she stood and carefully moved the magic so that it swirled near the edge of the fire.

"Thanks," she said to Ash as he handed her the bowl. She held it over her magic and tipped some of the batter into the midst of the bright sizzling sparks. Instead of falling into the fire, the batter spread out and began to take shape immediately, quickly forming something roughly square with perfect little square-shaped indentations. Silver watched with a growing smile. The waffle was golden brown in under a minute. "Oh yeah!" she crowed, raising her hand in Ash's direction. He slapped his palm against hers in a high five.

"Perfection," he said.

"Okay fine," Odette said from the other side of the fire. "I'm suitably impressed."

"In that case," Silver said, "you can have the first one."

"Ooh, yes please. Did you bring plates?"

"Oh." Silver laughed. "Oops, no. Sorry. Here, use the lid of the bowl." She dropped the waffle onto the lid and passed it to Odette. Then she got to work making more while Ash toasted marshmallows for toppings and Remy collected a few oversized leaves to use as plates before stealing the last piece of Odette's waffle when she wasn't looking.

"Aren't they the most beautiful things *ever*?" she was saying, her eyes fixed on the cloud of pink butterflies currently flitting across the clearing, glowing with their own enchanted light. "I love them!"

"They're just *butterflies*," Remy mumbled around the piece of waffle in his mouth.

"They're stunning. Every time I see them I decide they're my favorite creature."

"You are so weird."

When they were finally all sitting with their waffle desserts, Silver looked at Remy and said, "So, have you spoken about it yet?"

Remy avoided her gaze, frowning as he feigned confusion. "Spoken about what?"

"Come on." Silver squished her toasted marshmallow with her finger so that the crisp outer layer cracked and the melted sugary goodness oozed out the sides onto the waffle. "Your assessment this afternoon."

"He hasn't said a word," Odette supplied. "Kept saying he was waiting for you to get here."

"Hey, didn't we say we were coming out here to play Truth or Dare tonight?" Remy asked.

Silver looked a little more closely at him. "Was it bad?" she asked. "Is that why you don't want to talk about it?"

"No." Remy shrugged, then sighed. "It was …" He looked up with a grin. "It was brilliant. I aced it."

Odette threw a piece of waffle at him. "You idiot, why didn't you just *say* that? You had me worried!"

"Just drawing out the suspense—Hey!" he protested loudly when Ash leaned past Silver and threw a shoe at him. Remy tossed the shoe up in the air, spun it with magic, then pulled a glittering bow from the air and shot an arrow straight through the shoe. "See? It's pretty much automatic now. No more weapon retrieval problem."

Unlike the rest of them, Remy had found it surprisingly difficult to pull his guardian weapons from the air. Most trainees apparently learned how to do it within a week or two, if they practiced every day. Silver had struggled the first few days, but once her fingers had learned the feel of the weapons—the warm, almost comforting prickle—her mind had settled into that instinctive place where she could reach for something without really thinking about it. There would be that rush of heat and light and sparkles, and suddenly she was holding a guardian weapon, glittering like a thousand golden stars welded together.

Ash, of course, had been able to do it pretty much instantly. That was the Blackburn legacy right there. The knowledge of how to be a guardian was basically burned into his blood. When Remy had continued to struggle well into his third month of training, and the extra hours he was putting in with some of the mentors made no difference, Ash had quietly offered to help. Now, four months after the start of their training, one of the councilors wanted to know what was going on with Remy and had scheduled an assessment. Silver had been worrying about it the entire time she was making the waffle mixture, afraid that one of her friends was about to be kicked out of the Guild. But apparently, there had been no need for concern.

"Dude," Ash said. "You just shot an arrow through your own shoe."

Silver smacked a hand over her mouth, a snort escaping as she started laughing.

"I—what?" Remy stood and peered past Odette to where the shoe had landed on the ground, arrow still protruding from it. "Aah, man. Why'd you make me do that?"

"I didn't make you do anything," Ash said through his laughter. Silver wrapped an arm around her middle and tried to draw a breath, but it was pretty much impossible to do anything aside from shudder with uncontrolled laughter. Odette leaned back on one hand and tugged the arrow free with the other. It vanished when she let go of it.

"Here you go, moron." She tossed the shoe back to Remy. "Oh, hey, Silver," she added. "Did your parents catch that assassin guy last night? I forgot to ask you at breakfast this morning. Weren't you saying yesterday that they got some anonymous tip about him or something?"

"He got away again," Silver said, wiping tears from the corners of her eyes now that she'd recovered from her laughter. "My parents are super annoyed. They couldn't get close enough, and I heard them saying something about how it seemed almost like he was toying with them? Like maybe he was the one who'd sent in the tip, just so he could mess with them."

"Ugh, what is *wrong* with people?" Odette grumbled.

"I know," Silver said. The case that Zilph's brother had been arrested in connection with had grown over the past several months. Another councilor had been killed, this time from the Stormsdrift Guild, as well as someone high up in the Seelie Court. Silver wasn't supposed to know any of the details, but she overheard things at home when her parents thought she was asleep or in another room.

"My parents were talking about him this morning too," Ash said. "Sounds like the Guild named him the Scarlet Arrow?"

"Seriously?" Remy said. "That's gotta be the dumbest name I've ever heard."

"Yeah, well, the name might be dumb, but the details …" Silver grimaced. "The details are decidedly *not* dumb. I overheard my parents talking about the victims. They were all found with an arrow through the heart and … um … their heads cut off. So … lots of blood. Hence 'scarlet' and 'arrow.'"

Odette's mouth fell open. "Seriously?"

"I guess that makes sense if your target's a faerie," Remy said. "I mean, we're difficult to kill, so you'd have to cut the person's head off to ensure death."

"Okay, can we change the subject?" Odette said. "We deal with enough gruesome stuff during training. I'd rather *not* bring it up while we're eating."

"Yes, let's change the subject." Remy turned to her. "Odette. Truth or dare?"

"Ugh, come on. I didn't mean that you should start with me."

"Truth or dare?" Remy repeated with a grin.

She sighed. "Truth."

"Did you kiss Jerryn behind the potion manuals shelf in the library?"

"Ew, no!"

"You can't lie, remember."

"I'm not lying!"

"And since when is Jerryn 'ew'?" Remy added. "I thought we said he was hot."

"You and Silver said he was hot. I just nodded."

"Uh, pretty sure I also just nodded," Silver said, licking melted marshmallow off her thumb.

"Where was I during this 'Jerryn is hot' discussion?" Ash asked.

"It definitely wasn't a *discussion*," Silver said.

"I think you had an extra session with one of the mentors," Odette said to Ash.

"Okay, but I heard a rumor," Remy continued, speaking to Odette again. "So you must have kissed *someone* in the library."

Odette stared firmly into the fire. "I believe my turn is over now."

"Ah, so you *did* kiss someone!" Remy exclaimed.

Silver's grin stretched wider. "Oh, do tell! Who was it?"

Odette cleared her throat and looked up. "Silver. Truth or dare?"

Silver laughed. "Fine, you can tell me later."

A small smile made its way onto Odette's lips. "Maybe," she muttered. "Anyway, what will it be? Truth or dare?"

"Hmm." Finished with her waffle now, Silver drew her knees up and pulled the sleeves of her stripy sweater over her hands. Well, technically it was Ash's sweater. Silver had dug it out from among the dozens of other articles of clothing littering her bedroom floor, intending to return it to him this evening. But after taking so long with the waffle mixture, it had seemed easier just to quickly pull Ash's sweater on and hurry through the paths instead of going back upstairs to hunt through her clothes again for something of her own. "Dare," she said.

"Surprise, surprise," Ash said at the same moment Remy said, "Obviously."

"Yes, obviously," Silver said with a shrug. "Dare is way more fun than truth."

"Okay, um …" Odette tapped her chin and pursed her lips. "I dare you to send an anonymous message to that guy in fourth year telling him you like him."

"What guy?" Ash asked.

"Ody, that is *so* boring!" Remy complained.

Odette glared at him. "Call me that again and I'll stab you with this marshmallow stick."

"You know Silver's up for anything," Ash said, leaning forward to wrap his arms around his knees. "You have to dare her to do more than just a boring anonymous message. Like …" He looked at Silver. "I dare you to sneak into Councilor Eryn's office and steal that little unicorn figurine she likes to talk to when she thinks no one's watching."

"Ash!" Odette scolded. "You can't dare her to do that. She'll get into serious—"

"Done," Silver said, already rising to her feet.

"No, wait, Silver." Odette sounded genuinely concerned. "You don't have to—"

But Odette's words were cut off as Silver marched into the faerie paths. She walked out near the Guild's main entrance, skipped up the stairs, flashed her trainee pendant at the night guard, and was inside mere moments after leaving the clearing. She appreciated Odette's concern, but she wasn't about to back down from a dare, especially one issued to her by Ash. She would at least *try* to get that unicorn.

She climbed the massive staircase all the way up to the councilors' level, giving the two mentors she passed on the way up a friendly—and hopefully innocent—smile. Outside the second-to-last office along the corridor on one side of the councilors' level, she hesitated. This would be simple, she decided. If Councilor Eryn was here, then Silver would have to admit defeat and return without the unicorn. But if she wasn't, Silver would simply swipe it off the councilor's desk and hurry back to the clearing.

She cleared her throat and knocked on the door. Her heart leaped then, her brain suddenly floundering to come up with a believable story for why she would need to see a councilor in the middle of the night. She should have thought of that *before* she knocked on the door. But there was no response. She knocked again. Still nothing. Her heart rate slowed, and she allowed herself to smile. With barely a glance over her shoulder, she twisted the handle and stepped inside.

It was easy. The polished, hot pink unicorn was right there on the corner of the desk. Silver grabbed it, slipped it inside the loose sleeve of Ash's sweater, and held it, hidden, against her palm. Then she stepped silently back into the corridor and pulled the door shut.

And that was when she heard her mother's voice.

Her head whipped around. Mom hadn't reached this corridor yet, but she was somewhere close by. Silver's eyes landed on the two armchairs and the oversized potted plant at the end of the corridor. She darted toward it and slipped behind one of the armchairs.

It struck her suddenly that she knew very little about the Guild's security aside from the guards who stood at the main door and the enchantments that swirled above the main entrance hall. She'd heard that most areas within the Guild were 'monitored,' but what did that mean exactly? Was there some sort of observation device or spell currently watching her and relaying her activities to someone in a security room? Was a guard about to come running down the corridor looking for her? Well, if that was the case, she'd find out soon enough.

"… doing up here?" That was Iris's voice.

"Just waiting to see Ursula," Mom said. She and Iris sounded even closer than before. "I need to talk to her about that key."

"Key?" Iris asked.

"You know, the one she reminds us about every few months."

"Oh, that. Yes. Wait, did you discover something? Did you *find* it?"

"No, nothing like that. I saw an old painting in that cave Rowan and I were in last night, and it looked like the description Ursula gave us. Don't know if that's useful to her, but she told us to report anything that might be related to the key." The sound of footsteps came to a halt. Silver leaned lower and peeked beneath the bottom of the armchair. Iris and Mom were standing outside the last office, the one closest to the chairs. "Have you ever come close to finding it?" Mom asked.

"Nope. To be honest," Iris said, lowering her voice a little, "I haven't exactly gone out of my way to look for it. We have lives to save, criminals to apprehend, deadly creatures to stop, and illicit magic to hunt down, but we're supposed to find extra time in the day to look out for some old key that's apparently been missing for decades? A key that could be *anywhere* in the world? If I happened to see it—or a picture of it—I'd recognize it, but I haven't been actively looking. The Council will have to—oh, hang on." A cheerful jingle filled the air, and Silver recognized it as the tune Iris's little round pocket mirror played when she received a call. "It's Lennox," Iris said. "I'll see you downstairs when you're done?"

"Yes, I shouldn't be long," Mom said.

Iris strode away, and Silver's heart lurched as Mom approached the chair she was hiding behind. Mom shouldn't be able to *see* her, but what if she could somehow *feel* that Silver was hiding right there? Mom's feet turned, the chair moved slightly—that was probably Mom reaching for the armrests to lower herself to the seat—and then the nearest office door opened.

"Nel?" A pair of glossy high-heeled shoes appeared just outside the open door. "I got your message. You wanted to chat about something?"

"Yes. Thanks, Ursula." Mom walked away from the chair toward Councilor Bergenfell. "Just a quick thing."

"Sure, not a problem." Councilor Bergenfell's shoes disappeared back into her office—*click, click, click*—and Mom followed. The door shut, cutting off their conversation.

Silver didn't pause a moment longer. She crept out from behind the chair, rose silently, and walked as quickly as possible back to the main staircase. She barely allowed herself to breathe until she was back outside, walking away from the Guild's entrance. Even then, she managed to keep her jubilant smile to herself until she was back inside the faerie paths.

"There you are!" Odette exclaimed when Silver stepped back into the clearing. "What took you so long? We were just wondering how long we should wait before trying to find out if you got caught."

Silver pulled her sleeve back and displayed the pink unicorn on her palm. "Got it."

"Ohmygosh." Odette covered her mouth as she laughed. "I can't believe you actually did that."

Silver considered how close she'd come to being discovered not only by her mother and Iris, but by Councilor Bergenfell. Not that Councilor Bergenfell was particularly scary—Silver thought she seemed friendly enough on the two or three occasions they'd been in the same room—but she was in charge of the entire Stormsdrift Guild, so that made her a little intimidating by default.

Silver bit her lip and bounded back toward the fire, barely containing a squeal. "I can't believe I did that either. *And* I almost got caught."

"*What?*" Odette squeaked. "Holy fae, Silver! You could have got detention. You could have been *suspended*! Or worse!"

"Um … I guess?" A whisper of fear crept in at the corners of her mind. But she *hadn't* been caught, so what was there to worry about? She laughed as she dropped to the ground between Ash and Remy, the tiny hint of fear quickly smothered by the exhilaration of getting away with the dare. She pulled her knees up to her chest again and placed the unicorn on the ground at her feet. "Okay, your turn," she said to Ash.

"How am I supposed to follow that?" he asked with a laugh.

Silver shrugged. "You choose dare, I guess."

"Fine. Dare."

"Hmm." Silver pulled her sleeves down over her hands again before tucking her fists beneath her chin, pretending to be deep in thought. "Okay. I've got it. I dare you to go down into the Shadow Crypt."

Ash paused. "I …"

Silver raised a brow. "Scared?"

Firelight danced across his face. His lips curved into a smile. "Never. It's just that it's locked, isn't it?"

"And it's against the rules," Odette added.

"The councilors' magic can open it, right?" Silver said, ignoring Odette. "And this—" she picked up the pink unicorn with a smug expression "—must be *covered* in Councilor Eryn's magic. She touches this thing all the time."

"Um … don't know if it works that way," Ash said with a frown.

"So you *are* too scared to go down there."

He folded his arms. "You know I'm not scared of anything."

"So let's try it then. There's gotta be *some* magic on this thing. Even if it's just a trace."

"Okay." Ash stood and nodded to the unicorn. "Hand it over."

"Excellent." Silver passed him the unicorn before jumping to her feet. "Can I come too?"

Ash laughed again. "Whose dare is this, exactly?"

"Look, we have to at least go with you to the entrance of the crypt." She looked around at Remy and Odette. "Right? Otherwise how will we know if you actually go inside?"

Odette shook her head. "If you guys want to dare each other to break the rules, that's your business. I don't want to be hanging around waiting to get in trouble along with you."

"We're not going to get in trouble," Ash told her. "It's not like anyone monitors what's happening at the crypt. The only reason it's locked is because they don't want kids going down there and vandalizing it and being disrespectful or whatever. I'm just going to walk inside and walk out again."

"Well … someone has to stay here and keep the fire alive," Remy pointed out. "So I guess you can do that, Odette?"

"What? I'm not staying here *alone*."

"Why not?" Remy asked. "Isn't Stormsdrift supposed to be one of the safest places in the world?"

"Uh, *no*! Where'd you hear that?"

"I think you mean one of the safest places *that has a Guild*," Ash corrected, "since most Guilds were built in dangerous parts of the world. There are plenty of places that are safer than this."

"Okay, fine, I'll stay here with Odette," Remy said.

"Cool." Silver grabbed Ash's hand. "We'll be right back." Then she opened up a doorway to the paths and pulled him in after her.

The Shadow Crypt was a short distance away from the Guild and wasn't related to it in any way. It wasn't common for guardians—or any faeries—to bury or inter their dead. The deceased were generally placed in flower-laden canoes on the Neverending River and sent upstream to disappear beneath the Infinity Falls. This crypt housed elven bodies, and it had been here since before the Stormsdrift Guild was even built. Whatever building had once existed above it was long since gone. All that remained now was an overgrown opening in the ground that revealed a crumbling stone staircase leading down into the earth.

"Okay," Ash said as he and Silver stood at the top of the steps and looked down. It had begun raining just as they'd arrived, a gentle patter of fine droplets. "I guess … we just walk down there. And there'll be a door or a gate or something at the bottom."

"Yes." Silver looked at him. "Do you want me to go first?" She'd always been curious about this place, and her curiosity had only grown when she'd asked Dad about it one day before joining the Guild and learned that no one was supposed to go down there.

Ash met her gaze and arched a brow. "No way. You do not get to go down there first so you can tell Remy and Odette that you're braver than me."

Silver shrugged and gave him a wicked smile. "I mean … we all know it's the truth."

"You wish." Then he placed one foot on the first cracked step and began his descent. Silver watched him, contemplating whether she should sneak silently behind him and jump on him at the bottom.

"Whatever you're thinking of doing," Ash said without looking back over his shoulder at her, "don't."

Silver rolled her eyes. He knew her too well. "Fine. I'm not going to *do* anything. I'm just walking down behind you so I can also see inside." She wiped the rain from her face, then followed him down the ancient staircase, treading carefully in case the crumbling stone suddenly gave way. "It's dry," she said. "I mean, the steps aren't wet. The rain can't get down here."

Ash looked back up at her from the bottom of the stairs. "Must be some kind of protection from the elements. Makes sense, since there's a gate here, not a solid door. This place would be flooded all the time if there was nothing to stop the rain getting down here."

Silver reached the bottom and stood in the tiny space in front of a simple metal gate. It looked old enough to fall off its hinges with little more than a gentle pulse of magic. She was half afraid to even sneeze in case the gate crumbled beneath the force of the air moving against it. But she knew this wasn't really the case. She remembered being told at the beginning of her training, during the tour of the Guild and its grounds, that the Shadow Crypt was locked with magic and no one was allowed down there.

Peering through the bars, she said, "I can't see a thing."

"Well of course not," Ash said. "There's no light in there. It's the *Shadow* Crypt."

"You need *light* for there to be *shadows*, smart-ass," Silver said. "This is just darkness."

"Who's the real smart-ass then?"

Instead of answering, Silver looked pointedly at the unicorn in Ash's hand. He moved it closer to the lock on the gate. Nothing happened.

He touched the gate with it. Still nothing. He tried moving it in slow circles against the lock.

"You know you have to actually try and open the gate to know if it's worked," Silver said. She pushed the gate—and it swung forward.

"Oh." Ash stood there with his hand raised, unicorn still in his grip. "Sorry, I was waiting for a click or something." He lowered his arm. Silver lifted hers and conjured a globe of light over her palm. The light flickered a little—she had only used the spell a few times before—but didn't go out. She let Ash take a step ahead of her, then entered behind him.

The inside of the crypt was smaller than she'd always imagined. It was a single room with two stone caskets on the left and another two on the right. Symbols she didn't recognize were carved on top of each one. The walls were bare except for an arched pattern of stones set into the wall on the opposite side of the room. There were no other decorative elements. "Well," she said to Ash. "I'll admit this is a little disappointing."

"Yeah, I don't know exactly what I expected but … maybe …"

"More?" Silver suggested.

"Perhaps. It's still creepy, though. What if little creatures crawl in between the bars of the gate and start building their homes in here?"

"Maybe the magic on the gate keeps them out. I'd be more worried about the people who might be able to get past the magic—like we did —and hide in the shadows behind the caskets." She took a step past Ash, her eyes still on the archway pattern on the far wall. She couldn't say what, exactly, but there was something there that kept snagging her attention. Something that seemed to almost tug at her as if a string were attached to her chest.

"What are you doing?" Ash asked. "We should go now."

"Just … looking. Do you think there's something weird about that wall?"

"Weird in what way?"

"I don't know. I just … can't stop looking at it."

"Well that's weird." Silver felt his hand around her upper arm, warm and firm. "We should definitely go now."

"Yeah, okay." She let him pull her back to the door. They crossed the threshold, and Ash pulled the gate closed. He waved the unicorn near the lock in a random fashion, then tested the gate with one or two firm shakes to make sure it was locked again.

"Come on." He started up the stairs, and Silver cast a final glance over her shoulder. By the light of the orb that still floated above her palm, the wall on the far side of the crypt seemed to almost … flicker. For an instant, it seemed that the arched pattern was a real archway, leading to another room. But Silver blinked, and the other room was gone. There was only a wall.

"Are you coming?" Ash asked.

Silver paused for one more moment, waiting for the strange phenomenon to occur again. But it didn't. "Yeah, I'm coming." She extinguished her light and followed Ash up the stairs.

Fourteen

now

I wake with a sharp inhale, a nightmare still vivid in my mind. The last moments before my parents died. Our last moments together, shielding ourselves near the crypt. The pain is so real I can almost feel it. Radiating throughout my chest. Pressing, aching, *burning*. Dad shouting. Magic flashing. Mom whispering fiercely to me: *Don't ever come back here*. And then Bergenfell, looming over us, crimson eyes, sleek red hair sliding over her shoulder, a glittering sword raised and swiping through the air—

I push myself up with another quick breath, realizing suddenly that I'm lying on a bed I don't recognize. A four-poster with a gauzy white canopy above and intricate designs carved into each wooden post. My gaze darts across the room, my heart thundering, as movement catches my attention. But it's only Ash, rising hastily from a chair in the corner. "Hey, you're fine, everything's fine. We're at Ostin's."

I blink. "We—how did we—" I pause. "What are you wearing?"

Ash looks down at his loose stripy pants and plain orange T-shirt. The pants come to an end just above his ankles, and the orange of the T-shirt is brighter than anything I've ever seen him wear. "Oh. I borrowed some clothes from Ostin to sleep in. He's ... well. A bit shorter than I am." Yeah. That's an understatement. And yet Ash somehow still manages to look smolderingly hot in this ridiculous outfit. It isn't fair.

"Huh. Um …" I rub my eyes, my brain going back to my original question. "How did we get here?"

"You told me where he lives, remember? Firecove. On that volcano island. Drakkyn. It was easy to get here, and Firecove isn't a big town. The homes are out in the open, like in Stormsdrift. Fortunately. I knocked on the door of the first home I found and asked the guy if he knew Ostin Fairwend."

"And he just … told you?"

"He seemed suspicious—especially when he noticed the unconscious girl in my arms—but I showed him my guardian markings, and I guess people around here know Ostin used to be a guardian."

"Oh. Okay."

Ash moves toward the foot of the bed and sits on the edge. "I'm sorry. I know you weren't sure about coming here, about letting him know you're still alive, but you were in a bad way, and I couldn't take you to a healing institute or a Guild. I figured if your parents trusted him, then we can trust him too."

"A bad way?" I try to picture those last moments before I blacked out. It all seems horribly fuzzy. "What happened?"

He gestures at me, and I look down to find a bandage wrapped around the upper part of my right arm. "That creature that found us inside the Gauntlet changing house? It cut your arm when it almost caught you. Its talons must have been poisoned or something. You started getting a little bit … delirious. Then you passed out. I was trying to figure out what had happened to you, after I got us away from those guardians, and that's when I discovered the wounds. They were … not looking good."

I let out a grim sigh and run a hand through my hair. "Wonderful. So that creature has magic that can get past a shield, *and* it has poison that can incapacitate a faerie. That's fun."

"And rare," Ash adds. "Anyway, Ostin seemed to know what to do. He tried a variety of antidote spells until something started working."

I look down at my arm again, noting with some discomfort that my jacket is gone. Obviously. Ostin would have had to remove it to deal with the wound. Still, its absence leaves me feeling oddly exposed despite the fact that I'm decent enough in a tank top and pants.

My brain rewinds to something else Ash said. *After I got us away from those guardians.* I raise my eyes and tilt my head to the side as I frown at him, hazy memories swimming in my mind. "Did you … almost get *arrested?*"

He lets out a quiet groan. "Highlight of my career so far."

I shake my head and manage what feels like an actual smile. "Asher Blackburn. A Guild fugitive. Who would have thought?" I raise a brow and add, "Bet that's something your brothers never managed to do."

Ash's expression shifts to something … else.

"What?" I ask.

"Nothing." He looks away. "Anyway. There were two of them, and I fought them both off before grabbing you and getting away through the paths. I'll bet the Guild's about to hammer down my parents' door to find out whether we're hiding there—if they haven't done so already. That's the main reason I didn't take you to them. My mom did some extra courses in healing magic back in the day, so I figured she might be able to help, but … yeah. Not safe. Guardians must be crawling all over Stormsdrift now. That's the only way they could have found us at the clearing. By chance."

I nod. "I know. About the extra healing courses."

"Right. Yes."

I run my hands along my legs. "Is Ostin around? I should talk to him."

"Oh, yeah. But he's sleeping. It's the middle of the night here."

"Of course. Time zone differences."

"Yep. I, uh …" Ash rubs the back of his neck. "Sorry if it's weird that I was in here, but I couldn't sleep, and I thought you might freak out if you woke up and found yourself in an unfamiliar place with no one around to explain what happened."

I nod. "Thanks. Was I … asleep for a while?"

"About … a day and a half?"

"Oh. Wow. That's a long time."

"Yeah, Ostin said the cuts seemed to be taking longer to heal than regular wounds." He gestures to my arm again. "But they should be fine by now. You can probably take the bandage off."

I loosen the bandage and let it unravel. My arm is almost perfectly healed. Only three pink lines mark my skin.

"That's pretty," Ash says, and I'm completely confused until he adds, "The tattoo."

I stiffen, realizing his eyes are on my left collarbone. I pull my hair over my shoulder before he can look too closely, then climb out of the bed and move toward the open window. The room spins, and my head feels strange, but I manage to catch myself against the window frame without stumbling or falling. I shut my eyes as my body adjusts to the upright position.

"Does it mean something?" Ash asks quietly.

I press my lips together, thinking of the tattoo with its narrow stem, tiny blossoms, and little leaves and wondering what to tell Ash. Preferably nothing, but apparently my body language isn't enough to convey that I'd rather not talk about this. When I don't immediately answer, he says, "It looks a bit like those little white flowers your mom used to put in her hair."

I inhale sharply, steeling myself against the ache that always comes with picturing my mom and her beautiful smile and her windswept hair with tiny white blossoms caught in the tangles. She kept it braided when she was working—"I can't see past this wild bird's nest," she would complain—but otherwise, when she wasn't on duty, she left it down. "Gypsophila," I say quietly. "Baby's breath. We had it growing in our garden."

"I remember."

We're quiet for several moments as I open my eyes and stare out of the window. The house is on a hill, and by the light of a full moon, I can see over treetops and roof peaks to a beach and the sea beyond. I know this island is small, and that the majority of it is taken up by a dormant volcano, so does that mean this house is perched on the side of that volcano? Flecks of snow drift past the open window, and though I can feel the air moving against my bare skin, I can't feel the icy bite. Ostin must have placed a spell on his home that allows fresh air in while leaving the cold outside.

"I assume you had it done somewhere here?" Ash asks, presumably still talking about the tattoo. "In the fae realm?"

"No. Human realm, actually. Though not by a human tattoo artist, which I'm guessing is what you mean. It would have disappeared otherwise."

"Right. Faeries require enchanted ink for a tattoo to be permanent." Another moment passes, and then he asks, "Do you have any others?"

"No," I answer, a little too quickly. And then I close my eyes and shake my head, because this is all just so stupid. Why are we talking about *tattoos* when we should be talking about the faerie door, or the insanely dangerous monsters wandering around Stormsdrift, or all the things Ash shouted at me before—

And that's when I suddenly remember. The thing that punched the air from my chest. The thing that added another hole to my heart. The thing that seemed so utterly *wrong*. "Remy," I whisper, turning back to face Ash. "Did I dream that part?"

Ash looks down. "No. You didn't."

My next breath is a shudder. Tears well in my eyes. I return to the bed and sit on the edge, lowering my face to my hands. "I can't believe he's gone."

"I know. I mean … we all grew up knowing that it was a very real possibility. We didn't exactly choose a safe career path. But still. I don't think you can ever really prepare yourself for something like that."

"No," I mumble, shaking my head.

"We obviously all had counseling," Ash continues quietly. "The Guild is good about that, since they know this kind of thing might happen. So, you know, we all kind of dealt with it. In our own way. Eventually. But obviously it still …"

"Sucks?" I supply. Because I'm super eloquent that way.

"Yeah."

I'm silent for a long time, and I can't help thinking of Ash shouting *I lost you!* I almost ask him if he made peace with my death too, but I can't bring myself to say the words.

My stomach gurgles loudly then, which is more than a little embarrassing, but at least it breaks the silence. I straighten and push both hands through my hair. "Is there … maybe … some food? If I've been out of it for so long, I should probably—"

"Right, yes, sorry." He stands quickly. "You must be hungry."

He moves toward the door and I follow him, running my hands up and down my arms. I'll need to make a plan to get hold of some new clothes, seeing as all my belongings are now gone. I picture the journal, and my heart squeezes painfully. But even as I'm trying to push the hurt aside, my eyes land on a dark object sitting on the floor beside the chair Ash was in when I woke up.

"My backpack," I say in surprise. I meet Ash's gaze as he pauses in the doorway and looks over his shoulder at me. "You went back for it?"

"Well, the journal's in it, and we were still hoping to possibly get some answers from it. And also … well, I figured that if you weren't planning to go back to that apartment you were living in, then everything that's important to you is probably in there. So yeah. I went back for it after Ostin treated your arm and confirmed you'd be okay."

"And that creature?"

"Gone. I grabbed the backpack and slipped out just before a group of third years arrived. The place was a bit of a mess—furniture knocked over, and some claw marks running down one of the walls—but I didn't have time to fix anything."

"Well … thank you."

Ash leaves the room, but I take a moment to reach for my jacket, which is draped over the top of the backpack. The top of one sleeve has a few rips in it, which I'll have to figure out how to fix at some point, but for now, this is fine. I pull the jacket on and zip it up as I walk down the passageway, feeling more comfortable now that my tattoo is concealed. Vague memories nudge the back of my mind as I move through Ostin's home. I'm pretty sure I've been here before, though it must have been many years ago.

I walk into the kitchen to find Ash on the other side of the table looking inside one of the cupboards. "What do you want?" he asks.

"Um … whatever's easiest. But I can help myself. You don't have to do it."

He looks over his shoulder at me. "Waffles?" he suggests.

It takes me a moment to realize he's being serious. "No, don't be silly. It's the middle of the night. We don't want to wake Ostin while we're hunting for bowls and mixing up—"

"They're already made. We had them earlier for breakfast. Well, it was my breakfast, Ostin's afternoon tea."

"Oh. Well, in that case …"

I sit on one of the kitchen chairs, trying not to feel supremely awkward as Ash snaps his fingers to produce a flame for the stove, tosses a few waffles into a pan to heat up, and somehow produces all my favorite toppings: golden syrup, chopped nuts, and a jar of Mama Pixie's Marshmallow Creme.

A thousand memories of the two of us in a kitchen together flit through my mind. Breakfasts, late-night snacks, dinners, family gatherings with too many people walking into each other, talking over each other, Iris scolding Connor for tasting something before it's ready, my father and Lennox laughing over some stupid dad joke. It hurts so much it's almost a physical pain in my chest.

I stand abruptly and hunt through the cupboards until I find two glasses. I fill them with water, determinedly *not* thinking of the Black-burns' kitchen and all the bittersweet memories it conjures, and return to the table. "Thanks," I say when Ash sets a plate down in front of me. I pull one leg up, resting my heel on the edge of the chair and wrapping my arm around my shin. Then I pause, my gaze moving between the plate and the collection of toppings, and decide it's time to address the awkwardness. "This is weird, isn't it? A day or two ago I didn't want to see you ever again, and now you're serving me waffles."

He remains quiet as he pulls out the chair opposite mine and sits. "Look, Silver," he says eventually. "I'm really sorry about everything I said in the clearing, when you were trying to leave. I can't imagine how difficult it was for you, being in Stormsdrift again, all those memories of your parents. I understand that you wanted to get away. I was just …" He rubs a hand over his face. "'Happy' doesn't even begin to describe what I felt when I discovered you were actually alive, and then it hurt that you couldn't wait to get away from me. But I shouldn't have said—"

"No, you should have. *I'm* the one who's sorry. I … I understand your hurt." I pull the plate a little closer and tear a tiny corner off one of the waffles. "When I said, 'We're not doing this'—you know, implying that I didn't want to hear anything about you or your family or what's been happening since I left—it wasn't because I don't *care*." I break off another piece. "It was more … because … I was protecting myself."

"Okaaaaay. I won't pretend that makes sense."

"I mean, not protecting myself *from you*." Another tiny piece of waffle joins the collection on the edge of my plate. "Well, at first it *was* that, because I didn't think I could trust you. But then it was more that I was protecting myself from … getting attached. Because I can't stay. When this is over, I mean. And the more I know about your life, the more you tell me about your family and what being a guardian is like and … *everything*, the harder it will be to leave." I peek up at him between my lashes.

"Okay. I guess that makes sense. But if we do this properly—if *I* do this properly, I mean, because I know you don't want to be involved anymore. If I get rid of that door and stop those creatures coming into Stormsdrift, and if I manage to expose Bergenfell and Poppywood and the others for murdering your parents … If we essentially get rid of the entire Council the Stormsdrift Guild currently has, then why can't you come home? It would be safe for you. Nobody would be hunting you anymore."

I'm already shaking my head before he's finished. "Get rid of the Council? Get rid of *Bergenfell?*" A shiver courses through my body as I picture her face. The warm, friendly smile that hides the ruthless, cruel person she turned out to be. "That's never going to happen."

"Don't doubt me," Ash says quietly. "I will expose the truth about her if it's the last thing I do. I will make sure she pays for what she did to you."

I press my lips together and swallow. I reach the end of one waffle and begin pulling apart the next one.

"Stormsdrift is your home," Ash says quietly. "I know it hurts to be there, but won't it hurt more if you stay away forever? It's where you belong—"

"No. I don't belong there anymore."

"Why?"

Red begins to cloud the edge of my vision—blood, sweat, bruises, the click of high-heeled shoes—but I blink the memories away before they can overwhelm me like they did in the clearing.

Ash leans forward, arms resting on the table. "You said … you made it seem like … I don't know, like it's not the pain of losing your parents that's keeping you away. So if it's not that, and it's not because of a corrupt Council that seems to want you dead, then what is it?"

I *want* to tell him. I *want* to be as open with him as I was when we were younger. But he'll never understand the things I had to do in order to survive after I ran from Stormsdrift. He'll hate the person I became. "Can you just try to understand that there are some things I don't want to talk about?"

He's quiet for a moment before nodding. "Okay. I can try." Then he looks pointedly at my plate. "Are you going to eat any of that, or are you planning to shred each waffle into increasingly tiny pieces and push them around your plate?"

"Oh." I look down at my collection of waffle bits. "No, I'm—I'm going to eat." He doesn't continue speaking, which I assume means he's waiting for me to actually do the eating part, so I pour some syrup over the waffle mess, sprinkle nuts on top, and open the jar of gooey marshmallow. "You know what's super awkward?" I say to him as I scoop some out with a spoon. "When someone watches you eat."

He leans back with a quiet chuckle. "Sorry. Um, so, I need to decide what to do next. Perhaps you can check the journal again to see if there's anything inside it that might help me?" I nod as I place a piece of waffle in my mouth and start chewing. My stomach grumbles in appreciation, and I realize just how hungry I am. "And then I'll talk to Ostin," Ash continues. "I haven't told him anything yet about why we came to him. The conversation will obviously involve your parents, so I figured you'd want to be awake for that. Then, depending on what he says, I'll decide what to do next. I assume you'll leave after we've spoken to him?"

I pause with another piece of waffle halfway to my mouth. I *was* planning to leave all of this behind me and start over again somewhere new. Standing in that clearing in Stormsdrift, overwhelmed by memories so painful I could hardly breathe, my only goal was to run. But somewhere between passing out and sitting at this table eating waffles with Ash, that changed. Was it the news about Remy—that shockingly painful reminder that people I care about are dying because of the monsters creeping through the faerie door? Or was it the sinister, sickening thought that's slowly been taking shape at the back of my mind? The idea that this might all have been my parents' fault?

I don't know why they were there that night instead of at the Liberation Day Ball with the rest of us, but I know they had the key. What if they're the ones who opened the door in the first place? What if they ran before they could lock it again, and that's why Dad was so insistent, after he and Mom came to find me, that he had to go back? And what if he was interrupted before he could lock it properly, and that's what allowed the strange mist and all these creatures to start making their way through?

"Actually," I say to Ash, "I still want to help you. If there's something I can do, that is."

"Oh." Surprise is obvious in his tone. "That's—okay, thanks."

I shrug, intending to say, *You probably shouldn't be thanking me if this is all my parents' fault*, but my mouth is full of waffle, so I decide to keep it closed instead. I swallow and shovel some more into my mouth. "Sogood," I mumble.

Ash rests his chin on his hand and laughs quietly. "I should have known. All this time, you were just hangry. I should have walked into that fighting ring with a plate of waffles in one hand, and you would have forgiven me instantly."

I almost smile at that, but then I remember the precise moment I realized who had been fighting me in Riven's enchanted arena. The horror, the fear, the certainty that he was there to finish me off.

"Sorry," Ash says, sitting back and placing his hands in his lap. "I shouldn't joke about things like that."

I'm about to answer him when something catches my attention. A faerie paths doorway, opening in midair behind Ash. I'm on my feet in an instant, my chair crashing to the floor behind me. But it's Ostin who walks out of the paths, surprise registering on his face for only a second before his lips relax into a warm smile. "Silver," he says. "Silver Wren."

FIFTEEN

OSTIN FAIRWEND LOOKS AS THOUGH HE HASN'T AGED A DAY SINCE the last time I saw him. It never used to be strange to me that there's little physical difference between faeries who are hundreds of years old and faeries who are in their twenties. But now that I've spent time in the human world, where wrinkled skin and gray hair are a sign of age, I suddenly find it difficult to comprehend that Ostin is over two hundred years old. His eyes are a vibrant blue, startling against his smooth, dark skin, and though he's roughly the same height as me, he carries himself with the type of confidence that makes him appear taller. The same confidence he taught my father.

He crosses the kitchen and pulls me into a hug. I'm startled for a moment, but then I relax and bring my arms up around him. "I thought I was hallucinating," he says, stepping back, "when I opened my door and found someone holding a girl I thought was dead."

"I can imagine. I'm sorry."

"For what, dear child? I'm the one who's so very, *very* sorry for everything you've been through."

"Well, for … for never coming to see you. For not telling you the truth about what happened. I didn't know who to trust, so I ran away from everything and just let you believe a lie about my family."

Ostin shakes his head. "I may have believed the lie that you died that night along with your parents, but I never believed they were guilty. They would never have killed any of their fellow guardians. Defended themselves, yes. Immobilized someone who attacked them, certainly. But not murder."

I exhale. "Thank you."

"Now come into the lounge. It's far more comfortable there. And bring that plate of yours. I'm sure you're hungry."

I glance at Ash before picking up my plate and following Ostin into the lounge. It's vibrantly decorated with cushions of rich colors, lamps and colored glass vases placed around the room, and a fancy gold light fixture hanging from the center of the ceiling. A blue curtain, thin and translucent, ripples in the evening breeze, revealing a garden that slopes downward outside. Again, no glass or screen separates us from the outdoors, but the temperature inside remains comfortable.

"We thought you were sleeping," Ash says from behind me. "I didn't realize you'd left."

"Oh, I haven't been able to sleep easily in years," Ostin says, lowering himself into an armchair. "I like to wander the hill at night. Being outdoors … it calms a busy mind. I thought the two of *you* would be sleeping, which is why I was trying to sneak my way back inside through the paths instead of using the front door." He nods toward the door on the other side of the room as Ash and I sit across from him. Then he waves a hand toward a wooden cabinet behind his chair, and one of its two doors swings open. Out floats a diamond-shaped decanter filled with amber liquid, followed by three cut-glass tumblers.

"Oh, I won't have any," I say. I'm not sure exactly what I'm being offered, but my stomach needs more waffles, not alcohol. I pop another piece into my mouth.

"Me neither," Ash says. "But thank you."

Ostin nods, and two of the tumblers return themselves to the cabinet while the stopper pops out of the decanter and amber liquid sloshes neatly into the remaining glass. It glides through the air to Ostin's waiting hand as the decanter floats back to the cabinet. Then he looks at me, lets out a quiet laugh, and shakes his head. "I still can't quite believe you're here. It's incredible. Your friend Asher didn't tell me much, aside from the fact that the Guild lied about your death—which was clear from the moment I opened my door yesterday—and that they'd falsely accused your parents of murder. So … what really happened? And why are you here? Not that you aren't entirely welcome, of course," he hastens to add. "I'm only wondering what's changed to have brought you to my doorstep for help instead of to someone else's."

"Well, uh …" I glance at Ash, and he gives me a half-nod, half-shrug. Super helpful. But we're here now, and Mom and Dad trusted Ostin, so I suppose I should trust him too. "I was hoping that perhaps my parents had confided in you about something."

"Oh?" Ostin's eyebrows inch upward.

"So … they found a faerie door. You know, specific destination on either side. I don't know where the other side actually *is*, but the side my parents found is in the Shadow Crypt next to the Stormsdrift Guild. Hidden somehow, I guess, because I've been down there before and I didn't see it. And I know other people have been down there and not seen it either. And on the other side, there are … monsters. Terrible fae creatures, deadlier than any we ever learned about or came across in training. Anyway, my parents somehow ended up with the key that unlocks this door."

I detail the rest of what happened as quickly and emotionlessly as I can manage. How a creature came through the door and killed two guardians in front of my parents, and even though Councilor Bergenfell saw what happened, she pretended my parents had murdered them. Mom and Dad escaped, came to fetch me from the Lib Day Ball, and after we grabbed some stuff from our house—and Mom cast an enchanted fire to burn it to the ground—we returned to the Shadow

Crypt so Dad could lock the door. But guardians found us outside the crypt, and …

This is where I have to pause, take a deep breath, and blink a few times. After clearing my throat, I simply say, "You know what happened to them. Then guardians pulled me into the paths, we ended up in the Guild's greenhouse, I started a fire using some of my mother's leftover shadowfire potion, and then I escaped. Apparently everyone believes I died in that fire."

Ostin lets out a quiet exhale. "That is what was reported. I don't know if anyone ever thought to doubt the story was true."

"So … does any of this sound familiar? The part about the door and the key? Did my parents tell you about this?"

Ostin slowly shakes his head. "I can't recall them ever mentioning it."

I blink, my heart slipping down to my bare feet. I didn't realize how much I'd expected him to know something until this moment. "Seriously? They didn't tell you anything?"

"Well, perhaps in passing, but if I so, I've forgotten—"

"No, this wouldn't have been something they told you in passing. They would have made you understand the importance of whatever they were telling you and sworn you to secrecy."

"I'm so sorry, Silver. I wish I could help you. What kind of information are you looking for, exactly? What are you hoping they may have told me?"

"Well, mostly I'm hoping they may have told you if they knew of a way to destroy this door. It seems unlikely, because otherwise the Guild would have already done that. Although … it seems like the councilors from our particular Guild are trying to get through the door and they *can't*? So I don't really know what's going on."

Ostin's brow creases further. "This does all sound very strange. So your parents didn't tell you anything? Other than what you've already told me?"

I shove another piece of waffle into my mouth and mumble, "No.

Oh, there is a journal, though." I finish chewing and swallow so I can pretend I have at least *some* manners. "Perhaps you can help me figure out how to get it to show me what's hidden on its pages. If it's even possible to still read it. I'll go and grab it." I set my plate down and hurry to the bedroom where I dig inside my backpack until I find the journal.

Back in the lounge, I cross my legs beneath me on the couch and press the journal's clasp. "Dad put an enchantment on it to protect it," I tell Ostin as he leans forward and peers across the small space at the journal, "and I think that may have made all the words disappear when it ended up soaked after we took an unintentional trip down a river. Or maybe I'm supposed to do something else to——"

My breath catches in my throat as I flip the journal open and my eyes land on a drawing on the first page. A detailed sketch of my father. And then, before I have time to say a word, the sketch begins moving. "Silver, I … I hope I'm doing this right. Haven't tried this enchantment since … I don't know. Training days." Dad—in sketch form—rubs a hand across his brow. My heart pounds erratically as I stop breathing entirely. That's Dad's voice. *Dad's voice!* "Dammit, *dammit*, we made such a mess," he says, his gaze pointed somewhere beyond the journal. "I hope you don't ever have to see this. We're going to tell you everything tonight, after Mom finds you and we lock that damn door and we get as far away from this place as we possibly can. But just in case … in case something goes wrong …" He presses his lips together, then takes a steadying breath. I try to match it, but I can't. "I'm hiding Mom's journal in case you need to find out this way instead. But you won't. Because we're going to *tell* you everything. In person. Mom may have told you most of it already because she's probably found you by now. So … okay. I need to go. I'm coming to find you both. I love you, bug."

The drawing stops moving. I exhale in a rush, then inhale shakily. My face is hot and my hands are sweating and my very soul feels like it's trembling. The sketch begins moving again. "Silver, I … I hope I'm doing this right."

I slam the journal closed before the message can continue repeating itself. "I, um, I need a minute," I manage to say, my voice coming out oddly high-pitched.

Ostin, still leaning forward on the edge of his chair, says, "Of course. You can go outside. Get some air. Take your time, dear."

"Thank you," I mumble, turning away before he can see the tears welling in my eyes.

I pass through the spell that keeps the interior of Ostin's home warm, and an icy breeze kisses my face. I know I'll be shivering in under a minute, but for now, the chill soothes my burning cheeks. I wish there were doors that would close behind me, giving me a little more privacy than the translucent curtains gently undulating in the breeze. I wish I could hide in the dark somewhere and sob my heart out. But I can't. Not now. So I press my shaking lips together and let the tears stream silently down my cheeks. The nighttime colors of Ostin's garden fracture across my vision.

I hear footsteps, and then a shape I identify as Ash appears beside me. I blink and swipe at my cheeks, angry that he's intruding on this moment. I clear my throat before speaking. "Could you give me just a *tiny* bit more time before you—"

"Something isn't right," he says quietly. So quietly I almost don't hear him. He folds his arms and stares out at the night. "Ostin's been scribbling furiously on his amber since you came out here, and he keeps looking at the door."

My blood turns to ice. "What?" It takes everything in me not to turn instantly and look back into the lounge.

"I don't think we're safe here."

"Maybe he's just … answering a message." But even as I say the words, my instinct to run first and ask questions later kicks in.

"We should leave," Ash murmurs, and I nod because I've already decided the same thing. "I'm going to excuse myself and grab your bag. You tell him something believable, and hopefully we can get out of here without too much confrontation."

I turn and reach to brush the curtain aside. "Are you okay?" Ostin asks, standing as I step back inside. "That was …" He looks at the journal, still sitting on the couch where I left it. "I can't imagine what you must be feeling right now."

"I … yes, I'm okay." My heart thunders, my brain racing through all the excuses I could possibly give Ostin right now. Which one is he most likely to believe?

"I'm just going to grab that sweater for you," Ash says, moving past me and heading for the passage that leads to the bedrooms.

"Seeing my dad like that," I say once Ash is out of sight, "made me feel like … I need to go back home. I know the house itself isn't there anymore, but I want to stand in the space where it once existed. I think I need to *be* there. To properly say goodbye. To get … closure."

"I understand," Ostin says, his features tight with concern. I can't tell if he's lying. "Do you want me to accompany you? The Guild will still be looking for you, so it'll be safer if you have an extra—"

A soft sound pulls my attention to the front door. I frown, my heart thudding faster. My hands prickle as magic gathers at my fingertips. My gaze bounces back to Ostin. "Who's out there?" I ask him.

He looks at me, and something in his expression softens. He seems almost … sad. "I'm sorry, Silver. I always loved your parents. I loved you too. But your mother made the mistake of telling me the truth, and my loyalty is first and foremost to the—"

Ash is suddenly in the passage doorway, his jacket pulled on over Ostin's orange T-shirt, magic blazing above his open palms. "What did you—"

The front door bangs open.

Guardians. Seelie Court uniforms.

My hands are up already, hurling magic across the room at the same time as Ash. One guardian flinches sideways as sparks graze his cheek, while a second guardian goes down and doesn't move. A third and fourth race in behind the one whose face is now bleeding. I lunge out of the way as magic flies toward me. A second later, I see Ostin crashing against a wall. Did Ash do that?

Then furniture is flying, golden weapons are flashing across the room, and magic ricochets off the walls. No one has time to get a shield up in between the glass, flames, blades, and other deadly pieces of transformed magic zooming back and forth. Ostin groans from the floor, Ash swings a sword, and I drop down and swipe my leg out to trip the guardian rushing at me. He goes down. I roll away, grab a small side table by its skinny leg, and throw it at his head. His magic shatters it, and the splinters fly past him. Straight at Ash.

Without even looking, Ash sweeps a hand through the air and diverts the splinters across the room. His other hand is raising a crossbow, then shooting a bolt at one of the guardians. A woman. I jump up, distracted for a second by the sight of Mom's journal skidding cross the room and disappearing beneath the curtain—and then that same guardian is rushing at me again. I leap sideways onto an upturned armchair, grab hold of the light to swing myself around, and launch off the chair at the guardian. I'm on his shoulders, legs clamped around his neck, squeezing tight, tight, *tight,* my hands gripping his head as I prepare to wrench it right—

He throws himself backward and I slam against the wall, losing my grip on him. He reaches up and tugs my arm. Then I'm on the floor on my back, the air punched from my lungs. Something snaps around my wrists. My eyes catch the glitter of golden light before I blink and realize exactly what's forcing my hands together: guardian handcuffs. I can't access my magic anymore.

Fury rushes through me, chased immediately by burning hot shame. *I'm better than this, dammit!* A blade swings down toward me. I roll, shove against the floor, and jump back onto my feet. I face the Seelie Court guardian who was about to slice through me with a sword. "I can kill you with zero magic and my hands bound together," I wheeze, my lungs still struggling to find breath.

"I doubt—" Ash slams into him, and together they fall against the curtain, detaching the entire curtain rod from the wall above the doorway. It clangs against the floor as Ash and the other man land on the grass. My eyes land on the journal beside them. I lunge for it, but a streak of magic shoves me sideways as it slices across my thigh. I catch myself against the edge of the doorway just as Ash and the man stumble past me back into the house, still wrestling each other.

My gaze darts up, searching for whoever just threw magic at me. I see legs, unmoving, protruding from beneath a couch. And then the other guardian, the woman, rising to her feet behind the couch, an arrow drawn and pointed at me. She releases it.

My cuffed hands are already flying up—and then Ash throws himself in front of me. His body slams into mine. We land on the grass together, the full weight of his body crushing mine. And that's when I see the arrow protruding from his back. One part of my brain screams *nononono* while another part instantly jumps to *he's fine, he's a faerie, he'll be fine*. He falls away from me, landing awkwardly on his side. The arrowhead, glistening with blood, extends from his chest, just above —*please be above, please be above*—his heart. A little lower, and the arrow would have pierced me too. A little lower … and Ash wouldn't be moving at all.

My attention snaps back to the present. I roll the other way, ready to jump to my feet, but someone's already grabbing hold of my upper arms and pulling me up. I stretch forward across the grass and grab—and my fingers wrap around the journal just as I'm lifted from the ground. I swing it around, and it connects with something. A shoulder? A head? Whatever it is, the journal's protection magic kicks in, and the grip is suddenly gone from my arms as my attacker flies away from me and crashes into something inside the house.

Then something else grabs my ankle, and I almost kick it away until I realize it's Ash. There's a faerie paths doorway opening on the ground beside his other hand. Because the ground, of course, is *outside* Ostin's home. We have access to the paths out here. Ash tugs hard, and then I'm falling into the open space. I swing my gaze over my shoulder just as

Ostin staggers to his feet inside the lounge, one hand pressed against his chest. I meet his eyes. The eyes of the man my parents trusted. The eyes of the man who just betrayed me.

And that's when a Seelie Court guardian stops in front of him, swipes a glittering blade swiftly through the air, and slices right through Ostin's neck.

The darkness envelops me as a silent scream hurtles up my throat.

Sixteen

then

SILVER JERKED AWAKE, THE SILENCE STRANGE IN HER EARS AFTER the dream-scream that had woken her. The house was dark, and she was alone. Her parents were working late. She wasn't sure how she'd managed to fall asleep in the first place, anxious as she was. Mom and Dad were facing off against a fae *assassin*. A person believed to be responsible for the death of two Guild councilors, an advisor to the Seelie King, several other members of the Seelie Court, at least three politicians in the human world, and who knew how many others. It had been almost two years since the Guild first learned of this person, and he'd managed to remain one step ahead ever since. Silver's parents had sounded confident enough that they finally had the upper hand, but what if they were wrong?

Silver sat up on her bed, dragged a hand through her hair, and checked the time on her amber. It was still early. Barely even eight. Ash would still be up. She opened a doorway to the paths, walked a few paces through the darkness, and came out the other side in the Black-burns' garden. She could access the inside of their home via the paths—Flynn had helped Ash perform the permission spell years ago—but at some point over the past couple of years, Silver had stopped walking straight into Ash's bedroom unannounced and starting knocking on the outside of his window instead. They were getting older—almost fifteen, and nearing the end of their second year at the Guild—and barging into each other's private space without warning didn't seem quite right anymore.

Silver picked her way through the overgrown plants that grew along one side of the house, then pulled herself effortlessly up the wall, using the creeping vines and the cracks in the wall for hand- and footholds. When her head was almost level with the bottom of Ash's window, she paused and reached up to tap three times on the window ledge. She was perfectly aware that she could have used the front door. Any one of the Blackburns would have let her in without hesitation. Or she could have walked out of the paths into the passage upstairs, just outside Ash's bedroom door. But climbing through each other's windows had seemed like ridiculous fun the first time they did it, and, somehow, neither of them had outgrown the idea yet.

Ash appeared at the window. With a wave of his hand, the glass pane disappeared. "Hey," he said, stepping back as Silver pulled herself up the final distance. She swung one leg over the window ledge, then the other. "I thought you'd be here sooner."

"I would have," she said, "if I hadn't fallen asleep."

Ash threw himself onto the bed on his stomach, piled his textbooks on top of each other, and pushed them aside. "You fell asleep?" he asked, turning over to look at her.

"I know, right?" Silver looked around. As usual, everything was perfectly in place: clothes in the wardrobe, books arranged alphabetically on the shelf, notebooks and files in a neat pile on one side of the desk. Her own bedroom, in stark contrast, generally looked like a small whirlwind had just torn through it.

She moved toward the bed. "You'd think I'd be too stressed out to sleep. But I was so tired after the simulation ring. I ate something and then lay on my bed worrying about Mom and Dad, and then …" She shrugged and flopped down on her back into the space Ash had cleared for her on the bed. "I somehow fell asleep."

"Well, the simulation ring did kick your ass."

Silver rolled her eyes. "Whatever. That tidal wave came out of nowhere."

Ash laughed. "Yes, I think that was the point."

Silver sat up with a sigh. She tilted her head to the side, noting that Ash was already in pajamas. "Did Tobin make you go to bed early?" she teased. Ash's parents were also out tonight—they'd recently become involved in the Scarlet Arrow case as well—and Tobin, seen as the next most responsible Blackburn brother now that Flynn no longer lived at home, had been left in charge.

Ash let out an exaggerated sigh as he sat up. "As if any of us could go to bed early tonight." His tone was light, but Silver knew him well enough to note the tightness of his smile and the way he didn't quite meet her eyes. And now that she was sitting up and looking around a second time, she noticed what she'd missed before: a few shoes falling out of the half-open wardrobe, and the knocked-over laundry basket in the corner of the room that spilled a few items of crumpled clothing onto the floor. None of which Ash had tidied up yet. He was definitely anxious too.

Silver pulled her knees up to her chest and wrapped her arms around them. After a quiet exhale, she said, "They're going to be okay, right?"

"Of course they're going to be okay. Our parents are completely awesome. They can handle anything."

Silver rested her chin on one knee and met Ash's eyes. "I know you're worried too. You're just saying that because it's your turn to be the brave one." She and Ash had discovered over time—like most children of guardians—that concern for their parents was something they simply learned to live with. It wasn't something to obsess over, but rather an ever-present awareness at the back of their minds. A normal part of their day-to-day life. But every now and then, a particularly dangerous assignment came along, and they couldn't help letting the anxiety take center stage as it blotted everything else out. But if they both panicked at the same time, it only made things worse, so Silver had decided years ago that one of them should always be the brave one and reassure the other. They'd started taking turns after that.

Ash was quiet for a few moments before saying, "Yes, I'm only saying that because it's my turn. But that doesn't mean it's not true. They're always fine. You know they're always fine."

Silver let her legs slide down and lay back on the bed again. "I know. But it feels a bit different this time. Like more of a big deal. The Guild sent extra guardians along, so they're obviously expecting things to go badly."

"Or they're just tired of this guy evading them and want to make absolutely sure he doesn't get away this time."

Silver stared at the ceiling, which was covered this evening in rows of equations. Ash liked to make notes on his ceiling while studying. Silver had watched him dozens of times, lying on his back with his stylus held up, tracing words and numbers in the air and seeing them appear on the ceiling instead. Personally, she found writing in a notebook to be perfectly adequate—if she was going to put anything on her walls or ceiling it would be art—but there was something comforting about lying here and seeing Ash's handwriting above her. It was one of those constants in life.

"Potions homework?" she asked, pointing at the ceiling.

"Yeah." Ash lay down again and stared up at the numbers. "Have you done it?"

Silver nodded. "Remy and I worked together in the library this afternoon before I had the simulation session and he had a mentor meeting."

"Okay." Ash lifted his head and shoved a pillow behind his neck. "What did you get for the last question?"

"Three."

"Cool. Me too."

"Remy got thirty, but—"

"Not possible."

"Right? Even if you don't check the numbers, all you have to do is *think* about it. Thirty teaspoons of starroot powder wouldn't even fit in the flask."

"Exactly. And you can only get about five teaspoons out of one bottle of that stuff. If you had to use thirty for a single batch of burn salve, that would make it—"

"—impractically expensive," Silver finished, using the exact term their mentor had used in class that morning. "I told him that too, but he didn't seem convinced."

They lapsed into silence, and Silver found her thoughts wandering back to Mom and Dad. "Have you, um, studied for Friday's history quiz yet?" she asked in an attempt to distract her anxious mind.

"Yeah, a bit."

She smiled at the ceiling. "So, like, every single page. In painstaking detail."

"No," he protested. "I just read through it all quickly yesterday morning because I got to the Guild too early and none of you were in the dining hall yet. I had nothing else to do."

"You read through it *all*."

"I'm a fast reader!"

Silver laughed. The annoying thing about Ash was that he *was* a fast reader. He also had an excellent memory, perfected new combat moves in about five seconds, could perform insane gymnastic maneuvers in his sleep, and had the ability to complete his homework—correctly—in under half an hour. Which left him plenty of time to enjoy a social life on top of everything else. If he wasn't her best friend, Silver might have hated him just the tiniest bit for the way he excelled effortlessly at pretty much everything. But all the Blackburns were like that, and Silver kind of adored them for it.

"Do you think we need to know that ancient magic bit?" she asked. "That Like From Like principle? Seems like it's not really important these days if no one uses magic like that anymore."

"I don't know." His shoulders brushed against hers as he shrugged.

"It's a small section, though, and not exactly complicated, so just read through it anyway. And I think people do still use it sometimes, in certain circumstances, as a way of strengthening things."

"Because … two things created from the same type of ancient magic can only be destroyed by each other?"

"Yes. See? Easy concept. Like strengthens like. Like destroys like."

"Right. Cool, so I've done it now. No need to read that section."

Ash laughed. "That's not exactly what I meant."

Silence descended over them again. After a few minutes, Ash said, "You're still worried, aren't you."

Silver nodded. "Hey, um … have your parents set aside tokeharis for all of you?"

Ash sat up. "Silver," he said sternly, looking down at her. "Our parents are not going to *die* tonight. You know how hard it is to kill a faerie, right? Especially guardians who are as good as our parents."

"Yes, I know." They had been told this many times since beginning their training. Faeries' magic healed wounds quickly, even wounds that might be deadly to other creatures. It neutralized most poisons. It fought off illnesses so fast that it was highly unusual for them to ever get sick at all. Even when someone appeared lifeless, it wasn't necessarily the end for them as long as magic still pulsed through their body. Still, death was always *possible*. Look at the number of magical beings the Scarlet Arrow had killed.

"So why are you wondering about tokeharis then?" Ash asked, lying down again.

"Just … because. I don't think I've ever asked you before." Silver's parents had explained the concept of a tokehari to her when she was younger, and they had told her they'd each chosen a special item for her. Something for her to remember them by in the event of their deaths.

"Yeah, they've set aside things for us," Ash said quietly. "All guardian parents do that." He let out a heavy sigh, then turned his head to look at her. "I assume you're going to stay until they get home?"

"Yeah." It was what often happened when her parents worked late. "If you want to go to sleep now, I can go downstairs and lie on—"

"No, it's fine. I'll read for a while."

"Okay." She curled up on her side. Ash wiped his ceiling clean with a swipe of his hand, moved his textbooks to a neat pile on one side of his desk, and settled beside her with a book. Silver closed her eyes, but her mind was on the amber in her pocket, waiting for it to buzz. Waiting for Mom or Dad to let her know they were home. But no message came.

* * *

A noise woke Silver. Ash's lamp was still on, but the book he'd been reading was lying on his chest, and he was rubbing his eyes. He sat up, blinking. "I think they're home."

Adrenaline shot through Silver's body. She was awake instantly. Together, they scrambled off the bed and rushed down the stairs. Tobin was a few steps ahead of them, and Connor was standing up from the couch as they hurried through the living room. They found Iris and Lennox in the kitchen. Their faces were streaked with dirt and blood, and Lennox limped as he carried two glasses of water toward the table.

"Youreokay!" Tobin said in a mumbled rush.

"Yes, we're—oh, Silver, you're here." Iris reached out with a shaky hand and leaned against one of the chairs. "We thought you might be."

"Mom!" Ash rushed to her side. "Are you okay? Let me get that." He pulled the chair out so she could sit.

"Yes, yes, I'm fine," she said.

"My parents." Silver swallowed. "Are they—"

"They're okay," Lennox said before she could finish. He placed the two glasses on the table. "They're at the healing wing at the Guild, but they're—"

"*The healing wing?* Why? What happened?" Panic scrambled up her throat, making it difficult to breathe.

Lennox paused as he eased himself into the chair beside Iris. "We don't know exactly. They were inside that building longer than anyone else. And then, when they got out …" He glanced at Iris. "I think it was just severe depletion of magic. Nothing more serious than that. According to the healers at the Guild. But they're going to be fine, I promise. We were just there."

"Are you sure? Can I see them? Can I—"

"They're asleep now. You can stay here tonight," Iris said. "We'll take you there first thing in the morning, I promise."

"And the Scarlet Arrow?" Connor asked. "You got him?"

Iris and Lennox exchanged another glance.

"He got away?" Ash asked.

"*She* got away," Iris corrected quietly. "I would make a comment about the Guild's *assumption* that of course the successful assassin is a man, but … it feels too soon."

"But everyone's okay?" Ash asked.

They looked at him. Iris's features crumpled before she managed to take a breath and press her lips together. "Ash, I'm sorry. And Connor, Tobin …" Her gaze shifted to where they stood beside Silver. "I'm so sorry. Luke didn't make it."

Silence.

Silver held her breath as her mind replayed the words. As their meaning settled slowly into her brain. Luke was Ash's mentor. He was also mentor to Connor and Tobin. They saw him every day at the Guild.

Silver's gaze shifted to Ash as she took a slow, shaky breath. His jaw was clenched and tears lined the lower edge of his eyelids. Silver wrapped her arms around him and hugged him tightly, trying not to imagine precisely how Luke's life had ended. *You know how hard it is to kill a faerie, right?* That's what Ash had said earlier. That's what Silver had *believed* earlier. But they'd seen Luke just this afternoon, and now he was simply … gone.

SEVENTEEN

now

M<small>Y MIND IS BLANK WITH SHOCK AS</small> I <small>FALL THROUGH THE</small> darkness of the faerie paths, Ash's hand still tight around my ankle. All I see in my head is that blade meeting Ostin's neck. His wide eyes. The gush of blood. It's a horrifying frozen image, taking up all the space in my brain.

Ash must be thinking of a destination, though, because dim light begins to materialize around us. The next thing I know, we're landing on a heap of something round and soft. Ash releases an agonized groan and rolls away from me. A thump follows as he lands on the floor.

"Ash," I gasp, scooting hastily off the pile of what appears to be giant beanbags. I force my brain to focus on the present. "Are you okay?"

"Mm, totally," he grumbles. His hand reaches out blindly—fortunately missing the journal that's still in my hands—and stops near my fingers. Heat warms my wrists, and then the cuffs vanish.

"Thanks." I leave the journal on one of the beanbags and drop beside him, my gaze darting up as I take a moment to assess the spot we've landed in for any potential threats. Soft light, shelves of books, the scent of paper and coffee. A collection of armchairs and beanbags. Moonlight through a window. No magic in the air. Quiet. "Did—did you see what happened?" I ask, my shaking fingers reaching below Ash's shoulder for the arrowhead. "The moment before we got away. That guardian just … killed Ostin."

Ash's labored breathing fills the space around us as I slice neatly through the shaft with magic and catch the bloodied arrowhead in my hand. "What?" he gasps.

"Ostin betrayed us … and those were *Seelie Court* guardians … and then they *killed* him and …" I place the arrowhead on the floor and stand. "And what the hell were you thinking, jumping in front of an arrow like that? What is *wrong with you?*"

"Oh, jeez, forgive me for trying to save your life," he grunts as he climbs shakily to his feet.

"I'm a faerie. I would have been fine."

"And I'll be fine too," he wheezes, turning his back to me.

"Idiot," I mutter, moving closer and reaching for the end of the arrow. "Stand still."

"Like I'm really planning to dance around with an arrow stuck in my—aaah!" He lets out a cry and jerks away from me as I tug the remainder of the arrow free.

"Baby."

"Give me some *warning* next time!" He collapses onto the pile of beanbags, his eyes closed, and for a moment I think he may have passed out. I could hardly blame him if he did. I've been impaled by an arrow before, and the pain was … not fun. Then he murmurs, "They really … killed Ostin?"

"Looked like it," I answer quietly, picturing the blade flashing through the air and severing Ostin's neck. I blink the image away as I move the journal to an armchair so Ash doesn't accidentally touch it. "And why is the *Seelie Court* getting involved in all this? It's just … this is next level, Ash. I don't know what the heck is going on."

"Yeah," he answers quietly. "Me neither."

I sigh. "Almost killed by a river, almost killed by a monster, almost killed by the Seelie Court … I bet you're starting to regret the moment you decided to come looking for me."

He doesn't move. Doesn't open his eyes. Then he murmurs, "Not for a second."

For some reason, this makes me want to cry. For some reason … this makes me think of my parents. They would have gone through all of this for me. If they were still here.

I'm blinking away tears and trying to figure out what to say next when my eyes catch on something wrapped tightly around Ash's left forearm. Something that looks like a twisted wire bracelet with oddly shaped white beads. "What is that thing on your arm?" I step closer and crouch beside him.

"Don't know," he mumbles, eyes still closed. "One of the many unpleasant bits of magic that was flying around Ostin's lounge."

Up close, the 'bracelet' appears to be a tangle of skinny barbed wire and razor-sharp teeth. The pointy barbs and the teeth have both embedded themselves in his skin. Blood trickles in multiple rivulets down his arm. "Unpleasant indeed. I need to get this off you." I glance up. "It's going to hurt."

He manages a shuddering grunt that's probably supposed to be a laugh. "Didn't seem to bother you when you ripped an arrow out of me."

"Yes, well, that was quick. This is going to take a bit longer."

"Maybe I should do it." He struggles to sit up a little straighter. "Not sure I trust you to—"

"Lie back and stop being stupid. I've dealt with far worse than this. I can handle it."

"Of the two of us, I'm pretty sure I have more experience—"

"I have plenty of experience—"

"Oh, are you a healer in this world? A *doctor*?"

"I'm a pastry chef."

"A *chef*? Now I'm really scared. For multiple reasons. You definitely don't have the experience required to—"

"Would you just lie back down? Jeez, you're as stubborn now as you used to be."

"And yet *you*," he says, easing himself back, "are not nearly as fun as you used to be."

I pull a face. "Not sure why you'd expect anything else, given everything that's happened over the past few years. Tough to be *fun* when you've been through the kinds of things we've been through."

He's quiet for long enough that I think he's decided not to respond. But then, as I'm lifting his arm and coaxing a bit of magic to the tips of my fingers, he says, "I guess that's true."

I peer more closely at the mess of wire and teeth and flesh, focusing on the words required to fashion a tiny spark of magic into something that resembles the glowing tip of a tweezer. It's been a while since I used this particular bit of magic. My fights at The Gilded Canary generally leave me with little more than a few bruises and cuts, and my friends in the human world don't routinely get themselves stabbed by tiny objects. But the magic forms itself within seconds, as easily as if I did this spell yesterday. I let go of it, and it sits close to Ash's skin, gently nudging each tooth and barb of wire free of his skin with minimal damage, while my fingers slowly unwind the wire.

"Where'd you learn that?" Ash asks. I pause and look up to see that his eyes are open, his head raised enough for him to watch what I'm doing. "That wasn't part of Basic Intro to Healing Magic."

"No, it wasn't."

"Did you learn that at The Gilded Canary?"

I peer up at him. "Do you want me to remove the nasty sharp things from your flesh, or would you like me to reminisce about the past?"

He sighs and lowers his head, turning his eyes toward the ceiling. "I'll take that as an 'I don't want to talk about it.'"

"Great."

We're both quiet for a while, and then Ash says, "I'm trying to figure out what happened. I heard Ostin say he was sorry. That he loved you and your parents. That's when I knew something was about to go wrong.

I came rushing back as he was saying something about your mother telling him the truth, but his loyalty was to ... well, he didn't finish that bit, but I assume he meant the Guild, since that's who he contacted."

"Well, either he contacted the Guild and they alerted the Seelie Court, or he knows someone within the Seelie Court itself and he went straight to them. And then ... then they killed him." My stomach turns. I blink and refocus on the task at hand. Just another few teeth and I'll be done.

"So it's not just our Council that's trying to keep something secret. This goes all the way up to the Seelie Court. Maybe even the king himself. And that means ..."

My hands go still as I follow his train of thought. "And that means that no matter which Guild you go to for help, you'll be silenced."

"Yes," Ash whispers. Then he shakes his head. "No. We don't know that for sure. It could be a select group of Seelie Court guardians who are involved in this, acting without the rest of the court's knowledge, and without any other Guild's knowledge. That would make more sense."

"I hope you're right," I murmur. Then I carefully remove the final barb from his skin and add the tangle of wire to the collection of teeth and the broken arrow sitting on the floor beside me. "All done. Your magic should heal the wounds within a few hours, I think. The arrow wound in your chest will probably take a bit longer."

"Thanks for doing that."

I lift one shoulder in a small shrug. "Thanks for being a guardian. I'd still be bound by enchanted handcuffs and unable to use my magic if you weren't. And I'm sorry I don't have anything for the pain. I had some stuff in my backpack that would have helped, but ... yeah. We won't be going back for that."

"It's fine. It's not that bad."

"You're lying."

He doesn't argue. My eyes follow the half-dried rivulets of blood down his arm. Should I ... offer to clean him up? Should I look around for a kitchen area behind the coffee section of this shop and see if I can find water and a cloth and add in a soap spell? No. That would be weird. *Super* weird. Ash will soon be well enough to stand on his own two feet, and then he can clean himself up. It's not as though I need to be concerned about immediately disinfecting his wounds like I would be if it were Teddy or Duke lying here. Faerie wounds heal too quickly for infections to set in.

"Are *you* okay?" Ash asks.

"Me? Um … I think so?" I'm not sure, though. Between my shock over everything that happened in Ostin's apartment and my concern about Ash, I haven't had a moment to examine myself yet. I assume, though, that if I had some kind of life-threatening injury, my body would have let me know about it by now.

I shift out of my crouching position and straighten, becoming aware of several aches throughout my body as well as a sharp, stinging pain near the top of my left leg. A gash seeps blood into my torn pants. I spot a few other rips in my clothing, and my hands, of course, are covered in blood after helping Ash. "Yeah, I think I'm fine," I tell him. "Nothing serious. My leg should heal quickly. I think all the blood on my hands is yours, not mine."

Ash manages to push himself up a little on the beanbags. "Sorry. There's a kitchen through that door, behind the barista counter." He points to the other side of the bookstore. "If you want to wash up."

"You know this place?" I ask. Then, with a frown, I add, "You know what a barista is?"

"Of course. I'm not totally clueless about this world. I may not have lived here, but I've spent enough time hanging around during assignments to pick up on the vocab. Same as when we were training."

"So … you came here for an assignment?"

"Yes. A fairly straightforward one. There was some stolen stuff from the fae realm, and it was hidden in the back with all the extra book stock. It was recent, so I guess that's why it came to mind. Mostly, I just wanted to get us out of the fae realm."

"Oh. Did you know it would be nighttime here?"

He pauses. "No. I did not. Didn't really have time to consider that."

"I see. Guess we got lucky then." I look around. "It's … nice here. Cozy. Buy a book and a good coffee and curl up in an armchair. Or on a beanbag. Which—" I add with a look in his direction "—we should probably clean before we leave."

"Yes. Definitely."

"And you're right that I should clean myself up too. My hands, at least. Probably best not to wander around looking like I just stepped off the set of a slasher film."

"A … what film?"

Unbidden, a smile curves my lips. "Not *totally* clueless, but definitely a *little* bit clueless." Then I turn and pad on bare feet between the bookshelves, aiming for the door behind the barista counter.

In the kitchen, I fill the sink with warm water. The only soap I can see is the type for cleaning dishes, so I dig in the recesses of my memory and come up with the simple soap spell Mom used to use when we ran out of bubble enchantments at home. I watch the bubbles froth up beneath the running water as the spell takes effect. Then I close the tap, push my jacket sleeves up, and breathe in the comforting scent of lavender.

I'm just about finished scrubbing the blood from my hands—and I've decided I don't need to bother with my clothing, which is dark enough to hide blood stains—when I hear a sound behind me. I throw a hurried glance over my shoulder, my hands forming fists in the water, but it's only Ash moving slowly into the kitchen. "Hey, you shouldn't be walking around yet," I tell him.

"The arrow went through my chest, not my legs."

"Ash, you had a *hole* straight through your body. There's probably *still* a hole there, even if your skin has started healing over. You should be resting."

"Like I said, the hole is in my *chest*, and my chest is resting. It's my legs that are carrying me around."

"Fine. Be stubborn."

"I'm not being stubborn. You're just worrying too much. Which is sweet." And though his expression is neutral, there's that telltale glint in his eyes that lets me know he's holding back a smile. "I didn't think you cared at all, so it's nice to know you're so concerned about me."

My eyes narrow. "I'm not worrying. Go right ahead and walk around. Do some star jumps, for all I care. Maybe run a marathon."

He looks away, but the smile he's been fighting stretches his lips as he steps up to the sink. "I see right through you, Silver Wren."

I don't answer that. We both know it's true. He places his hands in the water beside mine—thank the holy courts this is a large sink—and begins rubbing them together. I think of a time when being this close to him didn't light a fire beneath my skin. When reaching for his hand was as easy as breathing. When the only cares we had in the world were how many points we might earn on the next assignment and what prank to play on his brothers next.

I long for that time more than I could ever put into words.

I'm busy trying to remind myself how to breathe normally when I notice something I missed before. A simple gold ring on the pinky finger of his right hand. He didn't have that before. I wonder who gave it to him and what meaning it holds. *Don't ask*, I firmly instruct myself. *Do. Not. Ask.*

He splashes the water a little too much, and I clear my throat. "I don't think you should be getting water on that yet." I point to the bracelet of tiny wounds on his forearm that have barely begun to close.

"I know, I'm just cleaning my hands and wrists. I'll leave that part dry for now." Then, as if the universe is mocking him, the next handful of water he scoops onto his arm runs all over the wound.

"Honestly," I scold quietly. "Just let me do it." And against my better judgement, I reach for his arm.

EIGHTEEN

then

SILVER REACHED FOR ASH'S OUTSTRETCHED HAND AND PULLED HIM through her window—a little harder than necessary, as it turned out. He tumbled past her, then rolled and sprang neatly into a crouch. Because he was Ash, so even falling looked good on him.

"Nice recovery," Silver said, stepping over her open training bag and plopping onto her unmade bed.

"Thanks."

"Here." She closed his history notebook and handed it to him. "Thanks again. Pretty sure I learned more from your notes than if I'd actually been in class." Her early morning meeting with her mentor had run late, and then a councilor had grabbed her as she'd been hurrying to class and sent her on an urgent errand. She'd ended up missing the whole of the first lesson.

Ash laughed. "I don't know if that's true, but—" A thump from the room next door interrupted him. "Are your parents home?" he asked.

"Just my mom." Silver moved to her open wardrobe, picking her way over discarded articles of clothing on the floor. "Dad's finishing off some paperwork at the Guild. Said he'd be home a bit later."

"Is your mom …" Ash paused, and Silver saw him look over his shoulder toward the open bedroom door. When he continued speaking, his voice was lower. "Is she doing okay?"

Silver sighed, running her hand down the sleeve of a maroon dress. "I think so. Sometimes she still seems a little … you know, quieter than she used to be. Like she's thinking about something. Or maybe … remembering something."

"Remembering that night, perhaps?" Ash suggested.

"Yes."

It had been a little over six months since the night Silver's parents had been trapped inside a warehouse in the human realm with the woman the Guild had named the Scarlet Arrow. Silver had sat beside her parents' beds in the Guild's healing wing for a full day, watching Dad toss and twitch, and listening to Mom mumbling nonsensical things about black weapons and stolen magic. When Mom woke the next morning, Silver had hugged her tightly and whispered, "Did the Scarlet Arrow steal your magic?"

Mom kept her arms wrapped tightly around Silver and shook her head repeatedly. When she sniffed a few times, Silver realized she was crying. *It's my turn to be brave*, she'd told herself, and then reassured Mom over and over that everything was okay now.

Later, when they were back home, she'd asked Mom if she remembered anything about black weapons. Mom had looked startled at that. "Where did you hear that? I … I haven't spoken to anyone at the Guild yet."

"You mumbled some things in your sleep," Silver said.

Mom's face, already so pale, had lost all remaining color. "What else did I say?" she whispered.

"Not much," Silver said quickly, wanting to erase that panicked look from Mom's face. "Hardly anything at all." Which was the truth.

Mom had gripped Silver's hand tightly as they sat together on the couch. "The woman … the assassin … she had weapons like ours," Mom said. "Like guardian weapons. But they were black. Like … black glitter, black diamonds." Mom shook her head. "I've never seen weapons like that before."

"So … no one else knows?"

"Dad knows, of course. And we'll tell the Council about everything that happened. But I don't think you should mention it to anyone else. It might worry people. And we don't even know what it means."

"Okay," Silver said. And then, after a pause in which Mom simply kept on staring at the floor, she added, "Did something else happen? Something you want to talk about?"

Mom had given her a weak smile that came nowhere close to matching the real thing. "No, Silver girl. Everything's fine. Thank you."

Dad seemed to return to his normal self within a few days, but something was different about Mom. She was more reserved. Her eyes didn't light up the way they used to, and she didn't smile as easily anymore. Silver eventually spoke to Dad about it, but he told her not to worry. "We went through quite an ordeal. It's just taking her a little longer to get back to normal. She's going to be fine."

And now, more than six months later, it seemed perhaps Dad was right. Mom wasn't a hundred percent herself yet, but it felt like she was close.

"Did she ever tell you any more about what happened?" Ash asked. "Any more than—" he lowered his voice further "—the black weapons?"

Silver had kept quiet about the black weapons with everyone except Ash. He was her closest friend, and she'd always told him everything. She knew he wouldn't say a word to anyone else. "No, she never said anything else." She turned from the wardrobe to face him. "But, I mean, something major *must* have happened. Dad used the word 'ordeal.' He didn't say anything more either, but … do you think … maybe they were …"

"Tortured?" Ash murmured. Silver nodded. "I know how much your dad loves your mom," Ash continued quietly, "so if something really bad had happened—if she needed help—he would make sure she got it."

Silver let out a long breath. "You're right. And Dad keeps telling me not to worry, and Mom honestly seems like she's just about back to normal, so … maybe everything's fine."

"And my parents care about your mom a great deal," Ash added, "so if they were seriously worried, they would also try to do something about it. But they seem to think she's okay too."

"Okay. So …" Silver nodded and smiled. "I think everything's fine." She turned back to the wardrobe and pulled the maroon dress out. "Should I wear this tonight?"

Ash angled his head to the side, feigning intense confusion. "Silver Wren, I didn't know you owned a *dress*."

"Shut up." She returned the maroon dress to its hanger. "For your information, I own *two* dresses."

"Neither of which you've ever worn."

"I've worn them! I think." She paused, thinking. "I mean, I'm pretty sure I have."

"What's the occasion?" Ash asked. "Do you have a date?"

"No. Odette's aunt got tickets to see some dancing show thing, and now she can't go, so Odette said she and I should go, because apparently the one guy is this super famous—" Silver cut herself off as she remembered something. She whirled around to face Ash. "Wait. Don't *you* have a date tonight?" She was fairly certain she remembered Ash mentioning that he and Kellee were going to that new restaurant with the amazing view of the Thunder Falls.

"Oh. No, that's tomorrow night."

"Don't look so excited about it."

He laughed and pushed a hand through his hair. "Sorry, I'm just distracted. I am excited about it. Or at least, you know, I'm looking forward to it. I guess."

"You *guess*? Wow, your enthusiasm knows no—Hey!" She ducked as Ash threw a cushion at her. It landed on a pile of shoes inside the wardrobe. "Okay, I've decided," she said as she straightened. "No dress. I'm wearing normal clothes tonight."

"I'm glad my input was helpful."

"Super helpful. And you need to leave now so I can bathe and get ready. I'm still stinky from training."

"Yeah, I can smell you from over here."

Silver stuck her tongue out at him. Then a buzzing sound caught her attention, coming from somewhere amid the chaos that lived permanently on top of her desk. "I think that's my amber," she said, moving closer to the desk and pushing aside a few notebooks and loose papers. "Ah, there it is." She looked down at Odette's handwriting, glowing gold on the smooth surface of the amber.

I'll pick you up in half an hour! P.S. Did you know Ash won that archery competition? I just heard!

Silver looked up. "You won the archery competition?"

"Oh. Yes." Ash stood and pushed his hands into his pockets. "I did."

"That's amazing! Why didn't you tell me?"

He shrugged. "It's not a big deal."

"Of course it's a big deal!" Silver leaped over the clothes littering her floor and threw her arms around him. The archery competition happened every year, with five of the Guilds taking part. A maximum of ten trainees from each participating Guild were invited. Due to some technicality this year, the final results hadn't been announced on the day the competition took place. Ash had returned last weekend and told Silver that the winners would be notified at a later date.

"It's really not," Ash said, stepping out of her embrace and pushing a hand awkwardly through his hair again. "Flynn won it twice when he was still training, and Connor and Tobin got first and second place one year. So … yeah. No big deal."

And there it was. Ash's only real fear in life: that he would never be as good at anything as his older brothers. It wasn't a fear he ever let anyone else see. Out there in the real world, Asher Blackburn was confident, even cocky at times. But when it was just him and Silver, the truth was harder to hide.

She used to think that he excelled at everything with little effort, but she'd slowly begun to notice in recent months what nobody else ever saw: the extra hours Ash spent studying late at night. The extra training he did early in the morning before breakfast at the Guild. The extra reading he did on top of everything that was already prescribed by their mentors.

She sat on the edge of the bed. "You don't have to be better than them."

Ash was quiet, and Silver wondered if he might brush this off and leave without talking about it. After all, she'd told him he needed to go so she could get ready. She was about to tell him he didn't have to leave yet when he sat beside her and said, "Don't I? Being *just as good as* isn't enough, so being *better than* is the only option."

"That's not true."

He sighed, staring down at his shoes. "Obviously I love my brothers—"

"I know."

"—but it's hard living in their shadow. Every success, every achievement—they've already done it. So it's no big deal when I do it. I know my parents are proud of me, but … it's not like they're impressed or anything. They just expect it. Because it's already happened before. *Three times. All* my brothers are amazing guardians, so I'm just … I'm never going to stand out at anything. I'm just … Number Four. No, I'm Number *Six*, since both my parents are guardians and they're amazing too. I'll only ever be Iris and Lennox's youngest kid. Flynn Blackburn's little brother. The *Wonder Twins'* little brother." He rolled his eyes.

"You know there is literally *nobody* who calls them the Wonder Twins."

"Yeah, but everybody's thinking it."

"Are they?"

"Yes."

Silver's hand slid toward the nearest pillow. "I'm not."

"Yeah, but you're—"

She whacked him in the face with the pillow. "Smarter than you?"

"Oh, you little—" He knocked the pillow aside and launched for her.

"Quicker than you?" she asked with a laugh, rolling off the bed and darting away before he could reach her.

"Absolutely not."

"Then come and get me!" she teased, leaping out of his way again as he lunged for her. With a burst of magic, she jumped onto her desk, knocking a dozen textbooks and files onto the floor in the process. She whipped around just as a cushion came sailing her way. She caught it, then cast a shield of magic in the air in front of her. The single shoe and the empty training bag Ash had just tossed at her bounced off the shield and fell to the floor.

"Fine," he said, lowering his hands. "You win." He flopped back onto the bed and stared at the ceiling.

"Hey, Blackburn Six." She let her shield vanish and threw the cushion at him.

He caught it and threw it back. "Yes, Wren Three?"

"Are you done feeling sorry for yourself?" Silver tossed the cushion back again and jumped off the desk.

Ash snatched the cushion from the air and dropped it onto the bed beside him. "You make it difficult, so yes."

"Good." Silver landed on the bed beside him and hugged the cushion to her chest. "Hey," she said again, waiting for him to look at her. "You know you're amazing, right?"

"Silver—"

"Seriously. I get that it's tough for you, following in the footsteps of your overachieving family, but you're still the most dedicated and talented trainee I know. I mean, you're not as good as *me*—"

He rolled his eyes and laughed. "That's the truth, you know. You breeze through everything and still manage to leave half the class behind you. If you put in just the tiniest bit of effort, you'd beat us all."

"*Not* true."

"*So* true."

Silver lay back and stared up at the ceiling. A half-finished painting of a colorful galaxy stared back at her. She'd started it few weeks earlier with Ash, Remy and Odette, and then they'd all become too busy with end-of-year assignments and studying to finish it. "I'm leaving that top spot for you, Blackburn Six."

He sighed. "It's … I don't know. It's not even about that. Not really. I mean, yes, I would like to be the best. But also … it's like the thing that's *really* pushing me is actually … the fear of failure," he admitted quietly. "There's just no room for that, you know? I can't mess up. I can't be the only Blackburn who doesn't do well."

Silver reached for his hand, but it was too far down the bed, so her fingers circled his wrist instead. "You're not going to mess up."

He paused. Then, even quieter: "And if I do?"

"It'll be okay." He didn't answer, and she knew he was probably wondering if it really would be okay, or if failing would somehow end the entire world for him. "It will be," she insisted. "I promise. No matter what happens—" she lifted his forearm and tapped one finger against his wrist "—you'll end up with those markings you want so badly. We both will."

He was quiet another few moments before speaking. "Thanks, Silver."

"Sure thing, B6."

"That's not going to become a thing."

"Oh, it's already a thing."

He shook his head, but when she turned to look at him, she saw that he was smiling.

Nineteen

now

I scoop water up in my hand and let it run down Ash's arm, watching it trickle over the dark markings that curl across his wrists. I rub gently with my fingers to remove the dried blood. *We've done this before*, I remind myself as heat rises to my face and my blood pumps too quickly through my veins. *Plenty of times. Numerous training injuries. Dozens of assignments. This. Is. Totally. Normal.* But of course, there's nothing normal about this at all. Not anymore.

And then I see something that distracts me from my internal freak-out. A small flourish on one side of the guardian mark. I lift his arm out of the water and lean a little closer. My finger traces the pattern down toward that extra swirl on the side. Ash is silent. Frozen. "You did it," I murmur. "You graduated top of our class." Something swells in my chest. Pride? He may have doubted himself at times, but I always knew he could do this. "Congratulations."

Ash clears his throat. "Um, thanks."

"I always assumed this would be my life," I continue, my finger still tracing a slow path along the dark lines and whorls. "I know I never worked as hard as you did, but being a guardian was still my dream. The only life I ever imagined."

"You should have been there," he says quietly. "You should have been standing right next to me when—"

"It's the last thing I want now," I tell him, lowering his arm and letting go. "Everything they stand for is a lie—"

"Don't say that. You know it isn't true. For some, yes, but not the Guild as a whole. *I'm* not like that. My family isn't like that. Your parents weren't like that." The warmth in my chest turns to an aching sadness at the mention of my parents. I know he's right. Mom and Dad only ever did their very best to protect people. "And plenty of other guardians stand by the words of the oath they made the day they graduated," Ash continues. "Don't hold the mistakes of a few against all of us."

"Mistakes?" I scoff, picturing once again the last horrifying moments of my parents' lives. "It was a little more than that, don't you think?"

He's quiet for several moments before answering. "Yes. It was definitely more than that. But that doesn't change what I'm saying. Their actions don't represent all of us."

Again, I know he's right. And maybe that's why it pierces my chest so deeply when I see the marks on his wrists and the weapons he so easily pulls from the air. Because a large part of me still wishes I had what he has. I look up at him. The perfect guardian. Everything he worked so hard for may be ripped away from him now. "I'm so sorry about how messed-up everything has become. You worked so hard for this. To be a guardian, to be part of the Guild. You finally got it, and now they're hunting you down. Because of me."

"They're hunting me down because they're trying to keep their secrets hidden. None of this is your fault."

"Okay, but … still. Would have been nice if you'd been able to live your dream for longer than a few months before your world turned upside down." I remove my hands from the water and reach for the small towel hanging from the knob of the cupboard above the sink. "But that's life, I suppose."

Ash shifts away from me to face the water again. "A few months," he repeats quietly. Then he sighs. "I need to tell you something."

"Um, okay." I continue drying my hands and arms.

"I wasn't going to bring it up after you made it clear we wouldn't be catching up on each other's lives, but now … now it just feels like I'm lying to you."

"*Lying* to me? About what?" He looks up. There's an uncertainty in his honey-colored eyes that causes apprehension to tighten my chest. "What, Ash?"

He pulls the plug out of the sink and reaches for the towel. I let him take it. "So, uh, after I graduated," he says, eyes focused on his hands, "I wanted to keep working for the Guild, but I felt like I needed to get out of Stormsdrift. I accepted a position at a small start-up Guild in … an unusual location."

"Small start-up Guild? I didn't know that was a thing. Haven't all the Guilds been around for, like, a really long time?"

"Yes, this is the first new one in over a century."

"Okay."

"Anyway. I ended up on this weird little island. It's … well … you know Kaleidos?"

I shake my head. "Should I?"

His eyebrows rise as he gives me a small smile. "Did you ever actually study for anything?"

"I think I mostly just used to wing it, didn't I?"

His smile stretches a little wider. "Yes, I think that pretty much sums up your approach to the entire theory side of our training. Anyway, I thought you might remember Kaleidos from the history lessons about Lord Draven and the prophecy and the Star and all that, which would make what I'm about to say less weird, but … never mind."

"Sorry." I kinda wish he'd just get to the point. The longer he takes, the more nervous I'm getting.

"So there's this other island," he continues. "Fennrock. Only discovered about a decade ago, so that's when faeries first started colonizing it. Also floating in the air high above ground, although this one's over a mountain range and not over the sea. It moves around on its own, so it's tough to know exactly where it is at any given time. Faerie paths don't work there. And … the *super* weird part …" He finally stops rubbing the towel over his hands, which must surely be dry by now. "Time moves differently there."

"O-kaaaaay. Different how?"

"Sometimes faster, sometimes slower. Impossible to predict."

"So …"

"So that's where I ended up stationed. Working at a newish Guild." He squeezes the bundled-up towel between his hands. "For two years."

"For …" I shake my head. "But you only graduated a few months ago."

"Correct. In *this* timeline."

"But—that doesn't—" Goosebumps prickle across my skin. I take a step back from him. "What exactly are you saying?"

He sighs. "I lived and worked on Fennrock for a little over two years, but out here, it was only three months. For me …" He finally looks up, meeting my eyes. "For me, it's been over four years since you died."

I stare at him. I stare a little longer. "So you—we're not the same age anymore? You're *older* than me?" I'm not sure why, but this throws me entirely.

"I guess, technically, yes." He waits as I continue to stare at him.

Well. No wonder he looks like he's changed more than I expected. "I … I don't know what to say to that."

"I suppose you don't really have to say anything. It was just starting to feel weird that you didn't know. So … now you know."

"I'm … I just … I think I need a minute." I turn slowly and walk out of the kitchen. When he joins me a few moments later, I'm pacing back and forth in front of the beanbags.

"I know it's weird," he starts.

"So, what exactly were you doing on this floating Fennrock island? How was there possibly enough to keep a whole Guild—even a small one—busy for two years?"

"This is going to sound weird too, but I don't actually know."

I stop pacing and look at him. "You don't know what you were doing?"

"No. Some kind of highly confidential work. There was an enchantment placed on the Fennrock Guild so that our memory of whatever work we were doing there was removed whenever we left the building."

I blink. "And that doesn't seem highly suspicious to you?"

"No. I'm guessing it seems highly suspicious to *you* because you don't trust the Guild anymore. But I know myself and my moral compass. I may not remember what work I was doing there, but if it was something I was ethically uncomfortable with, I would have left as soon as I got there."

I'm still frowning at him. I suppose I understand what he's saying, but if it were me, I'd be highly uncomfortable not remembering what I did for two years. Though perhaps, I think as my mind flashes backward for a moment, sometimes *not* knowing is better. "And ... you're *twenty* now? That's just so strange."

"Stranger than an island where time moves differently and a Guild where no one remembers what's going on inside?"

"Yes! You're old!"

"I'm not that old."

He's *twenty*, and I'm still only eighteen. He's lived an extra *two years*. I feel ... left behind, somehow. Unnerved. Unsettled. Un ... something. But whatever it is that I feel, I don't let it show on my face. "Okay. Whatever. This is fine. I'm moving on now."

"Silver—"

"We need to decide what to do next. And we need clothes. You're still dressed in a blood-covered T-shirt, pajama pants that don't fit you, and no shoes."

His lips curve up slightly. "Don't forget the jacket."

"And a jacket with a hole in the back. We shouldn't stay here much longer. I'm a little surprised someone hasn't shown up already to arrest us. I guess they don't have cameras inside. Maybe only an alarm on the doors."

"Oh. Yes, perhaps."

"Okay, let me think …" I rub my hands up and down my arms. I didn't notice the temperature when we first got here, but now that the adrenaline of the fight has worn off and my hands are no longer submerged in a sink of warm water, a chill is creeping into my bones. It doesn't help that I'm barefoot and the only thing I'm wearing under my thin jacket is a tank top. "Um, I think we should probably stay somewhere in the human realm for now, while we figure out what to do next."

"Here," Ash says. I look up to see him shrugging out of his jacket, which is considerably larger than mine and appears to be lined with something soft and fluffy.

"No," I say immediately. "I'm not wearing that."

He pauses, the jacket almost off his arms. "So … you happily wear my clothes for a decade, and now you suddenly have a problem with one jacket?"

"It isn't the jacket I have a problem with."

He pauses for only a second, his jaw tightening visibly. "Right. It's me. So you'd rather stand there shivering instead of the *horror* of touching an item of clothing that's touched my skin?"

My cheeks flush. Horror is certainly *not* what I feel when I think of wearing his clothes. "Look, it's just weird, okay? And besides, I can use magic to warm myself up. Which I know you can do too, but you're the wounded one, so all your magic should go toward healing yourself. Therefore, you should be the one wearing the jacket."

He sighs, shakes his head, and pulls the jacket back on. "Fine."

I turn to the armchair I left the journal on and bend to pick it up. Emotion rises like a tide inside me at the memory of Dad's message. I know it wasn't *him*, but it was his *voice*. It was almost as though he was sitting right there with me. Tears begin to form in my eyes again, and I blink them rapidly away.

"Did you see if there was anything else in there?" Ash asks, his tone softer now. "Or is the rest of the journal still blank?"

I clear my throat. "I didn't look. I saw Dad's message on the first page, and that was it." With my stomach twisting itself into a knot, I open the journal. Dad's voice starts up immediately. "Silver, I … I hope I'm doing this right." My fingers scramble at the edge of the page as I try to turn it quickly, not wanting to break down all over again. I finally flip the page over, and there—

My mother's handwriting.

This is silly. It feels silly. But it also feels … important.

I snap the journal shut, joy and heartache clashing inside me. My breath shudders past my lips as emotion tightens my throat even further. How am I still breathing right now?

"Did you see something?" Ash asks.

I turn slowly and sit in the armchair. Without looking up from the closed journal in my hands, I nod. My heart thumps a too-fast rhythm in my chest. Along with the thrill of seeing Mom's words, of the knowledge that I hold some tiny part of her in my hands, comes anxiety. Is it in here? The one thing I'm not supposed to tell anyone? It shouldn't be. She told me she tore that part out.

I will take this secret to my end.

"Did you see something your mother wrote?" Ash asks quietly. I nod again. "Silver …" He trails off. "You don't have to look at it now, if you feel like you're not ready—"

"It's fine. I'm fine." I clear my throat to rid it of the croak. "We need the information. If it's in here, that is. If they found a way to get rid of the door."

"Well, yes, but this is also deeply personal—"

"And I want to read it now," I say firmly. "Here, in this bookstore, in this reading corner, where there are comfy chairs set up specifically for consuming words on pages."

He pauses. "Okay then."

"And you're supposed to be resting, so we may as well stay here a bit longer."

With a quiet grumble, he sits, using one of the armchairs now instead of the beanbag pile. His gaze shifts past me. "Since we're staying a bit longer," he says, "I think that's a blanket that's folded up on the chair next to you. You might want to use that instead of sitting there shivering."

Right. I'd completely forgotten the cold. Seeing Mom's handwriting wiped away all thoughts of using magic to warm myself and the argument about Ash's jacket. It seems silly now. I pull the blanket around my shoulders, take a deep breath, and open the journal.

TWENTY

SWEAT COATS MY PALMS AS I OPEN MY MOTHER'S JOURNAL. I TURN swiftly past the page with Dad's animated sketch and swallow as my eyes land on Mom's first entry. It's dated about halfway through my first year at the Guild.

This is silly. It feels silly. But it also feels … important. Like I need to write this all down because it's going to end up being significant somehow and I don't want to forget things.

The key. I am starting an entirely separate journal because of a key.

The part that first started to seem strange to me is that Rowan and I were told about it years ago when we got here like it wasn't a big deal. But it MUST be if they remind us every few months to look out for it wherever we go. Anywhere in the world. Whenever I ask Ursula for more details, she brushes me off, saying that it holds historical significance to the Guild, and that she doesn't know any more than that. That her instructions come from someone higher up.

But I get the sense she isn't telling the whole truth. I get the sense that this missing key thing is far bigger than she lets on.

A couple of months ago I saw a painting on a cave wall (can't remember the name of the area. Will look it up after I get this down.) on the other side of the world. It matched the description we were given. Tonight, Rowan and I saw a carving at the Roth Ruins.

I told Ursula about the painting in the cave back when I saw it, but I didn't tell her about the ruins last night. It just didn't feel right.

Because ... it's silly, I know ...

Sigh. THIS REALLY IS SILLY. I didn't even tell Rowan that I've been feeling this way until this morning.

Okay. I'm writing it down. I'm putting it into words. Even if it feels stupid. Here it is:

I feel like I'm supposed to find this key.

There. I feel slightly less silly seeing it written down.

Here's the thing ... I always felt like I was drawn to Stormsdrift, like I was meant to be here. Rowan thought I was imagining it, but I don't think I was. Maybe this is why. This key. Because when Ursula first told us about it ... I couldn't get it out of my head. It stuck with me. Everyone else has to be reminded to look out for it, but I don't. It's often on my mind. And when I saw that painting, and then the carving ... I felt ... almost ... drawn to them.

It's strange. Very strange.

So that's why I'm writing this all down. Because it feels important somehow.

I let out a slow breath when I reach the end of the entry. "Find anything important yet?" Ash asks.

"Not exactly. It's more of an intro to the whole mystery. I think … can I read it out to you? Probably easier than me trying to summarize each entry. I mean, if you're interested. Otherwise I'll just let you know if I see any mention of whether the door can be destroyed."

"No, I'm interested," he says quickly. "Of course I'm interested. This is … it's your mom. She was like family. I want to know her story."

I blink away the sudden threat of tears and press my shaking lips together. I breathe. And breathe. And breathe again.

"But you don't have to read it aloud," Ash adds quietly, when I'm silent for so long. "If it's too difficult."

"No, I want to. I said I want to." I clear my throat *yet again*. Then I go back to the start and begin reading out loud.

When I reach the second entry, which turns out to be a description of the key, along with a drawing Mom did, my breath catches. My fingers rise to brush absently along the flower tattoo on my collarbone— my constant reminder of Mom—as I lean closer to examine the drawing. The key looks exactly as I remember it. Strangely elongated, the head of the key fashioned to look like some strange creature's head. A little bit dragon-like but with a snout that reminds me more of a wolf. My heart begins to patter faster as something occurs to me. "Ash," I say quietly, turning the journal to face him. "Can you see this? I'm still not sure if the pages are meant to appear blank to anyone other than me."

He leans forward. "I can see it. Perhaps because you're holding it. Oh, wow, that's the key? I think my parents gave me a vague description once, when we were talking about everything after … after that night. But I never had an accurate image of it in my head."

"Look closer. The top. Don't you think the head looks a little bit like that creature that came from the other side of the door? The one that knew my name and found us at the Gauntlet changing house?"

He stands and moves closer. His eyes narrow as he bends to examine the drawing. "Yes. It does."

"Interesting," I murmur as I turn the journal back to face me.

"I assume you already knew what the key looked like," Ash says as he returns to his chair. He groans slightly, his face twisting with pain as he leans gingerly back against the cushion.

"Yes," I say after a pause. "But I hadn't thought about it in a while. About exactly what it looked like. So when I saw that fae beast, I didn't make the connection. I was also a little bit preoccupied," I add wryly, looking down at the journal again, "with the fact that it knew my name and seemed to be trying to kill me."

I take a breath and turn to the next entry.

Oh my goodness. OH MY GOODNESS.

I found it! Not the key. The door. THE DOOR!

The door that the key is for. I don't know how I know that this is the right door, but I know. Without a doubt. It gives me the same feeling as that painting and that carving. THIS DOOR is why I was drawn to Stormsdrift.

It's in the Shadow Crypt. Something kept pulling me there. I thought I was imagining it, this NEED to go down there. For ages. I finally stopped resisting. I used an imprint of magic from one of the councilors (which I'd probably be fired for if anyone knew about it).

At first I couldn't see anything unusual. I walked right up to the wall that has that archway shape of bricks. I touched it. Listened. Pressed my hands against it. I was about to give up and then it just disappeared. The wall. It became an actual archway, and beyond it there's another room. And on the other side of the room is a door.

THE door.

And honestly … it's beautiful. Wood, with so many intricate carvings.

Rowan knows. But we didn't tell Ursula or anyone else. Again, it doesn't feel right. And she probably knows about the door already. Right?? She's been here for so long. And why would she be looking for the key if she didn't know about the door? She must know about it.

Drawing below. Couldn't remember all the details so I went back tonight.

My eyes travel over Mom's sketch of the faerie door. There's so much detail in the carvings. Flowers and swirls and winding vines. I turn the journal to face Ash again. "Is this what you saw? Inside the Shadow Crypt?"

He leans forward the tiniest bit, his eyes narrowing, and I feel bad for making him move at all. Despite his insistence that he's fine, he's clearly still in pain. I stretch further forward, holding the journal closer to him. "Yes, that's it," he says. "That's definitely it. Except for the holes I saw. I guess those are new."

"Yes, they must be. There's no mention of any holes here."

I sit back and return my attention to the next entry, which is dated sometime near the beginning of my second year of training. It's short, mentioning only that she saved someone's life during an assignment and felt some kind of connection with him. Something that drew her to him in the same way she was drawn to the door and anything to do with the key. A man named Anvi.

I turn the page, and the line at the top of the next entry makes my heart stumble over itself before speeding up.

I know everything.

I shut the journal, my heart suddenly in my throat.

"What's wrong?" Ash asks.

"Um …" I shake my head. "Nothing. Just … just give me a minute."

I reopen the journal to the same page and try to skim through the entire entry, absently twisting my Gilded Canary ring as my eyes search for the one thing I don't want Ash to know. But it shouldn't be here. Mom told me she took that part out.

I will take this secret to my end.

"She found the key, didn't she," Ash says, interrupting my anxious skimming of the words.

"No," I answer immediately, even though I haven't skimmed far enough yet to know whether this is true.

"That's why you don't want to read this one out loud," Ash guesses. "Because she mentions *where* she found it. And because that's where she hid it again that night after your dad went back to try to lock the door, and you don't want me knowing."

"No, Ash, that's—"

"Silver, I already know that you know where the key is, and I've already asked you *not* to tell me. I wasn't trying to trick you when I said that. I honestly don't want to know."

I examine his face, trying to discern whether he's hiding something, but all I see is truth. "Okay," I say slowly. "Well, I'm going to read this one in my head first then."

"That's fine. You can read the entire journal in your head first if that makes you feel more comfortable."

I know everything. There's SO MUCH. Anvi finally told me all of it.

Wow. Wowowow. Okay. I need to get this all out of my brain before I forget something.

The next line is a scribble so messy it's entirely illegible. Then:

Okay, I finally got the scribe spell working. Thank goodness. I didn't want to have to write out this entire story by hand. Think my fingers might fall off.

Anyway. It's been a few months since I wrote anything here. I see my last entry was the night we met Anvi. I visited him a lot after that night. Mostly with Rowan. Nothing inappropriate, of course. I couldn't tell WHY, but there was this connection. So yes, we became good friends.

Eventually, I decided to tell him about the key. It was … a difficult decision. Rowan and I were ordered never to speak of it with anyone outside of the Guild. In fact, we weren't even supposed to really discuss it with other guardians. Our only instructions were to look out for it or any news relating to it and report back to someone on the Council.

But something inside me just couldn't keep quiet. So I told Anvi about it, gave him the description, and asked if he knew anything about it. And the look on his face … Well, I knew instantly that he knew SOMETHING. He said he didn't. Said he'd never heard of this key. But I knew he was lying. Poor guy was terrible at it. Anyway, I could see he was quite distressed about it. So I let it go. This was … I don't know, maybe two months ago.

Then I asked him again a couple weeks later. He denied it again.

Today was the third time I asked him. I told him that I KNEW he knew something. That even if he didn't want to say anything about the key, he should at least stop denying his knowledge of it. So he did. He stopped denying it. And he said … I'm trying to remember his words … He said, "How did you know it's me? I've never told a single person."

And I found that a bit strange, because I didn't know what he meant when he said, 'How did you know IT'S ME?'

So I asked, "WHAT'S you?"

That threw him a bit, and he immediately clammed up. Didn't want to say anything else. So I told him that no one had ever said anything about him. I'd never even heard his name before the night I saved his life. And he wasn't even the target that night. He was an innocent bystander. Wrong place, wrong time, as they say.

Except, I keep thinking now that it was meant to be. I was meant to meet him. None of that was chance. The assignment was originally supposed to go to Lennox, and then he was running late, and then the Seer … um, I can't remember who it was. Sasha, maybe? Anyway, the Seer on duty gave the vision to ME and said she felt I was actually the better one to deal with it.

Anyway, Anvi asked me to leave then. So I did. I didn't want to upset him any further. I mean, I wanted answers, of course, but he's my friend as well.

Then he sent a message late this afternoon. He asked me to go back. I kind of felt like he wouldn't say as much if I had Rowan with me, so I went on my own.

"I was never supposed to tell ANYONE EVER," Anvi said. "But with you, I have this strange feeling. Almost as if the key is yearning to get to you."

That sent a shiver right through my body, I can tell you that. YEARNING for me? That's how I feel about the key and the door!

He said, "I have the key. But I will not be telling you where it is. What I will tell you is … everything else."

So here it is. The 'everything else.' The story no Guild ever told us. The story no Guild aside from ours even knows.

Long ago, when there was only one Guild in existence, in a place battered by storms, the guardians who worked there decided to experiment. From the shadows of the night, and from the storms that swept ceaselessly through their home, they pulled an unknown type of magic. They enchanted and cross-bred and created their own fae creatures. Their name, in Old Faerie, roughly translates to stormfae.

The Guild had noble motives, of course. There weren't many guardians, so they were trying to create creatures that could fight alongside those guardians. But they messed things up. Stormfae turned out to be even deadlier than the dangerous creatures that already existed. Deadlier and smarter. And they couldn't be controlled. They were monsters.

In the end, there was a battle. The first Guild was almost destroyed.

Many guardians died. What was left of the Guild was overrun by stormfae. The guardians who survived the fight managed to magically seal off the original Guild with all the stormfae inside. They tried to destroy it, but nothing worked. Eventually they figured out that the magic they'd used to seal the entire Guild was also protecting it.

But they couldn't remove the protective magic without risking the stormfae getting out. The Seelie ruler at the time gave them an order. The piece of land that this magically sealed Guild sat upon was removed and taken to the furthest reaches of the north, to a land walled off by enchanted mountains and unreachable by the faerie paths. I asked Anvi if he meant the Dark North and he said, "This land is so far away that even the witches of the Dark North know nothing of it."

Then they constructed a faerie door at the very edge of this land. A faerie door more powerful than usual, that required not only a key to lock it, but an elaborate series of hand movements and magic. They put the corresponding faerie door in the place where all of this began. A place that would one day be renamed in English as Stormsdrift. They concealed it below ground inside a building that was fashioned to look like a crypt, and then a new Guild was built next to it to protect it.

That's the Guild we work at now. The second oldest Guild in existence. The first one, as we've always been told, was NOT destroyed by shadowfire.

The guardians who remained locked the door and gave the key to someone trustworthy, someone not affiliated with the Guild. That person was told to take the key far away, to always keep it hidden, and to pass it on one day to someone who would be the next keykeeper.

So here we are, I don't know how many generations later, and Anvi is the current keykeeper.

So … in summary …

- *The faerie door leads to whatever remains of the original Guild, which was overrun by stormfae.*
- *No guardian or Guild is ever supposed to know where this key is.*
- *For some reason, the councilors at our Guild want the key.*
- *And by a strange series of chances, I found the man who has it.*
- *And finally … are any of those stormfae still alive today? Anvi doesn't know, because no keykeeper before him has ever taken the key back to Stormsdrift.*

My heart is pounding as I reach the end. I lower the journal and let out a long, slow breath. "So," Ash says quietly. "Is it what you were expecting? Did she write about the location of the key?"

"No," I say faintly. I look up and meet his eyes. "The Guild is responsible for the monsters forcing their way through that door."

His features crease. "What?"

"Guardians are the ones who made them."

TWENTY-ONE

ASH LISTENS IN SHOCKED SILENCE AS I RE-READ THE ENTRY detailing the Guild's experiments. The monsters they created and then tried to hide. "I wonder if this is why the Seelie Court is involved now," he says when I've finished. "They always knew about this. It was their plan to hide these stormfae, and they probably want them to remain hidden."

"I suppose that could explain why they killed Ostin. If he was aware of all this because my mother told him and not because he's part of the Council, then he isn't supposed to know any of it."

"I wonder why they didn't kill him before tonight then," Ash murmurs.

"Well … perhaps they didn't know. If my mom only spoke to Ostin about all of this just before she and my dad were killed, then he wouldn't have had time yet to go to the Guild and report them. And then once they were gone … well, he would have had no need to report anything then. But now, when you and I showed up and I started asking about the door, I guess he felt like he needed to alert the Guild or the Seelie Court right away." I rub a hand over my face. "I still can't believe they killed him, just like that. I mean, he had just proved that he was loyal to them above everything else, and then …" I shake my head.

"Makes the Seelies seem as ruthless as the Unseelies," Ash says quietly.

I look down at the journal again, managing to refrain from adding, *And that's the court you serve.* My eyes scan the page for the next entry, which Mom wrote about a week after the previous one.

Anvi showed me how to unlock the door. I'm still not sure why he trusts me with all of this. I mean, yes, I begged for information. But he could have continued to refuse. His job as keeper of this key is to keep it secret and hidden from EVERYONE. I'm pretty sure that includes NOT telling me all the things he's told me.

But I suppose it's because of this 'yearning' he says he feels. Not HIM, but the key. I'm not sure how he knows what the key is 'feeling.' He seemed to get uncomfortable when I asked, and he wouldn't look at me when he said, 'I just do.' And then later he admitted that he gets this uncontrollable urge to just TELL me everything whenever he sees me. That he has to fight so hard to keep from giving me the key as well.

Honestly, it's all quite strange. Anyway, I'm grateful, of course. I've longed to know all of this for years. And it's not as though I'm going to try and steal the key from him and run off to unlock the door myself. I may feel drawn to it, but I certainly don't want to know if monsters still exist on the other side.

So. Step by step, here it is. The way to unlock the door. Step 1 is straightforward. Then steps 2 to 5 require you to release magic into the door while doing the motions, otherwise the carvings on the door won't move.

1. Turn the key. (Obviously.)

2. Twist the top right flower clockwise three times.

3. Run your left forefinger down the third vine from the left (see diagram below). It will start to 'wiggle' if you've done it correctly. Anvi's word! He reminded me that obviously he's never done this. Makes me wonder how reliable these instructions are after being passed down for centuries.

4. There's a spiral near the bottom right corner that has a leaf at its center. Pull the leaf out a little bit, then turn it counterclockwise twice.

5. Take the vine that's 'wiggling'. You'll be able to pull it right away from the door, and it'll be softer now, like a real vine. It'll only be attached to the door at one end. Wrap the other end twice clockwise around the door handle.

You should now be able to turn the handle and open the door.
Perform the instructions in reverse to lock the door.

Below that is Mom's drawing, complete with arrows and little numbers. "Well," Ash says when I've finished reading the entry, "if your parents *did* manage to successfully unlock the door, this explains why they may not have been able to properly lock it again afterwards. Seems like it's easy to make a mistake if you're in a rush or don't know exactly what you're doing."

"Yeah," I murmur. I catch sight of the writing on the next page, noting immediately that there's something different about it. It's a hurried scrawl, with misshapen letters and jerky angles, as though Mom's hand was shaking as she wrote the words.

Something tightens in my chest. A sense of foreboding, as if what I'm about to read is bad. Very bad. A small part of my brain warns me to look away, to take a break, but I'm already scanning the words before I can stop myself.

I have the key. I shouldn't have the key. But I have it.

Anvi is dead. I don't know what happened. I don't know who it was. I must have been knocked unconscious by ... WHO??? I don't know. There was definitely a fight, but I don't remember who else was there. I heard something, but then ...

I don't know I don't know I don't know.

I can barely even think. I just keep seeing

He was dead when I woke up. Ripped apart. Literally ... And the key was lying on the floor between us. So I took it. Of course I took it. I couldn't just leave it there for someone else to get their hands on.

I just ... I can't even think right now.

It was all too awful.

I look up at Ash when I finish reading this short entry out loud, my voice shaking slightly. "Wow," he murmurs. "I'll admit, that is *not* what I was expecting."

"Me neither," I whisper, still staring at what I'm guessing are tear stains on the page. I keep turning, eyes running along the lines of text, hoping to discover what happened to Anvi. "She mentions sending an anonymous tip about Anvi's death, but that was the extent of her involvement in the investigation. No one except my dad knew that they were even friends." I keep scanning. "She says ... she and Dad were both extremely conflicted about whether to come forward and admit that she was there when Anvi died, but they were both afraid she might be blamed for his death."

"Isn't it crazy," Ash says, "that all of this was going on and we never had any idea?"

"I know. I was aware that their work caused them stress at times, and you know I used to overhear details sometimes, but I had no idea about any of this." I turn another page. "This next entry says she was looking into old Guild records to see if she could find out anything about storm-fae, for her own interest, but so far she hadn't found anything. Then ..." I turn again. "Another page of her basically saying the same thing. And then ... Oh. This might be important." I start reading aloud again.

I found something buried in the back of the dusty old archives underneath the library at the Guild. Like UNDERNEATH under-neath. I think we're all aware that there's a set of stairs at the back of the library that goes down to the archive level—I've been there multiple times recently—but I only just discovered that at the back of THAT room, there's another set of steps that leads further down to an even older archive section. It wasn't HIDDEN. It wasn't LOCKED. I'm pretty sure I was allowed to be there. But I'm also pretty sure that there aren't many people who know that level even exists.

ANYWAY. I think I found a book that may have something useful in it. It's super ancient, translated from Old Faerie. Kind of vague with the names—it doesn't specifically say 'stormfae' anywhere—but the details are enough to suggest that that's what the text is talking about. But I ran out of time to read more than the first few pages, and we're not allowed to remove archives. Will return tomorrow.

"Oh, the suspense," Ash says as I turn the page.

"Uh ..." When I see that the next entry has nothing to do with archives or a book or any major discovery, I glance at the date. "I think you're going to have to live with that suspense. The next entry is several months later."

"Oh. So she obviously didn't discover anything interesting after all if she didn't bother writing about it."

"I guess not."

"So what does the next entry say?" he asks.

"It's … a bit weird."

I keep feeling drawn to the door.
I sneak down there so often.
Rowan is worried about me.
I'M worried about me.
I know this isn't normal.

"I wonder if it was some kind of magical pull," Ash says, "or if it was just her fascination with the door. You know, just the fact that she was more intrigued by the mystery of it than anyone else."

I lift one shoulder and shake my head as I turn to the next page. "Oh, wow. Okay." I stop in surprise at the angry scrawl across the next page.

"What?"

"I'm not reading that out loud."

"What is it?"

"A bunch of swear words scribbled across the page. And possibly … some tears. There's a splotch or two at the bottom of the page." I turn the journal to show him.

He frowns as his eyes scan the page. "She was obviously really upset about something."

"Yeah. I wonder if …" I place the journal on my lap again and stare at the scribbled words. "There's no date on this page, but the previous entry was about two months before …" I hesitate, wondering why I've even brought this up. My stomach churns. My heart pounds so hard I start to feel lightheaded. "Remember when my parents were stuck inside that warehouse for hours with … with …"

"That assassin?" Ash says. "The Scarlet Arrow?"

"Yes. My mom wasn't really herself for months after that."

"Yes, I remember."

"The previous entry is dated about two months before that happened. So maybe *this* entry ..."

"Was written just after that confrontation with the Scarlet Arrow," Ash suggests quietly.

"Yes. Maybe. I mean ... I don't know how it would be related. I don't know why that whole ordeal would have anything to do with the key. It probably isn't. I just noticed the previous date, that's all. But she wasn't normal for months afterwards, so maybe ... maybe she just picked up the wrong journal when she scribbled all of ... this."

I swallow and turn quickly to the next page, feeling as though I've intruded on something intensely private. I realize that this entire journal is essentially a collection of private thoughts, but whatever that previous page was, it feels even more personal than everything else.

"Oh. This is it." My heart trips over itself at the sight of the next words. "This is the part you've been waiting for." I turn the journal to show Ash the single line of text.

I can't live like this. We're going to get rid of it.

"Oh. Wow. Yes." Ash sits a little straighter. "What did she say after that?"

"Uh, nothing else on this page." *Please, please let that not be the last entry*, I think as my fingers reach for the corner of the page and turn again. Relief warms my chest at the sight of a sketch and a short paragraph.

Everything else has failed. We need to find THIS. Belonged to one of the Seelie queens centuries ago. Contains some of her magic. Said to be incredibly powerful. It needs to be shattered and then all its power will be released. It might be the only thing that can destroy the faerie door.

The item Mom drew looks like an elongated gemstone or crystal, tapering at both ends. One end narrows to a deadly point, while the other end is blunt, sliced off, with a tiny hole through it as though it's meant to hang from something. An earring? A necklace? Something much larger? I don't know the scale. Tiny dots cover the drawing, and an arrow pointing to one of the dots has a note beside it that reads, *Specks of magic inside. Gold, glittering. Seelie power?*

"Do you know what that is?" Ash asks. He's standing beside my chair now, leaning over to look at Mom's drawing.

"No. I wonder if they found it." The next page is blank, and I turn the next few pages to see that they, too, are blank. The drawing was Mom's final entry. I sit back and look at it again. "And if they did find it, I wonder if they had a chance to try and use it." As I trace my forefinger carefully over the drawing, something stirs at the back of my mind. "I think … I think I've seen this before. I can't remember where. Some-where that was like … just part of the background. Where my eyes slid over it every day, not really registering it." I tilt my head, staring at the picture and prodding my memory, but still coming up with nothing. "The Guild, perhaps?"

Ash peers closer, then shakes his head. "I don't think so. I don't recognize it."

I breathe out heavily as my memory refuses to reveal anything else. Have I seen this icicle pendant more recently? Perhaps in the months straight after I fled the Guild? No. I shut that thought down immedi-ately. That can't be when I saw it. I'm pretty good at blocking out that period of my life, so if I *had* seen it then, I doubt I'd remember. No, I must have seen it before. "Perhaps it was in our house," I say suddenly. "That would explain seeing it on a daily basis. Perhaps they found it and hid it right out in the open. On a shelf, with other trinkets and books and things."

"But if they found it, why wouldn't they use it?" Ash points out. "Why display it in their home?"

"True."

"In this memory of yours, how large is the item? Tiny, like a piece of jewelry, or larger? Something you could hold in your hand?"

"I imagine it comfortably fitting in my hand," I say slowly. "With both ends sticking out on either side. That sort of size. But ... I don't know. Maybe my brain is making all of this up. Perhaps I'm only *wishing* I recognized this thing."

He's quiet a moment before saying, "Okay, let's assume your brain is indeed making things up. Then we need to find out more some other way. Exactly what this thing is and where it might be."

"And how are we going to do that? Run off to the Seelie Court—a place nobody can find unless they've been taken there before—and ask someone in the royal family to kindly share more about this thing with us?"

"Silver," Ash says patiently. "I know you were never particularly fond of studying, but you must have heard of this thing called a *library*?"

I give him a deadpan stare. "No. Never. Please enlighten me."

He sighs. "I think we should go to the oldest, largest library in the fae realm—"

"Where someone will no doubt attempt to arrest or kill us," I mutter.

"—and begin our research there."

I shut the journal and stand. "I think you need to rest somewhere safe first so that—"

"I told you I'm fine."

"Oh, is that why you keep grunting in pain every time you lean against something?"

He narrows his eyes. "I have not been *grunting*."

"What would you like to call it then?"

Ash pinches the bridge of his nose. After a pause and a shake of his head, he lowers his hand. "Fine. Since you're the one familiar with this world, where do you suggest we stay?"

TWENTY-TWO

I TAKE US THROUGH THE FAERIE PATHS TO A REMOTE CABIN THAT belongs to Teddy's family. Unsure whether anyone else might currently be using the place, I tiptoe out of the paths, keeping my glamor in place to conceal myself. I've stayed here several times with Teddy and Duke and a few other friends, but no one from Teddy's family has ever joined us, so I've always wondered what time of year they like to visit. If it's *now*, I'll have to come up with another plan.

But the cabin is silent. Cold. Very definitely empty. I'm completely confused now as to what time of day or night it is in any part of the world, so I can't tell whether the dreary gray sky visible between the trees outside is a morning or afternoon one. I look around for a clock, find one hanging on the wall above the empty fireplace, and discover it's midafternoon.

I leave Mom's journal on the kitchen table and point out one of the bedrooms to Ash, who says he feels weird lying on someone else's bed and aims for the couch in the main living area instead. As if it's somehow less weird to lie on something that far more people have sat on. I decide not to argue with him, instead hunting around until I find a pair of rubber boots that are several sizes too big for me. I carefully shrink them to the correct size. Then, after finding my one remaining spare stylus inside a slim inner pocket of my jacket, I head back out to get some food and clothes.

When I return several hours later, with a new pair of sneakers on and multiple bags over each arm, it's to a cozier scene than the one I left behind. Flames crackle and dance in the fireplace, and Ash is asleep under a blanket on the couch closest to the fireplace. I pause for a moment, watching him and listening to rain patter against the windows. Though this little cabin is nothing like the homes either of us grew up in, I can't help feeling as though we're in Stormsdrift right now.

I blink, give my head a little shake, and carry the bags to the table that separates the kitchen area from the rest of the living area. I push Mom's journal out of the way, move the clothing bags aside to unpack later, and aim for the bag with the containers of Chinese food. Ash's waffles may have been good, but I didn't consume nearly enough of them before we had to fight our way out of there.

"Sorry, I didn't mean to fall asleep."

I look over my shoulder at the sound of Ash's voice. He's sitting up carefully, one hand against his chest. "Why?" I ask.

"Uh, it seemed like an irresponsible thing to do, I suppose. Anyone could have shown up."

"Well, I'm here to protect you now, so never fear."

"Gee, thanks. I feel so much better."

"You should." I carry the two Chinese containers toward him. "In all seriousness," I add, "how are you feeling? And please don't automatically say 'fine.'"

He pauses, hopefully to honestly assess how he's feeling, then says, "Much better. Almost as if I was never impaled by a sharp object." He peers past me as I push aside the end of the blanket and take a seat on the couch. "Looks like you had quite the shopping spree."

"Yeah, well, we both need clothes and shoes. And food. Here." I hand him one of the takeout containers and a pair of chopsticks.

"Did you steal all this stuff?"

My mouth drops open. "No, I didn't *steal* anything. I have currency in this world, remember."

"But your bag is still at Ostin's. You don't have any money with you."

I exhale sharply through my nose and hold his gaze. "I keep cash tucked inside my bra at all times."

He hesitates, mouth half open, clearly unsure how to respond. It takes everything in me to keep a straight face. "That's … useful," he says eventually.

I roll my eyes and allow myself a breath of a laugh. "I'm kidding. I keep a credit card zipped inside this jacket." I turn my attention to the container in my hands and start opening it.

"Well, I suppose that's useful too." Ash opens his container as well, and for a minute or so we eat in silence. I notice the ring on his right hand again when I sneak a sideways glance at him, and I'm tempted once more to ask about it. But I have rules. We're not supposed to be sharing personal details. We're not supposed to be making it any harder than it will already be when we say goodbye.

Ash clears his throat and says, "So, uh, you have a job in this world?"

I look at him. "Yes. I told you that already."

He hesitates, frowning. "Oh, the pastry chef comment? I thought that was a terrible joke."

"Wow. Thanks."

"Wait, you're seriously a chef?"

I scoop some noodles up with my chopsticks and shove them into my mouth. "No joke," I say around the mouthful of food.

"How did that happen?"

I give him a look that's supposed to remind him that A, I'm not planning to share all the details of the past two years, and B, my mouth is full.

"Come on," he coaxes. "Tell me *something* about your life. What else are we going to do while we sit here eating?"

I finish chewing and swallow. "Um … we could just sit and eat? We could stare at the fire? I could dig through my memories until I find the one that tells me where I saw that glittering icicle-shaped crystal?"

"In my experience, memories rise to the surface when your mind is busy focusing on something else and *not* when you're trying to force them to appear." He watches me closely, amber eyes bright with something that might possibly be amusement. "Did this chef thing stem from your love of waffles? Because as far as I remember, waffles are the *only* thing you ever made when we were growing up. I didn't think you knew how to bake or cook anything else."

I sigh and poke at my food, deciding he's probably right about memories surfacing when they're not forced. And is it really such a big deal if I share this part of my life with him? We've already begun to venture down this path, sharing bits and pieces of the past two—four, in his case—years. It's already going to be monumentally painful to say goodbye to him. Why not add a dash more pain?

"You're right," I tell him. "I didn't know how to make anything else. Teddy taught me how to bake. He has this friend who owns his own little bakery. The Frosted Tart." I roll my eyes. "A silly name, but also kind of awesome. It was around about the time I'd just moved in next to Teddy and Duke, and The Frosted Tart was starting to get a little busier, and Anthony—the owner—was looking for another pastry chef. Teddy thought it would be perfect for me, because of course he didn't know me *at all* back then." I can't help laughing at the memory of the argument Teddy and I had when he first came up with the idea. "At first I thought it was ridiculous, but then … I thought about it and decided it might actually work well. I needed money, but I didn't want to bring attention to myself in any way. This was a behind-the-scenes kind of job, so I didn't have to interact with many people. And since it was a friend of Teddy's, I kind of had an in. It wasn't like I had to have an interview with a stranger who would see right through my lies and figure out I was a total fraud."

Ash chuckles. "I doubt that would have happened. You've never had a problem convincing people to go along with your crazy ideas."

My smile fades a little. "In our world, perhaps. But here, it was different. I barely knew anything about anything. And life had … you know, knocked me down. No way did I have as much confidence as I used to have."

"But it must have worked out."

"Yes, it did. I'm a quick learner, when I feel like applying myself, and I had magic on my side." I lower my voice to a stage whisper. "Don't tell anyone, but magic is the only reason my stuff doesn't flop every single time. And did you know you can make the most beautiful cupcake frosting designs with magic? I'm convinced that's what keeps Ant's customers coming back."

Ash's eyebrows climb. "Now *that* is—"

"Totally against the Guild's rules? I know." I shrug and shovel another mouthful of noodles between my lips.

"I was going to say 'smart,' but yes. Illegal too." Our conversation pauses for a bit as we both eat, and then Ash asks, "So you earn enough doing that?"

"Well, no," I admit. "That's why I started fighting at The Gilded Canary. I, um, earned quite a lot there, even fighting only a few nights a week."

"I assume your human friends don't know about *that* particular job."

"No," I say quietly. "Obviously not. I can't remember how I even discovered The Gilded Canary in the first place, but I got *that* job all on my own."

"And you didn't think you might draw unwanted attention to yourself?" Ash asks, leaning back and tilting his head to the side as he watches me. "You didn't think someone from the Guild might hear about this talented young fighter and want to take a closer look? I know the owner has some kind of deal with the Guild, but come on. You had to know there would be guardians hanging around, secretly keeping an eye on whatever was happening."

"Only one guardian," I correct. "Riven's contact. No one else from the Guild. Not officially, at least. Some of them snuck in sometimes, and clearly Markham was one of those guardians. And yes, of course I was worried about being discovered, but with a mask and a glamour enchantment for my hair, I didn't think I'd be recognized. I also changed my identity fairly regularly, and I made sure I never fought as well as I could have. Not even close."

Ash nods slowly, staring at the contents of his takeout container. "I wonder how Markham discovered you then."

"I wondered about that too, and I think he must have seen me back-stage before a fight. Sometimes, if I was late, I would only activate the glamour enchantment for my hair right before I went into the ring. I mean, I generally tried to be careful, but sometimes I was in too much of a rush and I just didn't think about the mask and the glamour until I was almost out there. So if Markham was hanging around somewhere in the backstage passageways—which he shouldn't have had access to, but I'm sure that didn't stop him—he might have seen me without any disguise on."

"And your hair is kind of a giveaway."

"I know," I grumble. "Which is why I tried to keep it hidden most of the time."

We spend another few minutes eating, listening to the comforting crackle of flames and the steady drum of rain. And then I decide … what the heck? May as well admit to *all* the things I've been doing since I fashioned a life for myself in the human world. "I also, um, had a third job."

Ash looks over at me. "Oh?"

"Not one that I received payment for, but probably the most satisfy-ing. And …" I pause for a moment, considering. "Yes, probably also the riskiest."

He raises his eyebrows in question.

"So, there's a lot of illegal stuff going down at The Gilded Canary."

"You don't say," he says dryly, leaning over to place his empty takeout container on the small table on his side of the couch.

"Riven's deal with the Guild is that he passes on some of this info in exchange for them leaving him and his club alone, but there's plenty that slips through the cracks. I … overheard things. Some truly terrible things. I didn't want to just turn a blind eye, but I was too angry and scared to go anywhere near a Guild to report what I overheard. So I started asking questions. About how I could possibly help. Very carefully, of course. A bartender here, an acrobat there. And I ended up getting involved with … well, I guess they're sort of a vigilante operation."

Ash cuts a sideways glance at me. "You know that's not legal either, right?"

"Yes, Ash, I'm aware of that. But at this point, I trust them far more than I trust any Guild. They heard that I was asking questions, looking for some way to make a difference, and they came to me. A woman found me after one of my fights. A faerie. Golden hair and eyes. She asked me straight out if I'd been trained at a Guild. I was terrified. I thought she might be an undercover guardian, but she had no markings. Turned out she had a bit of a history with the Guild, like me, but had been forced to leave and go into hiding."

"Also like you," Ash murmurs.

"Yes. Anyway, she gave me a job. Steal a necklace from one of the girls I was scheduled to fight and bring it to her. She gave me a meeting spot—somewhere far from The Gilded Canary, but still very public—which I guess was for both her safety and mine. So I did that. And then … one job turned into another and another. I never knew all the details. I was just a courier, a messenger. Passing notes and objects between people. I still don't know her name. People at the club who knew her just called her Goldilocks."

"But you had no idea if you could actually trust her," Ash said, his frown deep. "You may have just been playing a part in an even bigger illegal operation. You may have been *aiding* crimes, not *stopping* them."

"I'm not stupid, Ash. I know how to use my ears. If you're quiet and you hang out in the right spots, you quickly figure out who the bad guys are and what they're up to. And then, when you *do* something, and then you listen again later on and discover that their plans were thwarted, then you know you've made a difference."

"Still doesn't seem like the smartest idea to get involved with something like that."

"Look, you don't have to agree with my choices," I say as I stand and take my empty container to the kitchen table, "but I know I've helped people. That's what I always wanted to do, and the Guild made it impossible for me to do it by being a guardian, so I made another plan. And I have a lot to make up for after—" My hand tightens around the pair of chopsticks. My pulse thumps loudly in my ears. Did I seriously almost say that out loud?

"After what?" Ash asks. He's standing at the table now as well. I didn't hear him walk up beside me.

"Nothing." I clear my throat and push aside the empty takeout containers so I can pull the other shopping bags closer. "You know, I wonder if Goldilocks might know something about that Seelie crystal thing my parents were looking for. She seems to be involved in so many different things, and I've heard her mention the Seelies before, so perhaps she knows …"

I trail off, an image suddenly clear in my head: The Gold Floor inside The Gilded Canary, and the chandelier that hangs from its ceiling. An impressive sparkling structure created from dozens of cut-glass crystals shaped like icicles. My brain zooms in on the largest one, hanging from the center of the arrangement.

"Silver?" Ash prompts.

"I remember," I say faintly. Then I blink and focus on him. I grip his arm. "The icicle-shaped crystal. It's the centerpiece of a chandelier hanging in one of the rooms at The Gilded Canary. *That's* where I've seen it. At least, I think it's the same thing. It's the same shape as my mother's drawing, and I always thought it looked like it had little gold sparkles swirling inside it. I've never been able to get close enough to tell, but that's what it looks like from the floor."

Ash hesitates before answering, his gaze traveling my face. "You're sure it looks like the thing your mother drew?"

"Well of course I'm not *sure*. But it's the closest thing I can think of, and we don't exactly have any other leads, do we?"

Ash nods slowly. "So … are you proposing we steal it?"

"No, Ash, I'm suggesting we ask nicely for permission." I roll my eyes. "Of course I'm proposing we steal it. I have one more expensive charm on this bracelet—" I wave my right hand before reaching for one of the bags of clothes "—that might help, and I have an employee access charm in this ring. So as long as we're quick, we should be able to grab that icicle and get out of there before we're caught. Now you—" I give him the bag "—need to change out of those ridiculous pajama pants."

"First," he says, "tell me about this special charm that's going to help us steal something from above a crowded dance floor."

I remove the elastic band from my tangled, messy bun and begin scooping my hair up into something tighter and neater. "It can turn a room completely dark. I didn't have an exact purpose in mind when I bought it, but it sounded useful." I pause, my hands halfway through securing the elastic band around my hair again. "Now that I think about it, the moment you showed up unannounced in my bedroom two days ago would have been a good time to use it. I could have made my escape while you tripped over things in the dark."

"Right, because I've never created a light with magic before."

"Magical lights don't work in the presence of this charm. Neither do non-magical lights, like cell phones and flashlights. That's what makes it so useful."

"Okay, so you want to fill the room with darkness, jump up to reach the icicle while no one can see what's happening—which means *we* won't be able to see anything either—and then escape the club before anyone knows it was us?"

"Yes." I finish securing my hair in a neat bun and lower my hands.

"That sounds far too simple and almost certainly likely to go wrong."

"Well, you're welcome to stay here while I go and get it." I shrug out of my jacket. "I just need to fix the rips in this sleeve and change into some clothes that aren't caked in dried blood, and I'll be Gilded Canary ready."

Ash opens the bag I handed him and looks inside. "Okay. So we're doing this."

"We want to fix Stormsdrift, don't we? So yes, we're doing this." I place my jacket flat on the table and lean over the torn sleeve. "The Gold Floor is the fancier of the two dance floors, so we'll need to make a little bit of an effort. A torn jacket definitely won't do." I run my fingers over the ripped edges of the fabric, digging through my brain in hopes of finding a spell that can easily fix it. I may have to dig a little further and see if I can come up with some basic clothes casting spells as well. Something to change the style of the jacket a little bit. "Should have just bought a new one," I say to myself. "Except that all my small weapons are hidden inside this one. Would be too much effort to try and hide them all inside a new article of clothing."

"You told me you don't have any other tattoos," Ash murmurs.

"Hmm?" I freeze, my brain struggling to make the leap from jackets to tattoos. A second too late, as his fingertips brush the back of my neck, along the edge of my hairline, I realize what he's referring to.

I react instantly, automatically. Before I know what I'm doing, Ash is on the ground, face down, one arm pinned behind him as I shove my knee into his lower back. With his mouth half mashed against the floor, his words are a barely coherent mumble. "Whatthefreaking—"

"Crap, I'm sorry." I release his arm and climb quickly off him. My chest heaves with rapid breaths as I put a good few feet of space between us.

He blinks at me as he stands. "What the heck was that about?"

"It—I'm sorry. You just … startled me."

"Are you o—"

"I'm fine."

"You're not *fine*. You look like you're about to hyperventilate."

Breathe, breathe, BREATHE. "I'm fine," I repeat, grabbing my jacket and the bag with my new clothes and turning away. Before he can ask anything else, I'm striding away from the living area and into the bathroom, then slamming the door shut.

I press my back against it and slide to the floor. My eyes close. My breaths come a little more easily now. I raise my hand to the back of my neck and rub my fingers against the spot where the tattoo is, wishing I could scrub it away. I can't see it, of course, but I know what it looks like. A tiny dark shape. A little bird. If my hair was darker, the bird would be hidden better. Barely visible at a distance. But it stands out against my pale skin and silver-white hair.

That little bird is one of the reasons I wear a jacket so often, so that the collar conceals it. And when the weather is warm, my messy bun hangs low enough to hide it, or I leave my hair down. People generally don't notice it, or if they do, they don't say anything. But Ash ... of course he would notice. Of course he would comment.

I press my fists to my closed eyes, forcing tears away. When I open them again, my gaze settles on my wrap bracelet. On the tiny silver bird attached to one of the leather strips. So similar to the shape that marks my skin, and yet so different. The one on my wrist is too precious for me to put into words, while the one on my skin I would claw away if I could. I wonder if Ash noticed this one too. Probably not. It's so small, and my jacket sleeve usually covers it.

I force myself to my feet and move to the basin. Leaning forward, both hands gripping the edge of it, I stare into the mirror. My gaze shifts away from my red-rimmed eyes, sliding down to settle on the delicate flowers tattooed across my left collar bone. Another shudder ripples through my chest. I lift one hand and run a finger gently along the stem, the little leaves, the tiny blossoms. "I'm sorry, Mom," I whisper. "I'm sorry, I'm sorry." Then I take a deep breath, swallow, and face the shower.

Time to clean up. Time to steal a magical item powerful enough to destroy an ancient faerie door. Time to do for Stormsdrift what I couldn't do for my parents.

When I leave the bathroom, I'm clean and dressed, my eyes lined with dark, smoky shadow, my hair hidden beneath a new glamor enchantment, and all visible portions of my skin covered in glittery powder. The black sleeveless top I bought earlier is a little more club appropriate after I managed some sort of sparkly thread spell, and my sneakers, while certainly not *smart*, are at least inconspicuous after I managed to change their color from white to black.

Ash is standing at the window on the other side of the living area, looking out at the dark, wet landscape. He's changed into the clothes I bought him. He seems lost in thought, but when I walk out of the bathroom, he turns toward me. "Brunette?" he says, eyebrows climbing at the sight of the messy dark curls tumbling over my shoulders. "You look … very different."

"That's the point."

"Right. Of course." He continues watching me, and I sense he wants to say something else. Most likely about the part where I overreacted and attacked him. Fortunately, after another few awkward moments of silence, it seems he decides to keep his questions to himself.

"Are the clothes okay?" I ask. It's an unnecessary question, considering he looks like complete perfection in the shirt and jeans I chose for him. He also looks more 'normal' and less guardian, which is good. I need Riven's men to think he's just another average guy. Okay, maybe not *average*. There's no world in which Asher Blackburn could ever be average. But as long as he doesn't look like a guardian, we're all good.

"Yes," he says. "Correct size. Thank you."

"Well, after so many years of wearing your clothes, how could I not be familiar with your size?" *Oh holy fae, could you not just keep your mouth shut, Silver?* "I mean, you're … bigger than you were before. Like …" I use my hands to motion in the air near my own biceps. "Muscular bigger. But … it fits. So … that's good." *Just stop. Seriously. Stop right now.* With my cheeks flaming, I press my lips together and turn away before any more words can escape without my permission.

Behind me, Ash clears his throat. "Um, thanks. Did you manage to fix your jacket?"

"No." I take the jacket, which was hanging over my arm, and leave it on the table. "I just made an even bigger mess. Apparently fixing clothes is almost impossible, while making them super sparkly is easy." I look down at my top, which glitters wherever the light catches it. Teddy would say something like *Simply smashing, love.* The thought makes tears prick behind my eyes again. "Um, anyway, this sparkly thing looks kinda stupid, but I'm sure I'll blend right in with all the diamond decor of the Gold Floor."

"It doesn't look stupid," Ash says quietly from behind me. "You look good."

I hesitate, my back still to him, unsure what to say to that.

"What about weapons?" he asks, saving me from having to respond to his compliment. "That's why you wanted to wear the jacket."

"Oh. Yes." I finally turn back to face him. "I decided I'm fine as long as I have this." I point to the leather cuff with the moonstone. "My crescent-moon knife is yet to fail me. And, um, I may have a small blade strapped to my left ankle beneath my jeans."

Ash's lips curve into a smile. His eyes don't leave mine. "Of course you do."

I clear my throat. "Anyway. We should go. I figured out where we are in relation to the part of the world The Gilded Canary is in, did some time zone math, and I think it's late evening there."

"Okay." Ash nods, opens his mouth, pauses, then closes it, apparently deciding not to say whatever was on the tip of his tongue.

My eyes narrow. "What?"

He gives me a small smile. "You're going to hate me for saying this."

"Oh. Well perhaps you shouldn't say it then."

"This feels a little like the old days. Like getting ready for an assignment. It has a certain …"

"Don't say it."

"Nostalgia."

I hold a finger up. "I told you we weren't doing this." There's no venom in my tone, though, and I'm pretty sure a smile is fighting to make its way onto my lips. Because he's right. This does remind me of what it used to feel like to get ready for a group or paired assignment. There's a part of me that wants to grab hold of this feeling and never let it go.

"Too late," Ash says, walking toward me. He opens a way to the faerie paths and holds his hand out to me. "Ready?"

After a pause, I place my hand in his. "Ready."

Twenty-Three

then

THE WIND TUGGED STRANDS OF SILVER'S HAIR FROM HER MESSY bun and whipped them across her face as she stood back to back with Ash atop an enormous metal structure in the middle of a human city. Her arms were up, a bow positioned perfectly within her grasp, an arrow ready to fly. Heavy storm clouds had turned the afternoon sky dark and moody, and city lights twinkled at them from every direction. But now was not the time to admire the impressive cityscape.

Silver's eyes were pinned to the creature that flapped clumsily through the air, darting toward the structure she and Ash were balanced upon before reeling away. A nascryl. There were two of them, and Ash, she knew, was following the other. Small but deadly, they had skinny arms and clawed feet, leathery black wings, and a snapping beak for a mouth. Definitely not attractive, though Silver did envy their ability to fly. Perched way up here, alarmingly high above the city, she felt almost as if she could fly too. As if she could step off this structure into the air and wings would sweep out behind her.

The nascryl darted left, and she followed with her arrow. It was unclear how these two had ended up in the non-magic realm, but they'd already injured three humans on the viewing deck of this structure. And

231

the sparkly necklaces around their scrawny necks meant there had been death at some point; nascryls only took jewelry from those they managed to kill.

A guardian had already been dispatched to attend to the memory removal of the injured humans and enchant the others to leave the area when Silver and Ash were given this assignment. *A little late*, Silver had thought. Shouldn't one of the Seers have Seen this before it happened? But then, she knew it didn't always work out that way.

"We're going to have to shoot them down," Ash said from behind her. "The singing won't work. They're not coming close enough."

"I know. I really thought they'd find our shiny bangles more attractive, but apparently they prefer chunky necklaces."

This nascryl assignment was their final one before written exams began. Soon they'd be done with third year. "Since it's our last," Ash had said that morning, "we need to ace it. Let's not lose a single point." Silver had almost rolled her eyes. As if losing a single point was *ever* an option for Ash. He'd always been dedicated, but since his breakup with Kellee, he was even more focused on training and studying. "It's just nice not to have that distraction, you know?" he'd told Silver when she commented on it.

"So … it's not like you're secretly depressed and trying to hide it by working harder?"

He'd laughed at that. "No. I am completely fine. I *chose* to end things with Kellee, remember? You and Odette can stop worrying about me."

So when Reece, Silver's mentor, had given them the assignment details that afternoon, Ash had been the first to remember nascryls' affinity for shiny objects. Silver, at least, had contributed by mentioning the singing. "Good," Reece had said. "I think you'll manage this one easily."

But now they were here, with their glittery bangles doing little to draw the nascryls closer, which meant singing wasn't going to work. But there was still the opportunity to ace this assignment as long as they didn't shoot too many arrows astray and scare the nascryls away. Attempting to hunt the creatures down across the city would lose them points.

"They're tiring," Ash said. "We should be able to get them … in … just … another … few …"

"Now," Silver murmured, releasing her arrow. It went straight through one of the nascryl's wings. A victorious "Yes!" behind her told her Ash had struck his target too. She released her bow as both creatures began falling toward the wide viewing deck below.

"Quickly!" Ash said. They darted into the faerie paths and ran out a moment later onto the deck. Silver headed left toward the nascryl whose wing she had pierced. It had already snapped the arrow in half with its beak and was now flapping around, attempting to free the other half of the arrow. Silver skidded to a halt a few paces away and began singing. It was terrible, she knew, but this was the easiest way to defeat a nascryl. Somewhere behind her, Ash was doing the same, singing something completely different, and their jarring lack of harmony made the sound even worse. Which was perfect.

Both nascryls screeched as they attempted to cover their ears with their skinny hands. The one in front of Silver began to crumple in on itself, but then, with seemingly colossal effort, it straightened and leaped at her. She gasped in surprise, her singing coming to an abrupt halt as it struck her chest and knocked her down. She rolled, wrestling the creature away from her face as it tried to snap at her with its beak. "Silver!" Ash shouted. She gasped out another few words of the silly children's song she'd been singing, and finally, the nascryl disintegrated into a puff of foul-smelling smoke.

She rolled again and pushed herself up before taking a deep breath. "Got it," she said with a grin as Ash moved toward her. "I assume you got the other one?"

"Yes. Are you okay? I thought for a moment there that—"

"Nah, I'm totally fine." Silver looked down as she splayed her fingers. "A few scratches on my hands, but that's nothing."

"Good job, guys. That was fast." Reece stepped out from the shadows of the building constructed at the center of the viewing deck. Since Silver and Ash were still in their third year, it was a Guild requirement for a mentor to be present at their assignments. "Probably safe to lift the enchantment on this place now." Reece tossed a glance over her shoulder. The building contained a small restaurant, an elevator, and a few offices, all of which were empty after whatever enchantment had been used to convince people they needed to immediately vacate this gigantic monument of crisscrossing metal pieces.

"It *may* have been a little too easy for us," Ash said. "You should have given us a real challenge for our final assignment of the year."

Reece laughed and gave Ash a reassuring pat on the shoulder. "Don't you worry. There are *plenty* of challenges still to come in your training. It's not like you're in fifth year, about to graduate, where the final assignment is this *huge deal*. This was just like any other assignment, really."

"I think this might have been *easier* than the average assignment."

Reece sighed. "Stop complaining and be happy that you're going to get full points for this one."

"I just enjoy a challenge, that's all," Ash said, while Silver tried to communicate using her eyes that he needed to *stop talking* before Reece gave them extra work for the evening. Ash, however, wasn't looking at her. "I like to know I've actually *earned* the points I'm getting."

"Asher Blackburn," Reece said as she removed her amber from her pocket. "I don't think there's anyone who doubts that. Except you, perhaps. Ah, one of my fifth years has just finished a solo assignment," she added, staring at her amber's screen. "His last one before the *huge-deal* one." She waggled her eyebrows as she pushed her amber back into her pocket. "I need to go and assist with creature removal. You two can head back to the Guild and leave your tracker bands on my desk."

"Okay," Silver said. "See you tomorrow." The moment Reece was gone, Silver walked to the edge of the viewing deck and looked down toward the ground. Even though they weren't right at the top anymore, the ground still seemed very, *very* far below. She turned her gaze back to Ash and grinned. "Want to race me to the bottom?"

He folded his arms over his chest. "You know this is a national monument, not a ladder?"

Silver made a show of sniffing the air. "Is that *fear* I smell, Blackburn Six?"

"I thought we agreed to stop using those silly names, *Wren Three*. And no, you certainly do not smell *fear*."

"In that case …" She darted through an opening into the faerie paths and came out on the other side of the structure, stepping from the air straight onto the metal bars. Adrenaline raced through her veins, elevating her heart rate. She'd better be quick with her magic if she slipped from this thing.

"This seems like a silly risk," Ash said, stepping closer to the bars that separated them and peering through at her. Though there was an edge of concern to his voice, she knew he desperately wanted to take her up on this challenge.

"So you're giving me a head start then? Excellent."

"Never."

She grinned at him, the wind sending her hair sweeping across her face again. "Then come and get me."

Ash vanished into the paths, appearing beside her barely a moment later. They raced each other all the way to the bottom, hands rushing from pole to pole, feet reaching down for more footholds, adrenaline spiking each time one of them slipped and then caught hold of part of the structure. Silver's shoes hit the paved ground at the bottom a second before Ash's. "Yes!" She jumped and clapped her hands.

"Oh, come on, it was *so* close," he said.

"It was, but I'm still the winner."

"Yeah, yeah, whatever." He rolled his eyes, then added, "I mean, well done."

"Why thank you." She took a bow, then laughed as she pulled her stylus out. "I guess we should get back to the Guild."

"Yes. Oh, wait, there's something I was supposed to give you yesterday." He patted his pockets, then dug inside one of them.

"Yesterday? You mean … for my birthday?"

"Yes, obviously. Why else would I be giving you things and referencing yesterday?"

"I just mean that you already gave me something."

"That was from all of us. *This* gift—" he produced a small black box "—is super special. I had to have it custom-made. It only arrived last night."

She eyed him suspiciously. "Why do I get the feeling this is a prank?"

"Not a prank. A priceless item of jewelry that I expect you to treasure for the remainder of your days."

She placed her hands on her hips. "Definitely a prank. Or at the very least, a joke of some sort."

"The sweater my mom gave you was the joke gift. We all know you're never going to wear it as long as you can keep helping yourself to my clothes."

Silver opened her mouth to protest, then shrugged. "True. She should have given it to you, not me."

"She should have. But this?" Ash held the box out to her. "Not a joke at all."

She tilted her head, almost believing him until she noticed the gleam in his eye. He was such a bad liar. Whatever was in this box, she was certain it was not, as he'd said, a 'priceless item of jewelry.' She took it from him and opened it carefully, pulling her head back slightly in case something jumped out at her. When nothing did, she opened it fully.

Inside the box, on a little black cushion, sat a tiny silver bird with the number three engraved on its side. Silver threw her head back and laughed loudly. "Wren Three!" she exclaimed. "That's brilliant! I love it!" She lifted the metal pendant, discovered it was attached to a silver chain, and handed Ash the box as she used both hands to place it around her neck. "Also," she added as she did the clasp, "I was totally right about the joke part."

He smirked. "You were."

"But now that you've permanently engraved the name Wren Three onto something, it means I'm going to have to call you Blackburn Six for all eternity."

He groaned. "That is *not* what I was going for. I thought if I put the name onto a piece of jewelry, then we wouldn't have to say it out loud. And if I'm not calling you Wren Three, then you don't have to call me Blackburn Six."

She smiled sweetly and fluttered her eyelashes at him. "Thank you, Blackburn Six, for this priceless item of jewelry that I will treasure for the rest of my days." He shook his head and turned away from her, but not before she saw the adorable pink tinge in his cheeks and the smile he was fighting so hard to hide. "What?" she teased as he opened a doorway to the paths. "Isn't that what you said? That I must treasure it forever?"

"Let's just get back to the Guild."

"Sure thing, B6," she said, looping her arm through his.

They left their tracker bands on the desk in Reece's office, then walked up to the next level where their parents' offices were. Silver's mom had told her to check in when she was done with her evening assignment. "We might be working late this evening," she'd said. "So come by when you're done and check if we're still here. Iris said you can have dinner with them if your dad and I are still busy."

Silver stopped outside her father's office door, which stood ajar, and raised her hand to knock. "... confirmed it," her father was saying to someone. "But I'm still anxious about telling her."

"Well, you can't exactly keep it from her," a second voice said. Lennox. "She's been working this case for years, just like you. She'll find out soon enough, if she hasn't found out already."

Silver hesitated, her hand still raised. "What's wrong?" Ash asked quietly. He was leaning against the wall a few feet away. Silver shook her head, still not knocking. She knew she shouldn't eavesdrop, but she couldn't bring herself to step away.

"... not just worried about her being triggered by memories of the past," Dad was saying. "It's these new rumors."

"Which are just rumors," Lennox said.

"And if they're true? You'll be as worried about Ash as we are about Silver." Silver's gaze jumped to meet Ash's. He was frowning now, a silent question on his parted lips. "If this woman is stealing guardian trainees and turning them into assassins—"

"We don't know for sure if that's true," Lennox said, even as Silver's heart pounded faster. "The cases with those two missing trainees from the Bloodwood Guild ... they could be completely unrelated to the Scarlet Arrow."

"I know that. And they probably *are* unrelated. But I'm still concerned about Nel having a complete breakdown when she learns of this. Even if we can prove there's no link, I'm worried the rumors— coupled with the fact that the Scarlet Arrow has finally struck again after more than a year of *nothing*—will be enough to send her over the edge. I mean, the nightmares sometimes ... those black weapons ..."

Lennox spoke again, but his voice was lower now. Silver leaned closer to the door. "... underestimate her," he was saying. "She's strong. And a damn good guardian."

"You don't know what she went through." Dad's voice was quieter now too, and by this point Silver's pulse was almost too loud in her ears to make out anything.

"Because neither of you will tell us anything," Lennox said. Silver's gaze bounced to Ash again. Their parents were close, and she'd just assumed that Iris and Lennox knew what Mom and Dad had been through during their confrontation with the Scarlet Arrow. "And I respect that," Lennox added. "I do. And obviously you know her better than we do, so all I'm saying is that you ..." His voice grew even lower, and the only other word Silver could make out was 'trust.'

Then footsteps were suddenly moving toward the door, and Ash grabbed Silver's hand, pulling her hastily down the corridor. They had just slipped around the corner when Silver heard a door swing open. She and Ash came to a breathless stop, flattening themselves against the wall, a wide-eyed questioning look passing between them. Then, as if by unspoken agreement, they pushed away from the wall and continued walking, putting more distance between themselves and the conversation they'd just overheard. They made it all the way downstairs and outside before Silver realized Ash was still holding her hand.

Twenty-Four

now

I RELEASE ASH'S HAND AS WE STEP FROM THE FAERIE PATHS ONTO the moonlit sidewalk across the street from The Gilded Canary. It's hard to believe that only two days ago I sauntered confidently toward that dull brown door with no idea that my entire world was about to shift yet again. I look over at Ash. "How did you get in the first time?"

"You're not the only one who knows how to cast a glamour strong enough to fool faerie eyes." He extends an arm, pulls his sleeve up, and reveals his bare wrist.

"Ah. Smart."

"I didn't know anything about this place," he says as he lowers his arm. "All I knew was that I'd tracked Markham here. If I hadn't hung around long enough to see a group of fae cross the street and disappear, I wouldn't have known there was a glamour there. Once I figured out what was hiding beyond it, though, my next thought was that guardians were most likely *not* welcome. I figured it was best to hide my markings."

"A good instinct."

"I did some digging afterwards. After you vanished at the end of your fight, I mean. Found out a little bit more about this place then."

"Digging? What exactly did that entail?"

"Basically me just hanging around, chatting to the people behind the various bars, letting them know I was interested in the fighting ring. Most of them said I would have to try and get an interview with the owner, but I managed to have an early morning chat with the guy who's in charge of the fighting roster, and that ended up being my way in."

"Klyde?" I ask.

"Yeah, I think so."

I shake my head, looking across the street again. "What a hypocrite. Always reminding other people about Riven's rules, and then he goes and blatantly ignores them himself."

"Well," Ash says. "I, for one, am grateful he ignored the rules, gave someone else the night off, and slotted me in. After I proved I could fight, of course."

"What you should *really* be grateful for," I tell him, "is the fact that I'm Klyde's least favorite person. *That's* why he was so quick to let you into the fighting ring with me."

"I'm grateful whatever the reason," Ash says quietly. "Shall we go?"

"Uh, yes." We step off the sidewalk together, and I resist the crazy urge to loop my arm through his. The glamour peels away as we pass through it, revealing the grand entrance and its gold lettering. We climb the steps to the glass doors, and I reach for one of the glossy doorknobs. Inside, we're greeted by two bouncers. I recognize the guy, but the woman stops me before we can walk forward. "You just entered using an employee access charm," she says, brows lowering over her eyes.

"Yes."

"You should be using the employee entrance."

"It's my night off, and I brought a guest." Without stopping to consider whether it's a good idea or not, I slide my arm around Ash's and lean my head against his shoulder. I smile sweetly at the woman. "I didn't think Riven would like it if I tried to bring a guest in through the back. The main entrance is *so* much more impressive." I smile up at Ash before looking at the woman again. "He just got a promotion and I told him I knew *exactly* where we should celebrate."

"It's fine, she's cool," the other guy says, nodding to me.

"Thanks." I give him an even sweeter smile as we walk past him. We cross the polished floor, pass beneath the water droplet curtain, and then we're inside the vibrant, dream-like Rainbow Room. I release Ash's arm as we begin to make our way between the dancers. Bubbles drift past us, we dodge around a couple waving their arms in the air, and then we find ourselves walking into a cloud of butterflies glowing with their own pink light. I smile, my gaze caught by the many delicate, fluttering wings. "Odette's favorite," I say, my voice raised enough for it to be audible over the music. Ash nods but doesn't say anything. I look at him as we attempt to keep moving through the crowd. "Are you guys still friends?"

He opens his mouth, then hesitates. I can't tell if the color in his cheeks is from the cloud of pink butterflies still surrounding us or because he's blushing. "Uh … something like that."

I'm confused for a moment, and then it hits me: precisely what he's *not* saying. I almost trip over my own feet, which is quite something, considering we're barely moving. I catch myself against him, then immediately remove my hand from his arm. "Oh. Right. You guys are … together. That's …" *Possibly the worst thing that's ever happened in the entire world.* "That's great. I'm happy for the two of you."

"Oh, no, it's not like—I mean, we're not—not anymore."

A spark of hope. I hate that my silly heart grabs onto it like a lifeline. I dare a quick glance at Ash as I try to get past the butterflies. "Oh?"

He shakes his head and pushes a hand through his hair. "I'm sorry. This isn't coming out well. Odette and I *were* together. For a little while. She also worked on Fennrock for a few months. But it just …" He meets my gaze for a second before looking away. "It didn't work out."

"Oh." This seems to be the only word in my vocabulary right now. "I'm … sorry." I'm not. I'm so not sorry. And I hatehatehate myself for being so selfish. Odette is one of the best people I know, and so is Ash.

On the surface of things, they're perfect for each other. They *should* be together.

"There's nothing to be sorry about," Ash says. "It wasn't meant to be. And it ended a while ago. We don't really see each other much anymore."

"Um … right." I take a deep breath as we finally make it through the butterfly cloud and try to keep my tone light. "What did you do wrong?"

He looks at me, one brow raised. "Why do you assume it's something *I* did?"

I reply with my own raised brow. "Was it something *she* did?"

He takes a breath, then deflates. "No."

"Actually—" I hold a hand up "—you don't have to tell me anything. I shouldn't have asked. I'm sorry. It's none of my business."

Wonderful. This is just wonderful. Ash is two years older than me, Odette's probably older than she's supposed to be as well, and they've dated each other. They've moved on without me. But then … what did I expect would happen when I ran from my old life and decided never to go back? That they would all remain frozen in time and nothing would change?

I walk ahead of Ash, spying the mirrored passageway connecting the Rainbow Room to the Gold Floor and wishing I could have a moment alone to deal with my small internal meltdown. But since that isn't an option, I force it to the back of my mind and hope it stays there.

We make it to the end of the passageway without exchanging another word and enter the glittering sophistication of the Gold Floor. The room is a gilded forest, with golden vines curving around mirrors and across the walls and ceiling, complete with little gold flower embellishments. The reflective surfaces and diamond edges might be garish in another setting, but not here, where elegantly dressed fae sip sparkling drinks and sway to a sultry beat while soft golden light bathes the scene. Or perhaps it's simply the magic woven into this room that makes it feel as if this is the height of refinement.

My chest constricts as I look up, my eyes immediately seeking out the chandelier as I wonder if my memory has tricked me. If I'll see the crystal hanging at its center and realize it's nothing like the drawing in Mom's journal. But there it is, the largest icicle drop hanging from an impressive arrangement of cut glass crystals. And, as always, it seems to me as if tiny gold specks swim within it.

"What do you think?" I say to Ash, lowering my gaze so at least we aren't both staring at the crystal at the same time. I look toward the bar, curving elegantly along one side of the room. Mel doesn't appear to be working tonight. Thank goodness. She'd probably recognize me if she got close enough.

"That does look like the item your mother drew," Ash says. "I suppose we won't know for sure until we take it."

"Tell everyone in the room, why don't you," I murmur.

"Trust me," Ash says, looking around. "No one is listening to us. They're all caught up in the magical intoxication of this place."

I follow his gaze, my eyes traveling over the people moving in slow, rhythmic motion on the sunken dance floor, and the plush private booths around the edge of the room where heads are bent together. And that's when I see him: Riven. Reclined in one of the booths, speaking to a man and woman. "Keep walking," I say immediately to Ash, turning my head the other way as I step forward and walk as casually as I can across the room.

Perhaps it was something in my expression, or maybe the tone of my voice, but Ash doesn't say anything until we're through the arched passageway and beyond the private rooms. "What's wrong?" he asks as I turn swiftly past the employees-only door at the end of the passage. The same centaur from the other night is standing guard outside it, and I can feel his gaze on me as we continue along the corridor that leads to the small theater. I want to look over my shoulder to see if he really is watching us or if I'm simply being paranoid. But if his eyes *are* on me, I'll only look more suspicious if I glance back.

When we turn a corner into an atrium with a high glass roof and cherry blossom trees filling the space, I come to a halt. "I saw Riven. Back there. He was sitting in one of the booths. I doubt he'd recognize me unless I got right up close to him, but I'd prefer to stay away from the area until he's gone."

"Probably a good idea," Ash says. Then he looks past me. "Wait, this place has a *theater*? What kind of—actually, never mind. I don't want to know what kinds of shows are put on in a place like this."

I turn to face the theater entrance, which is illuminated by bright moonlight—or the enchanted equivalent—streaming through the glass roof. Unlike everything else we've passed so far, which is colorful, polished, or glittering, the theater entrance is an aged stone archway. Rough and uneven, with tendrils of ivy hanging from it and words in Old Faerie carved across the top, it evokes the feeling of stepping back in time. I can imagine walking beneath this archway and finding a world where faeries dance in flowing strips of fabric around stone circles and rings of toadstools. Instead, I see through the open archway to an empty stage on the other side of empty tables and chairs. Fortunately for us, there is no show tonight.

"'Bring this house down,'" Ash murmurs.

"What?" I look over and see him frowning up at the archway.

"The words. Carved into the stone." He gestures to the lettering in Old Faerie.

"Ah." Of course Ash would know what the words mean. Unlike me, he actually studied for that course we had on ancient fae languages. "Well, Riven is nothing if not arrogant. It's hardly surprising that he's etched a command into stone telling people to respond with enormous enthusiasm to whatever show they see inside this theater. To 'bring the house down.'"

"Mm. I suppose not." Ash turns and looks back the way we came. "Okay, so the plan is this: We'll dance until we're directly beneath the center of the chandelier, and then you'll twist that tiny yellow stone on your bracelet to cast the enchantment that will cover the room in darkness. I'll lift you straight up, you'll grab the crystal, and then we'll push our way out through the crowd."

"Which will be easy," I continue, "because I've walked through this place so many times I know exactly where the door is." I take a deep breath. "But we definitely need to wait for Riven to get out of there."

"Yes. That seems like the sensible option."

Silence descends between us, and Ash doesn't turn back to face me. I try to think of something to say. I try to tell myself this isn't awkward. I try *not* to think of Odette. Or, more specifically, Ash and Odette together. I open my mouth, on the verge of saying something about the precise amount of magic Ash needs to use to boost me into the air to grab the crystal, when I hear the clear clip-clop of hooves. A sound that seems to be moving closer.

Crap. The centaur. We must have looked suspicious after all. My brain bounces back and forth between the two available options: duck into the theater and hide, or pretend we came down this corridor for a good reason. Which would be …

"Is that a problem?" Ash murmurs, looking back at me and jerking his thumb in the direction of the sound.

"Yes, it's a problem!" I hiss. "And we—we need to—" I grab his arm and almost tug him toward the archway, but if we hide inside the theater, the centaur will come looking for us and we're going to have to sneak out without him seeing, and then if he returns to the Gold Floor and sees us before we manage to steal the—

"Silver," Ash says with more urgency, his voice tugging me from the turmoil of my thoughts as the clip-clop sound grows closer. "If you have no plan, then I'm going to make my own—"

"I have a plan," I mutter, my face warming, "and I cannot *believe* I'm actually about to suggest it." I pull him toward me and place his arm around my waist. The motion forces him to take an awkward, involuntary step closer.

"What are you—um—what?"

"What good reason could we possibly have for sneaking down this

246

passage on a night when there's nothing showing in the theater?" I demand in a whisper.

He blinks, his face far too close to mine now. "Seriously? You want me to *kiss* you?"

He says this like it's the most horrifying thing I've ever suggested. My face heats further. "You don't have to *actually* kiss me. Just pretend, you idiot!"

His expression darkens, and for a moment I think he's going to refuse. Then his hand tightens on my waist, while his other hand rises to my face. His eyes are still on mine as his fingers thread through my hair, pushing it over my shoulder. Then he's leaning closer, lowering his head toward my neck until he's so near I can feel his breath against my skin. But he stops there, lips barely an inch from the curve of my neck, and other than one hand at my waist and the other tangled in my hair, there is absolutely *no* point of contact between us.

The clip-clop comes to a halt. I hear the sound of a throat clearing. But Ash doesn't move away from me. His lips graze my neck as he murmurs, "Idiot? Really? If you wanted me to kiss you, all you had to do was ask nicely."

A shiver whispers across my skin. My eyes slide shut, and a breath escapes my lips—

"Ahem!" The throat clearing is louder this time. My eyes fly open as I shove Ash away from me, a little harder than necessary.

"Oh ... uh ... sorry," I manage to say, and it takes zero acting effort on my part to sound flustered.

"Apologies for interrupting," the centaur says in a bored tone, "but this is not the appropriate place for ..." He waves his hand in our general direction, his eyes focused somewhere past us. "Whatever this is."

"Right, of course." I manage a high-pitched laugh as I tuck my hair behind one ear. "I'm so sorry. We'll just, uh, head back to one of the dance floors." I reach out, catch Ash's hand in mine, and hurry past the centaur before he can take a closer look at us.

Ash waits until we turn the first corner before dropping my hand. He hasn't said a word, and I feel as though I should apologize or explain that that was *obviously* the easiest way out of there. The centaur barely looked at us once he realized we wanted nothing more than a quiet spot in which to make out. But I'm also flustered and defensive, and what the heck was that 'all you had to do was ask nicely' whisper-growl? Was that simply Ash getting back at me for putting him in such an awkward position? Because it *was* awkward. Super awkward. And hot.

No, Silver, NOT HOT.

By the time we reach the Gold Floor again, neither of us has said a word yet. So I decide, of course, that the most sensible thing to do is pretend the whole thing never happened. "I'm, uh, just going to casually wander across the dance floor and see if Riven's gone," I say to Ash, leaning closer so he can hear me, but pointing my gaze firmly past him as I speak. No way can I meet his eyes right now.

"Sure," he answers, his tone clipped.

I slip through the crowd of swaying bodies, giving in to the urge to move my hips in time to the slow, heavy beat as I go. I've never stayed long in this room, and I've never been on the dance floor. The magic here is … different. Stronger. The rest of the world and its cares begin to fade away beneath the warm glow, and though my eyes are still traveling the booths around the edge of the room in search of Riven, it suddenly doesn't seem to matter as much whether I find him. And when I *don't* see him anywhere, I relax further, giving in to the beat that slides like liquid gold through my veins.

I turn slowly, a lazy, languid motion, and see Ash coming toward me. Not hurriedly. He merely weaves his way between dancers with casual ease, as if he belongs here. "Is he gone?" he asks when he's finally in front of me. I nod. His eyes are on mine, and I can't look away, and I'm reminded suddenly of the last time we danced together. *That* didn't end well. At least … it did and it didn't. I wonder if he's thinking of it too.

I tear my gaze from his and let it slide over the crowd and up toward the chandelier. My arms lift away from my body and my fingers trail through the air as I sway. I imagine I can almost feel the threads of magic trailing around us. *You look stupid*, some tiny voice whispers at the back of my mind, but it's so small, so quiet, it's easy to ignore. I don't look stupid. I look like everyone else. And this was our plan, wasn't it? Dance until we're directly below the chandelier. I'm exactly where I'm supposed to be.

Ash is closer now, his body swaying in time with mine and his head angled toward me. But just like before, among the cherry trees outside the theater, he keeps a careful few inches of space between us. The magic, of course, urges us closer. It tells me to let go, to close my eyes, to lean into him and press my body against his. To forget everything else. And I could. It would be so easy, *so sooooo easy*, to lose myself in all of this. The beat of the music. The beat of my heart.

Thump-thump. Thump-thump.

His knuckles rise to brush against my jaw, my cheek.

My eyelids slide so low they're almost closed.

Thump-thump. Thump-thump.

His face is so close to mine, his lips a breath away from my ear.

"Stay," he whispers, and whether it's magic or the fact that he's so near, I hear him clearly over the music. "When all of this is over ... please stay."

Thump-thump. Thump-thump.

I want this. More than I can ever convey. I search my brain for all the reasons I'm supposed to stay away from him, from Stormsdrift, but here, in this moment, everything is slipping away from me.

Twenty-Five

then

Silver sat on the grass at the edge of the clearing, her knees pulled up to her chest and her face turned toward the last warm rays of sunlight streaming through the trees. Ash was beside her, and Tobin sat a short distance away, smiling as he wrote message after message on his amber, probably to the guy he kept blushing about. Their moms were a little further away on a picnic blanket, chatting with Flynn and Holly, and their dads were setting up the canopy enchantment for the storm that would inevitably roar through here before the evening was over. In the center of the clearing, Connor was dancing—terribly—with Rosie, a newly graduated Seer who had moved to Stormsdrift a few months earlier.

It was one of those perfect family evenings that had been so common when they were children but were few and far between now that Flynn no longer lived at home, Connor and Tobin had begun working, and their parents all seemed to take on more and more hours at the Guild. Silver was soaking up every golden second of it.

The entire summer had passed with barely a whisper of the Scarlet Arrow, and Silver had heard almost nothing about the woman since the night she'd listened outside Dad's office. Mom hadn't suffered any kind of emotional breakdown, and her concern that Silver might be snatched away at any moment and turned into an assassin seemed silly now. She'd only brought it up once or twice, and that had been months ago, at the end of third year. Now fourth year had begun, the Liberation Day Ball was coming up, and life was continuing as normal.

"Oh my gosh, he is *so* bad at this," Silver said, barely containing her laughter as she watched Connor stepping stiffly back and forth, struggling not to trample on Rosie's toes.

"I know," Ash said. "It's brilliant."

After Connor had spent years making fun of Flynn and his undying devotion to Holly, it had been a bit of a shock—to both him and everyone else—when he'd fallen head over heels for Rosie after meeting her at the Guild. Ash and Silver had taken great delight in teasing him mercilessly since the moment he'd begun sighing over her.

"On a scale of one to ten," Silver said, wiggling her toes in the grass as she watched Connor, "how mad do you think he'll be if we disable the canopy enchantment just before the storm arrives and they both end up drenched?"

"One hundred. No, one thousand. He's *super* into her."

Silver smiled. "It's kind of adorable."

"Uh, I guess."

"We *should* disable the canopy. We'd be doing them a favor. Kisses in the rain are so romantic, and I'm guessing Connor could use all the help he can get in that department."

Ash leaned back on his hands, laughing. "Kisses in the rain are so romantic? When did you kiss someone in the rain?"

"I haven't, but I've read about it in plenty of my mom's romance novels, and Tobin told me that when he went on that date with that girl from—"

"Okay stop. If you're about to share a story of one of my brothers making out with someone, I *definitely* don't need to hear it."

"You're such a *boy*," Silver said, poking Ash in the side.

He laughed again, leaning away from her and gripping his side. "I think you're missing the real question," he said as his laughter subsided, "which is … how mad will our *moms* be if we disable the canopy enchantment?"

"Okay, you're right. It's not worth it. Connor's on his own in the romance department."

"Yep."

A chilly breeze brushed the loose strands of hair across her face, and she scooped them back behind her ears. "I think that storm will be here earlier than predicted," she said, rubbing her hands up and down her arms. The temperature had dropped within the last few minutes.

Ash sighed. "Don't you *ever* bring anything warm with you?"

She stuck her tongue out at him before leaning back and grabbing the bundled-up gray hoodie from the grass behind him. "Why would I when *you* always bring something for me?"

"That's actually for me, nitwit."

She smiled sweetly before pulling the hoodie over her head and pushing her arms through the too-long sleeves. "Good thing you don't feel the cold."

He rolled his eyes, then returned his gaze to Connor, who was trying to twirl Rosie beneath his arm without tripping over his own feet. "Try to loosen up a little, bro," he called out, barely hiding his laughter.

"Hey, if you're so good at it, smart ass," Connor called back to Ash, "why don't you come over here and show us how it's done?"

"No problem," Ash answered, pushing himself up. "Silver?" he asked, looking down at her.

"Oh, absolutely." She jumped to her feet without pause, striding ahead of Ash. "I aced this one."

"That's not something to be proud of, Quicksilver," Connor said.

"You're just jealous," she answered with a sweet smile before spinning on her heel to face Ash. They clasped hands, and Ash counted them in. As they began moving, perfectly in step with one another, the music played through Silver's mind. This wasn't one of the old traditional faerie dances that had been around for centuries, like the ones used at Guild graduation balls, which had magic woven into the music. This one, like most of the dances that were included at Liberation Day Balls, had steps that actually had to be learned. They couldn't rely on magic to guide their feet. There was always a bit of a scramble every year in the weeks leading up to the ball as some of the Guild's training lessons were replaced with dancing lessons so that trainees who were attending wouldn't trip everyone else up. Ash, of course, had excelled at dancing the way he excelled at everything else, and Silver had found this one easy too.

His hand pressed against her lower back, and she twirled easily beneath his arm. Then they both spun, turning back to back for a moment, stepping around one another, and then catching hold of each other's hands once more.

She looked up and found him smiling down at her, his eyes warm, his dark hair falling across his brow. Their hands rose between them, palms pressed together, and as their fingers shifted and interlaced, she somehow couldn't pull her eyes away from his. Something inside her felt … different. A flutter of wings in her chest. A swoop low in her belly. A quickening of her pulse.

Their gazes remained locked together as Ash's right hand slid up her arm, over her shoulder and down to her waist, pressing her a fraction closer. That tiny movement was like a punch that knocked all the air from her chest. It hit her, out of nowhere, that this was exactly what she wanted. This moment, right here with Ash, his arm around her and his gaze burning into hers. She wanted this forever.

"Silver?"

She blinked and swallowed. Ash's expression had turned questioning. "Hmm?"

"What's wrong?"

"What?" she croaked, then cleared her throat.

"You stopped dancing."

"Oh." She hadn't even noticed. "Um, sorry." She tore her gaze away and forced her feet to start moving again, her face hot. And that's when she noticed all the asterpearls, those tiny white blossoms that permanently littered the forest floor, rising into the air around them. Instead of plain white, each one seemed to have a tiny glint of gold at its center. Which was most certainly not normal.

Crap. Was that *her* magic doing that? Bleeding out of her and creating fantastical things without her permission, putting her intense emotion on display for everyone to see? Crap, crap, crap, crap, crap. This was so embarrassing. Had Ash noticed? Had anyone else noticed?

"Thought you said you aced this one, Quicksilver!" Connor shouted from the edge of the clearing. She looked over at him, trying to blink her way out of this strange daze she seemed to have found herself in. He was standing behind Rosie, both arms wrapped around her and his cheek pressed against hers, and now that they weren't attempting to dance, they looked entirely at ease with one another. Silver found herself wishing, with an intensity that shocked her, that she could stand like that with Ash. His arms tight around her. His lips so close to her skin.

She sucked in a breath, returning her focus to her feet. Where the heck was this even coming from? Weren't they supposed to be *friends*? All around them, the twinkling asterpearls kept rising.

"Hey, knock it off!" Ash shouted at Connor, though Silver could hear the laughter in his voice.

"I'm not doing anything!" Connor yelled back.

Ash simply shook his head as though he didn't believe Connor for a second. *Thank goodness.* "Are you sure you're okay?" he asked in a quieter tone, looking down at Silver again.

"Yes, of course." She smiled at him and took a deep breath, determining to finish the dance without paying any more attention to the earth-shattering realization that had just crashed into her.

* * *

Two days later, on Monday afternoon, Silver dragged a towel across the back of her damp neck as Odette entertained her with the tale of the disastrous session she'd just had in the simulation ring. They were in the training center at the Guild, and Silver had just finished a session of push-ups, pull-ups, planks and weights. Hence the layer of sweat she was now covered in.

"I thought we were fighting *against* each other," Odette was saying, "because *my* mentor forgot to mention the fact that I was going in there with a *partner* not an opponent, and we were supposed to save a group of kids on the side of the mountain. And because the setting included an earthquake, when this giant rift formed in front of us straight after we got in there, I was like, 'Oh cool, this'll be easy.' And I managed to wrestle my partner to the edge and shove him right into it." She smacked a hand over her face. "And then of course I couldn't finish the simulation on my own, so the fictional kids didn't make it. So Jerryn and I *both* lost points for that session."

Jerryn, Odette's unfortunate partner, appeared at that moment, and Odette peeked through her fingers at him. "I'm sorry about that."

"Don't worry about it," he said with an easy grin, sliding a hand through his blond and blue hair. "We can blame your mentor for leaving out some key details."

Silver laughed along with them, but her gaze kept slipping past Odette to where Ash was doing archery practice on the other side of the training center.

She'd spent the remainder of the weekend agonizing over whether to say anything to him and had decided that her first, not-so-scary step would be to ask him if he wanted to go to the Liberation Day Ball with her. In the past, they'd always gone as a group of friends with Odette and Remy, but Remy had messed things up this year by asking someone else to go with him. Then Odette had begun talking about how much she hoped that guy in fifth year with the purple hair would ask her as his date. So perhaps it wouldn't be that awkward if Silver suggested she and Ash go together. Like, *together* together.

Ugh, even in her head, it sounded awkward. She needed to figure out exactly what to say before she opened her mouth in front of him. Which was … not normal. When it came to Ash, she'd spent a decade saying whatever came to mind.

"My mom put the finishing touches on mine yesterday, and it's *perfect*," Odette said, "but Silver's still not happy with hers. At this rate, she'll be going naked."

"Um, what?" Silver's already flushed face grew warmer as she zoned back in on Odette and Jerryn's conversation. "What did I miss?"

"I was just asking if you guys are planning to go to the Lib Day Ball," Jerryn said. His lips quirked up on one side. "Apparently you won't be wearing much more than your underwear."

Silver smacked Odette's arm. "She's talking nonsense. My dress is basically done. I was only hoping my mom could somehow add wings to it, but she said her clothes casting skills do *not* extend that far."

"Silver wishes she could fly," Odette explained. "Like *actually* fly, not just boost herself into the air for short bursts with magic."

Jerryn nodded. "Flying would be cool."

"Right?" Silver said, self-consciously rubbing the towel across her chest and around the side of her neck. "Thank you. Odette always thinks I'm being silly when I mention it, but that's because she was always too scared to jump off a rock and swing across the river, so she totally missed out on the thrill I'm always talking about."

Odette stuck her tongue out. "I was not *scared*. Anyway. Gotta get home. My mom asked me to do dinner tonight."

"Okay, see you tomorrow," Silver said. "Oh, message me about that history essay question."

"Oh, yes. Will do."

Odette walked away, and Silver looked past Jerryn to the other side of the training center, about to make an excuse so she could go and talk to Ash. But Ash must have finished his session and left already, because she couldn't see him anywhere.

"Uh, Silver, can I talk to you?"

Silver returned her attention to Jerryn, who was now twisting his hands together. "Yeah, sure," she said, looping her towel around her neck and holding onto the two ends. "What's up?"

"Um, so …" His gaze moved past her, paused on something, and then returned to her face. "Would you like to go to the Lib Day Ball with me?"

Silver blinked. Of all the things she'd expected to come out of Jerryn's mouth, this was not one of them. "Oh. Um." She lifted a hand to her sweaty hair and tucked a few strands behind her ear. She honestly thought Jerryn liked someone else, and *she* definitely liked someone else —all she could see in her mind's eye right now was Ash—so the obvious answer here was 'no.' But Jerryn was looking at her with such a hopeful expression, and somehow she found herself saying, "Can I … get back to you?"

Jerryn grinned as if she'd said yes. "Totally. Yeah. Thanks, Silver." Then he hugged her and hurried off, leaving Silver wondering if he'd genuinely misinterpreted her words, or if he was simply relieved that the scary part—the part where he'd actually asked her—was over now. She was certainly looking forward to that part when she finally found the courage to ask Ash.

* * *

It had been three days. *Three whole days.* Silver had been trying to speak to Ash, the person she'd spoken to in some form or other *literally every day* since they were old enough to get their own ambers, and somehow it hadn't happened. He'd been arriving at classes just as their lessons began, so she couldn't speak to him then. In the training center, he was too caught up in whatever session he was in or whatever in-depth discussion he was having with a mentor to exchange more than a few words with her. And apparently he was too busy studying at night to answer her messages with anything more than something brief and vague that included 'Chat later!' or 'See you tomorrow!' or 'Can I get back to you?'

Suddenly, and seemingly out of nowhere, there was more distance between them than there had ever been. Silver was starting to wonder if she'd done something wrong without realizing it. Had she been acting weird since her revelation while they'd been dancing? Crap, she'd tried so hard to just be *normal*. To act as though nothing had changed. This was why she hadn't been sure if she should say anything to him about how she felt. Because it would change things. It would ruin the easy, perfect friendship they'd always had. But perhaps she was being weird without knowing it and now things were messed up anyway.

She made it to Thursday evening before deciding she couldn't handle it anymore. She sent a quick message to Jerryn asking him to meet her the following morning—she had never meant to string him along, and she really needed to just get over the part where she felt bad and gently tell him 'no'—then walked through the faerie paths to the Blackburns' house. In the garden, she hesitated, looking up at Ash's window. She'd climbed up there too many times to count, but suddenly it didn't seem right. She walked around the side of the house instead and aimed for the front door.

"Silver?" Iris said, surprise creasing her features when she opened the door. She held a mug of steaming liquid in one hand. The scent of lemon reached Silver's nose. "Is there ... did something happen to the wall?"

"Um ... what?"

"The wall? You normally climb up to the window."

"I ..." Silver felt heat crawling up her neck. "You ... knew about that. Of course you knew about that."

Iris's smile was gentle. "Of course I knew about that." Then she stepped back. "Sorry, come on in. Is everything okay?"

"Yes. I just, um, came to see Ash."

Iris nodded, watching Silver closely, as though she didn't believe for a second that things were 'okay.' Silver crossed the living area, waving to Lennox who was sitting on the couch writing something on an amber tablet. She climbed the stairs slowly, her palms sweating and nerves chewing at her insides. This was ridiculous. *So* ridiculous. When had she ever been nervous about speaking to Ash?

His bedroom door was ajar. She tapped her knuckles against it and waited. "Yeah?" he called. She took a breath, pushed the door open, and stepped inside. He was lying on his stomach on the bed, making notes in a textbook. "Silver?" He looked even more surprised than his mother. "Hi."

"Hi."

He hesitated, mouth half open, like he wasn't sure what else to say. Or perhaps he *did* know what he wanted to say, but he couldn't bring himself to spit it out. The sight of that uncertainty made Silver's stomach turn over again. What the heck was going on between them? "Are you mad at me?" she asked before he could try to fill the space with something meaningless.

"What?"

"I don't think you've ever been mad at me before, so I can't quite tell, but you're definitely not happy with me. So what's going on?"

He scooted to the edge of the bed and stood. "I'm not mad at you."

"But you've been avoiding me."

He let out a short laugh. "I've just been really busy."

"But ... you're always really busy. This ..." She waved to the space between them. "Something is different."

"Well, it's ..." He pushed both hands through his hair, his gaze landing somewhere past her. "I guess things would have to start changing now. They can't exactly stay the same."

"What? Why? What are you talking about?"

"Because ..." There was color in his cheeks now as his eyes returned to hers. He rubbed the back of his neck. "If you and I are seeing other people ... I mean, if we're getting close to other people ... then our friendship can't stay the same. I mean, it would be weird. Inappropriate.

If you're dating someone, or if I'm dating someone, then that's the person you're supposed to be closest to, right?"

Silver blinked and shook her head. What the *heck*? This was like reading a book and discovering she'd accidentally skipped a page. Skipped an entire *chapter*. She was *definitely* missing something. "What are you talking about? Are you … dating someone new?" A gaping hole opened up inside her at the thought.

He frowned. "I … I meant you and Jerryn. But also—"

"What?" Relief and confusion collided inside her.

"I mean … people are talking about it. He asked you out? You guys are together now?"

She was so confused. Did Ash seriously think something like this would happen and she wouldn't *tell* him about it? She'd never dated *anyone* before. If she suddenly said yes to someone, it would be a big deal. Of *course* she would tell him. "No, it's—he asked me to the Liberation Day Ball, and—"

"Okay, that's great, because … Odette and I are going together, so at least now—"

"Wait, what?"

"Yeah." Ash gave her an uncertain smile. "Cool, right?"

No, not cool. Definitely not cool. But Silver couldn't say that out loud. She couldn't say *anything*. She was half convinced she'd wandered into a dream. "Wait, just …" She squeezed her eyes shut for a moment. "Just backtrack a bit. You're saying that you and I can't have the friendship we've always had because I might be growing closer to someone else, and you might be growing closer to someone else?" Holy crap, since when was there something going on between Ash and *Odette*? How had she completely missed that? "I mean, what about Kellee? You were with her for months, and our friendship didn't change."

"Well, yeah." Ash let out a soft laugh. "Exactly. Why do you think things didn't work out with her? She was never comfortable with me having two close friends who are girls. And I didn't want to stop being friends with you guys, so I told Kellee we obviously weren't right for each other."

Two close friends who are girls. Silver had always thought *she* was Ash's closest friend, but maybe he'd spent more time with Odette than she'd realized. Maybe they hung out alone together, the same way Silver and Ash did. Maybe Odette had been here, in his bedroom, alone with him. Maybe he'd been alone with her in her room.

Bitter jealousy, hot and entirely unexpected, burned through Silver's veins. She was so startled she took a step backward. She didn't want to think of Odette like that. Odette was her *friend*. She didn't want to be *jealous* of her. Ugh, how did this become such a mess?

"I'm just … a bit confused, Ash," she said eventually. Her voice was small, defeated. This wasn't her. She never sounded like this.

Ash sat on the edge of his bed, staring down at the floor. "I guess …" He let out a long, slow breath. "I guess this had to happen at some point. That you and I would start moving in different directions. That we wouldn't always be as close as we've been in the past."

No, no, no, no! That was not what was supposed to happen! But now that this had all gone so completely sideways, Silver had no idea how to turn everything the right way up again. Perhaps it wasn't even possible. "So you're … fine with all of this?" she asked carefully. "This is what you want?"

He looked up at her. "Well … if this is what *you* want, then of course this is what I want."

Okay. That was *not* what she'd asked, but she felt stupid trying to ask again. And if he was happy with Odette, then she didn't want to take that away from him. She didn't want to make him feel guilty about it. "Um … yes?" she said eventually, though *none* of this was what she wanted.

"Okay, great," Ash breathed, looking somewhat relieved.

No, not great, Silver wanted to shout. *Not great at all!* "Um, yeah," she said instead, feeling suddenly, horribly close to tears. Which was ridiculous. She didn't *cry*. Not often, anyway, and certainly not because of Ash. He was the one who made her feel better when something was wrong. And this? This was *all* wrong.

She cleared her throat. "I, um … need to finish some homework." She gestured over her shoulder as if said homework was sitting in the passage behind her. "So … I'll see you tomorrow?"

"Yeah. I'll see you tomorrow."

TWENTY-SIX

now

THE MUSIC WEAVES AROUND US, THROUGH US, BEATING IN TIME with my heart. Ash's fingers slide into my hair. He's so close still, his lips beside my ear and his whispered words landing softly, so convincingly, in my muddled brain. *Stay. When all of this is over ... please stay.* I could. I could stay here forever. If I allowed myself to, I could sway the rest of my life away with him. Nothing else seems important.

I blink. Something about that thought scares me, and the fear is enough to clear a fraction of the haziness from my mind. Other things *are* important. *Stormsdrift* is important. Ash's family is important. Isn't that why we're here? We're here to steal the ... the ...

I blink again and shake my head. "Ash, we ... we need to focus." I'm breathless. Lightheaded. I can barely think with him so near. With the intoxicating magic of this place threading its way through every thought. I tilt my head, my mouth so close to his skin that I'm a mere breath away from pressing my lips to the side of his neck. My eyelids beg to slide shut. "The ... ice," I whisper. "Icicle. Crystal." *That's* what we're here for. With an enormous amount of effort, I force myself to take a deep breath and step backward.

He catches my wrist, his fingers warm against my skin, just above the leather cuff with the moonstone. "What happened, Silver?"

"What?"

"*What happened?*" he repeats, his voice low, earnest. I was expecting to see hooded eyes and the same sluggishness I've been trying so hard to fight off, but his gaze is clear. "There's a gap. A space of time. Between when you fled the Guild and when you decided to start a new life in the human world. Approximately a year, as far as I can work out. What happened during that time? Where were you?"

My heart pumps blood in a galloping rush through my veins, clearing the remaining cobwebs from my mind. Is that all it takes to fight the magic of this place? Terror? Adrenaline?

I stare into Ash's eyes, so warm, so intense. *Tell him*, some inner instinct urges. *Tell him, tell him, tell him.* Perhaps I can. Perhaps I'm brave enough. And if I tell him, and he understands, then maybe … maybe I *can* stay.

"Eleven months, two days," I whisper, my mouth suddenly dry. "To be more precise."

"Okay," Ash says. "What happened?"

I shake my head. I can't have this conversation here, in this room that makes my brain feel like it's been tossed around and then put back inside my head at the wrong angle. Before I can change my mind, I grab Ash's hand and tug him through the crowd. I realize belatedly that I should be going slowly, not drawing attention by rushing out of here, but I guess it's too late for that.

We reach the edge of the dance floor, and I pull him past the bar and back into the passageway with the private rooms. I aim for the first open doorway—there's no door at all, in fact—and let go of Ash's hand once we're inside.

I realize then, at the sight of the soft blue light and tiny specks of neon blue floating in the air, that I recognize this room. Water runs down all four walls, and a stream travels from one side of the room to the other, tumbling over rocks and broken branches. The floor is earth and grass, and it smells real. Fresh. There's no door, but I know that if I press the little metal flower set into the wall beside the doorway, a sheet of water will come down, sealing us off from the rest of the club. I saw Riven do it when I was last in here.

This room is one of those that patrons pay extra to use, and once upon a time, back when I was the Diamond Knife, Riven hosted a private fight in here. A friend of his had taken a liking to both me and the Pink Lynx, and he paid a small fortune to see us face off against each other. I could have beaten her in under a minute, but that wasn't what Riven's friend was paying for. So I gave him a good show, dodging and dancing across the room, somersaulting over the river, sending magic streaking past the walls to create impressive arcs of water. And then, when I grew tired of throwing magic around and twirling out of the Pink Lynx's reach, I let her knock me out.

I shut my eyes for a moment, blocking out the violent memory. This room is so serene, so calming. Why did Riven make us *fight* in here?

I turn to face Ash. He hasn't said a word yet, which I assume means he's waiting for me to talk. My fingers can't stop fiddling anxiously with things, first turning my ring around and around, and then moving to the leather strips on my bracelet, twisting the beads and pearls as I try to figure out where to start. The next thing I know, silver-white hair is tumbling over my shoulders. My fingers freeze. My eyes dart down to the bracelet and the pearl I've unintentionally squeezed too hard. Wonderful. I'll have to redo the enchantment before we leave this room.

"So … uh …" I force my hands to my sides and look up again, deciding to begin with the worst, because if Ash can't forgive me for that, then there's no point in telling him the rest of it. "What if I told you I killed someone?"

He pauses, watching me closely, then says, "I would tell you I've killed someone too. More than just one someone. It's kind of unavoidable when you're dealing with dangerous fae creatures and criminals on a near daily basis."

A humorless breath of a laugh escapes me. "I don't mean like that."

"Then … what do you mean? Was it self-defense? Were you helping someone else?" He's so damn noble. He doesn't even question that my motives might have been anything other than pure.

I inhale a shaky breath. I *will* be brave enough to tell him the truth, dammit. "Not like that either."

"Okay."

"And it was more than one person. And I *wanted* them dead."

"They were bad people, I assume? They must have done terrible things if you wanted them dead." Still he refuses to see me for what I truly am: the very opposite of everything I always dreamed of being. "I think you're going to have to be a little more specific," he says. "I can't really be sure what you're getting at otherwise. But I feel like you're trying to say that you're a terrible person because you've done terrible things, and maybe—for some people—that's true. But for you?" He shakes his head. "There's no way."

I don't deserve this. I don't deserve *him*. He's far too good for me. Of course, at the heart of it all, I've only ever wanted to be exactly what he's describing. But looking back, knowing everything I know now, it was never going to be that way. *I* was never going to be that way. And I don't think Ash is capable of seeing that.

I push my shoulders back and look past him through the doorway. "We should go back to the Gold Floor and do what we came here to do."

"Wait, hang on."

"My head is clear now. As long as we're quick once we get back out there, we shouldn't be affected by the magic."

"Silver. You've barely told me anything. I still don't know what happened or what you went through."

My eyes snap back to his. "I am a monster, Ash."

"You're not a *monster*." He moves closer, lifting both hands, and before I know it, his palms are cupping my face. Out here, away from the intoxication of the Gold Floor, his nearness is startling. But his touch … it's warm, reassuring. I don't want to step away. "Whatever you did to survive," he says gently, "it was because you had no other choice."

I shake my head and push his hands away as I step backward. "I think this conversation is over."

"That's it? You refuse to tell me? You refuse to *trust* me?"

I don't look at him as I answer. "That's it."

"*What happened?*" he demands, and it isn't anger, it's something more like desperation.

The memories rise like a tidal wave—pain, sweat, blood, death, and red, *always red*—but I beat them back down into the shadows. I step around Ash, aiming for the doorway. "I don't want to talk about this anymore."

"So nothing has changed then," he says, and the hardness in his voice brings me to a stop. "Not since the moment I found you and you tried to run from me. You're *still* running."

I'm still running, and I still can't look at him. "Correct. Nothing has changed. We're going to go back in there, steal that crystal, and then we're parting ways. I'm going off on my own again while you take that thing back to Stormsdrift and use it to destroy the door."

"And then what? What am I supposed to do after that? Carry on with my life as if nothing has changed? As if I don't know that you're out there somewhere, very much alive?"

"Yes!" I swing back around to face him. "You can …" I gesture helplessly around me, searching for an answer. "I don't know, get back together with Odette."

His head jerks back as if I've just slapped him. "Seriously?"

"Yes, seriously. She's … she's amazing. She's clever and funny and a talented guardian, and … and beautiful." I feel sick to my stomach even as I'm saying it, but that doesn't change the fact that I mean it. Ash deserves to be with someone like Odette.

"Stop. Silver. This has nothing to do with—"

"I mean, she's basically perfect."

"She's not perfect."

"Oh, I'm sorry, does she have some tiny flaw that means she isn't good enough for—"

"She isn't you!" he shouts.

I stare at him. He stares back. I hear nothing but our heightened breaths and the whisper of falling water and his words ricocheting around my brain.

She isn't you.

She isn't you.

He finally breaks eye contact, turning away with a shake of his head. "Just … forget it. Forget I said that. Forget everything else. Silver, I just …" He looks at me, and his shoulders lift in an almost helpless shrug. "I just want my best friend back."

Something about the way he says this—as if it's *possible*, as if it's a request I could actually grant but I'm simply choosing not to—makes anger flare inside me at the unfairness of it all. "You think I don't want her back too? Your friend is *gone*, Ash! That fun, carefree, daring girl you grew up with? She's gone and *nobody* is ever getting her back!"

"Yeah, you've made that pretty damn clear. You're nothing like her. You're so *angry* and you hate everyone—"

"I HATE MYSELF!" I roar. Then I slam my palm against the metal flower set into the wall. A sheet of water crashes down, closing us in, and I clench my fists, open my mouth, and scream and scream and *scream*. I keep going until the scream becomes a desperate chest-heaving sob and my body starts to shake. "Do you have *any* … idea … what it was like," I gasp, barely able to breathe now, "watching the people you love … literally … cut down … in front of you? And I did *nothing!*" The last of the air is squeezed from my lungs, and I fight against the convulsive sobs and as I try to draw more breath. But it's all too much now.

I curl in on myself. My legs lower me down, and then I'm on my knees on the grass, my shoulders shaking and my chest shuddering. "I hate—I HATE—myself … who I am … and what I've done." The shuddering sobs won't stop, and tears keep streaking down my face. I lean forward and press my fingers into the grass. Into the dirt. "They gave up … their *lives*. And then I became … everything … they hated. Everything *you* hate."

Ash's hand is on my shoulder. Then he's on the ground beside me, slipping an arm around my back and pulling me against him. I don't fight it. I wind my arms around him and press my tear-stained face against his shoulder, and for the first time in *years,* I hug him.

He doesn't tell me everything's okay. He doesn't ask me to elaborate. In the end, all he whispers is, "I will never hate you." And maybe it's true. Maybe he would forgive me if he knew everything. Maybe he would understand. But I will fall apart completely if I tell him now.

I don't know how long we sit there, but eventually my sobs subside into shuddering breaths. "Tell me about your family," I whisper.

Ash lets out a confused laugh. "What?"

"You know I didn't mean it when I said I didn't want to know anything. I want to know every detail. Every single thing I missed." I carefully extricate myself from his embrace, sniffing as I swipe my hands beneath my eyes. "Are Flynn and Holly still together? Is Connor still the biggest pain in everyone's ass?"

Ash lifts one hand, smiling as he gently brushes his knuckles across my still-damp cheek. "Flynn and Holly broke up about a year ago, but it sounded like it was for the best. I think they grew up and grew apart." He lifts his other hand and sweeps his thumb delicately beneath my eye, making me wonder just how much mascara mess is currently streaking my face. "Connor and Rosie broke up, and then Connor did this all-out, grand-gesture proposal, and now they're forming a union."

"What?" I sniff-laugh in surprise. "Connor's getting *married?*"

"Right? Who would have thought he'd be the first? Mom made a bit of a fuss about him being young and impulsive, but you know Connor's adored Rosie since the minute he first laid eyes on her."

"Yes." I scoop my hair behind my ears. "And Tobin?"

"Tobin …" Ash's gaze shifts away from mine. "I don't see him much anymore. He left the Guild soon after …" He trails off, then sighs. "Soon after what happened with your family. Mom and Dad spoke about leaving too—not the Guild as a whole, just the Stormsdrift Guild —but then they decided to stay. It was just … things never entirely added up, like the story about how you and your parents were Unseelie spies, and we weren't really sure if we could trust everyone after that. But they decided in the end that if there was something suspicious going on at our Guild, then it was better to stay than to leave. My mom's also taken up knitting recently, which is completely random and also kind of funny, because she's terrible at it but she refuses to give up or use any spells to help her."

I laugh again, and it sounds closer to normal this time. "She'll be making you an ugly sweater any day now."

His smile stretches wider. "Yes, and then you'll steal it when you forget to—" He cuts himself off, apparently remembering that we're no longer living in the past. That it's been years since I casually leaned over and helped myself to whatever warm item of clothing he brought with him for the evening. "Well, anyway," he says. "Mom's going to be utterly beside herself when she discovers you're alive. They all will."

I look down at my hands as I nod. A few minutes ago, I was very firmly telling Ash that I'll be going off on my own again as soon as we get that crystal. Now I've allowed myself to soak up all the details I've longed to know for years, and all I want is to go home. Stormsdrift home.

"Silver," Ash says gently. "Are you okay? That was … a lot."

I roll my eyes. "That screaming meltdown?" I ask lightly. "That was nothing."

His hand rests on my knee. "It wasn't nothing. And it also wasn't your fault. What happened to your parents. You have to know that, right?"

I nod and try to swallow past the lump in my throat, but inside I still wish I had done *something*. Guardians are trained to act in the blink of an eye, in the space between heartbeats, and that's what I should have done. Instead I froze. I didn't even *try* to fight back.

"And the rest of it," Ash says slowly. "Do you want to talk about that?"

I'm not sure which bit he's referring to now. The eleven months and two days that I still haven't shared any details about? Or the *she isn't you* declaration? I look up at him as those words bounce around my head again.

She isn't you.

She isn't you.

The words make me warm and giddy, and I feel again the desperate longing that almost consumed me on the dance floor. It wasn't just the magic. *I want this.* Ash, Stormsdrift, his family. I want to stay. I want a life there. I want a life *with him.*

I look toward the sheet of water rushing down over the doorway. It won't be hard to steal that crystal full of Seelie power. Even if we end up having to fight our way out of here, we can do it. And if it works—if it destroys the door and Stormsdrift is safe again, and Ash and I go to another Guild and tell them under the influence of truth potion what really happened two years ago—then I can stay. If I bury those eleven months and two days in the past and never speak of them, I can stay.

Ash is watching me, waiting, giving me the space to speak when I'm ready. Perhaps he's hoping I'll finally talk about what happened after I ran from the Guild, but I have something else I'd rather tell him. Something else I'm pretty sure he'd rather hear. If I'm brave enough.

I take a deep breath. Then another. "Ash, I … I lied. When I told you I tried not to think about you at all the past two years. I was lying."

A quiet moment passes between us as I dare to meet his eyes. Then he says, "I know." His gaze moves down, his hand finds my wrist, and he gently lifts my arm. He turns the multilayered bracelet of crisscrossing leather strips until the little silver bird is visible. He touches the tiny number three etched on its side. "I saw it when I took you to Ostin's. After you passed out. He was trying to heal you, and I was going just the tiniest bit out of my mind thinking I might lose you all over again, and then this little bird caught my eye. And I figured … perhaps you didn't hate me as much as you wanted me to believe."

I let out a slow breath, my eyes still on the little bird. On Ash's hand holding my wrist so carefully. "I thought about you every day," I admit quietly. "I *missed* you every day. *Every single day.* Sometimes I thought I must have been mistaken, that you *weren't* following Bergenfell's orders, and other times I remembered the magic you threw at me the second before those guardians tugged me into the faerie paths and tried to kill me, and I was so heartbroken, so *angry*. But mostly … mostly I just missed you."

His finger moves from the tiny silver bird, tracing a path across the leather braids and over my palm. I can't help the shiver that dances across my skin and up the back of my neck. He interlaces his fingers with mine. "No words exist in any language to describe how much I missed you."

My next breath is a quiet shudder. Ash's eyes settle on mine, and his amber irises are like liquid fire. My blood rushes faster through my veins. My traitorous gaze dips, landing on his lips. It has been a very, very long time since I kissed him.

"Silver."

I jerk away from Ash at the sound of the intrusive voice, my eyes darting around for the owner. The curtain of water over the doorway is gone. In its place stands Riven Xeryth.

Twenty-Seven

I scramble to my feet. A second later, Ash is standing too. He grips my hand firmly, reassuring me with a brief squeeze. Riven regards us in silence, his dark gaze sliding over me, then Ash, then down to our joined hands, and then back to my face. "You know the use of this room comes at a price," he says, his silky voice cold.

I swallow. It's not as though I'm *afraid* of Riven. Not exactly. But there's something about him that's always reminded me of—

I blink and kick that thought clear out of my head. I'm not afraid of Riven, but my guard is always up when I'm around him. There's something unsettling about his direct gaze and the way he hardly blinks. And even though people say he's a faerie, he seems to have only one color: dark, almost black. It's a little strange. And while it's always seemed as though he wants to keep me around, I suspect that if I wound up on his bad side—by, let's say, *stealing* from him—he wouldn't hesitate to strike.

"We weren't using the room," I say, trying to keep my voice even. "We just came in here to talk, away from all the noise, and then I guess the doorway malfunctioned. Closed itself."

Riven inhales, exhales, continues watching me. "Talking," he says eventually. "I have to admit, that's not what it looked like." Heat crawls up my neck and into my face, but before I can respond, he continues. "I hope you're here to explain your exceedingly disappointing actions the other night. You can't simply jump up and run in the middle of a fight. The audience was most upset."

"I'm sure the audience loved the drama, and I'm sure Klyde wasted no time tossing the next pair of fighters into the ring."

"Klyde no longer works here."

I hesitate, unsure what to say to that. Unsure what to *think* of that. "Oh."

"Oh indeed. My assistant tried to contact you, Silver."

"I … lost my amber." A warning bell begins to ding softly at the back of my mind. Something isn't right here. I can't imagine Riven paying such close attention to all his employees. If people disappear, he just replaces them and moves on. At least … I always assumed he was that sort of person.

"You lost your amber," Riven repeats. "Well, how convenient then that you wandered in for a night of … conversation. Because that's exactly what you and I are going to have now. A private chat. Without him around." He gestures at Ash before stepping into the room and moving to one side. People begin filing in from behind him. Men and women I don't recognize. My eyes dart back and forth, counting. Five. Ten. Fifteen. Crappity crap crap. What is this?

"What's going on?" Ash demands as the newcomers move to stand around the edge of the room. He lets go of me, and I glance down to see him clamp his left hand tightly over his right.

"You," Riven says to him, "are a guardian who does not have permission to be in my club, and you—" my attention snaps back to him as he looks at me "—did not have permission to disappear."

He knows Ash is a guardian? And who the heck does he think he is, talking to me like he *owns* me? We're vastly outnumbered, yet I can't help the indignation that burns in my chest. "Excuse me? You may be my employer, but that doesn't mean I have to answer to—"

Riven snaps his fingers. At least half the men and women around the room move toward us. Ash's arms are up in a second, a crossbow in one hand, already loaded with a gleaming golden bolt, and a sword in the other. "Try it," he says, low and deadly, his eyes still on Riven.

A few people stop, sending questioning glances in Riven's direction. The others halt when I lift my hands, my own magic crackling around my fingers. "What's going on, Riven?" I ask, still trying to keep my tone calm, reasonable. "More than a dozen people? This seems a bit like overkill."

"I don't think so," Riven answers. "He's a guardian, and you …" He trails off, a hint of a smile on his lips. "Well, we both know what you are."

I blink at him, my heart pattering even faster now. Does he know I spent several years being trained at a Guild? Or does he somehow know more than that?

"Well?" Riven snaps, looking around the room. "What are you waiting for?"

They advance on us, and I move one hand swiftly to the leather cuff on my wrist. Definitely time to get my crescent-moon knife out. But I've barely touched the moonstone when my thoughts leap to my other wrist and the tiny stone that contains the darkness charm. I'm supposed to be saving it for the Gold Floor, but what's the point if we never make it out of this blue-tinged, water-filled room?

My hands cross over, my fingers aiming for the wrap bracelet instead, and Ash is shooting the crossbow, and his blade is sweeping through the air, and sparks of magic whizz past my head, and suddenly there are more people, more weapons, more bright, glittering gold.

Guardians?

Guardians I *recognize*?

What the—

Everything comes to a halt. Riven is standing at knifepoint, surrounded by three guardians. Another four have their weapons raised, aimed around the room. They're all councilors from the Stormsdrift Guild, as far as I can tell. Riven's people are brandishing weapons too. Magic is poised above dozens of hands. I'm frozen with my fingers near the stone containing the darkness charm. I could do it. I could fill the room with complete, instant darkness. But chaos would descend, and at least half of us would likely end up dead. What if Ash and I are among that number?

Riven is the first to move. His head whips back toward Ash. His dark gaze smolders with fury. *"What did you do?"*

Ash spreads his arms wide, palms up. His tone is clipped as he says, "What does it look like?"

"How *dare* you? This is not part of my agreement with the Guild."

"Yeah, well, you should have thought about that before you brought a bunch of your people in here and tried to attack me. This case is bigger than whatever deal you've struck with the Guild. We've been searching for her for years—" he jerks his head in my direction "—and I can tell you right now, there's no Guild in the world that's about to let you disappear with her."

I struggle to follow what he's saying. None of this was part of our plan, so he's obviously making this up on the spot, bluffing his ass off. Except … *he's* the one who called all these guardians here?

"Asher Blackburn." A guardian steps forward. Greenwood? He was new on the Council at the time I ran from the Guild, but I think that's his name. "You have some nerve, calling us here after you—"

"We can sort everyone's nerves out once we're back at the Guild," Ash says. And then he turns to me and snaps a pair of glittering cuffs onto my wrists.

Wait. What? What the actual freaking—

"Where's Ursula?" Ash asks.

Ursula? Since when are Ash and Bergenfell on a first-name basis? I remind myself that Ash has been a qualified, working guardian for some time. Years, from his perspective. So perhaps it's not weird that he calls her 'Ursula.' They're basically colleagues. And this strange exchange is all part of an impromptu plan to get us safely out of here. Right? That *has* to be what's going on. Because Ash is on my side. I *know* he is. There's no way he faked everything we just talked about, everything we've been through over the past two days.

Except … if he's on my side … why did he make sure I can't access my own magic?

"Ursula would like me to remind you," Greenwood says, "that you're also under arrest."

Ash sighs. "Yeah, we can fix up that little misunderstanding back at the Guild as well."

"Little misunderstanding? You tried to *kill* us when Singer and I showed up to—"

"That's definitely an exaggeration. And I got Ursula the girl, didn't I? So it was all worth it."

Excuse me? *The girl?*

"You're not the one who was supposed to be going after the girl, as far as I know," Greenwood says. "You're wanted for assault—"

"Another misunder—"

"Now that you've *ruined* the reputation of this place," Riven says loudly, speaking over both of them, "might I suggest that you take your domestic squabbles back to your little Guild and leave me and what's left of my club in peace?"

"Your reputation is fine," Greenwood snaps at him. "We came in quietly. No weapons drawn. Only your gatekeepers at the door and the people in this room know who we are."

"And if you let us *leave* just as quietly," Ash says, "your reputation will *remain* intact. No one out there needs to know that a group of guardians walked right through your club."

Tiny neon blue specks float past Riven. His eyes glitter as he watches Ash. "You're playing a dangerous game, boy."

My eyes dart around the room, taking in the raised weapons, the tense postures, everyone waiting, watching, hardly daring to breathe. Game or not, this is dangerous indeed.

"So that's a yes?" Greenwood says to Riven. "You'll stand back quietly while we leave?"

"While you take my silver girl?" Riven asks in an icy tone that sends goosebumps across my skin.

"She is not your silver girl," Ash growls, and his hand rises to clamp, almost painfully, around my upper arm. Part of me wants to tug free, to fight back, but the rest of me is too confused to act. I'm still trying to figure out whether this is all a big trick to get us out of here—or if *I'm* the one who's been tricked.

"You may not know this about me, *boy*," Riven says, eyes flashing dangerously, "but I always get what I want. In the end." His gaze shifts to me, and somehow, without him saying another word, I know that what he wants is *me*.

Ash pulls me roughly against his side. "Not this time," he says to Riven before marching me forward. "Oh, and one more thing," he adds, stopping and looking at Greenwood. "Actually, two more things. Firstly, she knows where the key is, so maybe don't kill her until you get that information out of her. And secondly, I noticed a stolen treasure from the Seelie Court hanging from a chandelier in that gold room. We should probably take that with us."

My stomach drops down to my toes. He told them I know where the key is? Why the hell would he do that if he's on my side? I'm about to shove an elbow into his gut or jerk my head back hard enough to break his nose, but Riven speaks first. "You will not touch the Icicle Pendant of the First Seelie Queen."

Despite my fury and confusion, I manage to be impressed by this. The First Seelie Queen? That thing really is a priceless treasure. How on earth did Riven end up with it?

"Well," Ash says, "thank you for confirming that it is, in fact, the icicle pendant." He drags me forward another few steps and stops in front of Riven. "How about this? You let us walk out of here with the girl *and* the pendant, and we all pretend we didn't see the highly addictive glimmX powder your bartender was busy sprinkling into every drink back there. You're happy, we're happy. Okay?"

Riven presses his lips together for several tense seconds. Then he drops his gaze, inclining his head ever so slightly.

"Great," Ash says, and then he's dragging me out of the blue room.

"Ash," I say to him in a low voice as I cling desperately to one last shred of hope. "Please tell me this is all—"

"Don't," he says, his tone short, his gaze pointed forward. "Please, Silver, just … you're only going to make this more difficult."

My mind spins. He's still acting, right? That's the difficult part he's referring to? The part where he pretends to betray me? I lower my voice further. "Please just give me some kind of sign—"

"There's no *sign*, Silver," he says abruptly. "Just stop, okay?" Still he won't look at me. "This isn't personal. This is my job. I swore an oath to the Guild and the Seelie crown. And you …" He shakes his head as he steers me back onto the Gold Floor. "You're nothing but an Unseelie spy."

My stomach drops. That has to be a lie. There's no way he believes that Unseelie nonsense. But even as I'm thinking this, the cracks begin to form in my heart. I knew, I *knew* when he suddenly appeared in my life again that I shouldn't trust him. That I couldn't trust *myself* with him. I should have stuck firmly to my initial gut feeling. I shouldn't have let myself get close to him again. I'm such an *idiot*!

Greenwood is suddenly in front of us, blocking our path. "Hold on, Blackburn. You're not leaving this club a free man."

"Are you kidding me right now?"

"No. I have my orders."

"So do I. From the Seelie Court. Because they got tired of waiting for Ursula to deliver."

Greenwood arches a brow. "I'm fairly sure you're lying through your ass."

"And do you think I'm lying through my ass about *that*?" Ash demands, pointing up at the chandelier.

Greenwood follows his gaze. He sighs. "I suppose not."

"Go ahead," Ash says, gesturing again to the Icicle Pendant of the First Seelie Queen. "We'll wait right here."

Greenwood gives him a do-you-think-I-was-born-yesterday look, then issues a few instructions to two of the other councilors. He remains at my side while the two women head onto the dance floor. Together, with hands raised and strands of magic weaving carefully through the air, they detach the icicle pendant from the rest of the chandelier.

If anyone in the crowd thinks it's strange that someone is removing part of the decor, they don't say or do anything. More likely they're too intoxicated to notice. I certainly wouldn't have, when I was the one swaying on the dance floor. The memory flickers across my mind. The beat of the music, the heat of Ash's body so close to mine, his lips whispering beside my ear. My face burns, and my heart breaks a little more. I push aside the pain and focus on the anger. No way in hell am I letting Ash haul me back to the Guild with the rest of these guardians.

He may have made it impossible for me to use my own magic, but the great thing about the enchantments I spent so much money on is that they all contain their own magic. The only thing I need to do is twist or squeeze the correct stone or pearl in the correct fashion. Not so easy, I discover, as I try to get the fingers of my left hand close enough to the items on my right wrist and fail miserably. And there's still the fact that once I escape—because I *will* escape—I'll still be stuck with guardian cuffs on my wrists.

"Perfect," Greenwood says as the councilors who retrieved the icicle pendant reach us. "Now, Blackburn, I'm afraid I need to cuff you."

Ash lets out a deep, low sigh that sounds almost like a growl. "Fine. Can you at least wait until we're outside? Don't make a scene in here. The Guild's deal with Riven Xeryth is, unfortunately, an important one."

Greenwood shakes his head, but all he says is, "Fine." Then his fingers wrap around my arm—the one not currently gripped by Ash—as he adds, "But I'm escorting this one out."

This one? Wow. I love the way they talk about me as if I'm not even here. If my brain wasn't so frantically preoccupied with trying to come up with a way out of this predicament, I'd be figuring out how to hurt this guy instead.

At first, Ash doesn't let go of my arm. I'm stuck there feeling like the knotted rope at the center of the most ridiculous tug of war. I look up to see his jaw clenched, his eyes burning. Then he releases me. "Sure," he says, somehow managing to make that single word sound like a threat. Typical Asher Blackburn. He never liked to lose at anything.

Greenwood pulls me forward, and Ash falls into step behind us, councilors flanking him. We make our way across the Gold Floor, through the mirrored passageway, and into the Rainbow Room. All the while, my fingers are scrabbling desperately at the multilayer bracelet. The stupid cuffs keep getting in the way, but I'm managing to turn the bracelet fraction by fraction. At some point, though, I'm going to have to look down to see if my fingers are close enough to the correct stone. Some point very, very soon, because we're almost across the Rainbow Room.

And that's when everything happens at once.

Someone screams behind me, then another scream, and then Greenwood lurches forward, an arrow straight through his left arm. Then I'm tugged backward against something solid and warm, and a hand is reaching down, grabbing my wrist, lifting it and fumbling with the bracelet. Fumbling for a specific yellow stone.

It takes my brain only a split second to put the pieces together. Ash shot Greenwood. He's aiming for the darkness charm. This was all an act. He's on my side. *He's on my side.*

And then the world vanishes.

Chaos.

Music and shrieks and angry voices. The sound of glass shattering and magic crackling in the air. Darkness pressing against my eyeballs. Ash's arm is around me, and I'm stumbling and skidding as he drags me across the floor, bumping into people, tripping over feet, fighting off elbows and hands and shoulders—until we collide abruptly with something solid. A wall?

Then a voice in my ear. Warm lips moving like a caress against my earlobe. "I'm sorry. I'm so sorry. Did I hurt you?"

"Yes," I answer without thinking. "You broke my heart. Again."

His hands, which were busy sliding down my arms, go still. His warm breath against my neck vanishes. Complete pandemonium fills the darkness around us, but Ash is frozen. It feels as though we exist inside a bubble. Then he says, "Did you really think I would choose them over you a second time?" He presses his lips against the skin beneath my ear. A real kiss this time. A shiver zings down my spine. "I will never make that mistake again." His hands slide down to my wrists. Warmth. And then the cuffs are gone.

I suck in a breath. "You alerted the Guild," I accuse.

"It was our only way out of here."

"You told them I know where the key is!"

"To keep you alive as long as possible."

"You said I'm nothing but an Unseelie—"

"I love you."

I stop. My lips are parted, but no sound comes out. I can't form words.

"I love you," he says again, a fervent whisper against my neck, and suddenly all I want is to *see* him. It's so dark, so utterly, completely dark, that it makes me question whether any of this is even real. What if I'm dreaming? What if I'm *dead*? What if he really did betray me after all?

Something shatters against the wall beside me, and I jerk away in fright. Ash's hand grips mine, and then he's pulling me behind him. I keep one hand up, sliding against the wall. He keeps bumping into people and I, in turn, keep bumping into him. Shouts and cries fill the room. Magic zings invisibly through the air.

Then suddenly I feel water. On my hands, my arms, my face. And then we burst through to the other side of the water droplet curtain and into the light.

But I've barely taken a step when a large shape lurches out of the Rainbow Room behind me. There are hands on my shoulders, tugging me roughly backward. I'm slipping, falling, hitting the floor, water frothing and bubbling on my face, before I'm yanked back into the darkness.

Twenty-Eight

then

Bubbles whizzed around Silver as she spun in a giddy circle on the dance floor. Someone had decided on an undersea theme for the Liberation Day celebrations this year, and the ballroom inside Mirrinvale Manor—the venue the Stormsdrift Guild had hired for this year's ball—was filled with glittery blue-green flowers, frothy white layers of tulle, impressive water displays arcing across the room, and silvery bubbles that were surprisingly difficult to pop.

Mirrinvale Manor belonged to some disgustingly wealthy family—distant relatives of the Seelie King—who apparently had an even larger and more modern home somewhere else. So the manor house, situated in a part of the fae realm that consisted of rolling green hills that went on for miles, sat empty most of the time. A pity, Silver had thought when she stepped out of the faerie paths and took in the grand old house with its endless gardens of rose bushes, water features and moss-covered sculptures. If she had a house this beautiful, she would never want to leave it.

She had lingered outside for a few minutes, smelling the flowers and trailing her fingers over the edges of statues, putting off the moment when she would have to walk into the ballroom and face the rest of the evening. "It's going to be okay," she had whispered to herself. "This is all going to be okay."

She had decided earlier that it was probably for the best, the way things had played out with Ash. Her friendship with him was one of the most important relationships in her life, and she did *not* want to mess it up any more than it was already messed up. But she knew that change was inevitable. Life couldn't stay as it was forever. Ash would find someone, whether it was Odette or someone else, who grew to be more important to him than Silver was. He and Silver would spend less time together, share fewer details of their lives with one another. It filled Silver with such deep sadness to think of it that she'd decided she'd rather not think of it at all. With time, she decided, she would get used to the idea of them growing apart.

After her private pep talk in the garden, she'd wandered into the ballroom where Remy had insisted on pulling her immediately onto the dance floor. "Okay, I think I'm done," she said breathlessly as the music came to an end. A few wisps of hair had escaped the elegant knot at the back of her head, and she tucked them behind her ears. "Thanks, Remy." She grinned at him. "I think your date wants a turn now."

Remy laughed and gulped in a breath. "I'm hoping my date will let me recover from this one first. Hey, um, I haven't seen Jerryn yet."

"Oh, I'm sure he'll be here soon. We said we'd meet here, and I was early. Oh, and there's Odette." She waved over Remy's shoulder as Odette entered the ballroom, her dark curls pulled into an elegant updo. Her dress, a deep shade of pink that was covered in thousands of tiny flowers, perfectly complemented her striking features. Ash wasn't with her, which caused a ridiculous amount of relief to flood Silver's veins. "I'm going to go and say hi."

She stepped carefully around Remy—her too-high heels were one of the reasons she was grateful to get off the dance floor; she would have wiped out multiple times if she hadn't been holding onto him—and headed in Odette's direction.

"Oh my gosh, Silver!" Odette squealed. "You look *amazing*! It all came together so beautifully! The little crystals on the bodice, and the lace on your arms, and—turn around—" She took Silver's arm and turned her carefully. "Aah, the back!" She clapped her hands. "It's *so* elegant. Your mom and I were totally right. This would have looked silly with wings."

"Fine, I know," Silver grumbled, picturing the way the ice-blue fabric swooped all the way down to her lower back, revealing a large amount of bare skin that Dad had said he wasn't exactly happy about. "You guys were both right. It does look amazing like this. The shoes are awful, though. They keep tripping me up."

"Well, at least they look amazing." Odette sighed and clasped her hands together beneath her chin. "Ash is going to *die* when he sees you. He's honestly going to forget how to breathe."

Silver blinked, blood rushing to fill her cheeks. "Ash?"

"I-I mean Jerryn. Jerryn! Oh, shoot." Odette pressed her hands over her face. "I'm so sorry, that was such a stupid slip. I totally meant Jerryn."

"Hey, stop that." Silver laughed as she reached over to pull Odette's hands away from her face. "You're going to smudge your makeup."

"Ugh, that was embarrassing. I'm sorry."

"Just a slip-up," Silver said with another laugh, though her insides were struggling to recover from the complete somersault they'd performed at the thought of Ash being breathless at the sight of her. "Um, anyway. *Your* dress looks incredible. I mean, I know my mom did a good job on mine, but your mom needs to win some kind of prize. All those tiny flowers? It's *amazing*. It totally looks like a professional clothes caster did it."

"Thank you." Odette beamed. "I'm *so* in love with it. I just hope Alaron thinks I look amazing too."

Silver paused again. Was that another slip-up? "Um … but aren't you here with Ash?"

"Oh, yes, kind of. He's meeting me here. But …" She peered a little closer at Silver. "You know we're only here together as friends, right?

We're not even really here *together*. It's more because Remy's here with what's-her-name, and you're here with Jerryn, and I really wanted to come with Alaron but he hardly even knows I exist, so …" She rolled her eyes and shrugged. "You know. Ash and I ended up coming together by default."

"Oh." An enormous weight lifted from Silver's shoulder. "Right, cool."

Odette frowned. "Didn't he tell you?"

"Um … he must have forgotten."

Odette pressed her lips together and inhaled sharply through her nose. "I'm going to kill that boy," she muttered.

"What? No, it's fine, it's not a big deal. Just a … misunderstanding on my part." Though that wasn't really the way Ash had made it sound when he'd said he and Odette were coming together.

"He's still in big trouble," Odette muttered. "Anyway." She cleared her throat and pulled a smile back onto her face. "Speaking of dates, where's Jerryn?"

"Oh, I don't think he's arrived yet. We also said we'd meet here."

"Okay, cool. Um …" Odette twisted her hands together. "I, um, I've actually been wanting to ask you something, but we always seem to be hanging out in a group these days, and I didn't want to make you feel awkward in front of the guys."

"Oh dear," Silver said with a nervous laugh. "What's this about?"

"Nothing major," Odette said quickly. "I just wanted to know how serious you are about Jerryn. Like, are you guys dating now? Or is it just a tonight thing."

"Oh, it's *definitely* just a tonight thing. I was actually going to say no to him, but … yeah." Silver's mind flashed back to that awful conversation in Ash's bedroom. She forced her thoughts back to the present. "And then … okay, this is going to sound weird, but Jerryn and I have hung out a little bit since he asked me to be his date, and he keeps talking about this third-year girl. Like *all* the time. I honestly think he only invited me to make her jealous."

"Oh." Odette started laughing, then shook her head. "There's a surprising amount of that going around tonight."

Silver frowned. "What do you mean?"

Odette sighed. Instead of answering, she said, "This is all so silly, you know? We should have just come as a group like we always do. Pairing off just makes everything a mess."

"You're telling me," Silver murmured. "Oh, I think—" She frowned as someone with blond and blue hair disappeared through one of the open doorways and onto the terrace. "I think I saw Jerryn."

"Oh, cool. Um, well, see you on the dance floor!"

"Yes!" Silver answered, a little too brightly. *Or not*, she thought as she hurried swiftly away, almost tripping on one of her stupid shoes. She caught herself against the edge of a fountain, wiggled her ankle a few times to check it was still okay, then set off again. The thought of having to watch Ash and Odette with their arms around each other on the dance floor made her feel a little nauseous. *Nooooo thank you. Not putting myself through that.*

Water arced high overhead as Silver skirted the edge of the dance floor. After nodding politely at Councilor Bergenfell, and then stopping to greet Iris and Lennox and explaining that her parents would be here later, she reached the doorway she'd seen Jerryn disappear through. She stepped out onto the moonlit terrace—and stopped.

Jerryn. And a blonde girl. Kissing. Locked in such a passionate embrace, in fact, that it was difficult to tell at first whether it was even Jerryn. But … yes. It was definitely him.

Silver stepped hastily back into the shadow of the curtains that framed the doorway, averting her gaze. She waited for hurt to pierce her chest. For anger to boil in her blood. But all she really felt was … relief. And annoyance. Did Jerryn really have to cause such a mess in someone else's life just so he could get this silly girl to pay attention to him?

Silver closed her eyes, leaned back into the folds of the curtain, and breathed out slowly. *This is okay*, she told herself. *I'm okay.* Honestly, she would probably have more fun this way. She would dance with Remy.

She would dance with Odette. Perhaps she'd even dance with Ash. It would be like all the other Liberation Day Balls they'd attended. If they could forget all the painful awkwardness of the past two weeks.

She turned back toward the ballroom, and there was Ash, standing with Odette. A gap in the crowd provided Silver with a perfect view of the two of them. He looked amazing, of course. Even more swoon-worthy than the last time she'd seen him in fae formal wear. He and Odette were laughing, and his hand was on her shoulder. A knife of pain slid straight through Silver's chest. It seemed as if all the air was punched from her lungs. Tears burned behind her eyes. Because of course *that* made sense. She saw her date kissing another girl and it didn't bother her. Then she saw her two closest friends laughing together, and now she wanted to dissolve into tears. Flipping ridiculous.

Breathe, just breathe. She spun back around, ready to leave immediately, but of course Jerryn and his crush were still there, trying to absorb each other's faces. Silver was so desperate to flee the ballroom that she almost marched right past them. But it would make things even worse if they saw her. Jerryn would apologize, and she would be crying, and he would think it was because of *him*, and … ugh. No.

Silver turned to face the ballroom again.

And Ash was coming toward her.

She froze, her breath catching. He slowed and stopped, a smile spreading on his face as he watched her. And she just stood there, unable to run, unable to think, wanting equally to wrap her arms around him and to get as far away from him as possible.

He closed the distance between them, his smile growing wider. "Silver, you look …" Then he trailed off, his expression falling. He stepped closer, his hand moving immediately, automatically, to her arm. "What's wrong?"

"Nothing," she answered quickly, swiping at the tears on her cheek. "Just … nothing."

His eyes slid over her shoulder, and his expression turned thunderous in an instant. She knew without having to turn what he'd seen.

Who he'd seen. "I'm going to kill him," Ash said, already stepping past her.

"Hey, no." She grabbed his arm. "Ash, stop. I mean it!"

He swung around to face her. "You want me to just leave—"

"Yes! Just leave it. Him. Them!" She sniffed, pulling him back inside the ballroom. "It doesn't matter."

"Are you kidding? Some asshole makes you cry and it *doesn't matter?*"

"*He's* not the asshole who made me cry!" she yelled.

He stared at her. Other people were staring too, she suspected, but she couldn't pull her gaze from him. His expression was frozen. Confused. And then she saw the way it shifted the moment he realized she meant *him*. He cursed beneath his breath. "I'm sorry. Silver, I— wait!" he called after her as she pushed past him. "Please just wait!"

She ducked past people, aiming for one of the other arched doorways. She had to get out. The gardens were extensive. She could lose herself out there. Cry into the rose bushes and then head back home through the faerie paths when she was ready. It was so *stupid*, really. How dare any single person have the ability to make her heart feel so crushed? It shouldn't be possible.

"Silver, just *wait!*"

Dammit, why was he still following her? She ducked past an arrangement of sparkly seaweedy-looking plants and onto a different terrace. Her left heel twisted sideways, and she almost toppled over. "Ugh, stupid, *stupid* thing!" She kicked it off, then attempted to send the other shoe in the same direction, but the damn thing was somehow stuck to her foot. She reached down, tugged it off, and flung it sideways with a furious yell.

"Whoa!" From the corner of her eye, she saw Ash duck low. "Did you just throw a *shoe* at me?"

"No! You were just—in the way! Stop following me!" She grabbed two fistfuls of her skirt and hurried across the terrace and down the steps, faster now that she didn't have to worry about her ridiculous footwear. The grass was cool and damp beneath her feet, and the evening air was fresh against her burning face. The moonlight was bright enough to illuminate her path between the roses and statues.

"Would you just *stop*?" Ash shouted. "What is going on? Silver!"

She came to a halt, her back still to him, breathing hard and forcing tears away. Just ahead of her lay a small round pool with a fountain at its center: two figures entwined, lips almost touching, rising from a frothing display of water that was probably supposed to be a wave. Wonderful. Completely freaking wonderful. Even the water feature was mocking her. She gritted her teeth and pointed her gaze determinedly at the ground.

"I don't understand any of this," Ash said from behind her. "You told me you wanted to come to this thing with *him*, and now he's kissing some other girl, but you're upset with *me*, and—" She heard the sound of his hands falling to his sides. "I don't even know what we're fighting about."

"You don't know? You *don't know*?" She swung back around to face him. "You and I were supposed to come together!"

He paused, a completely bewildered expression on his face. "We were?"

"Yes!"

"I—okay. I'm sorry, but I somehow missed that part."

"Because you were too busy being a silly, stubborn boy about Jerryn!"

"Because … you said you were coming to the ball with him. He asked you out. You … started dating?"

"No! We did not! He asked me to come with him to this stupid thing, and I did *not* say yes! I came to talk to *you*, and—"

"Wait. Hang on." Ash held both hands up. "You said this was what you wanted. Silver, I'm just … I'm really confused. The only thing I want is for you to be happy, and you said—"

"Seriously? *That's* the only thing you want?"

"Yes!"

"No! That cannot possibly be true. What about what *you* want?"

He paused again, looking a little startled now. "What?"

"What do *you* want, Ash?" She hesitated, then blurted out, "Is it Odette? Is that who you want?"

"No," he answered immediately. Then he shook his head. "I'm sorry. I can see how it might have seemed that way. I was—"

"How it might have *seemed* that way?"

"Odette is definitely just a friend."

"In the same way that I'm a friend?"

"No. Yes. I—I mean—"

"Ugh, this is all so STUPID!"

"Silver."

"WHAT?"

He pointed above her head. She looked up. *Oh.* A thousand fat droplets of water hung in the air above her. Above Ash. Above the space between them. She suddenly became distinctly aware of the absence of bubbling water behind her. And then, in the next moment, she became equally aware of the strands of magic bleeding invisibly from her body into the air above her. The magic that was holding all that water up there. She became aware of the effort it was taking to *keep* it up there.

Well. Crap.

"I assume that's you?" Ash asked carefully. "I don't think it's me."

"Yes, Ash, it's me," she snapped, biting down her embarrassment. She was too old for this kind of uncontrolled release of magic. "Remember years ago when you concocted a layer of syrup and brought it down over my head? Well, I figured it was time to get you back."

His eyes narrowed a fraction. "You wouldn't dare."

She inhaled deeply, and her voice was low and steady when she answered. "You know there's nothing I wouldn't dare."

His brows inched up. "Here? While you're wearing that dress? And with your hair and makeup all perfectly—"

She let go. And even though she was expecting it, she still gasped and tensed as the deluge struck her. It was over within seconds, every droplet now soaking into the earth, leaving her and Ash completely drenched. She couldn't help it. She started laughing.

He blinked at her through the water clinging to his eyelashes. "I can't believe you did that."

She laughed even harder. "Really? Do you even know me at all?"

He shook his head, but there was an undeniable smile on his lips now. "Okay. You're right. I can totally believe you did that." He wiped a hand over his face, then sighed. "Silver, I'm really sorry about—"

"Can we just pretend the last few weeks never happened?" she blurted out.

He hesitated for barely a second before answering. "Yes. Absolutely. Thank you. *Thank you.* And I'm *so* sorry. Things have been so weird, and I hated it."

"Ugh, me too. It was horrible. But I didn't know how to get things back to the way they were before."

"I know, me neither." He gave her a tentative smile. "So … are we okay?"

"Yes." If they could take a gigantic step over the past few weeks and all the embarrassing shouting she'd just done, then they were good. "I think we're okay. Or at least, we will be." She answered his smile with a hesitant one of her own. "Should we go back inside, or … I don't know, maybe you should go back and I'll go home. Pretty sure at least half the ballroom heard me yelling at you. I think I might get some strange looks if I go back in there."

"Have you forgotten we're both dripping wet? I don't think either of us will be welcomed back into the ballroom."

"Oh, right." Silver looked down at herself, then ran her hands over the damp lace that clung to her arms. Now that her anger had fizzled away, she felt terrible about soaking the dress Mom had spent her precious spare hours on.

"You didn't ruin it," Ash said, as if he could read her mind. "You still look beautiful."

"Oh. Um …" Her cheeks burned again. "Thanks."

"I-I mean ... objectively."

"Of course."

"I'm sorry. We're supposed to be working on *not* being weird, and I'm just making things worse."

She laughed. "Don't worry about it. Maybe it'll take a little bit of time."

He nodded. "Yeah. Maybe." Then he took a deep breath, looked around, hesitated, and then asked, "Do you ... want to dance?"

"Out here?"

"Well, we've already established we're probably not welcome in the ballroom."

"True. Okay, sure." She shrugged, hoping the movement looked natural. Inside, she was trying to figure out how her brain would continue sending commands to her feet with Ash standing so close to her. She forced herself to focus on other things: the damp grass tickling her feet, her wet dress brushing against her ankles, the music in the distance.

Ash moved closer, took her right hand in his, and placed his other arm around her. His fingers skimmed over her bare skin before his hand settled at the small of her back. *Also* bare skin. A tiny gasp of breath caught at the back of her throat. *Oh holy courts, please tell me he didn't hear that!* She swallowed and forced herself to take a normal breath. *Don't freak out, don't freak out, DON'T FREAK OUT.* She concentrated on the music emanating from the ballroom and cleared her throat. "Um, what dance is this?"

"I have no idea."

"Really?" She looked up at him and forced her lips into a teasing smile. "I thought you knew everything."

"I don't know *everything*."

"Right, sure." She laughed and felt herself relax a little. This she could do. Teasing, joking. This was their thing. This was *normal*.

Ash's eyes crinkled at the corners as he smiled back at her. "I honestly have no clue. Maybe we should just, like ... sway?"

"Okay." So they started swaying. And Silver kept breathing. And this was … okay. This was enough. There didn't need to be *more* between them as long as she had this. Her best friend. Not ignoring her.

"I really am sorry," Ash said eventually, as Silver made sure to keep staring over his shoulder instead of up at his face. "About the past few weeks. I never wanted it to be like that. I know we were still hanging out in a group, but somehow … I still missed you."

"I know what you mean. I missed you too. But now … this …" She dared to look up and meet his eyes. "It feels almost normal again." That wasn't entirely true, but perhaps if she kept telling herself this, she would eventually believe it. What was more important was that Ash believed it.

"Yeah," he said quietly, his honey-gold eyes never leaving hers. "Things feel right again."

Look away now, she told herself. *Look away, look away.* But she couldn't. Ash didn't look away either.

A moment passed.

Another moment.

Another moment.

Too long, Silver thought, as she sensed something change between them. But still she held his gaze, and he held hers, and somehow she felt it all the way down to her toes. Her heart thrummed faster, and she was hyperaware of his touch, the imprint of his hand against her lower back almost like a brand. Her every nerve ending seemed to be on fire. And then—

He kissed her.

It was featherlight, tentative. Somehow both strangely foreign—this was *Ash*!—and blissfully right. Her stomach dipped. Her eyes glided shut. Ash's lips moved with more pressure against hers, and his hand pressed firmly against her back. She wasn't sure how it happened, but she was vaguely aware of her own hands sliding around his neck and tangling in his damp hair. Then his fingers slipped beneath the edge of the fabric that skirted her lower back and pressed into the skin at her waist. Her breath caught—far more audibly this time—as he pulled her tighter against him.

This, this, *this*. This was what she wanted. How could she ever have thought that *just friends* was enough? It would never be enough. Not after this.

His mouth was hot against hers, and something like the delicate crackle and zap of magic tingled on her tongue as it touched his. A shiver rushed up her spine as Ash deepened the kiss. Seconds, minutes, an eternity—she had zero concept of time right now. Then he was dragging his lips along her jaw and pressing kisses against her neck and beneath her ear. "You," he murmured breathlessly. "You are everything I want." And her heart exploded with happiness.

"Silver?"

She sprang away from Ash, her face flushed. Blinking rapidly, as if she'd woken abruptly from a dream, she cast her gaze about for the owner of the familiar voice. And there she was, standing beside one of the rose bushes. *Not* dressed in her ballgown. "Mom?"

Mom hesitated, her eyes moving back and forth between Silver and Ash. And the look on her face … was that *sadness*? Then she took a quick breath. "I'm sorry, Silver girl, but we have to go. Right now."

Silver frowned. "Now? But—"

"It's urgent."

"There you are!" Now it was Dad stepping around the rose bush, and Silver barely had a second for mortification to crawl across her skin before Dad was darting past Mom and grabbing Silver's arm.

"Dad, what's—"

"Not here. Let's go."

"But what about—"

"Now, Silver!" It wasn't anger, but fear, and it was chilling enough to keep Silver from arguing any further as her father tugged her across the grass and away from Ash.

"What happened?" Ash called after them. "What's wrong?" Silver looked back to see him following hastily.

"Go back to the ballroom, Ash," Dad said. "Now." Then he and Mom were dragging Silver through the gardens and around the side of the manor house, refusing to answer her questions, muttering shaky half sentences to each other, and then before Silver could process what was happening—before she could even look back in search of Ash—they were disappearing into the darkness of the faerie paths.

TWENTY-NINE

now

A YELP ESCAPES MY LIPS AS I'M DRAGGED ACROSS THE FLOOR beneath the water droplet curtain and into the utter darkness of what is usually the vibrant, colorful Rainbow Room. "Got you." The voice is a labored grunt in my ear. Greenwood. "Figured I'd station myself by the door once I found it and wait for you to get there." His hands are hooked beneath my arms. "You won't be making it out of this club a—" I swing both fists back as hard as I can. He cries out as I strike his head.

Then another set of hands grabs my ankles, and suddenly I'm sliding swiftly back out across the polished floor of the entrance area. Unfortunately, Greenwood is with me this time, also on the floor now. Shouts greet my ears, and Greenwood scrambles close enough to hook an arm around my neck. His other hand is grabbing a guardian knife from the air, and my own hands are pulsing with magic, and—

Thwip.

Something shoots past my face, there's a yell in my ear, and then Ash is pulling me swiftly onto my feet. I spin back around to face Greenwood, magic still sparking around my fingertips. A glittering gold arrow has pierced straight through his shoulder, adding a second wound to his left arm. With his right, he releases the knife and grabs a sword instead—

Another *thwip*, and then another, and two more arrows protrude from his body. He collapses against the wall beside the water curtain. "You," he gasps, glaring at Ash. "You're a traitor to the—"

"Put your dirty hands on anyone I love *ever again* and I will kill you," Ash snarls. Then he reaches for my hand, and just before he can grab it, I release all the magic I've been gathering into a shield layer that ripples across the whole foyer. Then we turn and make for the pair of glass doors.

The two bouncers stand with magic sparkling around their hands. Their expressions suggest they're considering attempting to stop us, but Ash lifts one arm, displaying the now visible guardian marking on his wrist. "Guild business," he snaps as we push past them. "I suggest you don't get involved."

We hurry down the steps. "Faerie paths," I tell him.

"I know." He's already pulling a stylus out of his pocket. Once we're beyond the glamour layer and I can no longer see The Gilded Canary, he stops and raises his hand to the wall.

"Quickly, quickly, quickly," I mutter, half my attention still back inside the foyer where my shield magic feels like it's starting to take strain. If the other councilors found their way out of the Rainbow Room —if they're busy blasting my shield with their magic—we won't be safe for long.

A doorway to the faerie paths spreads across the wall. And then I feel an invisible snap. My shield is gone. "Ash—"

"Hey!" The shout comes from just behind us.

"Go!" I shout, and we dive into the darkness together.

"Don't think," he tells me as we fall through the nothingness, and I struggle to keep glimpses of numerous locations from flickering through my mind.

"*Oof!*" I strike the ground and roll a few times before coming to a halt. Earth, leaves, trees, moonlight. Wisps of mist. I pull a breath into my lungs. "Is this Stormsdrift?"

"Yes. I recognize this spot. We're close to the river. Faerie paths must be working right now."

"Stormfae," I say, pushing myself hurriedly to my feet. It's the first time I've uttered the word since reading Mom's journal.

A good few paces away from me, Ash is on his feet too. He has a crossbow raised. My hands are up, magic pouring to my fingertips again. We wait, breathing hard, eyes combing the shadows around us. I'm half expecting the councilors to follow us here—wouldn't put it past Greenwood to have placed some kind of tracking magic on me while we were still in the club—but the seconds tick by and no one shows up. No shadowy black mist seeps across the ground to morph into a ferocious creature. No threatening fae beast leaps from the shadows. Still, we wait. I hear the quiet rush of the river, and the buzzing hum of insects, and the distant rumble of thunder. I see glow-bugs dotting the fronds of a fern.

Eventually, Ash lets his crossbow disappear. I lower my hands. Slowly, we face each other. "I'm sorry again," he says. "About everything back there. I'm sorry I couldn't warn you. And I know it was a huge risk, but we were completely outnumbered. We wouldn't have made it out of there without the Guild's help. But look." He reaches behind him and lifts the back of his shirt. When he brings his hand back around, something sharp and glittering sits within his grip: the Icicle Pendant of the First Seelie Queen. "We did it," he says.

My lips part as I stare at it. We did it. We actually did it.

Ash places it reverently on a pile of leaves and takes a step back. "I'm half afraid this thing might break and explode all over me. Though I suppose if it survived everything that happened back at the club, it's not as fragile as it looks." He peers across the space at me. "Silver, we did it," he says again.

"We did it," I repeat in a whisper. He was on my side all along, and we got the crystal, and we're both alive, and he said he loves me, and *we can actually do this*. We can fix this entire mess. I can get my life back. Not the same as it was before—it'll never be the same without Mom and Dad—but as close enough as possible.

"Are you okay?" Ash asks tentatively.

"Yes." I'm better than okay. So much better than okay.

I love you.

The words ring in my head. The glow in my chest is so warm, so expansive, it's a wonder it hasn't burst from my chest to bathe the entire forest in light. "You love me," I murmur.

He hesitates, then says, "Yes. I'm sorry if I freaked you out with that. You don't have to say anything back to me. I just … I always regretted not telling you before. Another mistake I didn't want to repeat."

There is too much space between us right now. Way. Too. Much. Space. I start walking toward him, a smile tugging irresistibly at my lips. "Handcuffing me." I keep walking. "Dragging me through a dark room." Still walking. "Threatening my enemies." Just another few steps. "If you wanted me to kiss you …" I stop right in front of him and tilt my head up to meet his eyes. "All you had to do was ask nicely."

He blinks. And then his lips curve into a wide smile. His hands rise to cup my cheeks, to slide into my hair, to pull me closer. His eyes travel my face, drinking in … something. "*There* you are," he whispers, and then he kisses me.

I've spent so much time trying to convince myself I don't care about him anymore that I'd almost forgotten how much I want this. How much I want *him*. But it comes back in a startling, heady, heart-pounding rush. My lips are pressed hard against his, and my arms are snaking around him, my fingers digging into the muscles of his back. It's nothing like our first kiss outside the ballroom years ago that began so tentatively. This kiss is fevered, desperate, as if we're trying to make up for all the time we've lost.

His hands slide downward, moving from my back to my waist to my thighs, and then he's hoisting me up and my legs are wrapped around him. His lips drag kisses down my breastbone. My back is against something rough and uncomfortable—a tree?—and I honestly couldn't care less. There is, however, a tiny voice at the back of my mind that tells me we *might* have other priorities right now. I struggle to focus on it. "Should we ... um ... maybe ... save the world first ..." My breath hitches as he presses harder against me. Heat curls and liquefies low in my belly. I swallow. "And then get back to this?"

"You've chosen a very inconvenient time—" he presses his lips to my chest, just above my fluttering heart "—to be right."

"I, um, didn't plan this. Trust me."

He turns me away from the tree and lowers me gently to the ground. His hands rise to my face again as our brows press together and our heavy breathing fill the quiet. "Okay," he says. "Okay. This is ..." He takes another steadying breath. "You're right. We need to get this done. Or ..."

"Or?"

"No. Never mind."

"What?"

"It's a very bad idea."

My lips curve up before I press another kiss to the side of his mouth. "Sounds like my kind of idea."

He laughs. It's a low, breathless rumble. "So ... the faerie paths seem to be working right now, which means it would take only a few seconds to get to my place, and you've never been there before, so maybe you want a quick ... tour."

My flushed cheeks burn even hotter. I bite my lip. "A quick tour?"

He hesitates. Swallows. "Bad idea. I know. It definitely wouldn't be quick. I would probably forget the rest of the world exists, and we would never leave, and who knows what would happen to Stormsdrift while you and I were busy ... doing ..."

"The tour," I fill in, unable to keep the laughter from my voice. "Of your house."

"Right."

The idea is tempting. A little bit terrifying, but mostly oh so tempting. I'm about to tell him to hold that invitation for when we're finished with everything else when *PAIN*—shocking, slicing, sudden pain—punches through my chest. Then again, jerking me against Ash. His gasp matches my own. I drag my eyes from his horrified gaze down to the sliver of space between us. There are two golden blades, long enough to pass through both my chest and his. I catch movement from the corner of my eye, then behind him, then to my right. Guardians surround us.

I try to draw breath.

Screaming fills my ears.

And then darkness blots everything out.

I blink. I'm standing in the forest, moonlight still streaming through the trees, dark shapes on the ground around me. It's like I'm waking from a dream, except … was I asleep? How could I have been asleep if I'm standing?

I look down at the ground. Blood and limbs and mangled—

I gasp and stagger backward, slapping a hand over my mouth and forcing my eyes away as my stomach turns. *What the holy heck happened here?* My hand is wet. I pull it quickly away from my mouth, and—

Blood. There is blood on my hand. Both hands. And now it's on my mouth. My body heaves, and then I'm leaning over, palms pressed to my knees as I vomit on the grass. It's barely over when a sickening idea punches me in the gut: Did *I* do this?

The thought is so horrendous I immediately reject it. No. There is no way this was me. I've done terrible things before, but I've never done anything like this, and I've always been aware of my actions. And wasn't I impaled by a sword? Two swords? I would have been incapable of causing damage like this.

The thought brings my attention suddenly and sharply to the pain throbbing in my abdomen, just beneath my ribcage. I wonder how I'm even able to breathe right now, but I suppose I've started healing already. I'm not sure how long I blacked out for. I press my hand against the wounds, not wanting to take a closer look. I'm sure I'll be—

Where is Ash? The question hits me with as much shock and terror as the sight of all this gore surrounding me. Ash should be here. Why isn't he here? Panic clambers up my throat as I look around. Nonononono, where is he, why am I the only one standing here, *where is he?*

He can't … he can't be …

I let my gaze fall slowly to the bodies that are literally torn to shreds. My vision begins to turn white, and I blink hastily. I can't pass out now. With a sob in the back of my throat, I force myself to crouch down and take a closer look. I see Seelie guard uniforms. Parts of them, at least. Were all these guardians from the Seelie Court?

And then I see something that makes my blood drain instantly from my face: A hand. With a simple gold band on the smallest finger.

I'm breathing fast. Too fast. I'm going to pass out. This isn't happening. This is a nightmare. This *can't be real.*

A snarling howl.

A *yip, yip* and then a screech.

I scramble to my feet and whirl around. My head spins, and my chest aches, and I can hardly breathe, and—

A dark shape leaps from the shadows. I throw myself sideways, trip over something, and land among the roots of a tree. The wound in my chest screams at me, and my lungs beg for air. My fingers fumble with my back pocket, trying to find my stylus, and in my peripheral vision I catch a glimpse of the creature spinning around, kicking something aside, and moving closer. I think it's the same type of creature that chased us through the Gauntlet. *Stormfae*, my mind whispers.

I finally get hold of the stylus, but my fingers are trembling so badly I almost drop the darn thing. I write shakily, far too slowly, and then the thing lunges at me and I have to roll out of the way. It catches itself against the tree and swings itself around. Long claws rake the air. A doorway opens on the ground. I scramble toward it—

And I tumble into the darkness, my broken mind clinging only to the thought of safety, of *home*.

THIRTY

then

"THEY'RE ACCUSING US OF MURDER."

"What?" Silver blinked. She must have heard wrong. That couldn't *possibly* be what Dad had just said.

"Two councilors. Dead." Dad rushed across the living room and into the home study he shared with Mom. "Because of some—some fae creature we've never encountered before. Bergenfell saw. She *saw* what happened, but she's blaming us for—"

"We don't have time for this!" Mom interrupted as she grabbed a book from the shelf behind the couch. She turned back to Silver. "You need to change. Quickly. You can't run in that dress. Grab any essentials. We'll shrink everything and—"

"Stop, just stop," Silver said, her voice unnaturally high, her hands pressed to the sides of her face. "I don't understand any of this. Where … what are you talking about? What creature? Which councilors? Why are they blaming *you*?"

Mom ducked around the couch and stopped in front of Silver, taking her hand and gripping it tightly. "There's a door. In the Shadow Crypt. A faerie door. Usually hidden by a glamour. We found it and …" Mom's eyes darted past Silver toward Dad, and Silver remembered, with

306

sudden clarity, an evening long ago when she and Ash had snuck down to the Shadow Crypt and it had seemed, in the moment just before they left, that one of the walls inside had vanished to reveal another room.

"Something came through," Mom said, looking at Silver again. "This creature. It was …" She shook her head and pushed a few tangles of silver hair out of her face. Her eyes squeezed shut. Her face crumpled a bit as she whispered, "Storm and shadow. That's where they came from. That's what he told me. And he was right. But they're so much worse in reality."

Dad strode across the room and turned both Mom and Silver toward the stairs. "Like you said. We don't have time for this. We can explain everything later. And if … if we can't … Silver, there's a journal—"

"What?" Silver asked as Dad steered them toward the stairs.

"Mom's journal. She wrote about … about all of this."

"All of *what*? I thought this only just happened tonight. This—this *murder* accusation." Dad was ahead of her now, dragging her up the stairs so quickly she would have tripped if she hadn't been hanging onto him.

"Yes. But there's … more."

They reached the landing between the bedrooms, and Mom darted ahead. She dropped the book she'd been carrying onto the bed and grabbed an empty bag from the wardrobe. "Should have tried harder," she was muttering. "Should have just destroyed the darn thing."

"We *did* try!" Dad said. "You know we did. We've tried everything we could think of except—"

"Except the one thing that was impossible to find, I know."

"Dad, you … you said there's more," Silver said, blinking and shaking her head. "In a *journal*?" None of this was making sense.

"Okay, Silver, listen to me." Dad stopped in the doorway to the bedroom and gripped Silver's shoulders. "If something happens to Mom and me, you need to go to our spot. The study spot. Just off the Canopy Way. You'll find the journal there. It'll tell you everything about—"

"What do you mean *if something happens to you?* Dad, this is … this is insane. Why are we running from this? If you're innocent, then … then you tell them that. You take a truth potion and answer questions. Everyone will know Bergenfell's lying."

His grip tightened on her shoulders, but his tone was gentle as he said, "We're running, bug, because they want to kill us."

All she could do was stare at him. *Kill us.* This made *no* sense.

"Do you understand?" he asked. "They're coming for us. And not to lock us up. *We have to go.*"

She nodded. "O-okay." And then she ran to her room, already peeling her wet dress off. Such a waste of a beautiful gown when she'd been in the ballroom for less than half an hour. One half of her distracted, terrified, confused brain zeroed in on this silly thought, while the other half screamed at her that this was so *not important right now*! Who cared about a dress when people wanted to *kill* Mom and Dad?

And what if—what if she never saw Ash again? The thought hit her in the same way the deluge of water droplets had: sudden, cold, shocking. She stared across the room, standing in nothing but her underwear, seeing the rose bushes and the sculptures and Ash walking toward her. Their kiss already felt like it had happened in another lifetime. To a person who had all the time in the world, not someone who was—

No. She and Ash would still have time. This wasn't the end. Mom and Dad would fix this. They would run, find somewhere safe to hide, and fix this. There were plenty of other trustworthy guardians out there.

Silver shook herself back into action, grabbing the clothes she'd been wearing earlier—which she'd tossed onto the bed before getting ready for the ball—and pulling them back on. *Essentials,* Mom had said. She needed to pack essentials. But what was truly essential when your *life* was at stake?

Her eyes landed on the little silver bird from Ash, still attached to its chain and lying on the table beside her bed. She grabbed it and put it on. Of all the things she owned, this certainly felt essential. Her guardian trainee pendant was also on the table, and she looped that over her head too. She would need it at whatever Guild they ended up at. Another ache pierced her chest. The *Stormsdrift* Guild was where she was supposed to be. Not some other Guild without Ash and Remy and Odette and the rest of the Blackburns. *No, we're going to fix this*, she told herself again. *This is all just a horrible mistake.*

"Silver?"

"Freaking—" She whipped around, one hand pressed to her chest and the other reaching into the air for a knife. When she saw it was Ash standing behind her, she let go. The knife vanished with a faint sparkle. "Holy crap, you scared me," she breathed. Then she launched across the room and threw her arms around him.

"What's going on?" he asked, wrapping his arms around her just as tightly. "I came from the Guild. The things I overheard … I mean, none of it's *true*, is it? It can't be."

She shook her head, still holding onto him. And as they stood there, arms around one another, she quickly told him the few garbled bits of information her parents had shared.

"That's *crazy*," Ash said, stepping back when she was finished. He held her hands in his. "I didn't know what to believe when I heard Bergenfell addressing everyone."

Ice crystalized in Silver's blood. "What was she saying? What did you hear?"

"I went straight to the Guild after your parents took you from the manor house gardens. I know I wasn't supposed to be listening in, but—"

"*What did she say?*" Silver asked with more urgency.

"She was in one of the meeting rooms with a bunch of guardians, and she was telling them … she was saying that Nelina and Rowan Wren are highly dangerous and need to be brought in immediately. That two councilors discovered they're spies, and because of this, your parents killed those two councilors. Apparently your parents were already questioned under the influence of truth potion earlier this evening—"

"What? No they weren't."

"—and it was revealed that they've secretly been gathering information about various Guilds and passing it back to the Unseelie Court for the past ten years."

"*What?*"

"And then they escaped the Guild."

"This is absolute insanity."

"Silver, are you …" Ash searched her face, his beautiful amber eyes intent. His voice was lower when he continued. "Are you sure your parents have told you the truth?"

Silver's heart dropped like a rock in ice water. Her hands, still clasping Ash's, went cold. "You think I'm *lying* to you?"

His eyes widened. "No, absolutely not! I'm wondering if *they're* not being entirely truthful with *you*. I just … I don't understand why Bergenfell would say these things—why the whole Council would say these things—if they weren't true. Councilor Poppywood was there, and Councilor Eryn, and two others. And they were all saying the same thing."

"*What?*" Silver's hands slipped out of Ash's as she took a step backward. "They're all *lying*, Ash. I don't know why, but they're lying about this."

"Silver, who are you—" Dad was suddenly in the doorway, his startled expression quickly turning to something that looked a lot like anger. "How did he get in here?" he demanded, looking at Silver. "I didn't hear anyone come up the stairs."

"Through—through the faerie paths," Silver stammered. "He has access. From—from years ago. I gave him—"

"You *what*? Silver, I told you never, ever to do that. Your home is meant to be your sanctuary. The one place you can be certain you—"

"Dad, it's just Ash! He would never—"

"You need to go," Dad said to Ash as he strode across the room. He grabbed a stylus from among the dozens of items scattered across Silver's desk and used it to open a doorway against the wall.

"Um … okay. But—"

"Now."

After one last uncertain glance between Silver and her father, Ash moved toward the doorway. He turned to face her, walking backward into the paths. "I—I'll see you soon. Okay? I'll find you. I promise."

"Ash—" She stepped toward him, her hand rising automatically, but the darkness of the faerie paths had already swallowed him up. She blinked at the wall, her eyes filling with tears.

"Silver—"

"Dad, it's just *Ash*," she repeated in a whisper, tears in her eyes now. "He would never do anything to us."

"I know, bug, I'm sorry." Dad pulled her tight against him. "I'm sorry, I'm sorry. But we can't trust anyone. Not anymore. And we don't have time for lengthy conversations and goodbyes. Get whatever you need. You've got two minutes and then we're leaving."

Silver's brain was somewhere else as she grabbed a few items of clothing, her spare styluses, and some bottles from the bathing room. She had no idea if what she'd collected even made sense. All she could see inside her head was Ash's face as he disappeared into the paths. She kept replaying his words. *I'll see you soon. Okay? I'll find you. I promise.*

Back in her parents' room, she threw her things into the bag on Mom and Dad's bed. Dad zipped it and began the spell to shrink it, while Mom lifted the book she'd brought up here earlier. She flipped it open, and within a hollow space cut into the pages sat a small glass vial of orange-red liquid. It glowed, then shifted to black, then glowed again. It cycled repeatedly through these colors, like embers in a dying fire.

"What's that? Silver asked.

"Shadowfire potion."

"*Shadowfire?* Holy fae, Mom, doesn't that take days to concoct?"

"Yes. I brewed it months ago. I thought … I thought we might need to leave in a hurry at some point, and we can't have anyone finding any of the notes we may have left lying around. The journal isn't the only thing I wrote in. And there are … there are the pages I tore out."

"Wait, you—you're going to *burn our house down*?"

"Come on," Dad said before Mom could answer. He tucked the miniature bag into his pocket and took Silver's hand. They hurried downstairs, and before Silver could ask any more questions, Mom had pulled the stopper from the vial and tossed at least half the liquid into the center of their living room.

The flames were instant. Black and oddly translucent, they roared to life and devoured everything they touched. Silver took a hurried step back, along with Mom and Dad. She knew about shadowfire, but she'd never seen it before. It was difficult to make and absolutely *not* to be messed around with. It couldn't be extinguished. Not by anything. And now it was burning through her home, her world, her everything.

There was no going back from this.

THIRTY-ONE

now

I LAND WITH A THUMP ON THE FLOOR BESIDE A FAMILIAR COUCH. Teddy shrieks and leaps off the couch in a single bound. Duke is up a moment later. They pause, blinking at me. *"Silver?"* they both say at the same time.

Teddy and Duke. I thought of home, and the paths brought me to them. I sit up. *Breathe, just breathe, just breathe.* But my chest is so *tight*, and my body won't stop shaking, and Ash is … is … is he really *dead*?

I realize Teddy's crouching on the floor beside me. He or Duke must have turned the TV off, because it's suddenly quiet in here. "Hey, it's okay, it's okay," he says. But it's not okay. He has no idea how very *not okay* everything is. "You need to calm down so you can breathe."

But I can't. I can't breathe I can't breathe I can't—

Duke hunkers down in front of me and pulls me against his broad chest. One large hand presses my head gently against his shoulder while his other arm comes around me. "Cupcakes," he says in a voice so low I feel it more than hear it. "The ones with the rainbow frosting. Remember how you squashed one on top of my head when it was my birthday? And you know that TV show with the dumbass boss and all the useless employees? That one with the guy and girl who took forever

313

to figure out they should be together? Remember when we binged an entire day's worth of episodes and ate nothing but pizza?"

My breaths start to come easier as my brain latches onto his words and follows them, picturing everything he's saying.

"Sunflowers. Teddy's ridiculous bunny slippers. That time I tried to swat a fly with a rolling pin and left a hole in the wall."

I inhale another shaky breath. Part of my brain keeps forcing me to see those bodies and limbs lying in the forest—horrific images competing with cupcakes and sunflowers and TV show characters—but Duke's soothing voice shuts them out again and again. I can't forget Ash, though. I can't forget that he's …

"Whatever it is," Duke says. "You're going to be okay."

I shake my head. Now that it's easier to breathe, it's also easier to cry. Tears start to fall down my cheeks. I take a sniffly breath and swipe them away.

"Silver," Teddy says carefully. "There's blood on your face. And your hands."

"I know." I swallow. "It isn't mine. At least … I suppose some of it is. Two swords went clean through me, so—"

"What?"

"I'll be fine," I say faintly. "It hurts, but … it's already healing. It's not as though I'm—" *Like you*, I finish silently. *It's not as though I'm human.* I'd probably be dead by now if I was like Teddy and Duke. If I had no magic pulsing through my body.

My brain chooses this moment to remind me that I literally fell straight through the air onto their floor. *Also* something humans shouldn't be able to do. But if they're not going to mention it, then neither am I.

"Do you want to … maybe … clean your face?" Teddy suggests. "And your hands?"

All I really want is to curl up on the floor and never move again, but I suppose I should be grateful they're not calling an ambulance and insisting I go to hospital. So I climb to my feet, take Teddy's arm, and let him lead me to the bathroom. After a brief whispered discussion with Duke behind my back, he returns to my side. He fusses around me with a washcloth and some warm water while I try not to look in the mirror. My eyes land on the bottle of mouthwash, which brings my attention to the vomit taste in my mouth. I twist the cap off the bottle and rinse a few times.

When we return to the couch, Duke is busy moving aside a blue vase of flowers on the coffee table to make room for a sandwich on a plate and a glass of water. He hands me the water as I sit, and I take a small sip before leaning forward to set it beside the plate. And then I freeze. Like a shot of ice to my veins, I go instantly cold. There's something sitting on the other end of the coffee table. Two somethings, to be precise. Two somethings that *should not be here.*

"That's … an amber. And a stylus."

"Yes," Teddy says absently as he sits, tugging his fluffy robe tighter around himself.

I look at him. *Really* look at him. And I repeat the words slowly. "An amber and a stylus."

He frowns. "I know that's—" He stops. His eyes grow wide. He draws in a slow breath. "Shitness."

"You're not human," I whisper, and it's all I can do to get the words past my lips as the foundation of the life I thought I'd built over the past year and a bit crumbles to dust, leaving a gaping hole for every happy memory I share with these two people to fall into and disappear.

I am alone.

I am truly alone.

Teddy turns his panicked gaze toward Duke. "You didn't put them away!" he hisses.

Duke ignores him. He steps closer, watching me. "Firstly," he says carefully, lifting his hands and displaying his palms as if in surrender. "You should know that it was nothing personal."

"Nothing *personal?*" I start laughing. Somewhat hysterically. And then as quickly as it appeared, the laughter is gone and I'm yelling, *"It sure as hell feels personal right now!"*

"Silver—"

"Wow. *Wow.*" I'm vaguely aware that I should be getting the hell out of here. But I can't move. I can hardly think. Everything I thought I knew—the two most important relationships I've formed since leaving Stormsdrift—it's all been a lie. I thought I was finally the one in control, but that was never true.

"We didn't go looking for something like this," Duke says. "I swear. She came to us. And she didn't exactly give us a choice."

She.

She.

A shiver skitters across the back of my neck, and my hands are instantly sweaty. "So she's ... she's known all along where I was. I can't believe this. It doesn't make sense." I try to blink away the image of painted lips and glossy hair, but it doesn't work. My ears ring with the sharp echo of pointed heels—*click, click, click*—and even as I squeeze my eyes shut, I see her perfect silhouetted form sauntering down a shadowed hallway toward me.

I whirl away from the memory and push myself up from the couch. "When? When did she come to you? How long have you been spying on me for her?"

They exchange a glance before Duke answers. "For as long as you've been living in this world."

"When you slipped into May's Coffee Corner that evening," Teddy continues, "lost and desperate, we followed you. We put up the notice about the available apartment—when you weren't looking. We made sure there was someone friendly there to help you. To point out the vacant apartment. The apartment right next to ours that *she* made sure was vacant."

"Unbelievable." I'm shaking my head now, and my hands are twisting together. "You guys are good, you know that? I believed *all* of it. You were so kind, so welcoming and friendly. And it was because you already knew that I was a broken mess. You knew I'd fall for your charms because I was—"

"We didn't," Teddy says. "We actually expected you to kick us out the first time we came over and offered—"

"And when Ash showed up and those bloodtongues ripped half my apartment to bits a few days ago," I continue, "you pretended to be so shocked. So concerned. Demanding to know what was going on, what I'd gotten myself mixed up in." I let out a quiet scoff. "I believed every moment of it."

"We *were* concerned," Duke insists, his tone so earnest I almost believe him, "so of course we asked. I didn't think you'd reveal anything magical, but I thought you might tell us *something* that would enable us to help you in some—"

"*Help* me? Are you kidding? You've been spying on me since before I even knew the two of you existed, so why would you want to help me?"

"Because believe it or not," Teddy says, "we actually care about you."

"Oh please. Don't even start. It may have *seemed* like that when you were calling the cops to report whoever had attacked me—" I stop abruptly. "Except … you didn't call them, did you. You wouldn't have. That was *her*." Another shiver climbs up my spine.

"Yes," Teddy says quietly. "And we kept the rest of the nosy neighbors away. We obviously weren't the only ones who heard the commotion. We had multiple people up here wanting to know what was going on. And the cops showed up anyway because someone else must have called them."

"Oh, poor Teddy. Having to lie to the cops. I'll bet that was just *horrible* for you."

"Silver—"

"So you guys are—what? Halflings? Faeries whose colors I can't see?"

Teddy lets out a defeated sigh. "Faeries."

"Right, of course," I mutter. His hair is always dyed some shockingly bright color, and Duke's shiny head is always perfectly bald. There was no way for me to see the strands of faerie color in their hair that would have given them away. "Are you guys even together? Or is your entire relationship a sham too?"

"Of course we're together!" Teddy says, looking horrified. "You think we could fake a love like this?"

"I don't know, Teddy, you've been faking everything else!" I shout. "You pretended to believe that I was eighteen when I first got here, and that I had escaped a cult, and that my evening job was at a university library, and that I was actually *good* at baking. Which I'm not, by the way. The only reason I didn't totally mess up that job at The Frosted Tart was because I used magic whenever no one was looking. Which you probably knew all about! And you got me fake documents and a bank account and … and you even insisted I go to *counseling* after I told you I'd witnessed my own parents' deaths. I went there for *three months*!"

Teddy sniffs. "That really helped you."

"I know! You played this act so well that it literally changed my life!"

"That's because most of it wasn't an act," he says, blinking tears away.

"Don't," I tell him fiercely, pointing a finger at him. "Don't you *dare*. You do *not* get to cry about this." I let my hand fall to my side. "So what now? How does this end? Have you alerted her? Is she on her way?"

Duke shuts his eyes and shakes his head, but when he answers it's in the affirmative. "I've alerted her, yes. She'll be here soon."

"Well, thanks for the head start." My own stylus is probably somewhere on the floor near where I landed, so I swipe the one from the coffee table. I expect Teddy or Duke to try to stop me as I move to the nearest wall, but they don't. The reason becomes clear very quickly: the faerie paths don't seem to be accessible anymore.

"Ugh!" I throw the stylus onto the floor. "What did you do? Some spell to keep me in here? To block the paths? Is that what you were busy with while Teddy was so kindly helping me wash blood off my face?"

"Silver," Duke says, a wretchedness etched on his face. "You need to understand that we never—"

"I could kill you both. You know that, don't you? Even after being stabbed."

"Yes," he says. "We're well aware of that."

"So what's to stop me from doing that then?"

"Well …" Both their gazes land on the glass of water I barely took a sip of.

I nod in resignation, pressing my shaky lips together. "Fantastic," I whisper. "Your plan is to drug me." And even though I doubt a single sip is enough to knock me out, I heave a shaky sigh and feel myself give in. I can't do this. It's too much. Too hard. I have no family, Ash is dead, and my two dearest friends have been lying to me since the minute we met. I want out. Out. Out. *Out.* I don't want to live this life anymore.

"Guess I'd better get this over with then." I bend and pick up the glass. "Perhaps you could be so kind as to top it up with whatever nasty potion you added? Like, put as much as you possibly can in here. If I'm lucky, maybe it'll kill me."

They simply stare at me. I've never seen Teddy's gaze so wide. Duke's eyes shimmer with unshed tears. "Please," I whisper with shaking lips. "Please just make this all end." They don't move. I clench my jaw before taking a breath. "Fine." Then I lift the glass toward my lips.

"Wait!" Teddy lunges forward and smacks it out of my hand. It hits the floor and shatters.

There's a pause as we all stare at the broken pieces of glass scattered across a small pool of liquid.

Then Teddy jumps into action. He produces a stylus, snatches up the blue vase from the coffee table, and dumps the flowers onto the floor. He crouches down and begins hurriedly drawing patterns around the flowers while muttering at the same time. Anyone from this world would think him insane. Duke hesitates for another moment before his anguished expression smooths out and he joins Teddy in repeating the words of whatever spell they're doing.

I take a step back just as a bright flash illuminates the room. I squint, but the light is gone and something glitters on the walls. But that, too, vanishes a second later. Teddy rushes past me and writes on the wall, and this time, a doorway opens. He grabs my arm. "Go. You have to go. Now."

"Teddy—"

"Now!" He shoves me into the darkness. I see his lips moving, forming the words 'I'm sorry' as the edges of the doorway melt toward each other, and then he's gone.

Thirty-Two

I TUMBLE THROUGH THE ENDLESS VOID OF THE FAERIE PATHS AND this time, when I think of a location, my thoughts turn to the only other place I've ever felt safe and at home. A faint yellow-orange glow appears ahead of me. I stumble as I lurch from the faerie paths, but my footsteps are silent on the rug. The very same rug that's sat on this living room floor since I was a child. A lamp is on in the corner, the type that has an enchanted flame burning within a decorative glass cylinder. It bathes the aged, mismatched items of furniture in a faintly flickering glow.

I hold onto the arm of a couch and take a steadying breath. It smells like lemon tea and something warm and buttery sweet. The scent is so familiar that I'm instantly transported back in time. My breath hitches as a thousand memories bombard me. Tears ache behind my eyes. I do my best to blink them away as I look around. Aside from a few new items—different cushions on the two armchairs, the basket on the floor containing balls of wool and knitting needles, new plants placed around the room—everything I lay eyes on is achingly familiar.

A sob rises in my throat and I press a hand over my mouth, struggling to stifle it. This is all so *wrong*. Mom and Dad should be here. Ash should be here. How can this place—this perfect, cozy family room from my memories—exist in the same world where Mom, Dad and Ash *don't* exist?

The murmur of quiet voices reaches my ears. I turn, following the sound toward the kitchen. Iris and … Flynn? The second voice doesn't sound quite deep enough to be Lennox.

"… thought about contacting someone outside the Guild."

"Who?" Iris asks.

"I'll be honest, Mom. The less you know, the better. I'll do it when I get home later."

"Flynn …"

"Okay look. As far as I can tell, it's someone connected with those Griffin Gifted rebels. Someone with a special … well … gift. For finding people."

"I don't think that's—"

"And that's why I don't want to tell you anything more. Look, I don't want to go outside the Law any more than you do, but he's my *brother*. I'll do whatever I can to find him."

I squeeze my eyes closed and tears fall down my cheeks. What if they never find Ash because he's *dead?*

"I hope you're not suggesting that I *wouldn't* do anything—"

"No, Mom—"

"All I'm saying is that we need to tread very carefully now. We're *all* involved with the Guild. Well, aside from Tobin, but I'm sure they'd find a way to implicate him too. If we're seen to be going against the Guild, it won't end well for any of us."

I'm close enough to see her now, sitting at the kitchen table with her hands wrapped around a mug. Again, this scene is so familiar that I feel for a moment as if I've been flung back into the past. But that deep frown … the way she's staring into the steaming contents of her mug … that's the part that pulls me back to the present. The Iris in my memories never stared at her lemon tea like that.

I haven't quite reached the doorway yet, but if they look up, they'll see me. A ghost shrouded in the warm glow of their living room. I take one more step. "Iris?" My voice is smaller now than it's ever been inside this house. "Flynn?"

They're on their feet the second they lay eyes on me, chairs crashing to the floor, Iris's mug following a split second later. It shatters, sending steaming hot liquid across the floor. Flynn has a crossbow in his hand, glittering and deadly, pointed straight at me. Iris seems too horrified to do anything but stare. My next word is little more than a wobbly whisper. "Hi."

"Silver?" Iris says in a shaky tone. "It … can't be."

I press my trembling lips together as I nod. "It's me."

All they do is stare. Flynn doesn't release his weapon. I imagine what I must look like to them: a slightly older version of the girl who died more than two years ago, with puffy eyes, streaked makeup, and a torn, blood-stained, glittery top. I need to say something else. I need to explain. "They … they lied. The councilors. They killed Mom and Dad, but … I got away. I've been … hiding, and …" I press a hand to my mouth as more tears fall and speaking becomes harder. "And, um … Ash found me."

Flynn's crossbow vanishes. "Quicksilver," he murmurs.

Iris shoves her way past the fallen chairs, and then she's across the kitchen faster than anyone should be able to move, scooping me into her arms. "I can't believe it," she whispers into my ear. "I can't believe it."

I can't speak anymore. I wrap my arms around her and let myself cry the way I did when Ash held me in the water-filled room at The Gilded Canary. I cry the way I wish I could have cried straight after my parents died. I cry for all the time I've lost with these people I love so dearly. I cry for the life I used to dream of but will never have.

I feel more arms around me, but my eyes are squeezed shut, so it's only when my tears finally subside and I blink through puffy eyes that I see Lennox is here as well. He and Flynn lower their arms and move back as I attempt to disentangle myself from Iris. She wipes her fingers beneath her eyes, and when I turn to Lennox, he takes my face gently in his hands. "I thought I must have been imagining things when I heard Iris say your name. I can't believe it's really you."

I sniff and manage to say, "I kind of can't believe I'm here either. But, um …" I shake my head as a fresh wave of tears threatens to spill from my eyes. I haven't told them the worst part yet. "Ash," I whisper. "I think he's … I think he's …" I can't get the word out, but from the expressions on their faces, they've figured out what I'm trying to say.

Iris goes pale as she grips the edge of the table and lowers herself into a chair. But Lennox remains steady. His hand moves to my arm as he guides me to one of the other chairs that's still standing. "Why do you think that? Tell me exactly what happened." He sits beside me while Flynn rights the two fallen chairs.

In halting tones, I tell them about how we were ambushed in the Stormsdrift forest by guardians, and when I get to the part about seeing a disembodied hand with a gold ring on the smallest finger, I can hardly get the words past my shaking lips.

"That doesn't mean anything," Lennox says immediately. "Everyone at the Stormsdrift Guild has a ring like that now." He lifts his right hand to display his fingers, and I see the simple gold band he's wearing. My eyes dart to Iris's hand and then Flynn's, and I see the same thing. "Because of the monsters," Lennox says. "The unusual fae creatures. It's an emergency alert thing. So it could have been anyone from our Guild."

"I … oh." The relief that floods me is so powerful I feel lightheaded. Or perhaps that's due to the fact that the only decent meal I've had in the past two days is now sitting on the forest floor. Or because of the two swords that were shoved through my body not that long ago. I press a hand gingerly to my abdomen, but the pain isn't as bad as I expected.

"You said you were stabbed?" Iris says, her gaze following my hand. She stands quickly and moves around the side of the table. Her tone is businesslike now that we've established Ash might not be dead. But if that wasn't him … then where is he? And what if it *was* him?

"Silver?" Iris prompts. She's standing beside me, leaning down.

"Oh. Um, here." I lift the lower edge of my top.

"Come and lie down. On the couch. I can't see properly while you're sitting like that. Flynn, please get my emergency kit from—"

"On it," Flynn says, already halfway out of the kitchen.

"And Lennox, we should probably—"

"Contact the Guild to find out what they know about that attack. Definitely. Doing that now."

"Iris," I say, gripping her hand hard as she leads me out of the kitchen to one of the couches in the living room. "What if it *was* him? I saw Seelie Court uniforms on the guardians that attacked us. And they wouldn't have had those rings, would they? They're not from our Guild. I don't want to believe that that hand belongs to *him*, but what if—"

"Just lie down please," Iris says. Though her voice is still gentle, there's a tightness to it. "Lennox will find out as much as he can."

"Here, Mom," Flynn says, hurrying into the living room and dumping something I can't see onto one of the armchairs. "And I figured you'd ask for this in about five seconds, so …" He hands her a glass containing clear liquid. My brain immediately conjures an image of the glass Duke handed to me. The glass Teddy shattered. I blink the image away. Iris and Flynn are certainly not about to drug me.

"Thanks," Iris says, taking the glass while I carefully prop myself up on a pillow so I'm at enough of an angle to drink.

"Ugh, that's disgusting," I tell her after one sip.

She manages a smile as she digs through her emergency kit. "That's how you know it's the good stuff."

"I assume you want me to drink it all?"

"Yes. It's the equivalent of a hearty meal, with extra healing properties." She pushes my top up a little higher and examines the wounds I still haven't looked at myself. "These don't seem to be that bad," she says. "How long ago did this happen?"

"I … I'm not sure. Like I said, I blacked out for a bit. But I don't think it's been that long."

"Hmm. These should be far worse. The kind of wound you're

talking about … it should take you several *hours* at the very least to heal from something like that. Maybe even a day or more."

"That's … kind of weird. Maybe I just heal really quickly."

"Maybe," Iris says, though she looks doubtful, and I'm guessing we're both wondering what exactly happened to me during the time I blacked out. "Anyway, I don't think you need any extra healing magic. Just some food and a good sleep."

"Does that mean I don't have to drink this?" I ask, raising the glass I've had little more than a few sips from.

Instead of answering, her face twists with emotion and tears fill her eyes. She takes my face gently in both her hands and presses her brow to mine. "Silver, Silver, Silver girl, I can't believe it's *you*. Here on my couch. As if the last two years didn't even happen." She hesitates, then says, "Your parents …" I shut my eyes and take a deep breath, willing myself not to start crying all over again. "I'm so, so, so sorry. I can't imagine what you've been through. We miss them every single day. We never believed what the Guild told us. It just didn't make sense. The details didn't fit the people we knew your parents to be. And I know you must have found it almost impossible to keep going after losing them, but I'm so, so, so glad you survived, precious girl."

I fail. No way can I hold back tears when she's saying things like this. I lean forward and hug her again, careful not to spill the contents of the glass. "Thanks, Iris," I manage to whisper. "I missed you too. Like … *so* much." I let out a snuffly laugh. "I was, um, confused about so many things after I left." I decide to leave it at that instead of bringing up the fact that I believed Ash may have tried to kill me. "I didn't know who I could trust. So I never came back. I almost ran again when Ash found me, but … well, he convinced me things were getting bad here."

"Things *are* getting bad here. These *monsters* …" She pulls back, shaking her head. "Sorry, they're technically fae, but they're so savage, so bloodthirsty. Everyone around here just calls them monsters now."

"I've, um, met one or two," I say as I sit up properly and swing my legs over the side of the couch. "And I'm pretty sure it was one of them who tore all those Seelie Court guardians to shreds," I add quietly.

"Yes," Flynn says, and I realize he's still in the room, sitting on one of the armchairs. "I was thinking the same thing."

"Same here," Iris says. "And as for your question about *that* …" She points to the glass in my hand. "I strongly suggest you drink it all *and* eat some food. We've had dinner already, but I can heat up leftovers for you if you'd like."

"I just spoke with Ursula," Lennox says, walking into the living room before I can answer Iris. At the sound of Bergenfell's name, a chill crawls across my body. I lift the glass to my lips, shut my eyes, and force myself to focus on the revolting flavor and not on the image of Councilor Bergenfell swinging a sword down toward my mother's—

I swallow, try not to gag, and force myself to drink again.

"And what did she say?" Iris asks. "Does the Guild know about this attack in the forest?"

"Yes, they're aware of it. She wouldn't confirm any names, but she said they don't believe Ash was one of the victims."

Iris sucks in a breath and gasps, "Ohthankgoodness."

I press my hand to my mouth as tears threaten yet again. I honestly shouldn't have any left at this point. Part of me feels terrible for the guardians whose lives ended out there in the forest tonight. I'm sure they had families, loved ones. But they also tried to *kill* us, so I can't muster complete heartbreak for them. Mostly, my relief that Ash wasn't among them is blotting everything else out.

"She made some subtle comment," Lennox adds, "insinuating Ash might be partly *responsible*—"

"*What?*" Iris demands.

"—but I ended the call before I could ask her if she really meant what it sounded like she meant."

"How *dare* she?"

"Well, she's already made accusations about Ash over the past few days. It's hardly surprising she's adding one more."

"Wait," I say, leaning forward and resting my elbows on my knees. "Those rings you were talking about. You said they're some kind of emergency alert? So that means they can be tracked, right? Can we use Ash's ring to find him?"

They're already shaking their heads before I'm finished, and I realize this is so obvious that if it were possible they would, of course, have done it by now. "They don't work that way," Lennox says. "At least, they *can* be tracked, but only when the emergency charm inside a particular ring is triggered."

I think back to that moment inside The Gilded Canary when Riven's people surrounded us and Ash let go of me so he could press one hand tightly over the other. He must have been doing something with his ring. That's why a bunch of councilors from the Stormsdrift Guild showed up soon afterward.

"Someone at the Guild crafted them after the monsters started getting out of control," Flynn explains, "so we can call for assistance if we're out in Stormsdrift alone and happen to be attacked. Everyone else wearing a ring is alerted. Whoever's available can respond."

"Okay, so … I think Ash triggered his emergency alert charm earlier this evening. We were at a club. In, um, a difficult position. He figured it was the only way out. But it was only councilors who showed up. Were you all busy then?"

"Ash was the one who sent that?" Lennox says. He looks at Iris. "We didn't know. When the signal comes through, we can't see who sent it. We can only follow it to its origin if we choose to. But the Council *can* see who sent it. So they must have seen it was Ash and then immediately disabled the alert. We were about to respond, and then it disappeared."

"Because they all know by now that I'm with him," I murmur. "And no one except the Council is supposed to know that I'm not actually dead."

With a decisive sigh, Flynn pushes himself to his feet. "I'm going to contact someone. About finding Ash."

"Wait, Flynn," Iris says as he moves toward the kitchen door. "Is that the person you mentioned earlier? Someone Griffin Gifted? Because—"

"Mom, we're desperate, okay? I don't care if we have to go outside the Guild for this."

"I know, honey, I was only going to say that there's a—" she lowers her voice slightly, as if someone might be listening in on this conversation "—there's a new amber in the drawer on your dad's side of the bed. Use that one. No one knows it's linked to us."

Flynn gives her a small smile. "Thanks, Mom."

"Silver," Lennox says to me, "do you know what happened a few days ago to make Ash just disappear without any explanation? Did he tell you?"

I hesitate before nodding. "I do, but … he wanted to keep you guys out of it. To keep you safe. So you wouldn't end up like … like my parents. And now I've messed that all up by coming here—"

"Hey." Iris reaches over and grips my hand. "Don't you dare think like that. I wish Ash had come to us sooner. I wish you both had. Instead, you were out there on your own, trying to deal with—whatever this is. And now he's—" She presses her lips together before inhaling deeply. "He's still alive. We'll find him."

I nod, but before I can begin explaining anything, we hear the sound of a chair scraping loudly across the kitchen floor. "Darn, stupid—who left this thing here? Doesn't anybody push chairs back in around here?"

I sit up straighter. Was that Connor?

Flynn's voice reaches us next. "Oh, you're here. I thought you might call first to—"

"You send a message like *that* and you think I'm not going to get my ass over here immediately? I swear, man, if this is some kind of sick joke—"

"You think I'd *joke* about this?" Flynn demands.

I release Iris's hand and rise quickly. Connor stops in the doorway. He stares at me. Then he curses. Loudly. Then again. And again. And then his eyes begin to well with tears, and I'm crying too as we meet halfway across the room and he pulls me tightly against him. "You little brat. How are you *alive* right now?" he says hoarsely into my hair.

"It's a long and unpleasant story," I mumble against his shoulder.

"Somebody tell me this isn't a dream," a quiet voice says from somewhere behind me. I pull away slightly from Connor and see a duplicate of him on the other side of the room.

"Tobin," Flynn says in surprise. "You came."

Tobin doesn't answer. He presses his lips tightly together, walks around the furniture, and wraps both Connor and me in a tight embrace. His face is buried in my neck, and though it doesn't sound like he's crying, he's inhaling deep shuddering breaths. I shift so I can get one arm around each twin, and for an unknown amount of time we simply stand there. It's only when I hear Iris's voice, a little further away now, that I open my eyes and lift my head.

"Where have you *been*?" she demands, her voice thick with emotion. "Do you have any idea how worried we've been? Don't you *dare* disappear like that ever again!"

My heart leaps, and I turn abruptly within the circle of Connor and Tobin's arms. And then I hear his voice. *Ash's* voice. "Figured … it might be time … to ask my family for help."

THIRTY-THREE

"You're here," Ash says, his entire expression changing the moment he sees me. "Thankthecourts," he exhales in a single breath. He reaches for me, and I want to throw myself at him and never let go. But he's leaning heavily against the wall and appears to be having difficulty breathing, so I hover anxiously beside him as Lennox and Flynn rush to help him to the couch.

"What happened?" I ask. "Where were you?"

"I was hoping ... you ... might be able to tell me ... what happened. And how are you so ... *fine*? Weren't we both stabbed? Twice? Ow, wait, Mom ..." Iris is trying to get him to lie down, but he reaches behind him and removes something. The crystal. The Icicle Pendant of the First Seelie Queen. Which I somehow managed to completely forget about until this moment.

"You still have it," I say in surprise.

"It was lying next to me ... when I woke up."

"Woke up where?"

He leans back on the same cushions I was lying against not long ago. "Somewhere in Stormsdrift. A short distance away from ... from ..." He shuts his eyes and swallows. "I managed to stagger back there. The whole area was sealed off. Guardians all over the place. I saw ... bits of ... bodies. I thought ..." He places a hand over his eyes as Iris leans over him to examine his injuries. "I thought you might be one of them," he whispers.

I move to kneel beside the arm of the couch, where Ash's head is resting on a cushion. I take hold of the hand he's currently covering his face with and wrap my hand around it. "I thought the same about you," I tell him quietly. I want to kiss his brow, his fingers, his lips, but his entire family is in this room with us, so I settle for holding his hand against my cheek as I speak. "I couldn't even think straight. I ended up at my friends' place—Teddy and Duke—" Another ache pierces my chest as I remember the truth about them. But that's a story for another time. "And then I came here. I know you didn't want to get your family involved, but I didn't know where else to go."

"And I've already told you that was the right thing to do," Iris says. "Now this looks more like what I'd expect to see if you were run through with a sword or two," she adds quietly, frowning at Ash's abdomen. "You'll be fine, of course. It'll just take some extra magic and rest."

"Ash," I say to him. "You said you woke up a short distance away. Do you remember how you got there? For some reason I blacked out, and when I became conscious of things again, you were gone. So I'm not sure what happened."

"I don't know. I think I was hit on the head, so things got ... kind of fuzzy. And then ... it was so odd. I think I remember ... flying."

"Flying?" Lennox repeats sharply. I look around at him.

"Like something was ... carrying me ... through the air."

Iris and Lennox exchange a worried glance. I'm wondering if their concern is to do with whatever creature could have carried Ash away or the fact that this tale speaks more to his mental state. I look at Flynn, Connor and Tobin. Flynn is sitting again, Connor is standing beside his chair, and Tobin is leaning against a wall, arms folded tightly over his chest. It's unusual that they're all so quiet. Well, unusual for Connor and Flynn, at least. The Blackburn boys used to talk over each other all the time. It was almost impossible to get a word in.

My gaze shifts back to Lennox. "Do you know what it could have been?" I ask. "*If* something was carrying him? Do some of the stormfae have wings?"

"Stormfae?"

"Um, the monsters," I add quickly, realizing he wouldn't know that word.

"Possibly," Lennox says. "Some of them we haven't seen close up. They dart through the shadows, strike quickly, and then they're gone. What did you call them?" He frowns at me. "Stormfae? And what is this crystal thing?" He turns the icicle pendant carefully in his hands, examining it. "And you were about to tell us why Ash disappeared in the first place days ago. I'm hoping one of you can explain why half the Council thinks Ash attacked a fellow guardian."

Ash sighs. "Probably because I did."

"Ash!" Iris admonishes quietly, her hands still pressed against either side of his abdomen as she sends magic into his body.

"He was going to kill Silver, so, you know. He should be grateful I didn't kill *him*."

"Sounds like a good enough reason to me," Connor mutters.

"Indeed," Tobin adds quietly, which might be the first word he's uttered since he got here.

"Can I tell them everything?" I ask Ash. When he nods, I start at the beginning with the night he first saw the faerie door and discovered I was still alive. It's all happened over the course of only a few days, but I'm exhausted by the time I finish telling Ash's family everything. Well, not *everything*. I leave out a few, uh, intimate moments that occurred along the way.

Silence fills the room after I'm finished. Iris has completed whatever healing magic she was performing on Ash, and he's sitting up now, breathing a little more easily. I'm on the couch beside him now, still holding his hand. Everyone else seems somewhat at a loss for words.

"So let me get this straight," Lennox says eventually. "The first Guild *made* these creatures that are currently wandering around our forest, tearing people limb from limb? The faerie door Ash told us about years ago—that none of us has ever been able to see, despite sneaking into the Shadow Crypt multiple times—is real, and that's where these stormfae are coming from. And that—" he points at the icicle crystal "—is supposed to be able to destroy it?"

I nod. "Yes, I think that pretty much sums it up."

He lets out a long breath and shakes his head. "This is … a lot. I think we need to go to another Guild. Tell them everything. This feels … bigger than us. I think we need different councilors from a different Guild—and the head councilor who oversees all the Guilds—to decide on a course of action once we've presented the truth. We can wait until tomorrow—I think you both need to rest tonight—and then, if the faerie paths are still functioning, we can go straight to another Guild. The one your parents worked at before moving to Stormsdrift might be a good option."

After a pause in which no one else says anything, I ask, "Do you think that's … wise? I agree that this feels bigger than us, but … if the Seelie Court is involved—if they're killing people who know about the door and the key and all of this, people like Ostin—and if every Guild answers to the Seelie Court, then …" I look at Ash, then back at Lennox. "I just don't want us all to go off to another Guild, wind up locked away in a cell while they contact the Seelie Court to find out what's really going on, and that's the end of us."

Lennox rubs a hand across his brow. "Yes, I agree that would be less than ideal."

From the corner of the room, Tobin lets out a frustrated sound.

"I hope that wasn't an 'I told you so,' dear brother," Connor says. "Because we already knew something fishy was going on. This just confirms it."

Tobin raises both hands, eyes still pinned to the floor. "I'm not looking to argue with anyone."

"Although," I add, "we did wonder if perhaps the Seelie Court guardians who killed Ostin and who tried to kill us were acting on their own, without the knowledge or permission of the court.

"That would certainly be less alarming," Lennox says. "I'd obviously prefer to believe we can still trust the other Guilds and the Seelie Court."

"You know," Ash says quietly. "We could do it ourselves. Take that icicle pendant thing down there, smash it against the door, and destroy it. Or *I* could. I'm already in trouble with the Guild. Now that I'm breaking rules instead of following them, I may as well continue the streak."

"Ash," Iris chides quietly at the same time Connor says, "That's the spirit, little bro."

Lennox frowns at Ash, angling his head slightly. "How were you able to see the door? We've been down there numerous times. We could never see anything beyond that wall."

"Uh … I'm not sure. Perhaps because the councilors were down there. Bergenfell and Poppywood. Perhaps they had lifted some sort of glamour."

"So if we go there ourselves, how are we going to get through this glamour to where the door is?"

"Oh. I hadn't thought of that. Wait—" He looks at me. "Your mom got through. Before she even found the key. She thought it was just a wall at first. She touched it and nothing happened, but eventually it just … vanished? I think that's what she wrote in the journal. So it must be possible." He looks at his father again. "Maybe we just didn't wait long enough. Or maybe we need to send some magic into the wall."

"Perhaps," Lennox murmurs, still frowning.

"Am I the only one wondering if we're still safe in our own homes?" Connor asks. "We know now that at least one type of monster—sorry, stormfae creature—can become some sort of shadowy mist and pass through the protective enchantments on buildings—"

"Not to mention through a faerie's shield," Flynn adds quietly.

"Right," Connor says. "So should we be worried about them getting into our homes and slaughtering us while we're safely tucked in bed?"

"They've been around for almost two years," Lennox says, "and that's never happened before. Faerie homes are well protected. The Gauntlet changing house won't have the same level of magic on it, since no one's ever lived there."

Connor doesn't look convinced. "You sure about that, Dad?"

"Yes. I'm the one who made certain you all had the most up-to-date protective enchantments on each of your homes when Ash moved out. And I know for a fact that the Guild hasn't done anything to the security of that Gauntlet building in decades."

Connor hesitates, then says, "Okay. Thanks, Dad."

"I'm still offering to take the crystal right now and get rid of that door," Ash says.

"Sure, because you're in peak health right now," Connor points out. "So when the guardians who are watching the Shadow Crypt—because I'm sure Bergenfell would have posted someone there by now—try to kill you, you'll *totally* be able to fight them off."

Ash flicks his hand and sends a cushion flying through the air to whack Connor on the side of the head. "Fine. So maybe I need a few more hours of recovery time before I do that."

"Okay, how about this?" Iris says as she stands, catching the cushion Connor promptly tossed right back. "We all go into the kitchen and sit at the table together, because we haven't done that in, you know, *more than two years*. Ash and Silver can eat something—and so can the rest of you, if you're still hungry—and then they can go to bed. Because being stabbed is no joke, even if Silver's pretending to be fine and Ash is breathing normally again. Then, in the morning, when everyone's thinking a little more clearly, we can decide what to do."

I suck in a breath and decide not to wait for anyone else to answer. "Honestly, that sounds amazing."

We all stand and begin filing through to the kitchen. Halfway there, I glance up at Ash, and the moment our eyes meet, I remember the last moment we were alone. In the forest, breathless, a kiss that was trying to make up for several years' worth of kisses we never got the chance to experience. I almost pull his face down toward mine and kiss him again, but then Connor swings an arm around my shoulders and says, "So what exactly have you been doing for the past two years?"

For a second, I'm paralyzed by an image of *red*. But I blink it away and force a laugh. "Hey, can you let a girl eat some food before interrogating her?" I shove him playfully away. "And congratulations, by the way. I heard you're getting *married*, of all things."

"Thank you. Crazy, right? I'm such a grown-up."

"Well, I wouldn't go so far as to say *that*." I roll my eyes, and my laugh is genuine this time. "Where's Rosie tonight?"

"Oh, she has this extra training thing. Some kind of Seer conference. She'll be back in two days."

We sit at the table and Iris bustles around the kitchen, grabbing plates and food, until Lennox gently takes her elbow and guides her to a chair, telling her he'll sort the food out. When there's a moment of quiet among the boys, Tobin leans forward on his elbows and says, "This is so weird. So, so weird."

"Well, if you came home more often," Iris said, "it wouldn't feel so weird to you. I *do* invite you every time we have a family meal, you know, which is at least once a week."

He looks at me, then back at the table. "You know that's not what I'm talking about, Mom."

Iris sighs. "Yes, I know." Her eyes move to mine. "It is strange to have you here, Silver. And yet …" Her expression turns thoughtful. "On some level, it feels as though you never left."

"I know what you mean," I say to her. And then I meet Ash's eyes again, because somehow, my gaze keeps getting drawn back to him. His hand is on my knee beneath the table. His right thigh is pressed against my left thigh. My fingers slide down his wrist to entwine with his. We're like opposite ends of two magnets, unable to resist the physical pull toward one another. With his eyes still on me, he lifts our joined hands and kisses mine.

"Oh thank *goodness* that finally happened," Connor says, loud enough to startle me.

"What?" Ash asks.

"That," Connor says, pointing to our interlaced hands, which are still only a few inches away from Ash's mouth.

"Oh!" Iris exclaimed. "I completely missed that earlier."

"I don't know how, Mom, since you were probably the first one to predict they would end up together one day."

"You did?" Ash asks, looking at Iris.

Before she can answer, Connor leans across the table toward Flynn, hand outstretched, palm up. "Time to pay up, bro."

"Oh *come on*," Flynn says, leaning back in his chair and folding his arms. "That was years ago."

"A bet's a bet."

"I can't believe you even remember that nonsense," Tobin says, elbowing Connor in the ribs.

"You remember it too. You bet the same thing as me!"

Tobin turns a little red. "Okay fine," he admits. "Maybe I did."

"I can't believe you were *betting* about your brother's relation-ships," Iris says. "I don't think we want to hear anything more about this."

"I do," I say, a wide grin stretching my lips.

Connor pulls his arm back and turns to me. "Okay. So it was *so* obvious Ash was hopelessly in love with you—"

"It was *not*!" Ash objects.

"But he was always so darn sensible. So we made a bet with Flynn that Ash would be too scared to say anything to you while you were

338

both still training. That it would definitely take him until after graduation to work up the courage to tell you he was totally heart-eyed—"

"You are such an ass," Ash says, but he's fighting a smile.

"And Flynn said—"

"Oh please," Flynn interrupts, "like you remember what I said three years ago."

"I remember *exactly* what you said. You said, 'No way he'll last that long. They'll be together by fifth year, trust me.' And now look? Ash's graduation is *months* behind us. Years, actually, if you take into account that weird time-warping stint he did on Fennrock. And he's only *now* got up the courage to tell her."

"Yeah, because he only just found me," I argue. My gaze turns back to Ash as my mind conjures up our first kiss in the gardens at Mirrinvale Manor. "But at the Liberation Day Ball two years ago, the night everything went so horribly wrong …" Everyone goes quiet around me, but I'm determined not to turn that night into a taboo subject that everyone's too afraid to speak of. "Something else went very, very right that night," I say quietly, smiling at Ash. I squeeze his hand. He smiles back at me and leans closer to gently press his brow to mine. For a moment or two, it feels like we're the only two people in this room. Then—

"Aaaaah," Connor says loudly. "Aren't they just the *cutest*?"

There's a commotion under the table, most likely someone—or multiple someones—kicking Connor as everyone starts laughing. "So what I'm getting at, Connor," I say to him, "is that I think you *lost* that bet."

He tries to glare at me, but I can tell he's too happy to make it work. "You're still a brat, you know that?"

"Yes."

"Connor, stop it," Iris scolds. "I can't believe I have to tell you not to call people names when you're supposed to be an adult now."

"I'll never be an adult, Mom."

She sighs and shakes her head. "Yes, that's what I'm afraid of."

I lean back, watching them all. The smile on my lips is so wide it might actually split my face, and the ache in my heart is equal parts brokenness and absolute joy. It hurts so much that Mom and Dad aren't here, but I have dreamed of sitting at the Blackburn kitchen table with Ash's family for so very long.

When Lennox brings plates of food to the table, I pull mine closer, pretend the past two years never happened, and dig in.

THIRTY-FOUR

AFTER WE SAY GOODNIGHT TO ASH'S BROTHERS AND THEY HEAD off through the faerie paths, Iris gives me some clean clothes and insists on getting the bathing room ready for me, despite my protests that I'm perfectly capable of doing it myself. "She just wants to look after you," Ash whispers to me, before Iris tugs him away and tells him he'll be sleeping on the couch tonight. It's his turn to protest then, reminding her that he has his own place he could sleep at. And that he has a spare bedroom I'm totally welcome to use. Though Iris doesn't see me roll my eyes at that, I doubt she believes for even a second that I would actually use that spare bedroom.

I hear her firm voice just before I close the bathing room door: "And if something goes wrong with your recovery? Or someone finds a way to break through the protective magic on your home? And the faerie paths stop working and we can't help you? Nope, sorry. After the past few days of being sick to my stomach wondering where you were and what happened, I'm not letting you disappear again tonight. Not while there are people out there who apparently don't give a second thought to *ending your life*."

I float in the steaming water amid mounds of bubbles, trying not to think of the two faint scars just below my ribs. The scars that will probably be gone by morning. A quiet sense of dread nudges the back of my mind. Faeries have impressive healing powers, but those wounds should not have healed so quickly. I don't have answers though, so I slide beneath the bubbles and focus instead on the fact that I'm *here*. I'm *safe*.

We didn't go looking for something like this. She came to us.

With a jolt, I open my eyes beneath the water. I push against the bottom of the pool, breaking the water's surface with a loud splash. Even inside my own head, I can't escape her. Even when I want to believe I'm safe, my memories step in to remind me that this will never be true. I wipe water off my face and rub my eyes. I have to tell Ash. I have to tell Iris and Lennox. They will never look at me the same way again, but perhaps that's better than living in fear for the rest of my life.

When I'm finished in the pool, I dress in the clothes Iris gave me. They're not pajamas, but they're comfortable enough to sleep in. Though after everything that's happened recently, I could probably wear a chest-constricting corset and have no problem sleeping. It's been too many hours, too many time zones, too many near-death experiences since I last had a restful sleep.

I step into Ash's old bedroom just as thunder cracks and rumbles. After leaving my shoes and dirty clothes in a pile beside the door, I pad toward the window and look out, trying to see past the rain slamming against the window. Is it misty out there? Are stormfae prowling around, looking for something or someone to rip their claws into? How many more of them have seeped their way through the faerie door?

We're going to fix this, I tell myself. The same words I repeated years ago, the night we tried to run. I believed those words then. I believed my parents could fix anything. And then ... well, then I didn't believe anything could be fixed for a long time after that. But now, here inside this safe, cozy bubble that is the Blackburns' home, I somehow find it in myself to truly believe that everything will be okay.

Thunder booms again, and I shut my eyes and let the grumbling rumble wrap around me like a blanket, familiar and comforting. That sound will always mean home to me.

I turn away from the window and look around. Ash's bedroom is even neater now than it used to be, given that he doesn't live here anymore. My eyes pause when they land on the wardrobe. If I open those doors and find an old sweater or hoodie inside there, I am *so* putting it on. Just for old time's sake. Okay, maybe not just for old time's sake. Maybe because I'm completely aware now of just how much I *want* to snuggle up inside something of his, whereas back then it was something I did without even thinking.

I open the wardrobe doors, and … yes. On one of the shelves is a pile of old clothes. I lift the edge of a pair of pants and then a T-shirt— and then I recognize the gray hoodie I wore the evening we danced in the clearing and it hit me like a kick to the chest that I was in love with this person I'd been friends with almost my whole life. I may not remember what I wore three days ago, a week ago, a month ago, but I remember precisely what I was wearing that evening.

I pull the hoodie out and leave the rest of the clothes on the shelf. There's a tear along the bottom edge at the back, which might be why Ash didn't take it with him when he moved his things, but that doesn't matter to me. I push my arms through the sleeves and pull it over my head. It smells a little bit musty and a little bit him. Soft and well-worn, with sleeves that are too long for my arms, it's perfect.

"Stealing my clothes again?"

I turn to see him standing in the doorway, smiling in a way that makes my stomach do a flip. Heat crawls up my neck as I tug the sleeves over my hands and attempt a teasing smile. "Aren't you supposed to be on the couch?"

He leans in the doorway. "Are you asking me to leave?"

I close the wardrobe doors and press my back against them, tilting my head to the side. "What do you think?"

He pushes away from the doorframe, strides across the room, and picks me up. A squeal escapes my lips as he tosses me onto the bed.

Then he's on his hands and knees beside me, covering my mouth with his hand as he laughs—not exactly silently—into my neck. "You should have closed the door, moron," I try to whisper through my giggles. His hand slips away from my mouth, and I turn my head in an attempt to muffle my laughter in the pillow.

"Ah, that actually *really* hurt," he gasps, only half laughing now as he curls in on himself and presses a hand beneath his ribs.

"Yeah, well, nobody told you to pick me up and throw me across the room, Tarzan."

"Tarzan?"

"Never mind." I prop myself up on one arm. "Seriously, are you okay? Do you need me to call your mom?"

He inhales slowly, eyes closed. When he looks at me again, his amber gaze is burning. "I definitely don't need you to call my mom."

He pushes himself up into a sitting position and glances at the door as he slides one hand slowly through the air. The door closes with a quiet click. Then he looks down at me. I look back up at him. "This is kind of strange, isn't it," I say quietly. "In some ways, being back here, lying on your bed and wearing your clothes, it feels like no time has passed. And then I blink and I remember that so much has changed."

He leans the tiniest bit closer to me. "Lying on my bed and wearing my clothes," he repeats slowly, his tone low, the beginnings of a smile on his lips. "Were you aware that you were driving me crazy? Or were you totally oblivious?"

"What?" I ask, laughing again. "You talk such nonsense."

Instead of answering, he pushes a hand into my hair and lowers his lips to mine. I respond instantly, my hands winding around his neck to pull him down over me. "Not nonsense," he murmurs against my lips as his hand slides down my side and grips my hip. "Definitely not nonsense."

"I don't believe you."

His hand finds the edge of the hoodie and slips beneath it, and then he's trailing his fingers slowly over the curve of my waist and the side of my ribs, sending a shiver dancing across my skin. "You have no idea," he breathes, his lips on my neck now, "how many times I longed to reach across this bed, pull you closer, and do exactly this."

That surprises me enough that I pull away slightly. Just enough to properly see his face. "Really?"

"Yes, really." He's somehow frowning and smiling at the same time. "Why is that surprising?"

"I just thought … I thought it was only near the end, around about the time of the ball, when Jerryn asked me to go with him, and then everything became really weird between us. I thought you only realized then, at the ball, after we yelled at each other, that maybe you … liked me. As more. Than, you know, a friend." Wow. My eloquence is astounding. I blame it on the fact that Ash's hand is still beneath my clothing, tracing patterns across the bare skin of my back. It's distracting in the best possible way.

"Uh, nope," he says with a quiet chuckle. "That is not when it happened."

I smile at him. "You loved me before then."

I watch the color rise in his face, but he doesn't look away. "I have loved you forever," he says simply.

I shift closer, kiss him, and whisper, "That can't be true. We met when we were six."

He laughs again. "Okay, fine. I wasn't in love with you back then. I guess it happened slowly over time until one day I just … knew. Somewhere near the end of third year, I think."

"Oh, wow. I had no idea."

"Yes, I know. That was the point."

"Why?" I ask, though I remember my own reasons for wanting to keep quiet, and I suspect his are probably the same.

"Why?" he repeats, looking at me like this should be obvious. "Silver, you were everything to me. Our friendship was so easy, so perfect. What if I had told you and it messed things up? I couldn't face that. I just … I wanted more, but I also really, *really* didn't want to lose what we already

had. I wanted … I just wanted you hanging out in my room forever, totally oblivious to how amazing you truly were. Wild and adventurous. Bold and daring. Always up for a challenge."

"That was *you*," I point out. "Physically incapable of backing down from a challenge."

He rolls his eyes. "I suppose we spurred each other on in that department. And then there was my *family*—"

"What do you mean?" I bat my eyelashes. "They're crazy about me."

"Exactly. My parents love you. My brothers are scarily protective of you, even if they always liked to pretend you were a pain in the ass. On some level, it felt like you were already part of our family. What if I had started something with you and then messed things up? It wouldn't have been just *our* friendship that was ruined. The way my entire family interacted with you would have changed. Or at least, that's what I imagined. It felt like a huge amount of pressure."

I lift a hand and run my finger along his eyebrow and then down over his cheekbone. "You always used to think things through far too much."

"And you didn't think at all. Blindly leaping into everything with unabashed zeal. Which I adore about you, by the way."

A small sigh leaves my lips. "I don't think I'm like that anymore. Life has taught me to be … careful."

His eyes travel my face. "I'm sure."

This is it. The perfect opening to tell him more. To try to explain all the awful things I did after I first left Stormsdrift. The things that changed me. But this moment … this moment … I want to hang onto it forever. So I continue the path I'm tracing across his face, my forefinger following the curve of his lips, dipping over his chin, traveling up the line of his jaw.

"What are you doing, Wren Three?" he whispers.

I smile at his use of that old nickname. "I don't know. Just … savoring the fact that I get to do this. That I can lie this close to you and touch you like this, and it isn't weird because I know you love me."

His hand traces down to my lower back before pressing me closer to him. I shift my head across the pillow so our lips are almost touching. "I don't think I told you in words earlier," I whisper, "but I love you too."

When our lips meet, his fingers splay across my back, pressing me even closer. I know we should both be old enough by now to control our magic, but I'm fairly certain the delicious tingles dancing across my skin are tiny sparks. Light flickers at the edge of my vision: faint gold wisps looping and tangling in the air close to our faces. Perhaps I should be embarrassed by this, but I'm so lost in a dozen other sensations that I can barely focus on a little bit of escaped magic. My fingers tangle in his hair, his tongue moves across mine, and my heart pounds a heavy beat in my chest.

"Isela …" he whispers against my mouth, sending a shiver across my skin. "Silver … How did you end up with not one, but two beautiful names?"

My laugh is quiet, breathless. "You know you're the only one who's called me that in years? I'm not even sure when my parents last used that name."

His lips are on my cheek, and then below my ear. "I think I like the fact that I'm the only one who calls you that. Except—" He goes still, and a second later I remember something. The same something, most likely, that's just occurred to him. He's *not* the only one to call me Isela recently.

"The stormfae," I murmur.

He breathes out slowly, then says, "Well, that killed the mood."

"Yeah." I manage another breathy laugh. "Probably a good thing though." I pull slightly away from Ash. "I hate to be the sensible one—"

"You're definitely not the sensible one."

"—*but* we were both badly injured and we need to sleep instead of … you know, wherever this is heading if we don't stop now."

He pauses, considering my words. "Okay, perhaps you are the sensible one when it comes to … this. Though I would like to point out that kissing you is an excellent distraction from the rather intense pain still piercing through my abdomen, so perhaps we should continue."

I frown. "You're still in a lot of pain?"

"Yes. How are you *not* in a lot of pain?"

"I … I don't know."

We simply watch each other for another few moments, and then he says, "It's … unsettling, isn't it? Losing a gap of time like that." He's talking about the moments—minutes? Hours?—during which I blacked out, but I suspect he's also talking about his time on Fennrock. All the work he did at that Guild that he has no memory of.

"Yes," I answer. "It is." I stare at him a moment longer, then turn over and shift closer to him so that my back is against his chest. His arm tightens around me, and I lace my fingers between his.

"I've only dreamed of sleeping next to you like this a hundred thousand times," he murmurs against the back of my neck.

I lift our joined hands and press a kiss against his knuckles. Rain patters against the window. My eyes slide closed. "You probably don't remember this," I say quietly, "but there was an evening, at the beginning of fourth year, when we were dancing in the clearing. Our families were there. Connor and Rosie were practicing, and they were terrible."

"I remember. And we volunteered to show them how it was done, because of course we had perfected that dance, and then you ended up stumbling through the second half of it."

"Yes." I take a breath. "Because I had just realized—quite suddenly and totally out of the blue—that you were everything I wanted."

"Oh." He's quiet a moment, and then: "All those little flowers in the air. That was you."

"Um, yes. Possibly. Probably." I bite my lip. "Almost certainly."

"So it was my dancing skills that won you over."

I laugh quietly. "Yes, that must have been it."

He's quiet for a while before speaking again. "Okay, things are starting to make sense now. You started acting strange soon after that, and I thought it was because you liked someone else. That you'd started dating that guy who asked you to the ball, so you were pulling away from me because our friendship was … well …"

"Very close."

"Yes."

"I'm sorry," I say. "I should have been brave enough to tell you."

"*I* should have been brave enough to tell *you*." He shifts a little closer and says, "For me, it was one night when you were sleeping over here. Near the end of third year sometime. Definitely after Kellee and I broke up. You'd fallen asleep on my bed while your parents were working late unexpectedly. I went downstairs to sleep on the couch because, you know, we were fifteen, almost sixteen. Sharing a bed was not appropriate."

"Obviously."

"Obviously. The next morning, Tobin got up early to go out running or something, and he asked if I wanted to join him. I came in here to quietly grab some things, and I just … I looked at you lying here, fast asleep, in my bed, in my clothes …" He lets out a quiet chuckle. "Because you were *always* wearing my clothes. And, I don't know. I just suddenly felt … different."

"Different?" I tease, squeezing his fingers with mine.

"Like … I wanted to climb into bed next to you and wrap my arm around you and pull you against me. Exactly the way we're lying right now. Like all of a sudden, even though I'd never considered it before, I really wanted to kiss you."

I turn enough to see him over my shoulder. "And you managed to *not* kiss me for several months? I'm impressed."

"Right? I mean, how did I manage to resist your charms for so long?" He leans far enough over my shoulder that his lips *just* graze mine.

"It's unfathomable. I truly don't know how you lasted until the Lib Day Ball."

"I plan to make up for it in the very near future. Trust me.

Except ..." He lies back down with a groan. "Maybe not *right* now, because that was a super uncomfortable angle."

"I *told* you you need to rest, old man."

"Hush, you."

"I mean, who says 'hush' unless they're at least a hundred and thirty-seven years old?"

"Twenty. I am effectively twenty."

I laugh silently and pull his arm tighter around me, and though I know there are many things I still need to tell him, I decide rest is better for both of us right now. I shut my eyes, breathe him in, and let myself fall asleep.

Thirty-Five

I wake with a jolt.

"Ash? *Ash?*"

I'm disoriented for a second, unsure who's calling Ash's name or where I am or why something heavy is draped over my middle.

Oh. Ash's arm. We're in his bedroom. We fell asleep next to one another. I push myself up, slow enough that his arm doesn't slide away from me. My body, my brain, my face, *everything* floods with a happy warmth.

And then the bedroom door bangs open. "Ash, *there* you are," Iris gasps. For a moment, I think we're in trouble because we ended up sleeping in the same bed. Such a silly thing, but still kind of embarrassing, since Iris clearly wasn't comfortable with us—

Something slams against the window. I jerk back instinctively. Long claws scrape at the glass and a snarling snout with bared teeth snaps viciously. "Holy *crap*!" I gasp.

Ash is up too, and the arm that was loose around me is now tight. He's pulling me off the bed and toward the doorway before I can even comprehend that this creature is *right here*. On the other side of a pane of glass and an enchantment that's supposedly strong enough to keep any creature out.

"They're surrounding the house," Lennox calls to us. Over Iris's shoulder, I see him reach the top of the stairs and stride toward us. "I counted at least six, but it's difficult to know for sure while it's still dark out there and they keep moving. I've never heard of so many in one place. Two, perhaps three, max, but this?"

"And you think the protection on this house is enough to keep them out?" Ash asks.

"We're not sticking around to find out," Iris says. "The paths are still working. Grab shoes and something warm, and let's go."

I dart back into the room and snatch up my sneakers from just inside the doorway. The clothes I'm already wearing are fine. The stormfae at the window—the same type that found us at the Gauntlet, as far as I can tell—is still slashing and snarling at the window. I step hurriedly back out of the room and grab Ash's hand as we make for the stairs behind Iris and Lennox.

"What's the time?" Ash asks as we descend.

"About an hour before dawn," Lennox answers.

"Are you feeling okay?" Iris asks, directing the question over her shoulder at Ash. "You must have got a good few hours of sleep. I-I mean … assuming you … I wasn't trying to pry or suggest that—" Though the fact that Ash and I shared a bed last night is the least of anyone's concerns right now, Iris still manages to get flustered over it. "Never mind," she mutters quickly as we reach the living room. She drops onto a couch and summons a pair of boots with a flick of her hand.

"Yes, we slept," Ash confirms. "I feel fine. No more pain."

"Good," Iris says, tugging her boots on. "Did we decide which Guild we're going to?" she asks Lennox as I sit on the edge of an armchair and shove my feet into my sneakers.

"Yes, I still think Bloodwood is a good option. And there's that—"

"—woman who was friends with Nel who still works there."

"Yes.

"Oh, here, don't forget this." I stand as she throws an amber across the room. Lennox catches it neatly.

"I saw yours in the—"

"Got it already."

This speaking over each other, the rushing around, grabbing things, it all reminds me far too much of the night I fled with Mom and Dad. I can almost see their shadowy figures darting around. Can almost hear the fear in their voices. *We're running, bug, because they want to kill us.* I press my hands to my cheeks, panic clamping around my throat and squeezing, squeezing—

"Hey, it's okay," Ash says, taking one of my hands and pulling it away from my face. "This isn't like that night. I promise." Then he kisses the back of my hand.

I blink and focus on him. He's wearing a jacket now—one of Lennox's, I assume—and I can just make out something bright and sparkling behind the top of the zip. "Is that … the crystal? The icicle pendant?"

"Oh, yeah." He pulls the zip down to reveal the Icicle Pendant of the First Seelie Queen. A chain has been threaded through the hole in the blunt end, so that now it really does look like a pendant, albeit a ridiculously large one. Once again, in the panic of things, I'd forgotten all about it.

"Please don't let that thing explode all over you."

"After what it's been through since we stole it, I'm guessing it's going to take a big jolt of magic, at the very least, to break this thing."

"Okay, everyone ready?" Lennox says.

There's a pause as we all look at each other. I notice all of a sudden that the scratching of claws against glass and the muted snarling sounds have vanished. The rain is a soft patter against the windows. And then we hear it, a whisper from somewhere outside. *"Iselaaaaa."*

My skin prickles. A shiver crawls up my neck and into my hair. "Not again," I murmur.

Lennox is frozen with his mouth half open. Iris looks utterly horrified. "Did one of those creatures … just say … your *name*?" she asks.

"So … I may have left that part out when I was giving you the summarized version of everything that's happened over the past few days." I tell her. "When one of the stormfae broke into the Gauntlet changing house, it … seemed to know who I am."

"How?" Iris whispers.

"I don't know. I think … I'm guessing … that my parents went through the faerie door. It's the only thing I can think of. How else would these stormfae know my name?"

Iris closes her eyes and shakes her head. "Okay, but … even if they did go through … why would they tell these monsters about their daughter?"

"I'm guessing they didn't give the information willingly, Mom," Ash says.

"And even if they know your name, how do they know that name belongs to *you*? And how did they know you were *here*?"

"Okay, as disturbing as this is," Lennox says, "we don't have time to stand here and discuss it right now. I'm—"

We all freeze as a strange sound reaches us over the quiet thrum of the rain. I look around, trying to figure out where it's coming from, what it is. Then I realize, a moment before my eyes land on one of the windows, exactly what I'm hearing: the slow splintering crack of glass.

Lennox curses beneath his breath. "We're going. Now." He's at the wall in a second, writing quickly with a stylus. I half expect the doorway that opens to blink out of existence before we can run through it, because that's the way life works, right? But it remains open, a yawning hole of darkness. Iris grabs Ash's other hand, then lunges for Lennox's outstretched arm, and as glass shatters behind us, we dive into the faerie paths.

THIRTY-SIX

then

TANGLED TREES AND BEAMS OF MOONLIGHT MATERIALIZED UP ahead, and Silver hurried out of the faerie paths with Mom and Dad. "Wait," she said, tugging them to a stop without thinking. This wasn't some unfamiliar forest in some distant part of the world. They were still in Stormsdrift. Close to the Guild and the Shadow Crypt. Close enough, in fact, that if she squinted through the trees, she could see the spot where a hole in the ground led to the crypt's ancient stone staircase. "Why are we here? You said we have to run. That they want to *kill* you!"

Dad ushered Silver and Mom behind a tree before taking a deep breath and facing Silver. "Mom and I had to leave earlier before we could properly lock the door, so I need to go back and do that. If I don't, more terrible things are going to come through it. So you and Mom are going to hide here while I run back down there. I'll be quick."

It sounded so simple, but Silver knew with a cold sense of dread that it would not be that easy. "Do you think Ursula's stationed someone there by now?" Mom said.

"Possibly. I'll gather enough magic for a stunner spell. Just give me a minute and then I'll have enough—"

"And if there's more than one person? I should go with you."

"No," Dad said firmly. "You can't go near that door again."

"I won't enter the crypt. I'll just go with you to the entrance. With stunner magic gathered. There'll probably be at least two guardians hanging around. If there are more, we'll have to fight off the rest."

"Mom," Silver said, her voice shaking. "Dad. Is this worth it? Why don't we just leave?"

Mom looked at her. "We have to do this. I don't know why Ursula wants to open that door, but if she does …" Mom shook her head. "She can't control what will come through. None of them can." She turned to Dad, reaching with one hand to pull a chain from beneath her sweater. At the end of it hung a key Silver had never seen before. Longer than the average key, a dull metallic gray, with the head of some kind of beast on one end. "I'll hide it as soon as you're done," she said to Dad. "No one will ever find it."

"I don't think you should—"

"I've been practicing. I know the words perfectly now."

"It isn't our kind of magic, Nel—"

"And that's why no one will ever find it! Here." Mom pressed the key into Dad's hands. "Just lock the darn thing and let's be done with this. You remember all the motions and the magic?"

"Yes, of course."

"Okay, Silver." Mom looked at her again. "You need to hide here while—Actually, perhaps you should wait somewhere else, far from here. We'll decide on a meeting spot. You can go through the paths—"

"No," Silver interrupted. She couldn't bear the thought of being separated from them, not knowing what was happening, not knowing if she would ever see them again. "I'll hide here. I'll be fine."

"Silver—"

"Mom, just go. Quickly!"

"Okay." Mom looked at Dad, her hands raised as magic began to leak from her fingertips. "Let's go. I'll have enough magic gathered by the time we get there."

Dad nodded. He already had a sparkling mass of magic collected above one palm. With his other hand, he pulled Silver closer and pressed a hurried kiss to her head. "Love you, bug," he whispered, and as he dashed away through the shadows with Mom, she wanted to shout, *Why did you say that?* Why, if he thought everything was going to be fine, would he tell her that he loved her?

She crouched behind the tree and began counting, her lips moving silently as she tried to focus on the numbers instead of whatever was happening in the Shadow Crypt. But it wasn't long before she realized her lips had stopped moving and her eyes were fixed on a tree with oddly interlaced branches, and her brain was conjuring up images of her parents lying dead on the—

No, stop. We're going to fix this. We're going to fix this. Everything's going to be fine. A light mist of rain began to fall. Silver peered around the side of the tree. What was taking so long? It was just a door. Surely all they had to do was turn the key and leave? She pulled her head back around and shut her eyes again, wondering if she should bother trying to shield herself from the rain or if she should reserve her magic. Perhaps she should follow her parents' lead and gather enough for a stunner spell. Just in case someone—

Shouts. The sizzle of magic. An agonized cry.

Silver's heart slammed against her chest, pounding with such ferocity that it almost hurt. But she was a guardian—*almost* a guardian—and she was trained to act, not hide. She gripped the tree and peered around it once more.

Her parents were racing toward her, Dad in front, Mom hobbling slightly behind him, a bloody gash on her forehead. Then Dad spun around, hurling blade after blade he grabbed straight from the air. Mom ran past him, and she was close enough now that Silver could see her eyes, wide and wild. Shock froze Silver to the spot. Never in her life had she seen that kind of fear, raw and untamed, in either of her parents. "Doorway!" Mom screamed at her.

The cry jolted Silver to life. Her hand fumbled over her pocket. Then her other pocket. But she didn't have a stylus. *She didn't have a stylus!* She'd been in such a rush, such a panic, and she'd thrown several into the bag that Dad had shrunk, but then she hadn't grabbed another one before they left. *How had she left the damn house without a stylus?*

Mom crashed into her, and then they were both kneeling on the ground, hands grasping for each other, and Dad was skidding to a halt not far away, both hands sweeping overhead in an arcing motion. The shield he created was almost invisible, but moonlight caught on it here and there, and Silver saw enough to know that it formed a dome covering the three of them and the tree she and Mom crouched beside.

"I don't have a stylus," Silver gasped. "Where's yours?"

"Jacket. Left pocket." Silver's hands went to Mom's pocket immediately—and pulled out two halves of a single stylus. Mom breathed out a curse. "Must have snapped … when I fell. Someone pushed me down the stairs." Well that probably explained the gash on her forehead.

"Crap. Dad!" Silver shouted. "Stylus!"

He shook his head and didn't answer, grunting as he held both hands up to reinforce the shield. On the other side of the near transparent layer of magic, three guardians were hurling magic, shooting arrows, slicing at it with their golden swords. "His is gone," Mom gasped. "He tried to open a way to the paths—after he locked the door —but someone blasted it out of his hand."

"Okay. The … the bag. The bag he shrank."

"Here." Mom patted her other pocket, pushed her hand inside. But all she withdrew was the vial of leftover shadowfire potion. "Dammit, *dammit*. Must have fallen …" She sucked in a breath. "I will kill whoever pushed me down those stairs," she hissed.

"So we … we have no stylus?" The reality of what this meant for them sank into Silver's being with sickening clarity. *We're running, bug, because they want to kill us.* "Okay, Mom, I … I have to help Dad with the shield. Can you draw enough magic for another stunner spell?"

"I … don't think …" She sagged against Silver, one hand forming a fist that she pressed tightly against her middle. Blood seeped through her clothing and dribbled over her fingers. An alarming amount of blood.

"Mom! Are you okay?"

"I'm fine, I'm fine." But she was blinking repeatedly in a way that certainly didn't seem fine. "You and I … we're stronger. I'll be fine. But … if I'm not … you'll have to take this." She uncurled her clenched fist to reveal the key, now covered in blood, in her palm. "And don't ever let them get it."

"What? No, just hold onto it for now." Still kneeling beside Mom, Silver raised her hands and pushed magic up and out, sending it into the shield her father had created. "Or just destroy the darn thing," she added, not looking down. "Then no one can use it."

"We've tried that. Your dad can't. And I … I think I can, but I can't. I just *can't*."

"Mom, that doesn't make—"

"Silver, I need to tell you—"

"Mom—"

"In case—"

"Mom, please just sit, okay?" Silver tried to make her tone firm, but all she heard was the shudder in her voice. "So I can help Dad. So they don't get through the—"

"Just listen to me. *Listen*." Then Mom pulled Silver closer and began whispering into her ear, and all Silver could do was stare at her father straining, *straining* beneath the onslaught of magic pummeling his shield as Mom's words sank heavily, one by one, into her mind. A story that surely belonged to someone else. A secret that couldn't possibly be hers. "Swear to me you will never come back here," Mom said when she reached the end of her tale. "Swear to me you will take this secret to your end."

And still, all Silver could do was stare. A dozen questions battered her mind, but she couldn't bring a single one to pass her lips. She was vaguely aware that magic was still bleeding out of her into the shield, but she couldn't focus on that either.

"Silver, did … did you hear me?" Mom gasped, her breathing growing more labored.

In the end, the only words Silver could utter were the same words Mom had begged of her: "I … I will take this secret to my end."

Mom pulled back, pressed one hand to Silver's cheek, tucked a strand of hair behind her ear, and kissed her brow. "My beautiful … brave … determined girl," she managed to say. "My Silver girl. May it be many … *many* years before you meet your end."

Then she looked down at her clenched fist. "Don't ever come back here," she whispered again. "Don't ever let them get the key."

Silver swallowed and nodded. "I'll take this secret … to my end."

Then Mom pulled her close again and pressed a hand above Silver's heart. "Forgive me," she whispered. And then Silver's body was *burning* and she was screaming and her flesh felt as if it would melt off her bones. And then, in an instant, the pain was gone. She knelt there breathless, utterly spent. And in that moment, with a small and entirely anticlimactic pop, Dad's shield vanished.

Things happened almost too quickly to follow then. Dad dodged a blade, then grabbed a bow from the air and shot an arrow. A guardian jerked backward. He threw a knife, dodged again, threw two knives in quick succession, and the other two guardians staggered backward. A second arrow. A third arrow. The other two guardians were down. There was just enough time—perhaps a second or two—for hope to flare inside Silver. Was it possible they might actually survive this?

And then a figure in an ivory ballgown stepped straight out of the air, a guardian sword gripped in both hands. She swung with all her might, and the glittering deadly blade sliced clean through Dad's neck.

Silver couldn't breathe. Couldn't move. Screaming filled her ears. She wondered distantly if it was coming from her, but then Mom pushed herself up and lunged past Silver, her scream turning into a guttural cry as she grabbed a sword from the air and slashed wildly at Councilor Ursula Bergenfell.

There was a darkness at the edge of Silver's vision, trying to pull her under. Things seemed to flicker out of view. Something growling inside her head, the sound of wings fluttering. Then she could see again, and that long, gleaming blade was cutting through the air—

Mom. Her head there. Her body there. Separate. And Silver wished the darkness would take her forever.

But it didn't. Time kept ticking. Her heart kept beating.

Councilor Bergenfell, still in the dress she'd been wearing at the Liberation Day Ball earlier that evening, dropped onto one knee, breathing heavily. Silver dragged her gaze a little higher and saw that there were multiple bloody slashes all the way down her front. When had that happened? Had Mom somehow done that before she'd … before …

The other three guardians, all of them councilors, Silver saw now, were attempting to stand, gingerly removing arrows and knives from their bodies. In the distance, other guardians were gathering. Shouting, moving closer, some of them starting to run.

Flee, a tiny, distant voice whispered to Silver. But still she couldn't move. Councilor Bergenfell looked up. Her gaze landed on Silver's. With a rasping breath, she said, "Kill her."

As if suddenly released from an iron grip, Silver staggered backward. She tripped over something—a root or a fallen branch—and landed hard on her left wrist. And there, on the ground barely a few inches from her fingers, was the vial of remaining shadowfire potion. She grabbed it, pulled the stopper out, and tossed some in Councilor Bergenfell's direction. Translucent flames leaped into existence in an instant. Silver shoved the stopper back in, pushed herself up, and ran.

THIRTY-SEVEN

now

SOMETHING IS WRONG. WE'RE FALLING THROUGH THE FAERIE paths when I feel as if I've been jerked to a halt. I see a flicker of … *something*. Which shouldn't be possible. The faerie paths are meant to be utterly black. Then another tug and stutter, sideways this time.

"Silver, are you—"

"I'm here!" My hand is still in Ash's, but I reach over blindly with my other hand and make sure I'm hanging onto him with both. And then we're dropping. We fall out of the faerie paths with such force that I stagger forward and drop onto my hands and knees. Ash is on the ground beside me. "What happened?" I gasp as my eyes do a quick scan of the area. No guardians, no fae creatures, but I'm pretty sure we're still in Stormsdrift. Trees surround us, moonlight struggles to filter through the branches, and a thick fog is creeping in. And …

Yes. We're definitely in Stormsdrift. Without even looking, I know the Shadow Crypt is close. So very, very close. I feel the pull now in a way I never felt it when I was growing up.

Don't ever come back here. Don't ever let them get the key.

"I think the paths stopped working," Ash says, pushing himself up into a crouch. I blink and try to clear my jumbled thoughts, watching

362

him as he tries a doorway spell on the ground. Nothing happens. "Yep, it was the paths. But I think …" He looks around. "I think we're close to the Shadow Crypt, which is odd. If the paths aren't working, we generally find ourselves thrown out somewhere outside of Stormsdrift." He puts his stylus away and stands, extending a hand toward me.

"I think … maybe it was me," I say as I take his hand and let him pull me up. "I can't get the memories of that night out of my head. I was thinking about how we hid here, just before … you know." His hand, still holding mine, squeezes a little. "So maybe in the moment before the paths stopped working, I broadcast my thoughts a little too loudly. But your parents …" It's my turn to look around. "If I'm the one who ended up directing the paths, then they should have come through with us."

"Mom's hand was pulled out of mine when that jolting feeling happened inside the paths. That seems to happen if you're trying to travel when they stop working. Mom and Dad must have dropped out somewhere else."

We wait, listening, but there's no sound aside from a distant chirrup, chirrup. And there's that tug. That silent, invisible, inexorable tug toward the door that ruined my life.

Ash looks at me. "Silver … this is where it happened, isn't it?"

My eyes slide over the misty scene and land on a tree with branches that are interlaced in an almost braid-like pattern. My chest tightens. My throat begins to close. Ash is right. This is *exactly* where it happened. Because that tree … that's the one I stared at while I counted desperately in my head, waiting for Mom and Dad to come back. Which means that that tree over there—my gaze slides to the left—that's the one Mom and I knelt beside. That's where Dad stood, trying with everything in him to hold back the councilors. That's where he and Mom …

My chest is heaving rapidly, trying to draw air in, and Ash's arms are around me now as he presses my head gently to his shoulder. All the thoughts that have tormented me for the past two years—the thoughts I usually stamp down the second they try to surface—flood my brain. If only I'd had a stylus, if only I'd helped Dad hold the shield for longer, if only I'd reacted as quickly as a guardian is meant to react and thrown a weapon at Bergenfell the instant she stepped out of the paths. If only if only if *only*.

Instead of forcing aside the memories like I usually do, I let them filter in. I let them overlay my vision as my eyes dart back and forth across the area. I see where we hid. I see Bergenfell stepping from the faerie paths. I see where Mom fell … where Dad fell …

And for the first time, I let myself think of other 'if onlys.' If only someone hadn't pushed Mom down the crypt steps and broken her stylus. If only Mom and Dad hadn't opened that door. If only Mom had never saved Anvi's life and become his friend and discovered he had the key. For the first time, I let myself think of all the things that were beyond my control. For the first time, I think … perhaps it wasn't my fault the way things turned out.

My next breath shudders its way through my body. I wind my arms around Ash's waist and hold on tight. Tears slip down my cheeks as the fog shifts around us, revealing more of the forest. My heart still aches. But eventually, the tears stop falling. Eventually my breath no longer hitches. Eventually, we're simply standing here quietly.

"Are you okay?" Ash asks.

"I think … I think I am."

"You know," he says hesitantly. "We're so close to the crypt. We should just finish this. Take the crystal down there and destroy the door. We can stop more of these monsters from getting through. Stop them before they overrun our home entirely."

I shift enough to look up at him. Doesn't he remember what I told him at the start of all this? "Ash, I can't go down there. To the Shadow Crypt. I can't go near the faerie door. I already told you that."

He frowns at me. "You mean … you physically can't go down there? I thought it was more … because of the memories of this place. That you didn't want to face any of this."

"I, um … that was part of it." I stare firmly past him, my heart pattering faster.

"Silver. What are you not telling me?"

"I …" I press a hand to my collarbone where the tattoo that is a reminder of my mother is inked into my skin. I picture the slender stem with its tiny leaves and flowers. The same flowers that so often adorned her hair. *I will take this secret to my end.*

"Silver?" Ash prompts.

I exhale slowly. "Remember how my mom said she felt drawn to the door? How it became harder and harder to resist? Well … I feel it too."

His eyes travel my face, his brows pulled low. I'm assuming that whatever he guessed I might say, it wasn't this. "You never said anything when we were growing up. Did you always feel it?"

"No. I didn't feel anything when I was younger. Except … there was that one time we snuck down there when I dared you to go inside. I remember feeling …" I look past him, thinking of that night. "Something. A sort of … pull. And if we ever played or trained in this area, I felt like I wanted to be closer to the crypt. I always thought it was simply curiosity."

"Maybe that's all it was. Maybe you're imagining this 'pull' because of everything you read in your mother's journal."

I shake my head. "What I'm feeling now … being so close to it … I'm not imagining this, Ash."

"Okay. And you're worried that if you get too close to the door that you'll … what? Want to go through it?"

"Maybe? Yes? I don't know. I think that's what happened to my mom, and I don't want to repeat her mistake."

"Okay." He runs his hands up and down the sides of my arms. "That's fine. You don't have to go down there. I can do it."

"Ash—"

"I can. It's not a big deal. My only concern is—"

But whatever he was about to say, it's lost as a piercing shriek cuts through the quiet. A storm rumbles nearby. I swing around to face the ruffling, flapping sound, instantly alert. The creature that lands a short distance away is like a giant bat. Its wings, however, are covered in shiny black feathers. When it extends those wings, I hear … a sort of thrumming sound. Falling rain, I realize.

"That," Ash says, his hands already gripping a crossbow. "My only concern is leaving you out here alone with things like that."

I quickly pull his hoodie over my head and toss the oversized garment to the side. Perfect for snuggling in, not so perfect for fighting dangerous fae in. The top I have underneath, the one Iris gave me to sleep in, is simple, dark, long-sleeved. Not about to flap around and get in the way. "I'm offended," I say, keeping my tone light as my thumb brushes an X over the moonstone on my wrist. "You think I can't take that thing down on my own?" A moment later, the two interlocking curved blades of my crescent-moon knife are tight within my grip.

The bird-bat stormfae creature rears up, flapping in a way that causes a sound like rumbling thunder, then darts forward with needle-sharp fangs bared, lightning flashing from its tongue. Ash and I jump aside, and the lightning strikes the spot we just vacated. "Would you prefer me to stand back and leave this one to you?" Ash asks.

"I suppose I can share." I swing my knife in a figure eight pattern. "Wouldn't want you to feel left out."

"How very generous of you." Then he lifts his crossbow and shoots. The creature bleeds instantly into the shadows, and the bolt flies straight through black mist. The mist slides closer to us, and then suddenly it's shifting into feathery bat form again, and it's *right there*. It leaps off the ground, clawed feet coming at me, and I slash wide with my knife.

It falls back with a high-pitched shriek, and I catch a glimpse of glittering gold in its right wing. Ash must have shot it. With an angry sweep of the creature's wings, the sounds of rain and thunder intensify and the bolt flies loose and vanishes. But Ash is on its other side now, and as the creature rebounds between the two of us, flitting from bat to shadow and back again, I let myself sink into that state of flow where my limbs and magic act on instinct rather than directed by conscious thought. I swipe, dodge, leap away, and hurl magic. And all the while, the creature continues shifting form, evading our weapons and magic with apparent ease. We're going to have to get more creative if we hope to defeat this thing.

This thought has barely crossed my mind when the bird-bat swipes a little too close to Ash with one enormous wing, and he slams hard into the ground. "Ash!" I shout as I lunge closer and swing my knife in a wide arc. My blade meets the creature's furry chest, but then it has my arm wrapped in the oversized claws of one of its feet, and suddenly it's launching upward, lifting me from the ground.

I switch my knife to my free hand and swing wildly at the creature's leg while sending magical heat into my other hand. Hot, hot, hot, *hot*—and then its claws open and I'm falling toward the earth. I manage to slow my fall so that when I strike the ground, I can tumble and leap straight back up.

"Ash?" I look around. I'm so close to the crypt now that I can almost see the opening in the ground where the stone steps lead down. The pull is even stronger here, something inside me longing to move closer, to walk down those steps. *Stop it!* I shout silently at myself. *Focus!*

The creature swoops overhead, and I throw up a layer of shield magic before remembering it's most likely useless. "Here!" Ash calls, shouting from a short distance away. I'm pretty sure he was calling me, but the bird-bat seems to take this as an invitation to send a bolt of lightning streaking in Ash's direction. Then it sweeps back around toward me, just in time for me to fling a hailstorm of sharp stones straight toward it.

It banks sharply to avoid the stones, but they slice through part of its wing. I'm already gathering more magic as it lands heavily not too far from me. Ash yells, catching its attention again with a few throwing stars and magical flames.

Get creative, I tell myself again. I throw my hand out, magic shooting across the ground ahead of me and scattering into a spray of water. *Ice*, I think, and it transforms in an instant. The bird-bat wheels around, clearly surprised by the temperature drop near its feet. But I'm already running, skidding, sliding. I drop, my crescent-moon knife sweeps up, and I slide clear beneath the creature and slice right through its belly.

The shriek it emits is unearthly. As I reach the end of my ice-skating maneuver and leap to my feet beside Ash, the creature tries to become shadowy mist again. But its form seems to flicker and remain bird-bat instead. "Looks like it's too injured to change form now," Ash says, a little breathlessly. We jump apart as another bolt of lightning strikes the ground between us. "Can you gather stunner magic?" he asks me. "I'll keep it away from you. Otherwise we might be fighting it all night."

"Can you handle it on your own while I do that?"

Ash grunts out a laugh. "Should I be offended by that?"

"Okay, hang on." I dart around a tree and press my back against the rough bark as I release my knife near the moonstone and let it shrink itself back into hiding. I gather power above my palms as fast as I can draw it from my core, trying not to focus too much on the grunts and cries coming from the other side of the tree. I want to yell out every few moments and ask if he's okay, but I also don't want to distract him.

When I've gathered what I estimate to be enough power to stun the bird-bat stormfae, I peer around the tree to see what's happening. The two of them are near the crypt entrance again, and in the moment that I step out around the tree, the creature slashes across Ash's side with one of its clawed feet. He cries out, stumbling one or two steps to the side.

"I'm ready!" I shout, running closer. "Move out of the way!"

"Wait!" he gasps. And as the creature rears back again, he jumps up, thrusting his hand forward in an upward motion. A sword is in his grip a second later, and then the blade is driving straight through the creature's chest. It staggers backward. The sound of rain thrashing against a hard surface fills the air as its wings shudder. And then it crashes down. After a few twitches, it stops moving.

Ash collapses onto his knees, breathing hard. He presses a hand to his side. "Ash—"

And then up from the crypt staircase, just behind him, emerges a figure. Councilor Ursula Bergenfell. Her red hair is shorter, and she obviously isn't wearing an ivory ballgown, but this is so close to the way it happened last time that I freeze. The past and the present are merging in my mind again. I'm that terrified sixteen year old, rooted to the spot, too horrified by what she's just done to my parents to even breathe.

No. I'm *not*. I am deadlier than she can ever imagine, and this time I'm not running. I raise my hands and hurl everything at her. My magic, my pain, my anger. The ball of stunner magic hits her square in the chest. She staggers backward, shock registering on her face for an instant before her eyes slide shut. She collapses on the ground beside the crypt entrance. She doesn't move.

I exhale in a rush. I just stunned Councilor Bergenfell. I *stunned* her. I stride past Ash as he pushes himself up from the ground, his hand still against his side as he breathes heavily. It's been barely moments since the fight with the bird-bat stormfae ended. I stare down at her, at her expression that seems almost peaceful. How *dare* she feel any sort of peace after what she did to Mom and Dad? "I could kill her."

"Silver," Ash says, almost cautiously. "I know that's what you want to do. I know she took everything from you. But killing her isn't going to end any of this. It will only make things worse."

My lips tremble. My jaw clenches. "I just want her to pay for all the pain she caused me," I whisper.

"She will pay. Trust me on that. If it's the last thing I do, I will make sure every councilor at this Guild pays for what they did that night." He steps around me and hunches down to snap a pair of golden handcuffs onto her wrists. "This ends now." He stands, moves behind her, grabs hold of her beneath her arms, and pulls her away from the crypt entrance. With a grunt, he drops her and presses a hand to his side again. "Don't know why I'm not using magic for this," he mutters. I lift my hand, about to help him with my own magic, when I hear the voice.

"Hello, little bird."

Ash looks around, but I go utterly still at the memory of that silky voice. That whisper in my mind. Emerging suddenly from the depths of my nightmares to taunt me.

"It's been too long," she says.

Ash's head jerks to the side, his eyes darting about, and I realize … I realize …

No.

No.

Her voice isn't in my head. It's *here. She's here.* I stop breathing. My body begins to shake, and I know I need to act, to run, to fight, to movedammitMOVE! *Turn around, Silver. Turn around, TURN AROUND.*

Too late, I feel cool fingers on the back of my neck. Cool fingers pressing the tiny bird tattoo. And everything inside me … relaxes.

My eyes slide shut. Warmth spreads throughout my body, down my arms, my legs, reaching to my fingertips and toes. And then … I am suddenly awake, vibrating with life, a tight coil ready to spring open.

I inhale. Exhale.

Aaaaah.

It is so good to be myself again.

When I open my eyes, everything is brighter, sharper. My gaze travels along my arms to my fingers. I turn my wrists, loosening my joints, and then I reach into the air with both hands. When I pull them back, I hold a dagger within each fist, glittery black like polished shards of obsidian.

My gaze rises slowly. Vivienne is standing behind Ash, a black blade against his throat. She must have moved lightning fast to get so close to him without him fighting back. Then again, she mastered the art of killing a very long time ago. Asher Blackburn may be good, but he's no match for a woman who can step literally in and out of shadows.

I meet Ash's eyes, and in them I see the story unfolding. His shock is replaced by understanding, resignation, as he puts the pieces together. As he figures out exactly where I ended up when I ran from Stormsdrift. "I know who you are," he says through gritted teeth. "Scarlet Arrow."

Vivienne's glossy black hair slides over her shoulder as she rolls her glittering eyes. I have to admit I agree with her. The Scarlet Arrow is one of the stupidest names the Guild ever came up with. "And I know who you are," she says to Ash, tracing the tip of her blade along his jawline. "Nothing but a silly guardian." She looks at me. "We don't need him, do we?"

Well, I don't know about her, but I certainly never needed him. Thank goodness Vivienne showed up to remind me of this. My lips curve into the smallest smile. Vivienne shoves away from Ash, her blade leaving a thin red line across his cheek, and vanishes into the shadows behind him. I asked her once to teach me how to do that, and all she said was, "It can't be taught. You simply can or you can't."

Ash grabs hold of a sword the instant he's free. He's breathing fast now, tilting his head a fraction lower, watching me with uncertainty.

My gaze slides lazily down to my weapons again. I spin both blades. Sparks of magic fall like tiny black diamonds. Then I brace myself, lift my gaze to his, and utter the words I know will pierce his heart. "Come and get me."

Thirty-Eight

I swipe my blades through the air, but Ash doesn't move. "I won't fight you," he says.

"Then I guess this will be easy for me."

"Eleven months, two days." He repeats my words from the club. From a time that already feels like ages ago. "You were with her. The Scarlet Arrow. That's what happened."

I smile at him, slow and savage. "Bingo."

"Little bird," he says quietly. "The tattoo on the back of your neck."

"Little bird," I repeat, my smile twisting. I toss both daggers into the air, watch them spin for a second, then grab a bow and shoot an arrow at one and then the other. Twinkling black sparks rain down as the blades and arrows vanish. I twirl on the spot and take a bow. "That's me."

"Why didn't you tell me?"

"Why didn't you figure it out, Asher Blackburn?" I counter, dancing around him. I fling the bow aside and grab a sword from the air instead. It's as black and glittering and deadly as the daggers. "You know, for all your skill and intellect, you can be rather slow at times."

He shakes his head. "Did you think I wouldn't understand? That I would look at you differently?" He's looking at me differently already, the stupid, sappy boy. "I wish you had told me. And then I could have told you the things I've done. The things that haunt *my* nightmares."

Nightmares. For a brief moment, a flicker of something cold and clammy and terrifying presses against my mind. But it's gone a second later. If that sad, pale version of myself—the one who's lost without Vivienne—experienced nightmares, I have no concept of them. To have nightmares, I would have to be afraid of something. And I am afraid of nothing. "Sounds like a sad, boring conversation we'll never get to have." I lunge closer and slice an X through the air, but Ash dodges backward.

"I won't do this."

I let out a heavy sigh. "Do you know why you were always top of the class, Ash? Not because you were the best." I toss both blades aside and grab a throwing star in each hand. "But because I never even tried." My hands flash forward, releasing both stars, and though Ash swings aside, they skim the top of his shoulder before vanishing.

His hiss of breath makes me smile. "I know," he answers, and I hear the sting of pain in his voice. "Didn't I always tell you that?"

"You did. And I was always polite enough to pretend to deny it." I reach for another sword and swing it back and forth between us, but every time I dart toward him, he steps sideways or lunges back. It's a ridiculous dance I need to put an end to quickly. Vivienne will be growing tired of this. "I'm disappointed, Ash. I've heard you're one of the best around here. I was hoping you could show me what you're made of. Come on, I want to show you what *I'm* made of."

"I already know what you're made of."

My laugh is bold, wild. "You have *no* idea."

"This isn't you."

"Is that really what you think? Don't be deceived. This is the real me. All my doubts and insecurities peeled away to reveal the true monster I am inside. I was made to hunt, to maim, to kill."

"No you weren't."

"I was. This is my nature, Ash."

"This is not your nature, Silver," he says fiercely.

I smile at his anger. Perhaps if he loses his temper, he'll fight back. "Yes, it is," I say simply.

"So kill me then." He throws his weapons aside and spreads his arms wide. "If that's what you were made to do, then do it. I would rather you kill me than I let myself hurt you again, so go ahead."

I breathe out a sigh. He thinks he's calling my bluff. He thinks I won't do it. Or perhaps he thinks that I *can't*.

Somewhere not too far away, a howl rises above the quiet, answered immediately by a *hiss, hiss, hiss*, and then a distinctly *non*-monster-like shout. Well. Sounds like this place is keeping Vivienne busy. I'll take care of Ash and then help her with the rest of the stormfae.

"You are so sure, Asher Blackburn, that you're right. Interesting, when you were always so afraid of being wrong. So afraid of failure. Well, guess what?" I drag the tip of the sword lazily across the ground as I saunter toward him. "This—" I lift the sword and bring the tip of the blade to rest against his chest "—is the moment you fail."

Then I drop the sword, grab a knife from the air, swing my arm back and swipe, fast and vicious, straight across his thro—

THIRTY-NINE

then

Screams echoed in Silver's head as she ran blindly through the forest, the tiny glass vial clenched in her closed fist. All she could see was Mom's head, Dad's body—

Don't think don't think don't think don't think don't—

There were shouts behind her. Shouts all around her. Guardians catching up. They could travel through the paths and she couldn't. They could show up anywhere, at any moment, stepping out of the darkness with a sword exactly the way Councilor Bergenfell had done.

A golden blade, Dad's head falling—

Nonononono.

With a gasping sob she forced herself to *see* the forest, the branches she had to duck beneath, the leaves and twigs her feet were slamming against, the rocks she had to jump over.

"Silver? Silver!"

She whirled around at the sound of her name on Ash's lips. Her breath was ragged in her chest. She felt so sick, so utterly sick, and nothing in this world would ever be right again, but if she could just get to Ash—

"Silver!" he called again, and this time she heard running footsteps.

She turned toward the sound, shoved a leafy branch aside, and there he was, a shadow among the trees. Though he was too far away for her to clearly make out his expression, she knew the moment he saw her. The moment he turned toward her. And then instead of racing faster, he stopped. He lifted his hand, and above his palm blazed a mass of sparkling magic.

She jerked around to look over her shoulder, because Ash must surely be aiming for someone behind her. Someone about to attack her. But there was no one there. She looked back at him—

—and his magic was flying straight at her.

Straight. At. Her.

She flinched aside at the last split second, feeling the heat of the magic before it struck a branch and burned a hole right through it. Before she had time to process the fact that *Ash had tried to strike her with magic*, a yawning black hole opened up beside her. She yelped in fright as arms tugged her into the darkness of the faerie paths.

She kicked, elbowed, and yelled. Jerked her head back hard and struck something fleshy. But she couldn't escape the numerous hands that held her tightly within their grip, keeping her from reaching into the air to take a weapon. Everything became a jumble as she fell out of the faerie paths along with her captors. Herbs and flowers and dozens of tables covered in plants. Glass panels all around. Arms and fists and elbows and teeth. Hands clamping fiercely around hers. Golden cuffs snapping wildly and missing her wrists multiple times. And then a stabbing pain in her side. A blade sinking deep before pulling back out again.

She shrieked and the sound was unlike anything that had ever escaped her lips. It was piercing, and it seemed to reverberate almost visibly in the air. She felt herself shoved backward against her assailants. They crashed into a table of plants together, and Silver took the opportunity to jam her elbow backward yet again. The guardians' grips were looser now, and she finally managed to tear free.

Her knees and palms hit the floor. The glass vial rolled away. She scooted around to face the guardians as she felt once again that strange sense of darkness gathering at the edge of her vision. Something pulling irresistibly at her. *I will not pass out now. I will kill these people before I let myself pass out at their feet.*

There were three of them, she saw now. The same three who'd been battering Dad's shield magic. All lunging toward her, weapons glittering, magic sparking. She threw a shaky hand up, releasing as much shield magic as she could manage. They slammed against it as her other hand groped wildly for the fallen vial. And there, at her feet, was somebody's stylus.

Her fingers wrapped around the tiny cylinder of glass. Then she lurched forward and grabbed the stylus. Her shield magic was already slipping away from her mental grasp, stretching, stretching as if it were a balloon and someone was pressing a finger further and further into its surface.

She pulled the stopper from the vial.

Her shield popped.

She tossed the vial onto the floor and whirled away. Behind her, flames whooshed and crackled to life. Without another thought, she scribbled as quickly as possible across the floor. When the doorway opened, she didn't look back. She fell into the darkness and pleaded with the paths to take her far from Stormsdrift.

FORTY

now

I SUCK IN A QUICK BREATH AND BLINK AS MY FEET SKID ACROSS the ground. I stumble to a halt, utterly confused, as the whisper-beat of wings sounds behind me. I whip around, but I'm off balance somehow, and I land in an ungraceful heap on the ground. My eyes dart around as I hurriedly push myself up, searching for a creature with wings. But whatever it was is gone.

Like last time, several motionless shapes lie on the ground around me. Bergenfell, the birdlike stormfae creature … and Ash. I race toward him, fear clamping around my heart with an icy fist. I remember what I did to him. With frightening clarity. That's the way it always happens with Vivienne's control. There is no escaping what I've done when it's over. The blacking out, though … that part's never happened with Vivienne before.

I look around for her as I drop to my knees beside Ash, but she's nowhere in sight. I know there's no possible way she's *gone*, but I can't focus on her when the last thing I remember doing is slicing a blade through Ash's neck. I lean over him, my hands shaking against my thighs as I take a closer look. Blood stains his skin, but the wound only goes partway across his neck. Something must have stopped me before I could slit his throat completely.

Disappointing, Vivienne's voice whispers in my mind. *You can do better than that. You know how to remove a head from a body.*

I do know. And I came terrifyingly close to doing it to the person I love more than anyone else in either world. I shove aside that memory—which will no doubt haunt me for the rest of my days—as I feel for a pulse on the uninjured side of his neck. Either it's too weak for me to find, or there's nothing there. And like the last time I blacked out, I have no idea how much time has passed. Perhaps his heart stopped beating a while ago.

No, no, no, NO! a voice screams inside my head. *It is NOT too late!* It's hard to kill a faerie. That's what I was taught. And despite the fact that I now know precisely how *easy* it actually is, I refuse to give up hope as I slice carefully through the collar of Ash's T-shirt with a spark of magic. I pull the two sides of the fabric apart and press my palms just below his neck, my fingers spreading across his collarbones. Magic bleeds through my skin and into his. *Please, please, please*, my heart beats out. *Please let it not be too late.*

I can't do what a healer would do, sending specific types of magic to different areas within a person's body to guide the healing of organs and tissue. And I can't do whatever Iris was doing last night to rapidly heal a specific site. But I can at least send as much of my own magic as I can spare into Ash's body to give him a chance to heal before his own magic reserves run dry. That is ... assuming they didn't run dry a while ago.

I lean down and press my brow to his chest, pleading with him to be okay as I continue pouring magic into his body. I keep going for longer than I should. Longer than any of the Guild mentors would ever have advised, especially given the distinct possibility that Vivienne will show up again soon and I won't stand a chance against her if I've exhausted myself. A tiny, taunting part of my brain reminds me that I don't stand a chance against her even in peak physical and magical condition. True.

So either way, I'm screwed. And I'm too tired now to stop the flow of magic. Too … lethargic. Too cold. Too …

Ash's chest moves. A gasping breath shudders from his lips. The sound is enough to jolt some sense back into me. I raise my head quickly, pulling my hands back. The world spins, begins to turn white, but I blink furiously a few times and things come slowly back into focus.

"S … Silver?" Ash mumbles, his voice raspy. It's possibly the best sound I've ever heard.

"Ohmygoshareyouokay?"

He lets out a long, low groan, lifting one hand to his neck. He prods gently at his skin, which, as far as I can tell, looks like a thick scar now. "I don't think I've ever been so gravely injured so many times in such a short space of time."

I half laugh, half cry. "Yeah, I don't think I'm particularly good for your general health and wellbeing."

He sits up and pulls me against his chest. His breath is ragged against my cheek when he speaks. "You are good for me in every possible way. I will never regret finding you."

I'm crying now, so it's difficult to get the words out, but I manage. "Ash, I … almost … killed you."

"No. You didn't. *She* did." His voice is starting to sound a little more like normal. "Silver … all that time … you were with *her*."

"I'm so sorry," I manage to whisper as I shake my head against his chest. "I'm—so, so, so—"

"No, stop. I … I can't even begin to imagine. You had just witnessed your parents' deaths, and you were all alone, and then … then she took you. Why didn't you *tell* me?"

I'm still shaking my head. All those memories are flashing through my brain again. Running, tears, heartbreak, slamming into her in the dark. That room we used to train in, with the sweat- and blood-stained mats on the floor and the stained-glass window that turned everything red. The rewards, the punishments, the way we had to outcompete each other. "I … I tried. I did." I sniff and swipe tears from my cheeks. "When we were at The Gilded Canary. I told myself I could do it, but then you were so convinced that none of the terrible things I'd done were my fault, and then I just couldn't—"

"And they weren't." He pulls back so he can look at me. "She *made you* do those terrible things."

"That doesn't matter! I still did them! So many terrible things, Ash, and I *wanted* all of them. That's what she does to you. She makes you believe that you *want* exactly what she wants. And afterwards, you don't forget. It's not as though it's a hazy memory. It's all still horrifyingly clear, and you're left trying to separate the threads of what *she* wanted from what you wanted, but it's all so tangled that … you just can't. So in my memories, I *wanted* to kill you earlier. I remember how I pitied you, how cold I was—"

"Then what stopped you?"

"I … I don't know. I blacked out again. Like with the Seelie Court guardians. I don't know what happened. There were—flapping wings, and now Vivienne's gone, and … I don't know."

Ash looks past me, a frown on his face as his eyes comb the forest. "I wonder if … maybe it's one of the stormfae. They seem to be able to do all kinds of other things. Pass through shields, enter homes that are protected, change form, stop the faerie paths working. Maybe some of them can make people black out as well. I mean, I don't remember what happened either after you came at me with that knife, so maybe I blacked out too."

"Or maybe you just collapsed because I almost *killed* you."

"Well, I seem to be pretty much fine now." He lifts a hand to his neck again, but he still has that frown on his face, his gaze directed past me. "Those weapons …"

"Those weapons," I repeat softly, my eyes sliding shut. My fingers curl around air as if I could reach for them now. The feel of them beneath my hands is so right, so addictive. Like a drug, I simultaneously long for them and hate them.

"So much like a guardian's," Ash says. "It's crazy. Do you only have access to them when …" He trails off, leaving the question hanging.

"When I'm under her control, yes." I open my eyes, swallow, and reach up to gently pull his hand away from his neck. "Are you sure you're okay?"

"Yeah, I feel almost fine. I think you hardly injured me at all."

I can't help the way my eyebrows shoot up automatically. "That's not true. At all. Ash, I think … I think you would have died if I hadn't given you a whole load of magic."

His eyes narrow. "A whole load?"

"I mean, not *too* much, just—"

"Silver—"

"What was I supposed to do? Keep all my magic to myself and let you die?"

"That's incredibly dangerous! You know there are limits you're supposed to stick to when it comes to sending magic into someone else."

"Yeah, well, I'm not particularly good at following the rules." I rub my hands over my face again, but my tears are mostly dry now. "Thank goodness. Or we might not be having this conversation."

He stands, pulling me up with him. For a moment or two, the world seems to tilt. "Are you kidding me?" he says. "You can't even stand up straight? Silver, you gave me *way* too much magic. How are you going to defend yourself if that woman comes back?"

"I can stand up straight," I say, a little defensively.

He mutters something that includes the word 'stubborn,' then shakes his head. "Okay, look. Obviously I have a lot of questions about this whole assassin thing, but now is clearly not the time. We need to get out of here." He pats his pockets until he finds a stylus. He writes a doorway spell on the ground, and for a moment, it seems as though it's working. But then the doorway flickers and vanishes.

"Well," I say with a sigh, "I guess there's nothing else to do except take the Icicle Pendant of the First Seelie Queen down those steps and throw it at a really old door."

Ash looks up sharply. "Are you saying that because it's what *you* think we should do, or because some creepy, ancient magic is pulling you down there?"

I'm about to say that of course it's *me*, but … is it? That urge is still there, that need to go down the crypt steps, to get closer to the door. It's been there this whole time, a nudging sense at the edge of my mind, a gentle tug in the center of my chest. But fear for Ash's life kept me from focusing on it. "I think it's probably both," I say eventually.

He straightens. "I don't think you should go down there."

"I won't go inside with you. I'll just wait at the entrance." It hits me, as the last word leaves my mouth, that this is almost exactly what Mom said to Dad when we came back here that night to lock the door. This should concern me. It *does* concern me. But the feeling is outweighed by my growing desire to go down those steps.

Ash looks around. "Honestly, I think we both need to get the heck out of here before—"

"Ash, it'll be quick. We're *right here*."

He releases a frustrated breath. "Fine. Let's do it quickly and then get as far away from this area as we can. If that assassin woman comes back—"

"Stop wasting time," I say, catching hold of his hand and pulling him toward the opening in the ground that leads to the ancient stone staircase. We step past Bergenfell, still passed out on the ground with a pair of gold handcuffs encircling her wrists, and begin our descent below the earth. The last time we came down here, it grew darker the closer we got to the bottom of the stairs. This time, there seems to be a faint glow at the bottom.

We continue down. Gone is the thread tugging at the center of my chest. It's more like a rope around my middle now, pulling me forward with far more force. I think I could resist if I really wanted to, but … I don't.

Don't ever come back here, Mom said. Her voice is so quiet at the back of my mind. So easy to ignore. Did she tell me this because she found it impossible to resist the pull and feared the same thing for me? I tell myself that I'm stronger than her. I can resist. Of course I can resist.

We reach the bottom of the steps, and I suddenly remember the gate. The gate that could very well have been locked. But Bergenfell was down here earlier, and it seems she left the gate open. It stands ajar, as if she pulled it behind her as she hurried from the crypt to see what was going on above ground but didn't stick around long enough to ensure it was properly closed. What was she doing down here? Standing guard? Waiting to kill any stormfae that came through?

I lift a hand and push the gate open, remembering the first time Ash and I crept down here. There are several things that are different this time: First, the inside of the crypt is illuminated by two lanterns just inside the doorway, one on either side. A flame flickers within each one. Second, there is an archway on the other side of the room. The archway I thought I caught a glimpse of the first time we were here. And third ... I see the faerie door.

It's set into the wall on the far side of the second room, a rich, textured wood covered in intricate carvings, with a large round door-knob and keyhole of the same metallic gray I remember the key being made of. Lamplight dances across its surface, making the curling vines and flowers appear to come alive. The only imperfections are the holes. Several of them, perhaps a little smaller than my palm, dull light shining through each one.

But despite these flaws, the door is beautiful. So much more beautiful than Mom's drawing, and I want *so badly* to cross the distance and touch it. I'm moving forward without even thinking when Ash catches my arm in a firm grip and holds me back. "Nope. I don't know what's going on here—what kind of weird magic you and your mom seem to be susceptible to—but I'm not letting you any closer than this."

I almost fight him. *Almost*, until I realize what an absurd thing that is. Am I seriously going to fight the person I love, the person I gave almost all my magic to, so I can get closer to a *door*? Besides, I'm probably too weak to fight him off at this point. I need a good night's sleep to replenish my magic stores. "Right, sorry." I clear my throat. "Thanks."

"Now that we're here," he says, tugging down the zip of his jacket to reveal the icicle pendant, "I'm not entirely sure how we should do this. We need to break the crystal, which probably requires a large magical force. And then, if I remember what your mom wrote, the crystal's power will be released. But is that, like … an explosion? I mean, do you think we should throw this thing and then quickly conjure shield magic to protect ourselves?" He removes the chain from around his neck and holds the pendant up. The tiny gold specks within it glimmer in the lamplight.

"Probably a good idea to—" I pause, a sound reaching my ears. Snapping twigs, rustling leaves. Our heads turn at the same moment. Bergenfell, standing at the top of the stairs, hands raised—

All I have time for is a surprised intake of breath before I shove sideways into Ash. He grabs hold of me in the same instant, and we tumble together inside the crypt between the four stone caskets. The crystal hits the floor and slides to a halt beneath the archway.

Ash is up in an instant, weapons brandished. The perfect recovery. I, on the other hand, seem to be suffering the effects of parting with too much of my own magic. My limbs are sluggish and my head is spinning again. I blink rapidly, scrambling backwards toward the crystal.

Bergenfell is down the stairs already—she must have jumped or used magic—throwing herself into the small space. And then blades are flying, fists are swinging, magic is sparking. I grab the crystal and push myself to my feet, reaching for the edge of the archway in case the world starts to spin again. When I'm steady, I raise my hand, ready to throw whatever small spark of magic I can muster—

And then as quickly as it began, the fight comes to a halt. They're frozen, Ash with a knife pressed against Bergenfell's side, and Bergenfell with a blade curved like a claw against Ash's neck. "If you didn't want me coming after you," Bergenfell grunts, her eyes darting toward me, "you should have finished me off when you had the chance."

"Believe me, I wanted to," I tell her. "He's the one who stopped me."

"Who released you from the cuffs?" Ash demands.

"I did. Guardian cuffs don't work on councilors."

"What? Since when?"

"Since always. We have extra rights and privileges. I'm surprised you don't know that, Ash. You seem to know far too many other things—including things you *shouldn't* know."

"Have you always been in the habit of *murdering* people for knowing things they shouldn't know?" I demand. I take a step toward her, but she presses the deadly point of her curved blade harder against Ash's throat, breaking the skin.

"Come any closer," she says, "and I'll swipe this thing across his throat in the blink of an eye."

Ash's next breath is almost a growl. I see his grip tighten on his knife. "I wouldn't be so quick to—"

"Oh trust me, I'm in a better position than you are, Ash. Older, stronger, faster. You may injure me, but I'll—"

"Then why haven't you killed me yet?" Ash demands. "You must be afraid of *something*, otherwise you would have made your move by now."

They both stare at each other, breathing hard. Then she utters a single word, too quiet for me to hear. Ash's brows draw lower. He doesn't respond.

I can't handle this any longer, simply standing here with the faerie door begging for my attention and my parents' killer *right there*, and doing nothing about either. "You are not going to get away with any of this," I tell her, my voice shaking with suppressed emotion. "Even if you kill us both right here and concoct another story about it being an accident. There are people who know the truth now. People who know you *murdered* my parents. The other Guilds will find out what you've done. Then the Seelie Court will find out, and you'll—"

"The Seelie Court already knows."

I pause, my blood growing cold as she confirms one of the fears Ash and I had. Those Seelie Court guardians weren't acting alone. They were acting on the orders of the Crown. "You—you're lying."

"I am not. The Seelie Court helped us cover up your parents' deaths."

My throat constricts beneath the tightening fist of grief, rage, help-lessness. I want to scream at her, *hurt* her, but I can't muster the energy. I'm just so tired of all of this. "I trusted all of you. And look what you did with that trust."

Her blade presses harder against Ash's neck, but she's fully facing me now. For a moment I think I see something real and raw in her eyes, an unexpected agony, but then her expression hardens. "You think I'm the villain in all of this, but I've only ever done what I swore an oath to do. I have *always* kept my vow to the Guild and to the Seelie Court. *I follow orders.*"

"What about *protecting* people?" Ash demands. "What about *that* oath?"

She swings her gaze back to him. "If you think obeying the Seelie Court doesn't come before everything else, then you're mistaken about who it is that you serve. I, however, am under no such illusion. If they said guard the door, that's what I did. If they said never allow anyone to open it or go through, that's what I—"

"Are you kidding?" Ash interrupts. "You've been trying to *get to the other side*! You've been telling all your guardians to look for the key!"

"Because my orders changed!" she shouts. "Because the door isn't keeping the monsters out any longer!" She looks at me again. "Because your parents screwed up!" Then she swipes one leg out and hooks it hard around Ash's ankle. He staggers backward, falling, a hand thrown out to catch himself against one of the caskets. He drives his other hand up, shoving the knife into Bergenfell's side, but in a single swift motion she's discarded her weapon and grabbed a pair of cuffs from the air. *Snap*—around one wrist. *Snap*—she's tugged his hand off the knife still in her side and cuffed that one too. Then she kicks him hard, and he goes down with a furious cry.

"Damn you!" he yells.

But she's whirling on me now, pulling the knife from her side and tossing it away as if she barely felt it. It vanishes with a faint sparkle. "Your parents *really* messed up. When they came back to lock the door they never should have opened, they didn't complete the locking enchantment. That's how the monsters on the other side were able to get so close to it. To start burrowing tiny holes that have slowly grown over the past two years. That's how they started coming through. And now, even if we knew where the key was, it's too late to properly complete the locking enchantment. That damn door—" she points angrily past me "—is magically disintegrating because *your parents messed with the magic that's supposed to keep it shut!*"

For several moments, I can't speak. This is the fear that's been growing in me over the past few days: that the presence of all these monsters in Stormsdrift is Mom and Dad's fault. But still … something else Bergenfell said doesn't add up. "But … you've had people looking for the key for *years*. Since long before we moved here and my parents got involved in the search. Monsters weren't coming through the door then. It was still perfectly intact. You wanted the key for another reason that had nothing to do with my parents, so don't make out like you're the hero here."

"Not that I'm required to explain any of this to you," she says, advancing on me, "but that *reason* was because we were given orders during Lord Draven's time. The survivors of the first Guild never planned for the key to be in the possession of any future Guild or court, but during Draven's time, the Seelie Queen decided she needed it in her possession." I take a few hurried steps back as Bergenfell continues toward me. "Then Draven was defeated, and the need to find the key became less pressing, but our orders have not changed. A new ruler sits upon the Seelie throne and he, too, wants the key. So we kept looking." She's right in front of me now, and the door is inches from my back. "Then your parents showed up and ruined everything. If your mother had just followed orders, remained loyal to the oath she made—"

"Don't you dare speak about my mother like—"

"You know I'm right! She should have given me the key. Instead, she and your father decided to play their own game, and now the whole of Stormsdrift—*and beyond*, if we can't kill the monsters that have already come through—is in danger."

"So you *killed* my parents because they screwed up? You tried to kill *me*, even though I had no part in any of it? You couldn't have, oh I don't know, *arrested* us?"

Her hands are suddenly on my shoulders, gripping me tightly and tugging me closer, and I know I should fight back, but I also know I don't have nearly enough magic to call on right now. "You know why I had to kill them," she says fiercely. "Why I have to kill *you*. Because you—"

There is a spray of blood. Bergenfell is swept aside. Then two sickening thumps in quick succession: her body, her head. Separate. I'm so horrified I can't move a muscle. I stand there clutching the icicle pendant in both hands, staring at Bergenfell's lifeless gaze, until my eyes manage to slide slowly upward. And land on Vivienne.

"I'm disappointed, little bird. There was a time when you could have done that in your sleep."

FORTY-ONE

BERGENFELL IS DEAD.

Ash has vanished from the crypt.

Vivienne is here.

Adrenaline kicks in and I dart sideways, out of Vivienne's reach. I slam into the corner of the room and use the last of my magic to cast a hasty shield in front of me. I'm stuck now with nowhere to go, but at least she can't get close enough to activate the mark on my neck.

"Well." She cocks her head, watching me. "That was silly."

It's difficult to deny the pure terror she elicits in me. It's almost a tangible thing. But I force myself to swallow and speak. "Where is Ash?"

"Waiting outside."

Waiting outside? Alive? Dead? Still cuffed but with stormfae creatures prowling around him? I'm too terrified to force the questions past my lips.

"Oh, relax," she says. "He's still alive. You know I don't kill unless I'm being paid for it." Her gaze shifts to Bergenfell lying in two pieces on the floor. "Well. Not usually. But this woman threatened one of my own."

I shake my head and shrink as far back against the wall as I can go. "I never wanted to be one of yours."

"I know." She smiles at me. "Silver Wren, little bird. Of all my students, you fought back the hardest."

"Students," I scoff as the anger that hid beneath my fear for so long tries to make a stand. "You kidnapped and brainwashed us. I think there's probably a more appropriate name for us than *students*."

She leans against the wall beside the door, folds her arms over her chest, and continues watching me with something like curiosity. She's dressed simply tonight—no heels or fancy dresses for the forest—and yet she's still the picture of perfection. Painted lips, flawless face, not a hair on her dark, glossy head out of place. "Even under the influence of my magic," she says, "you wouldn't part with the secret you held so tightly within your broken heart. And that secret, Silver, is the only reason I chose you."

"W-what secret?"

"The key, Silver. That is what I want. That is why I took you in the first place. I tried my best to learn its location from you, but you fought back with everything you had."

"I don't remember that part," I say faintly. Odd, when so many of the other terrible things from that time are still horribly clear.

"Because I blocked that part out for you." Her lips turn up in a wicked smile. "You were an excellent little killer—one of my best—but it was difficult to tame you. In the end, it was easier to let you go. Easier to let you *think* you were free while keeping an eye on you from a distance. I knew that in time, you would be drawn back here. That's what happens with people like us."

"People like … us?"

"I didn't mind waiting a little bit longer. After all, I've waited a very long time already. What's another few years? Another few decades?"

"I don't know what you're talking about."

She lunges closer, suddenly fierce, her face right on the other side of my rippling shield layer. "'I will take this secret to my end,'" she hisses.

"That's what you used to whimper in your sleep, caught in the grip of another nightmare."

"This … secret," I repeat shakily. "The key."

"Yes." She looks at me as if I'm a bit slow. Admittedly, right now, I kind of am. "After a while, I had to admit defeat. You would never share this secret with me. And even if you did, you would then have to *willingly* give me the key. It can't be taken by force. If it were that easy, I could simply drag that boy back in here and threaten his life. But no." She sighs. "The guardians of the original Guild were smarter than that. I knew I had to wait instead. I knew the magic on the other side of this door would draw you back here eventually."

I shake my head slowly. "*It* didn't pull me back. Ash did."

She leans away from my shield, resting her shoulder against the wall again. "If he hadn't, the magic would have. Eventually. And now that you're here, you're succumbing to its power. I see you edging slowly toward the door."

She's right. Without even realizing it, I've been inching closer to my very weak shield layer. I'm almost touching it. I force myself to retreat until I feel the wall against my back again. I grip the icicle pendant tighter against my chest. "But … Vivienne … *why?*" I dare to ask. "How do you even know about all of this? Did you … oh." A memory leaps to the front of my mind. "The Guild—when they thought they were about to catch you—years ago. My parents were part of that team, and they ended up trapped inside a building with you long after everyone else escaped. Is that when you discovered all of this? Did my mom … tell you?" I remember my mother's haunted expression. My whispered fears to Ash that she may have been tortured. "Did you force information out of her?"

Vivienne gives me a pitying smile. "You're looking at this the wrong way, little bird. You're so concerned about the things she may have told me, when you should be wondering what *I* told *her*. Would you like to know? I don't mind sharing the details with you. I don't mind indulging in a lengthy conversation while your shield magic slowly peters out and you find it harder and harder to deny the pull toward this door."

I shake my head again. "That's not how this is going to end."

"That is precisely how this will end. I won't have to convince you of a thing. You will unlock this door yourself, and we'll both walk through it."

I'm still shaking my head, but inside, I'm terrified that she's right. After all, isn't that what happened to my mother? And I can't, I can't, I *can't* let that happen to me too. But I'm so tired now. I have barely any magic left, and I realize suddenly how silly it is that I'm wasting it on a shield. A shield that's so weak Vivienne could probably obliterate it with a mere blink if she chose to. I look down at the glittering icicle-shaped crystal in my hands. If I have only a tiny bit of magic left, then I know what I should be using it for.

I don't pause to think it through. I hold the crystal in one hand and in the other I draw as much magic as I dare from my core. I'm vaguely aware of Vivienne laughing. "I hope you don't think you're going to fight me off with—"

I drop my shield, hurl the crystal past her, and then throw my magic straight at it. The crystal strikes the door, and my magic pierces it an instant later. It shatters. A bright burst of gold flares across the room. And then—

I'm on the floor, Vivienne half covering me, a roaring in my ears and gold flames rushing overhead. Rumbling, cracking, screeching, and then … it all dies away. The flames are gone. Dust hangs in the air, and I see the faint ripple of something. Shield magic. Vivienne's? She's climbing off me now, looking around, and I push myself slowly up. The room spins around me, but I see the cracks that now run through the walls. I would have expected this whole place to come down on us, but the walls must be well reinforced with magic.

On the other side of the archway, the stone caskets didn't fare so well. They lie in jagged, crumbled pieces, Bergenfell's body partially concealed among them. Not a single bone in sight, though. But I suppose this was never really an elven crypt. That was just a story the first Guild came up with.

I blink and turn my gaze toward the right. Toward the faerie door. Which is …

Still perfectly intact.

My last hope dies inside me.

"You stupid girl," Vivienne snaps, shoving me hard as she climbs to her feet. "What a *stupid*, unnecessary risk. That was never going to work! Don't you know how old this door is? What magic was used to create it? There is an ancient power here that is almost impossible to break. Only like can destroy like."

"W-what?" Those words ring the vaguest of bells in the furthest reaches of my mind, but I can't grasp hold of what they mean. And the door … the promise of whatever lies on the other side … I have no strength remaining now to resist the pull. I stand and take a shaky step toward it.

"Yes," Vivienne murmurs, so quietly I almost don't hear her. And I hate that she's right about this, about *me*.

"How do you know," I say in a faint voice, still staring at the light beaming through the holes in the door, "that I even have the key with me? What if this is all a waste? We both just … stare longingly at this thing … but can't get through?"

"Because just like you and your mother," Vivienne says softly, "I have a connection to all of this. I've always been able to sense that you've hidden the key somewhere close by. No matter where you go, it always follows you. Perhaps you used the same ancient magic the Guild used when they first figured out how to hide weapons in a space beyond sight. The same magic I stole from them so very long ago to craft my own hidden weapons."

I shake my head. She thinks far too highly of me if she believes I have any knowledge of magic that complex and secret. Still … she's right about the key. It hasn't left me since the moment Mom gave it to me. And now … I can't resist any longer.

I step up to the door. I close my hand around the doorknob. *I'm sorry, I'm sorry, I'm sorry*, I think desperately, wretchedly, as I break my promise to my mother and turn it. Along my collarbone, something begins to burn. I lift my other hand to touch the simple tattoo. The slender stem and tiny flowers. The mark that hides a faint scar beneath. A faint scar in the outline of a key.

The burning pain intensifies. The same agony from that night. My head is splitting, my flesh is melting, my mouth is open and I'm screaming. But through it all, I don't let go of the doorknob. Then power rushes from me in a pulse. A bright flash of light radiates across the door. I'm thrown backward, and the only reason I don't slam onto the pile of crumbled stone on the far side of the crypt is because Vivienne is there to catch me. I breathe heavily, weak in the wake of all that pain. And the door … is open.

"Well," Vivienne murmurs, still holding me up. "*That's* how you hid it. I certainly wasn't expecting that."

I remember what Dad said to Mom that night. *It isn't our kind of magic.* He was right. That kind of agony doesn't belong to any sort of magic I've ever learned. Melding metal with bone. But it worked. It hid the key and the enchantment that went along with it. And it worked to unlock the door.

An icy breeze curls across my face. The mist on the other side of the door shifts to reveal hazy shapes. Trees, rocks, glittering snow. The distant shadow of something moving. It shouldn't be possible. One should have to step into the nothingness of the faerie paths before reaching the other side of this door. But the stormfae monsters' magic has pushed so far. It's penetrated right through the paths to this door.

Vivienne moves to stand beside me. She sighs. "Home."

That single word lodges itself like a knife into my brain. Sudden clarity, sudden horror, sharp and clear and painful. *Home?* Then she grabs me and pulls.

"Silver!"

I hear the shout as Vivienne tugs us both across the threshold.

Suddenly, we're in a winter world. It is icy cold, a bone-deep chill that has me shivering within seconds. And yet something here feels so *right*. It's the way I've always felt at home in Stormsdrift, but stronger. I look around at the snow-dusted trees. I turn my gaze toward the clear blue sky.

"Silver!"

I want to stay. I *need* to stay. But …

"Silver, look at me!"

I turn toward the voice. Toward the doorway. Ash is there inside the crypt, Lennox and Iris just behind him, and his hand is stretched toward me. I stare at him, and in his amber eyes I see our life together. I'm jumping from a rock, plunging into the river, and there are bubbles and lights, sunsets and laughter, the stickiness of marshmallows, training and sweat and pain and trust, hands touching, a dance, a kiss, a promise. *I'll find you.*

I blink.

And then I shove away from Vivienne and lurch toward that outstretched hand. A blade spins past me, its golden edge glimmering, and behind me, Vivienne cries out. An arrow follows swiftly, and it's Iris who has her bow raised. Vivienne's second cry is more of anger than of pain.

And then I grab hold of Ash's hand. He tugs me back inside the crypt, enfolding me in his arms and spinning me away from the door. My final glimpse of Vivienne is her furious face, magic roiling suddenly in a sparking mass between her palms. Lennox shoves the door, and the last thing I see before it slams shut is Vivienne's magic streaking toward us. Ash hunches over, his back to the door as he holds me tight against him, and then the shock of an explosion flings us forward.

His magic catches us an instant before we hit the floor, dropping us gently the final distance. Iris and Lennox tumble to a halt beside us, arms raised as splinters and dust rain down on us. I'm not sure if it's the magic or the fact that I'm so lightheaded now, but for a while, everything seems to shudder and spin.

Then it all grows still and quiet. Ash's arms loosen. I twist within his embrace and look over his shoulder. The door is gone. And so is the desperate longing to find my way through it.

A sob of relief catches in my throat. How did she do it? How did Vivienne destroy something that only minutes ago she told me contained the kind of power that was almost impossible to break?

Only like can destroy like.

Home.

An idea whispers at the back of my mind, but I'm too mentally spent to try to pick it apart to see if it makes sense. And does it even matter? She's gone. Trapped in an ancient land so distant that even the occupants of the Dark North apparently know nothing of it.

Making no move to get up from the crypt floor, I wind my arms around Ash and let my exhausted head drop onto his shoulder, finally daring to believe—for real this time—that it's over.

FORTY-TWO

"DAD, I THINK THE POTATOES ARE BURNING," FLYNN CALLS ACROSS the kitchen. "Quicksilver, toss that oven mitt over here, would you? Not sure how it ended up there."

"Here," Tobin says before I can remove my hands from the sink. He walks past, grabs the mitt, and throws it to Flynn. I turn back to the sponge in my hand and the pot Ash has just passed me. Lennox and Flynn are getting lunch prepared, Iris is busy making waffle batter for dessert—my request—and Ash and I are washing up as they go. Partly so that the kitchen isn't a dirty dish war zone by the time we sit down to eat lunch, and partly because standing next to him doing such a mundane everyday task makes my heart trip over itself with happiness.

"You guys are *still* washing those pots?" Connor says from somewhere behind me. I glance over my shoulder as he heads into the kitchen with two empty glasses and aims for the jug of fruity purple cocktail Rosie mixed up earlier. "You know there are spells for that, right?"

"Don't be such a lazy ass," I tell him.

"It's called making productive use of your time, *actually*," Connor corrects.

398

"I am making productive use of my time." I lean over, interlace my wet soapy fingers between Ash's, and press a long, slow kiss to his lips.

"Get a room," Connor says loudly.

"Connor, please," Iris complains.

"We did that already," Ash answers.

"Ash!" Iris and I exclaim at the same moment.

"What?" he asks innocently. "I got Silver a room. My guest room. Like you said—"

Connor emits the loudest snort-laugh in history, and Iris chases him out of the kitchen with a hand towel while her waffle batter keeps mixing itself. With cheeks burning, I toss a glass full of soapy water at Ash. He dodges back with a laugh, and the water slops across the floor. "You are the worst," I tell him, but I'm laughing too.

"Hey, no water fights in this kitchen," Iris says, marching back in.

"Sorry, Mom." Ash loops an arm around my waist, presses a quick kiss to the side of my neck, and reaches around me for a dry towel. He quickly wipes up the mess, then returns to my side.

It's been a day and a half since everything that happened down in the crypt, and I still can't quite believe it's over. Even the stormfae that should still be prowling around Stormsdrift don't seem to be a threat anymore. Those that surrounded the Blackburns' house before dawn yesterday morning were gone by the time we returned, and numerous stormfae bodies have been found around the forest since then. *Not* in the prettiest state. No one knows who slaughtered them, though I have my suspicions.

But I suppose none of this is really *over* yet. Not with the Guild in a giant mess because of Bergenfell's death, rumors that I didn't actually die two years ago, stories about a mysterious door being the source of all the monsters, and conflicting accounts all over the place from the rest of the Council members.

I heard Iris and Lennox muttering earlier about inquiries and other Guilds getting involved, but I stepped away before the details could cause me too much anxiety. They know the truth now about my time with Vivienne, about some of the things I was forced to do, and about how my mother hid something from the Guild *literally* within my bones. A long list of criminal activity and illegal magic. I know they're already trying to figure out how best to keep me safe during the investigation that's about to unfold, and I'm grateful for it. I'm grateful I'm not alone in all of this.

But for today, I want to enjoy my freedom from Vivienne and Bergenfell without thinking about the Guild. I don't want to worry about the details of exactly how I'm going to return to having a normal life in this world. I don't want to wonder why the Seelie Court has been completely silent about all of this so far and whether they still want us dead. Flynn suggested they might be backing off now because the door is gone and there's no way through to the other side, and I'm hoping he's right. Perhaps, now that the stories about the door have spread so far, the Seelies will give up on getting rid of everyone who knows about it. They can't very well kill us all, can they?

Well. I suppose they can.

Banishing that unpleasant thought from my mind, I glance up at Ash and catch him looking at the flower tattoo on my collarbone. "Sorry," he says, flushing slightly as he looks away. "It's just … I keep trying to see the scar now. The key shape. But it's hidden so well."

"That was the point," I say quietly. When he doesn't answer, I add, "I would have told you about it at some point. I just hadn't got there yet."

"I know." He leans down to kiss my cheek. "A lot's been going on. There are things I want to tell you too."

I remember what he said to me when I was under Vivienne's control. About how, if I'd told him, then he could have shared the things that haunt his nightmares too. I remember Bergenfell uttering that single word to him in the crypt instead of just killing him immediately. "Fennrock," Ash told me late last night while we were talking. "That's what she said." I wonder if there are things he *does* remember about his time there. Things he hasn't yet been brave enough to tell me about. Just as there are things I haven't yet been brave enough to tell him.

Before he can pull back, I turn my head and kiss his lips. "We have time," I whisper against his mouth. And I love this so much. The fact that I can casually lean over and kiss him whenever I want.

We finish washing as many dirty dishes as we can gather up while Tobin starts clearing books and ambers and random articles of clothing off the kitchen table. "Oh, don't touch that!" I say quickly as he aims for my jacket and Mom's journal. "It'll stun you. Literally. I'm sorry, I shouldn't have left that there. I thought it was wrapped up inside my jacket." I dry my hands quickly and swipe the journal and jacket up from the table.

"When did you go back for that?" Ash asks.

"Oh, Rosie was teaching you her cocktail recipe earlier and I suddenly remembered we left some things at that cabin. It was just a quick trip through the paths. Which are still working perfectly fine, by the way. I, um … I don't know if I'll ever see Teddy and Duke again … Who knows if that cabin even belongs to any real family of theirs." I shake my head. Though they broke my heart, I hope desperately that Vivienne didn't have any time to hurt them after they let me go. Now that she's gone, maybe they can get back to living whatever life they had before she roped them into spying on me. "Anyway. The journal means a lot, so I didn't want to end up losing it. I'll leave it upstairs for now."

I walk past Connor and Rosie snuggling on a couch in the living room and climb the stairs quickly. In Ash's old room, I drop the jacket and journal onto the bed. And then, because all the memories are so near, and because I miss Mom and Dad even more now that I'm back here, I lift the journal, open the clasp, and flip idly through it, watching Mom's words flick past.

I'm about to put it down when I stop. There was something there, near the end. On a random page roughly halfway through the empty half of the journal. Well, the half I thought was empty. I sit down, my heart fluttering a little faster, determined to find it again. I turn the pages one at a time. I did *not* imagine those extra few words.

I reach the right page eventually. Mom's written at an angle across it, her letters slanted and half-formed, as though she scribbled this down in a rush. I read the lines, and my blood drains from my face. My hands go cold. Prickles crawl across my fingertips. An odd silence presses against my ears.

"Silver?"

I drop the journal and look up. Ash is standing in the doorway. The chatter and activity from downstairs flood my ears abruptly. "You okay?" he asks.

"Yes, fine, sorry." I force a laugh.

His eyes move to the journal, then back to my face. "Are you sure?"

"Yes." I shove the journal under my jacket and stand, tucking away my ice-cold panic to deal with later. "Is, um, is lunch ready?"

"Yes. And Mom just revealed that she whipped up three different types of marshmallow topping this morning, which I think is overkill, but she wanted to be sure the waffles would be perfect for you."

I take Ash's hand and hold on tight. "That sounds amazing."

* * *

When the day is over, when I've savored every single warm, happy moment, and when Ash has fallen asleep beside me, I finally take a deep, shuddering breath and let the panic back in. I know what I have to do, and it's slowly breaking my heart into a thousand pieces.

I gently disentangle myself from Ash's embrace. Then I sit beside him for a while, memorizing the angles and contours of his face and replaying every moment from today. With featherlight touch, I smooth the hair away from his brow. His even breaths don't change. He won't wake. I hummed a sleeping spell earlier to be sure. The one Mom used to use whenever I woke from a bad dream in the middle of the night.

"We did it," I murmur. "We made our home safe again. But if I stay …" I shake my head. "It will be for nothing. Because no one is safe as long as I'm here." I reach for Mom's journal, which I left on the bedside table earlier. "I will take this secret to my end," I whisper, my lips barely moving, the words almost inaudible. Then I flip through the journal until I find that random page she scribbled on. My heart thuds painfully as I re-read it.

I remember now.
What happened when I blacked out.
It was me.
I killed Anvi.

I shut my eyes, letting this knowledge sink into me. I remember the times I've blacked out in the last few days and the things I found when I woke.

With the faerie door and Vivienne and Bergenfell gone, I was so desperately hoping I could hide from the terrible truth Mom whispered to me mere minutes before she died. But I can't. Four simple lines, and the harsh reality of exactly what she was—of what *I* am—came rushing back in.

I turn backward in the journal. I find the entry where she wrote about discovering something to do with stormfae in the Guild's archives. Something she was going to go back and read more of the following day, but then the next entry was months later. I spread the journal flat, run my finger down the middle, and discover what I missed the first time I read this journal with Ash: the ragged edges of torn paper. This was the part she told me she removed.

I will take this secret to my end.

I close the journal and stand. Then I pull on my jacket, which still has a sleeve partially torn, tuck the journal inside it, and zip the jacket up. I know I'm taking the coward's way out by leaving like this and I hate myself for it, but I can't let Ash talk me into staying. I can't risk something terrible happening to the people I love so desperately.

I lean over him and press a kiss to the side of his mouth. "Forgive me," I whisper, my lips shaking as I try not to cry. And then, because I feel too guilty to leave without at least *some* explanation, I remove the journal from my jacket, tear a page out, and transform my stylus into a charcoal tip so I can write with it.

You'll never be safe if I stay.
I'm so sorry.
I love you.

I leave the page on the bedside table, then remove my silver Gilded Canary ring and place it on top. Selfishly, I want him to have something to remember me by, and I don't have much else I can leave behind. I return the journal to the inside of my jacket.

Then, before I can change my mind, I cross the room, open a doorway to the faerie paths and walk into the darkness. And finally, after years of shutting out Mom's final words, of convincing myself that they don't matter, that they don't dictate who I am, I allow them to replay in my head. I allow myself to accept exactly what I am.

I know the Guild's biggest secret, Silver girl. Their biggest mistake. There are monsters on the other side of that door. Monsters that should never have existed. Monsters the first Guild couldn't get rid of.

So they did something terrible. A horrible, awful mistake. They created a new kind of faerie. Faeries who were supposed to control these monsters. Faeries who turned out to be even deadlier than the creatures whose minds they could communicate with. Faeries the Guild thought they eradicated centuries ago. But they were wrong.

Those creatures on the other side of the door, Silver ... they are not the true monsters. We are.

RACHEL-MORGAN.COM/STORMFAE-BONUSES

NEW TO RACHEL MORGAN'S WORLD OF GUARDIANS?

FIND OUT WHERE THE MAGIC BEGAN!

ACKNOWLEDGMENTS

First thanks, as always, goes to God. For giving me an imagination, for helping me find alllll the words, for protecting me from every daycare germ this year until the day this manuscript was finished (particularly grateful for that one!), for blessing me with ten years (*ten years!*) of publishing, and for so much more.

Special thanks to my beta reader and proofreader team: Rachel Debty, Mimi Parker, Yousra El-Gaafarawy, and Graham Downs. You helped make this book better.

Thank you to the advance readers who took the time to write early reviews for this book (and for sending screenshots of typos!). I appreciate you more than I can say.

To AJ Skelly: Thank you for helping me organize a cover reveal and book reviewers for this book. (And for making sure I never feel alone in the juggling-publishing-and-parenthood department. I have no idea how you get everything done!)

Thank you to my sweet, smart, funny, feisty sparkler child Riley for *not* hitting that key that magically deletes an entire manuscript every time you climbed over me while I was trying to write something!

Thank you, Kyle, for taking Riley on fun daddy-daughter outings when I *really* needed to get this book finished. You know the bike park well now! I love you.

And lastly, thank you to every reader who loved Creepy Hollow enough to want to return. You are the reason this magical world has become so much more than just a single series.

Rachel Morgan spent a good deal of her childhood living in a fantasy land of her own making, crafting endless stories of make-believe and occasionally writing some of them down.

After completing a degree in genetics and discovering she still wasn't grown-up enough for a 'real' job, she decided to return to those story worlds still spinning around her imagination.

These days she spends much of her time immersed in fantasy land once more, writing fiction for young adults and those young at heart.

Printed in France by Amazon
Brétigny-sur-Orge, FR

18486567R00243